Dear Reader,

It is hard to believe that a month has passed since I last
wrote to you. I do hope that you have been looking
forward to reading this new batch of *Scarlet* titles as
much as I have enjoyed selecting them for you.

Do keep those questionnaires and letters flooding in,
won't you? It is extremely useful for us to receive
feedback on how you like the mixture of books we
present, whether you are finding them easily in the
shops each month and so on. It is only by hearing from
you that we can be sure *Scarlet* continues to please
you.

I know that authors, too, like to have readers' comments
on their work, so if you wish to send me a letter for
your favourite *Scarlet* author, I'll be happy to pass
it on.

Till next month,
Best wishes,

Sally Cooper

SALLY COOPER,
Editor-in-Chief – *Scarlet*

About the Author

Vickie Moore lives in Wichita, Kansas with her family and assorted pets. A full-time writer, she enjoys the enticing mixture of romance and suspense. Her family has become quite accustomed to finding references to homicidal intent jotted down anywhere . . . including on recipe cards!

When Vickie's not plotting love and murder, she enjoys being outdoors, gardening and painting.

This Time Forever is Vickie's first novel for *Scarlet* and we are sure that readers will enjoy the exciting blend of mystery and romance contained in the story.

VICKIE MOORE

THIS TIME FOREVER

Enquiries to:
Robinson Publishing Ltd
7 Kensington Church Court
London W8 4SP

First published in the UK by Scarlet, 1996

A copy of the British Library Cataloguing in
Publication data is available from the British Library

ISBN 1-85487-721-6

Printed and bound in the EC

10 9 8 7 6 5 4 3 2 1

PROLOGUE

Kansas, 1878

The man stroked his thumb across the dead girl's cheek. She had been twenty-four and beautiful; now her skin had paled to a porcelain hue, her blue eyes vivid in a mask of white. Even death could not steal from her the radiance of her delicate features.

A droplet of his grief fell to her face. The moisture slowly caressed her skin. The shimmering bead gave her the tear she would never be able to shed. Yes, he could still grieve for the loss of that vitality which had attracted him to her. But the all-consuming wonder of this 'power' of death carried an exhilaration beyond any earthly measure. God had given life to Allysa when she had been conceived; he, however, had struck her down, then watched in shock as her eyes had dimmed in death.

Beauty is only temporary, he thought. Images of his mother swam before him, blurring with Allysa's pale face. Then she becomes useless. Unwanted. Dead.

He touched his lips to Allysa's forehead; the silk of her hair caught at the stubble of his rough beard. The

1

man's gaze moved from her to the jagged shards of the porcelain mask that lay within reach of her fingers. The face lay broken in two, the black holes of the eyes grimacing accusingly.

He straightened the chalky porcelain, arranging each piece to match with its mate. Studying the arrangement, he clucked his tongue. He then pulled the lower section away only enough to leave a small, hollow divide to run through the middle of the face.

'My sweet, Allysa, you deserve perfection.' His words were low and soothing.

Tidying the folds of her long skirt, he tucked them modestly around her ankles. He smoothed an errant lock from her brow and adjusted her curls in a becoming style.

The killer stood to admire his work. Allysa's body lay on the coarse colors of the rug, her blonde hair pooled beneath her head. Her eyes staring unseeingly at the broken mask.

The mask *he* had given her.

He chuckled to himself. Even in death Allysa's tenacious spirit sought to accuse him. But would these insignificant, ill-bred townsfolk have the intelligence to figure it out?

This time he laughed at the thought. He had come to this miserable, buffalo-wallow of a town to dig out a new start for his career. Allysa's intelligence and vibrant personality had been like the exotic bird he had once seen back east at the docks; a vision of color in a backwash of brown.

He frowned as he thought of the dirty, louse-infested

population. No, they would never be able to grasp the subtlety of it. Except, perhaps, for Allysa's brother.

Although he had never met the man, the people of the town spoke highly of him. And often. Now he wondered if perhaps they had been trying to warn him. The brother, Trevan, was known for his honesty and good character. And for his uncanny knack of solving things. At the thought, he moved cautiously to the window and pulled the thin material of the curtain aside. There, riding down the street, as if conjured by his own speculation, was Allysa's brother. Trevan Elliot.

He studied the rider as the man swung from his horse at the livery down the street. Elliot's expression was hard. Focused.

The killer turned to the portrait nestled in its frame on the mantel. Yes, it was him.

Pulling his watch from his pocket, he noted the hour. Damn, he had thought he would have more time than this. Quietly he slipped to the back of the theater where his horse was tied. Shreds of conversation filtered to him from the front porch. The horse-like laughter of Maybella Lovejoy meant Elliot would be occupied for a few more moments.

Thank goodness for flirtatious, ugly women, he thought.

Suddenly he heard the front door open, then the deep voice of Trevan Elliot calling to his sister. He chuckled to himself, little did the brother know that his words fell on dead ears. He heard Elliot call her name softly, a thick thread of anguish woven through it.

Allysa's killer laughed, then let the door slam behind him.

Trevan Elliot pulled his hat from his head and slapped it against his leg knocking a cloud of dust from it. He ran his hand through his hair and replaced the hat on his head.

'Damned if it isn't hot,' he muttered as he stepped up on the smooth planks of the theater's porch.

'Mr Elliot,' wheezed a shrill voice behind him.

He glanced to see Maybella Lovejoy patting her hair into place as she stepped in front of him.

'I apologize, Maybella, I didn't see you.' Or I would have gone the other way, he thought. He took a deep breath and raised his eyebrows expectantly. The town's busybody looked as if she was about to burst. In more ways than one, he thought wryly.

'No need, Mr Elliot, I fully understand that a strong man such as yourself who's been out on the range as long as you have might have all sorts of pent-up urges,' she giggled with a meaningful flutter of her eyelashes.

'Yes, well, that's still no excuse for forgetting my manners,' Trevan said, looking to the theater where his sister Allysa usually spent her afternoons. Out of the corner of his eye he caught a movement that caused his brows to dip into a frown. One of the curtains had been pulled slightly to the side, then it fell quickly back into place as if someone had been watching him only a moment before.

'A gentleman. That's what you are, Mr Elliot,' Maybella said. Pulling a fan from her bag she began

4

to wave the stale hot air toward her red face. Suddenly she slapped it closed and pointed it at him. Trevan looked down at the object wondering if she were about to hit him with it.

'Ruth said I should mind my own business, but I told Ruth. I told her, that you were a gentleman and you would want to know. That's what I told her, so I did.'

He frowned down at her shiny expectant face. 'I would want to know what?'

Maybella leaned toward him and lowered her voice. 'Your baby sister Allysa has been seeing that handsome stranger. The one who arrived not too long at all after you left for the drive.'

Trevan shook his head, then met Maybella's eyes. 'We both know she's old enough to see men. Besides he's probably one of the actors she hired for her show.'

Maybella's lips pursed together with her anger. 'I would think, Mr Elliot, you would be concerned for your sister's reputation. Why, she practically spends all her time with that man. They've been together day and night.'

With the last word she nodded her head firmly with a meaningful widening of her eyes.

Trevan knew his sister would resent his getting mixed up in her affairs. Allysa was as strong-headed as she was smart. Still, he didn't appreciate the town's gossip, Maybella Lovejoy, fanning the fires of the rumor mill that she had already started working on.

His gaze hardened and he was pleased to note Maybella's look of self-righteousness dim a little.

'I would hope, Maybella, that the people in this town

had more to do than just sit around and speculate about people. Some might just think they were jealous.'

He turned and started toward the theater when her voice rose behind him. 'We'll just see who's jealous, Mr Elliot, when you find out what your betrothed has been up to in your absence.'

Trevan shook his head, disgusted with the woman and her petty talk. His anger dimmed a little when he heard her snort in annoyance, then the heavy sounds of the large woman as she lumbered off. Suddenly he felt the weariness from the long drive settle over him. He longed for a bath and a steak dinner, but realized it would have to wait, at least till he talked to his sister.

Opening the door to the theater, Trevan was met with silence. Allysa was usually at the theater at this time and never was his little sister quiet. The unease he had felt earlier returned.

'Allysa,' he called, his voice loud in the quiet of the empty theater. His spurs clinked against the wood floor as he moved down the hall. He walked to the back of the theater and started to move past the backstage area to the prop room when something caught his eye. Trevan stepped back and felt his heart tighten within his chest.

It was a woman's foot.

Dread forced him to move slowly toward it and gradually the rest of the body came into view. His chest heaved with his shock. Pain and intense anger speared through him. Anguish caused his voice to catch as he called to his dead sister. Distantly he heard a man's laughter and the loud slam of the back door.

He moved quickly to the hallway, then turned his

head to the door. The red curtains were just settling back into place and he heard a horse gallop off.

Trevan Elliot's eyes hardened. He ran through the theater and pushed the front door open with a shove. He hadn't stopped to look at his sister; he didn't need to; it was an image he would carry with him for the rest of his life. Untying his horse, he climbed into the saddle and spurring the horse on he started after his sister's killer.

He swore to the memory of his dead sister that if it was the last thing he did, he would find the man who had done this. In that moment, the hunter had unknowingly become the hunted.

The man spurred his mount on. He didn't bother with any of the traveled roads, but plowed into the dark range.

The brittle spikes of prairie grass were occasionally shaded by cottonwoods or elms. As he drove the horse on, the land became more dry. More flat. Too exposed.

Dust swirled around him. The turbulent tossing of the wind caused the tiny particles to bite at his face. He pulled a handkerchief from his pocket and tied it around his head. It didn't keep the choking grains from hitting his face, but it did at least allow him to breathe.

He guided his horse northwest where the flatland began to roll and wave into hills. The alternately rocky and wooded terrain could prove exceptionally helpful, should the need arise to take cover.

The ground began to slope under the steady clip of his horse. He was beginning to feel the tingle of exhilaration as the thrill of escape moved through him. It was then that the rhythmic noise caught his attention. He turned to see Elliot riding relentlessly across the dark prairie. The man's gaze focused on him.

'Damn it,' he muttered. He drove his horse deeper into one of the many ravines that riddled the hills.

The thunder of the stranger's horse's hooves chipped into the ground, then reverberated, providing an ominous rhythm to the building storm. Foam was flung from the beast's mouth as it pushed into the rising wind. Dark clouds tumbled heavily across the land as the storm's fury was mounting to a release.

He quickly glanced over his shoulder to check Elliot's progress, then turned to study the land around him. An outcropping of rocks jutted from the ground ahead of him. Excellent refuge, he thought, as he guided the horse behind and down the ravine cut deeply into its shadow. The muscles of his horse bunched and strained as it stumbled on the dangerous slide of pebbles, only to regain its footing at the base.

He spurred his mount again. The hoofbeats of the beast following him hesitated at the edge, then continued past him on the ridge above. He noted with small satisfaction that the ravine curved, then widened into a gully. The trail carved its ruts between two hills before smoothing into open prairie. He eyed the gun-smoke gray of the sky and hoped the rain would hold off at least till he could make his escape. The water could prove to be very dangerous for him and the horse until they reached the dry cake of the flat land. Once there, the dim curtain of the storm would only hide the signs of his escape.

Lightning sliced from the darkening sky, exploding in a flash of sparks as it struck a dead tree. The large hulk fell in a sputtering hiss of fire, blocking the ravine.

The man pulled his horse short. 'Curse this wretched storm,' he seethed, as the cold fingers of dread wrapped around his throat.

Thunder bellowed nature's war cry, the air thick with the oppressive push of the storm. His heart beat a wild tattoo in his chest, matching the turbulent rolling of the murky clouds.

He eyed his only option, the steep wall to the top of the bluff. The thunderstorm shook the ground with its wrath. The first fat drops of rain hit his face; he could see the dark sheets of the torrent coming behind. The opportunity would be lost in only seconds if he did not act. He spurred the horse on, momentarily fighting the animal as it resisted the idea. His mount then began to move up. Pebbles fell in a spray from its hooves as it pawed and found purchase. The horse's mane slapped into his face as the animal climbed, then dug into the grass at the top.

The smile spreading wickedly across his handsome face was his only concession to the feat just performed. His heart lifted as the salvation offered by the open prairie came into view. The flat ground offered an excellent run for his thoroughbred's long stride.

His goal was there before him and he began to move toward it. His deliverance. The dry grass crunched beneath the prancing hooves of his horse. The man leaned forward, ready to spur his horse into a long legged dance with the wind. The report of a rifle whipped towards him in the chaotic gust of the storm, a spray of dirt kicked up before him. His horse pulled short, rearing into the air as it shook its head side to side in terror. He lost his hold, his arms flinging wildly in front of him. His back connected with the stiff mat of the grass below and the wind rushed from him.

With a hard groan, he rolled to his knees, then stood shakily. The sight of his horse running riderless in the direction of his escape caused spears of fury to shoot through him. Now he would have to make it on foot. He started to move forward when the sharp ridge of a rifle barrel nudged the base of his neck.

'Die now or die later. Doesn't matter to me.' Elliot's voice was low and vehement with fury.

'I have no money, sir,' the killer said, his voice cool and polite, with a touch of fear, as he feigned ignorance. He started to turn when the hard lip of the gun jabbed into his skin, stopping him.

'You bastard. You know who I am and why I'm here.'

'I'm afraid I don't under – '

'This isn't a social call. You killed my sister.' Elliot's control and fury threaded through his words. 'The only thing stopping me from dropping you where you stand is that the sight of seeing you swing is too damn enticing.'

The air was stifled in his lungs, he could not discern whether it be from the terror clutching at his heart, or from the oppressive shift of the storm.

The killer noticed the sky glowing with the eerie hues of orange and green like a beautiful backdrop. The wind picked up around them, small twigs and branches

10

whipped into the air. His body swayed from the push and pull of the rising tempest. In a sudden moment of detachment, he found himself thinking that the weather was perfect for such a dramatic encounter.

He turned his head and caught the movement of Elliot's gun shift away from him as his captor reached for a rope. A low growl escaped from the murderer as he twisted, then sprang on his opponent like an angry cougar. They fell together in a writhing heap on the dirt. The ground vibrated beneath them. A roar built, the deafening sound engulfing them. He felt the whip-lash of hail as it cascaded onto their contorted forms.

Together they rolled, until he found leverage to pull himself on top of the man. He gripped Elliot's throat, feeling his adversary's skin compress as he tightened his hold. His breath sputtered as Elliot found a grip on his own. Like two snakes, their muscles coiled and worked to dislodge the other. Their arms shook with their effort as they continued their deadly hold on each other.

A black haze begun to swirl in his vision as Elliot's strong hands clamped around his throat, then tightened even more. He hated the show of weakness as he gasped for air. He forced his eyes to remain on the man, determined to allow nothing else to diminish him as a coward.

The hand released his throat suddenly, causing him to drop to the ground on his back beside Elliot. His breath came in short, hoarse gasps. He turned to Elliot and saw that the raw emotion had vanished from his face; only his dark eyes expressed his loathing even as he too worked for air.

He rolled to his stomach away from Elliot to shield his face from the hail, his handkerchief slipping from his head. Suddenly the icy shower was gone, the roar of the storm engulfed them. Elliot's horse bolted away wildly, like the erratic fingers of lightning.

The killer lifted his head, then felt the blood drain like icy water from his face. The murderous black swirl of a tornado roared deafeningly toward them. He opened his mouth to scream. His lungs strained with the effort, but the sound was sucked from him before it could reach his own ears.

The twister swept them into its frigid clutches like the shadow of death. The killer's body spun helplessly, tighter and tighter. Pinpoints of lights formed in his vision, the tiny spots moving together, melting into a blinding hot, white flash.

His breath heaved within him, and his body contracted. The cells of his being pulling inward as his essence became part of the funnel of light.

The sound of the storm ceased, light ceased, feeling ceased. Only the resonance of his heart beating rhythmically existed. Suspended in a black limbo, he struggled to form a thought, anything to remember who he was. What he used to be.

Thunder boomed as sparks of color foamed around him, growing into a hazy cloud of shimmering shades of red and blue. He felt himself falling heavily; pain returned cloudily as his perception cleared.

His body prickled with pain. Opening his eyes, the black fog of his gaze shifted, then focused on his gloved hand. He reached for his face, squeezing his eyes shut.

His head felt as if it were splitting. Taking deep breaths, he forced his eyes open to squint at his surroundings.

The rain beat around him, pelting noisily on the black surface below. Gone were Elliot and his threat of retribution. The curtain had closed on that scene of his life. Now he had a new drama to play out.

And a new audience . . .

CHAPTER 1

Kansas, 1996

Jocelyn Kendrick tilted her head to study the corpse as it lay nestled in a green field of grass within the secretive gaze of tall cottonwoods. A forensic technician pushed past her, forcing her to step back quickly and juggle her notebook.

'Goat herder reject,' she mumbled under her breath, as she tossed a withering glance at the woman's blue-clad back.

Personnel had been kept to a minimum, allowing her the opportunity to examine the body more closely. She had needed the solitude so she could push past the mental barrier of encountering her first body in the field. All the other bodies had been at funerals.

Her brows knitted into a frown as she studied the corpse. Jocelyn had to admit this killer did seem to have a desire for cleanliness, but she didn't think that in this case it would count as a virtue.

Taking a deep breath, she tried to focus on the physical remainder of what used to be an individual. She tried not to think of whether this woman had been shy, or how she might have felt being the center of such frenzied activity. This part of her research made her feel like a vulture, circling in the beauty of the warm sky as death lay beneath her, cold and black.

She couldn't help thinking of Katrina, her best friend in high school. 'Focus,' she reminded herself quietly, 'focus on the part. Not the whole.' Sage words of advice from a veteran officer. Advice she was beginning to understand.

Carefully she positioned her feet in the area the tech had already covered. Kneeling beside the victim, she studied the facial features. Her gaze then moved to the dead woman's forearm lying across her chest. She hesitated only slightly before she gently prodded the purplish-liver color of the skin. Jocelyn bit her lip lightly in concentration as the color remained. Now, with more confidence, she lifted the index finger on the victim's right hand and wiggled it up and down.

Mumbling to herself, Jocelyn rested her own arm across her jean-clad knee.

'What's your assumption, Kendrick?' a gravely voice rattled from beside her.

She glanced up and then rose quickly to face Bill Wilson, the county coroner. Carefully she cleared her throat, 'Well the victim's skin is cold and clammy, it looks like rigor mortis has almost resolved, and there is evidence of fixed lividity. It's, well . . . it's only a ball park figure, but I would say about eighteen to twenty-four hours.'

He too surveyed the body, then grunted in agreement. 'I'd say good guess.'

Jocelyn accepted his meager compliment with a small smile. 'Thank you.'

'I'll have to see about getting you in on an autopsy,' the portly man said as he bent down beside the body. The floodlights, set up by the sheriff's department, gleamed off his balding head as he started his own examination.

'Bill, I really wouldn't want you to go to any trouble,' she swallowed. Her stomach lurched at the thought, but she was not about to mention that to him. A few graphic images remembered from textbooks flashed through her mind. 'Really,' she assured him.

She wasn't even a rookie cop, only a graduate student working on her masters in sociology. Her emphasis: deviant behavior. She could only call it a miracle when the homicide department had accepted her request for an internship. Her morbid fascination with death, however, had not come with a steel stomach. Not yet anyway.

'Really, Bill. I'm sure you're very busy,' she nervously repeated a little louder, afraid he hadn't heard her the first time.

'It's not a problem at all. In fact, I'll be doing her tomorrow,' he said as he gently touched the girl's face. 'I'll just give you a call when I'm ready.'

She moved to the other side and knelt to face him; she would work past that particular problem when it presented itself, definitely try to be busy at that moment. No matter what 'moment' it happened to be.

Bill studied the dead woman's features closely, then his brows drew together in a frown. Returning her attention to the corpse, Jocelyn also studied the woman's face which was in what could only be described as a mask-like condition.

During her undergraduate work she had been fascinated by forensic medicine. She had done a lot of elective work in forensic pathology but most of her experience had come from textbooks. Pictures and pages of graphic information could never prepare a person for the 'feel' of death, the shimmering sensations of brutality and the cold fear of finality. Here and now she attempted to put her education to use, hoping to learn from Bill's experience.

'Female, Caucasian, early twenties. Pupils fully dilated, mask-like expression, bruises probably from tetanic convulsions before her demise and there's no external evidence of cause of death,' he said, offhandedly. He peered over the glasses that had slipped down his nose, giving him an owlish expression. 'What would you surmise, Kendrick?'

She took a deep breath, her gaze on the dead woman's face. The pupils were extremely dilated, giving the eyes the look of a dull, hypnotic, drug induced stare. The face. Jocelyn had never seen anything like it. The victim's features and skin appeared waxen and chiseled, like a mask. An image worked its way through her imagination: Mardi Gras. She swallowed and shook herself free of the vivid image. This mask was not worn in celebration. It was a death mask.

'Poison,' she answered finally with a shrug of her shoulder. 'It would have to be something unusual or exotic.'

'You missed your calling,' he nodded as he raised an eyebrow, 'but we won't know for sure until I do a toxicology. Unfortunately, it also means I'll have to work with the damned FBI.'

Frowning, she met his gaze, noting the slight disgust in his eyes, 'Why?'

His eyes never left hers, his words cautious and direct like his manner. 'It would mean we now have a serial killer in our neck of the woods.'

Jocelyn's heartbeat accelerated at his words. She didn't know if it was from fear, or excitement. 'The Porcelain Mask Murderer.'

'Exactly,' he stated as he got heavily to his feet

She glanced down to a clear, plastic forensic bag lying beside the body. Her gaze fell on the fine, chiseled features of a white mask sheathed within; its garish red lips twisted in a sardonic smile. The killer's calling card. Her textbook experience would have several explanations as to why he left the small objects beside the bodies. Part of a ritual, or more likely a sort of identification of his work. Or perhaps to taunt those determined to find him.

Bill took a tissue from his pocket to wipe his glasses. He placed them back on his bulbous nose, then sighed. 'Well, it's going to be a long night and they're going to buzz my butt until I get this done,' he grumbled as he waved his hand to the detectives milling outside the taped area. 'And I already have two priority cases to do before this one.'

He shifted to leave, then hesitated. 'Hey, kid?'

She turned to the older man whose image reminded

her more of a kindly grandfather than one of the nation's best forensic pathologists. She raised her eyebrows in inquiry.

'Be careful.'

She nodded, unable to speak past the emotions swelling within her. He was concerned about her and she appreciated it. It was because of his concern that she began to feel a sliver of fear work its way into her thoughts.

'Time for me to get back to work too.' She spoke in a low voice. She put the image of the body, over which they were now draping a blanket, from her mind. Jocelyn wasn't here to study the dead, although she had a lot of training in it. It was the people who were alive that interested her and how they reacted to the situation.

Deviant behavior. Some people were appalled by it. Others were drawn to it. Some chose to ignore its very existence in society. Jocelyn, however, studied it, analyzed it, and hoped that maybe, just maybe, she could make her part of the world a little bit better.

She stepped over the yellow crime tape and made her way around the crowd to stand beside a police car. Leaning back against the vehicle, she propped her notebook in front of her as her gaze moved from face to face.

'Lurking are we?' a man said beside her.

Jocelyn turned and found Thomas Cohen moving to stand next to her. 'In sociology we call it observing.'

'You do it so well,' he murmured as he leaned against the car.

'At least my subjects are still breathing,' she smiled.

She looked nervously at his hands encased in rubber gloves. Thomas was holding something and with an assistant coroner, you could never be too careful.

'Sometimes I consider the fact that mine don't as a fringe benefit, Kendrick,' he said. He shifted the object to one hand, then scratched at his chest with the other.

Jocelyn watched this, remaining silent till curiosity finally overcame her. 'Thomas, what are you holding?'

'This?' He looked down as if suddenly remembering he was holding the item. 'Oh. You don't want to know.'

Jocelyn leveled her gaze on him. 'Trying to protect my innocence?'

Thomas chuckled and shook his head. 'I'm afraid it's probably too late for that. Not that you aren't just the sweetest little thing, but this is pretty gross.'

She swallowed, turning his comment over in her mind. She seriously considered for a moment whether she really wanted to know what was in the bag. Again, curiosity won out.

'Come on, Thomas, you have my interest piqued,' Jocelyn said earnestly. She leaned toward him to try to look into the bag. 'Just let me look.'

He leaned away holding the bag out of her reach. 'No. Really, Jocelyn. Not only are you nosy, but you're morbid.'

She wrinkled her nose at the word. 'So it's something gooey or gross you picked up from over there and you're taking it to the lab.'

'Wrong,' Thomas chuckled. 'See you don't know everything. Besides you would never be able to guess what is in this bag.'

Jocelyn grinned, she had always loved challenges. 'How much would you want to bet me that I can?'

He tried to pretend he was studying her seriously. 'You're on, Kendrick, and it will cost you five bucks.'

She looked the bag over, noting the size and shape. She nodded, then poked the bag before Thomas could pull it away.

'Hey, no messing with the evidence,' Thomas said. He held the bag in front of him with both hands as if holding a prize possession. 'Time is up, Jocelyn. What is in the bag?'

She looked at his eyes filled with humor and took a deep breath. 'Okay. I feel, no, I believe what you are holding is a sample or samples which you will use for entomological testing,' she said with a firm nod of her head.

'Sorry, no bugs in this bag,' Thomas laughed with a self-satisfied look on his face.

'Then what is in the bag?'

Thomas held the bag out to her and she opened it. Jocelyn frowned and looked again. 'It's your lunch?' She couldn't believe it. She looked at his grinning face in amazement. 'You bet me five bucks to try to guess that it was your lunch? You said it was gross.'

'And it is too,' he assured her. 'Besides you're the one who thought it was something to do with this case. Well, actually it does pertain to this case. It belongs to the guy who found the victim.'

Jocelyn folded her arms over her chest. 'Don't try to play nice, Thomas. You said it was gross. What else was I supposed to think?'

'Here, take a whiff,' he said, putting the bag under her nose. 'It's liverwurst. That by definition is gross.'

The unmistakable odor made its way to her before she could jerk her head back. 'Okay, okay, you'll get your five bucks tomorrow.'

'Where have I heard that before?' Thomas settled back against the car. He remained silent for a while as she started noting her observations. 'Did you write down John's unusual behavior?'

She smiled as she noted John Cartland's scowling expression. One of his hands waved expressively in the air as he talked with another detective. She jotted a note about his body movements, even the motion of his other hand as he scratched constantly at his stomach, chest, and elbows.

'What is wrong with him anyway? He's been grumpy all day and he keeps scratching all over himself,' Jocelyn said. 'You would think he has poison ivy or fleas.'

'He does,' Thomas answered with a knowing nod. 'Poison ivy, I mean. He got it while he was turkey hunting. Apparently didn't know he was lying in wait in a bed of poison ivy.'

Jocelyn made another note, then continued studying the people around her. A patrolman wearing white rubber gloves patted the shoulder of a county worker who sat on the step plate of a brush hog. Noting the pale complexion and the obvious distress, she wondered if he was the unfortunate 'first arrival' on the murder scene.

'What's the story on that guy?' she asked Thomas as she nodded in the man's direction. Cohen did seem to know what was going on.

He followed her gaze. 'That's the guy who found her and the proud owner of this lunch. According to one of the detectives I talked to earlier, this man literally stumbled over the body as he walked through the trees.'

Jocelyn had to admit she probably wouldn't be doing much better than the shaken man if she had been in his shoes. 'Sounds like he had a bad day all around.'

'Yes he did.' Thomas pushed away from the car. 'Not that I haven't enjoyed your company, Kendrick, but I better get this over to that guy and get back to work. Remember you owe me.'

Thomas walked off with a wave. Jocelyn shook her head, then glanced at her notes. It was time she got to work also.

All around her trained men and women performed their duties. Each person did his or her assigned task, some with emotion, some without. Whether the job was as a forensic technician, or a local reporter covering the scene for the evening news, no one could completely hide his thoughts. Their faces might appear nonchalant and professional, but it was the slight tremor of their hands that gave away the anger or fear that welled up within them. That was what she was searching for. The deep, personal part of an individual that they could not hide. Or change.

Anger, fear, caution, disbelief, and morbid curiosity. There was a wide range of emotions displayed at a crime scene, whether it be a robbery, or murder. Society had been desensitized by the media and movies, except when the reality brutally happened in their own back yard. Then it became personal.

Jocelyn studied the people present while remaining in the background of activity. Her gaze moved purposefully from individual to individual, noting behavior, perhaps occupation, if identifiable. Her analysis stopped abruptly, however, when she saw one man. One she had never seen before. He was tall, at least six foot, and broad shouldered. The stranger's dark hair was cut short in thick waves from his face. Quietly, he stood at the edge of the yellow tape and studied the corpse. The man's stance was rigid, even though the hands in his pockets suggested a relaxed posture. His expression hard, his eyes dark, he slowly turned and focused unwaveringly on her.

Jocelyn's heart beat with a very primal rhythm, as she exhaled slowly. She was unable to move her gaze from his as everything and everyone seemed to fall away like filmy strips of satin. Analyst met the scrutiny of the analyzed and felt what it was like to be studied. Determination, vitality, and warning; impressions that assaulted her with their power. His inspection was as physical as hot fingertips burning along her skin.

The man's eyes widened as if in fear, or perhaps shock. She frowned as his lips moved as if saying something. A shimmering wave of disorientation moved over her as what he had said sank in. She wasn't sure, but it seemed like her name.

He suddenly turned and moved away from the tape. Like her, he too had stood at the edge of the activity. Unlike her, he passed unhindered through the crowd. People parted in front of him as if his animal grace backed them away. He was focused, and moved with purpose. The purpose to leave.

'Driven.' She said under her breath, habit causing her to make a list. 'Focused, rigid control, most likely private with his thoughts . . . and damn good looking.'

Her feet were moving before her mind stopped its analytical processing long enough to realize she was following him. The strong urge to hesitate and plan a strategy pulsed through her. Uncharacteristically, she pushed caution aside and continued working her way through the crowd after the dark-haired stranger. Why would a man, whom she was quite sure she had never met, react as if he had seen a ghost, and more importantly, possibly know her name? Shouldering her way through the people she could see the top of his head appear here and there. The crowd began to thin, giving her the opportunity to pick up her pace.

She couldn't explain why she was now walking briskly enough to catch up with him other than his seeming to know her identity. Her thoughts clicked down the mental notes of her momentary study of him and found the answer. It was the look on his face. He hadn't shown fear or even anger at the result of a serial killer. She had found detachment and determination. The look of a hunter. Why?

She was ten feet from her goal of reaching the tall stranger when a large shoulder bumped into her. Jocelyn landed very ungracefully with a splatter into a puddle of dark, soupy liquid. Her mouth came open as she drew her hands up in front of her. She was covered with a thick layer of mud.

The movement of a blue truck pulling onto the dirt road caught her attention. The stranger was gone. Her questions would have to remain unanswered.

Now her attention focused on her current situation. She turned an angry glare to the apologetic man who had bumped into her.

'I slipped,' he explained as he motioned to his shoes, also thick with gooey layers of mud. 'Please forgive me, madam. Allow me to help you.'

She closed her mouth and swallowed her anger. It had been an innocent mistake made by an imbecile, she reminded herself. She accepted the offer of his hand and took great pleasure in the slime covering his grip as she let him haul her to her feet.

'No problem.' She smiled almost sweetly. She felt a momentary sense of misgiving as his hand remained holding hers a little longer than custom dictated.

'Please let me pay for the cleaning of your outfit,' he said. His voice was smooth and cultured, making her think of Hamlet.

'Don't worry about it. It happens . . .,' Jocelyn started, then found herself unable to finish. The man was almost as tall as the one she had been following. He also could be described as handsome, except for one thing. His eyes. The icy blue of his gaze held no warmth or emotion.

The boor who had graciously picked her up from the mud studied her with the unnerving sensation of a telepath. It was as if his gaze probed with gentle fingers into her deepest thoughts.

Jocelyn shook herself, breaking the hold of his eyes.

She rolled her shoulders to loosen the tension that had begun to tighten in her neck.

Impressions. She didn't always understand them, but she did tend to trust them. It was the cold she felt to her bones when she looked into this man's soulless eyes that cautioned her.

'I do apologize for such an imbecilic mistake.'

His choice of words, as if he had read her thoughts, caused a flush of embarrassment and fear to move through her. She stepped out of his grasp. 'It will wash out, really. Now, please, excuse me.'

Quickly she moved away, keeping her stride confident and determined. She passed John Cartland, and received the expected teasing remark. Her nerves were still vibrating. She knew if she looked back she would find the man's gaze still on her. Taking a deep breath, she smiled and turned to remind John that she was riding back to the station with him. This had the desired effect of shutting him up.

Jocelyn pulled her duffel bag from the back seat of Cartland's car to retrieve her gym towel. She cleaned up as best as she could, then later discreetly slipped her jeans off in the back of a police van. She grimaced as she pulled on the sweats she had put in the bag earlier. They were still damp from her work out, but at least it beat the grime of the mud. She emerged feeling somewhat crusty and tired.

This day had been a long one. She had been preparing herself for her first body in the field, but hadn't expected it to be the result of some twisted ritual by a serial killer. She wrapped her soiled notebook in the dirty towel she had used and tossed it on her bag in the back seat. The mess of her notes would have to be sorted out later.

Jocelyn sat in the passenger seat of John's car and leaned her head against the head rest. Her eyes burned and her shoulders ached from tension. She wanted desperately to go home and shower, before she could allow herself to quietly sort out the events of the evening. A killer with a whim for masks, and the unsettling impressions of two strangers, their effect on her similar, but for completely different reasons.

The thought of going home wished its way into her mind. She pushed the desire away with a sigh and resigned herself to the hours that she would have to remain at the scene. There was a body to take care of and an investigation to start.

And a madman on the hunt.

CHAPTER 2

Jocelyn rubbed a distracted fingertip across the throbbing of her temples. Sleep, if a restless nap filled with dark shadows could be called such, had left her feeling drained.

Last night, as she stared down at the corpse, she had been able to persuade herself to think of it only as a container of the soul. Once the soul was gone, the body became merely an empty vessel; the mortal remains of spiritual life. The thought had allowed her to work past her unease with death . . . until they had learned the victim's name.

Carrie Carter once was a 23-year-old college student studying for a degree in photojournalism; now she was dead.

Sitting in Veronica Figueroa's house, Jocelyn found several pictures of the victim scattered around the family room. Carrie and Veronica had been friends since childhood. They had remained close even when their lives took different directions: Veronica's to marriage and a family; Carrie to college and a killer.

'She was like a sister to me. We've always thought of

each other as sisters,' the dark-haired woman sniffed into her tissue. Her eyes were red-rimmed and swollen with grief. 'We even did the blood sister thing. You know where you cut your finger and put them together.' Her voice hitched and she reached for a new tissue, 'I still can't believe . . . she's . . .'

John placed a fatherly arm around Mrs Figueroa's young shoulders and led her to the couch. Reluctantly he had allowed Jocelyn to accompany him, but only with strict instructions to keep her mouth shut. 'I apologize for disturbing you during all this, ma'am. I know this is an extremely hard time for you.'

'Carrie's mother has been sedated since they told her last night.' She swallowed, then blew her nose. 'Her dad died only three months ago, so this has hit her mom pretty hard. Very hard.' The young woman yanked another tissue and wiped at the tears on her cheeks. 'I'm sorry . . . I know I'm rambling.'

'We understand, Mrs Figueroa.'

'Please call me Ronnie,' she said as she ran a trembling hand through her thick, dark hair.

John took a small notebook from his pocket and flipped it open. 'Can you tell us about any new acquaintances Carrie might have made recently?'

Ronnie's eyes turned to hold Jocelyn's. 'It was that Porcelain Mask guy, wasn't it?'

Jocelyn stiffened, then glanced uneasily at John, not knowing what to say. The woman's eyes demanded honesty. John leaned forward to pat Ronnie's hand on her knee, his voice soft with calm authority. 'We have reason to believe it was.'

'I thought so.' She looked to the tissue twisted in her hands. Her lip quivered for a moment as if she were going to cry again. Quickly, she cleared her throat and took a deep breath. As if she had made a mental resolve to help her dead friend, the young woman straightened her shoulders, her voice calm. 'Yes, Carrie had met this new guy.'

'Did she mention a name?' Jocelyn asked. It was only natural for a woman to turn to a woman to share grief. John tilted his head slightly, the subtle move his belated permission for her to join in.

'Jefferson Kerndon, I think.' Ronnie said, her voice edged with frustrated anger. 'She met him at the Renaissance Fair at the college. They were both wearing period costumes and started talking. Really hit it off I guess.'

'How long had she been seeing him?' John asked, as he noted her information.

'Two, going on three weeks maybe.'

'Did you ever meet this boyfriend?'

She shook her head, a protective hand moving to her swollen belly. 'I'm due in two months and the doctor doesn't like me running around too much. There've been a few complications.'

Jocelyn's gaze scanned the room taking in all the pictures. A new family's memories were on display on every available surface. She stood to study the arrangement on the mantel. The composition of the candid shots was beautiful, the color vivid. Better than the average point-and-shoot automatic camera.

She turned to Ronnie. 'Did she ever show you any pictures of this man she met?'

'No.' Frowning, she bit on her lower lip. 'Wait a minute. She brought a roll of film over last weekend for my husband to develop. He owns a photographic equipment store. Carrie is majoring . . .' She hesitated, swallowed, then took a deep breath to continue, her voice husky with emotion, 'was majoring in photojournalism. He hasn't taken it in yet.'

Ronnie shifted her pregnant frame forward on the couch, then pushed herself from the cushions. She moved to the kitchen and quickly returned with a black canister of film.

'Thank you, this could be very helpful.' John accepted it and tucked it into his jacket pocket. 'I'll return it to you as soon as possible.'

Jocelyn pointed to a picture of two smiling girls in their teens, their skinny arms draped around each other, 'Is this Carrie?'

'Yes.' Ronnie moved beside her and took the frame from the mantel. Her smile was warm with the memory even as her eyes shimmered with grief. 'Carrie was a picture taking fool. She even taped my last scan. Now she won't –' Quietly she replaced the picture, stroking a finger across the smooth frame. Her voice was low, determined. She turned to Jocelyn with a hard, compelling gaze. 'Just catch the bastard who did this.'

'We'll do our best,' Jocelyn said, as she turned the woman away from the pictures. She had to give the young woman the pretense of confidence, but guilt bit at her. It would not help the woman to know that she would have little, if anything, to do with the case. She was only allowed to go along as an observer.

Ronnie rubbed at her belly as she moved to pick up the box of tissues. She returned to the couch and slowly lowered herself. 'I remember her mentioning this guy, Jefferson, and she joked about how opposites attract each other. I guess it was because she liked taking pictures and he didn't like having his taken.'

'Did she ever say why?' John asked, looking up from scribbling in his notepad.

'No. But she did call about a week and a half ago to ask if she had dropped a roll of film off. I told her I didn't have it. Carrie told me that she had finally talked Jefferson into posing and later that same evening she couldn't find the roll. It had disappeared.'

'Was she in the habit of losing film?'

Ronnie shook her head quickly, 'Carrie was meticulous about her work. He must have taken it.' Her accusation was vehement.

John glanced through his notes then turned to Carrie's friend. 'She attended college full-time at a private university. How did she manage that sort of tuition?'

'Her dad was the founder of Carter's Grocery Stores. They have hundreds of locations in Kansas.' Ronnie studied the detective. 'Do you think money had something to do with it?'

He raised his shoulders in a shrug. 'I honestly don't know. But we like to check all the possibilities that we can.'

The woman studied him for a moment, then went on. 'Carrie's dad didn't want his children to grow up expecting to have it all,' she explained. 'He instilled a work ethic and a financial discipline in her and her brother. They worked summers at the stores. Not as managers, but as clerks or grocery sackers. He taught them to manage their money.' Ronnie nodded with a firm tilt. 'Check her records at her apartment. She kept track of everything.'

That is exactly what they did after they left Veronica Figueroa's comfortable little house. Carrie Carter had been as thorough with her finances as she was meticulous in her work. Neatly labeled file boxes were stacked in the corner of her walk-in closet. The victim's purse had never been found, but her returned check stubs and bank records confirmed that Jefferson Kerndon had received a considerable amount of money from the young college student. They had found several documents regarding Carrie Carter's loan to him. Jocelyn shook her head; apparently the killer had no qualms about breaking his word either.

Sitting at her desk at the station, Jocelyn held the loan papers in her hand. They had already been dusted and the dark soot clung to her fingertips as she studied the documents. The fingerprints had been smudged, giving them no evidence to follow. Carrie Carter had typed the paper on her computer and at the bottom of the printout the carefree flow of her signature was beside that of the thin, spiky alias of the killer. Their research into Jefferson Kerndon had turned up another dead end.

A large, brown envelope dropped on her desk. 'Here are the pictures from Carrie Carter's roll. Very disappointing.'

'How so?' Jocelyn asked as she picked the packet up

and opened it, pulling the pictures out to lay them on the desk.

John sat on the edge of her desk. The desk wasn't 'officially' hers, but just happened to be empty. Just like she didn't 'officially' work there, but that didn't stop the detectives from treating her like a slave. 'Take a look for yourself. The guy was very good at avoiding the camera.'

She examined each picture closely as she went through them. Frowning, she shook her head with frustration. 'He's either looking away or has his hand on his face.'

'Exactly,' he said, as he scratched at his arm, then moved on to his knee.

She looked at the grainy enlargement of their alleged killer, his head turned away and his hand effectively blocking his profile. Her attention was caught, however, by a face in the background. It was the man with the thick dark hair and mustache; his eyes were hard and focused at the camera. Focused as if studying her through the surface of the picture. She had called him the hunter. A feeling of apprehension moved through her, just who did he hunt? A murderer? Or unsuspecting women?

Her heart beat a wild tattoo in her chest as she studied the tiny image hidden behind the shoulder of their suspect. She straightened and laid the picture down in front of her.

'Do you see something?' John's voice broke into her thoughts as if he had sensed her unease.

'I don't know,' she said as she shook her head slowly,

releasing an uneasy breath and pointing to the stranger in the background. 'I may have seen this guy before.'

'He's a college guy. You could have seen him at college,' John shrugged distractedly as he studied the previous photos.

'Kendrick, line two' a man boomed from across the room. 'It's the coroner.'

John's shocked expression swung to her, his eyes wide with disbelief. 'Bill Wilson is calling you?'

'He's invited me to sit on the Carter girl's autopsy,' she explained, lifting her shoulder in a shrug. She suppressed a shudder, but was unable to stop the grimace from appearing on her face. 'I was really hoping he had forgotten.'

'The hell you do.' John's hand came down hard on the desk. 'Get your butt over there ASAP. Bill Wilson very reluctantly, do you hear me, reluctantly allows us in his department. He's never called anyone over here to just "invite" them to an autopsy. Never.' He hit the desk again for emphasis, then leaned toward her. 'Now listen to me, Kendrick. You go, you watch, you listen, and you better damn well take notes.'

Her stomach tightened with dread. 'Yes, sir.'

'I'll be damned,' he muttered. John turned to walk away, shaking his head as he looked at another detective. 'I can't believe it. Did you hear that? Bill Wilson called.'

Several detectives turned their attention to her, studying her with new interest. She looked at them, feeling like a bug under a microscope. 'It's not that big of a deal.'

'None of us have ever been invited, Kendrick,' Gary Pemberton stated. He was one of the best looking detectives she had ever seen and he possessed a sense of humor unlike some of the other cops in the department. He wadded a piece of paper into a ball and threw it at her from across the room. 'We practically have to get a court order just to walk into the morgue.'

'Perhaps if you weren't so obnoxious,' Jocelyn said, then leveled her gaze on him trying to keep a straight face. Failing, she laughed. 'Of course, it could just be your personality.'

Several detectives chuckled at her comment. Pemberton was known for his killer personality with the women. The man attracted women in herds and she knew several had made bets on how long it would take her to succumb. Some may have considered it sexual harassment, but she saw it as nothing more than what it was. People trying to find something humorous in a work day where the things people were doing to hurt each other were getting worse. She had also been the one to win the bet.

An hour later, Jocelyn swallowed the unease she had tried to avoid. She rolled her shoulders to try to ease the tension, then pushed the down button before she could change her mind. 'Why do they always put the morgue in the basement?'

She stepped into the elevator and grimaced when the doors slid closed. The efficient hum all too quickly stopped and the door dinged open. Taking a deep breath, she wrinkled her nose as she smelled the unpleasant odor of formaldehyde. She made her way to the opaque glass door with the black stenciled letters indicating the coroner's turf.

With a firm twist she turned the knob and walked into the office. Fifties style green vinyl furniture was situated around the room. 'I guess decor isn't real important down here,' she mumbled to herself.

She heard a sharp twang of something metallic hitting the cement floor, followed by an equally sharp curse. Bill Wilson's voice reassured an apologetic intern that it was quite all right; that dropping the brain pan and the brain would not hurt anything.

Jocelyn closed her eyes, then took a slow, steadying breath. She jumped when Bill boomed with enthusiasm, 'Jocelyn, come in. I am so glad you could make it.' He motioned with his hand for her to join him.

As if I had a choice, she thought. She followed him into the sterile hallway, devoid of any color, past two examination rooms with draped tables. She didn't dare ask what was under them. From the outline of the shapes she already had a pretty good idea what they were. What else would be lying on a table in the coroner's room anyway? He stopped at the third room where a young man, his face covered with sweat, worked.

'This is one of our new interns,' he said introducing the man to Jocelyn.

The young man raised his arm in a small wave, a dark, liver-looking object in his hand. She nodded, then continued after Bill. Her steps faltered as a thought hit her. 'My God, it probably was a liver.'

'I'm sorry I didn't quite catch that, Jocelyn.'

'I said I'm starting to shiver,' she stammered as she held her hand over her stomach protectively. 'I mean, I hope I'm not getting a cold. I wouldn't want to . . . uh . . . give it to you,' she said hopefully.

'Don't worry, dear,' Bill waved aside her concerns good-naturedly. 'You won't hurt anyone down here. I can guarantee it.'

'Good, I was so . . . worried,' she said disappointed. Taking a deep breath, she remembered John's order to thank the reclusive coroner for inviting her. 'I wanted to tell you I really appreciate this opportunity.'

'Nonsense.' He waved his hand as he entered the examination room at the end of the hall. 'I'll enjoy the company. I don't get much conversation from my patients.'

Jocelyn swallowed several times as she tried to dislodge the cold wad of apprehension sticking in her throat. A table draped with a faded green sheet dominated the room; the distinct form of a body hid beneath the thin material. Shivers of apprehension caused goose bumps to well up on her skin. Although the room was very cool, she knew the icy feeling seeping through her didn't come from the air.

'The dead, silent type, huh.' She said in a feeble attempt at humor. Obviously very feeble.

'That's good,' Bill hooted with laughter, then nodded. 'Good sense of humor. You're going to need that. A lot of rookies tend to suffer from "fall out" once I get started.'

Jocelyn cringed at the term. The detectives had relished teasing her about 'fall out'; an all too common experience for first-time observers of autopsies.

'Got my five bucks, Kendrick?'

She turned to see Thomas Cohen standing in the doorway wearing an apron splattered with dark stains. She frowned trying to focus on his question. 'What? No. No, I forgot.'

Thomas studied her for a moment. Without looking away from her, he spoke to his boss. 'If you don't mind, Bill, I think I will stay in here for a few moments.'

He peered over his glasses at Jocelyn, then nodded. 'Probably a good idea, Thomas.'

Bill switched on the overhead lamp and the autopsy began. He flipped back the sheet like a magician revealing a trick. The nude physical remains of Carrie Carter lay on the shiny surface of the chrome table. A shimmering sensation of light-headedness began to tingle down like a shower from Jocelyn's head to her toes. She locked her knees to keep them from folding under her. Images of all the detectives and the uniforms teasing her about fainting like a rookie flitted through her thoughts. She had promised herself she wouldn't pass out like the cops in the opening of the show *Quincy*.

Bill's voice took on a distant quality as if he were speaking from another room while Jocelyn tried hard to concentrate on what he said. She wasn't sure, but she thought he was reading stats from the chart. She heard something about height and age muddled within terminology she was probably familiar with, but just could not comprehend right now.

She held her breath as he made the incision down the girl's front. Even as the surgical saw whirred through the breast bone and she felt her body began to sway, she was proud to still be standing. Fortunately, her vision began to blur like sand in an hour glass when he began removing items to examine and weigh.

'Now here we have everybody's favorite, our friend, the stomach,' Bill said with such innocent enthusiasm.

Jocelyn's rump connected roughly with the cement floor before she realized she wasn't standing any more. 'That's better,' she mumbled thickly.

Thomas chuckled softly, but his voice was filled with understanding as he knelt beside her. 'Are you all right?'

Her vision began to clear, and the rushing whoosh-whoosh of her heartbeat was fading from her ears. Her thoughts and Bill's words were now beginning to make sense. She nodded, hoping Thomas would not make a big deal of this. 'That's definitely better.'

Above her and across the table she heard a meaty plop and the unmistakable sound of knife cutting through sinewy layers as he dissected the organ. 'Nothing unusual here.'

She lifted her eyes in a silent prayer of thanks that she was unable to see what was going on. John had made her come and had told her to stay. She may be sitting on the floor beside the table, but she was still there. That counted in her book.

'Jocelyn, where are you?' Bill called. His face appeared over the top of the chrome surface. 'Oh, there you are. Don't worry, dear, spending your first autopsy on the floor is not uncommon. A lot of those hard cases in your department weren't even conscious by the time the autopsy was complete. Isn't that right, Thomas?'

Thomas grinned, meeting her gaze. 'Just ask Pemberton about his first autopsy.'

She tried to smile, but was not quite able to accomplish the task.

'Not unusual at all. Now we'll go on to the kidneys,' Bill said with jolly enthusiasm.

An instrument clanked to the floor and skidded beside her. She turned warily to it and sighed with relief. It was still shiny, which thankfully meant clean. Unused.

'Now what happened to that pesky . . .'

Jocelyn picked the item up and straightened her arm to hold it above the edge of the table.

'Why thank you.'

She wiped the cold sweat from her brow, retrieved her notebook from her bag, and began to take notes.

The Porcelain Mask Murderer smiled as he clipped the picture from its dominating position on the front page. He liked the name. It had such a dramatic lilt to it.

'A double memento,' he chuckled in amusement as he shifted his gaze to a similar article regarding the killing. Written by a psychologist, it had stated that serial killers often kept items from their victims as reminders, or trophies.

Lifting his head to study a painting on the wall of his small apartment, he pursed his lips in thought. Serial killer sounded too, well, rough handed; working class. He was an artist.

He returned his attention to the grainy image from the paper. Carrie, dear, sweet Carrie. Only her foot could be made out in the dark picture. Standing over her were two people; an old man in a coroner's jacket and the young woman with a clipboard.

The familiar yearning tightened in the pit of his stomach. A need that soon would not be satisfied except by the power. The God-like power of life and death. He took a deep breath, and focused on the woman's young face in the picture. The concentration cooled the fire; the control returning even as his thoughts began constructing the scenario for his next drama.

As he studied her face, he felt the veil of time slip silently away. The image merged to that of another woman standing on the wooden porch of the dry goods store. A smile lifted the corners of his mouth as he remembered her lively spirit and wit, then his lips slowly hardened as he recalled her continued rejection of him. She had called him cold and unfeeling. A man without a soul. Choosing instead a man who she had said would give her all that she could ever want. Or need.

He shook himself from his thoughts and returned his gaze back to the clipping. This one would be perfect. This woman who bore the likeness of the girl from his memories. He remembered the smooth texture of her skin and the defined, delicate features of her face as she examined the body. The woman's hair was a tad short for his taste, but he admired the thick, luxurious curls as they framed the passionate green of her eyes.

That's what had caught his attention. His desire. The range of emotions which had been displayed in her eyes;

anger, tolerance, and an unknowing fear. He would have to be careful around her. The girl was intelligent. She saw too many of a person's thoughts. But the risk was part of the role. The excitement.

Yes, she was perfect. Soon he would know her name. Then the curtain would rise again . . .

CHAPTER 3

Trevan Elliot watched the building as he sipped the remains of his lukewarm coffee. He had followed the woman here a couple of hours ago and had been drinking coffee since. He took his watch from his pocket to check the time. Again.

'Five-thirty. My, how time flies when you're having fun,' he muttered, shifting to replace the item. 'Watching a building, which has air-conditioning, while I sit out here roasting my a . . .'

The woman he had been waiting for began to descend the steps, stopping his words and focusing his attention. Her short, dark hair bounced in the breeze as she slowly made her way to the sidewalk. Trevan squinted as he studied her. Her skin was a little too pale, her manner too subdued. He set his cup on the dash as he watched her with concern. She stopped, grasped the rail of the steps, and lifted her face to the sun as if enjoying the caressing warmth on her face.

His mouth dried as hot images involving the creamy column of her throat pulsed through his thoughts. The irony hit him as he remembered feeling her gaze on him at the scene of the murder. He had been studying the body until he felt the prickle of caution on the back of his neck. Turning, he had found her watching him intently. Looking into her eyes, he had found himself needing. Wanting. A distraction he could not allow. But it was her face that had caused the blood in his veins to turn icy with foreboding.

The moment his gaze had touched her face he had felt the cold wash of shock and then the warm joy of recognition, until he realized her eyes had reflected no knowledge of him. The woman she had reminded him of was only one of the many sacrifices that fate had forced him to make. To leave behind his fiancee. He held so many clear and moving memories of her from a time so long ago and forgotten by those around him.

He had seen the questions in the stranger's eyes and the shift of her stance as she started to move toward him. Then he had caught the glint of her scene pass – she was a police officer. Police asked questions. He could not risk either one; officers or the questions they would surely have.

Yet, now he was keeping an eye on her. From a distance, of course.

Trevan mumbled a dark curse and shook his head, his gaze following her to her vehicle. He didn't *want* to want her. Didn't understand why something like this would affect him now. The hunter the press had shamelessly dubbed the 'Porcelain Mask Murderer' would keep on killing until he was found. Trevan growled as his thoughts continued to assail him, and as fate would have it, the madman was after the very woman who had affected him so completely.

Instinct. His body had hummed with its warning since he had encountered the probing stare of the woman named Jocelyn Kendrick. The 'PM' murderer would focus on her beauty, her intelligence, and hate her for them. Trevan knew without a doubt that the madman would not be able to resist the urge to take this woman away from him as Trevan guessed the man had tried unsuccessfully to do so long ago.

Starting the car, he waited until her black Jeep Cherokee pulled from the curb before he moved to a discreet distance behind it. With a grim, humorless smile he thought of his informant and sometimes accomplice, Cargo, who had often warned him that, 'Beauty bears a price'.

The words of caution pulsed through him as Jocelyn Kendrick's delicate, fineboned features remained in his thoughts. She was beautiful, that he could not deny. The soft curls of her dark, almost black hair framed the green of her eyes. Even now he could very well imagine the silky texture swirling around his fingers as he cupped her face.

'Get a grip, Elliot,' he muttered. The effect of this woman had done nothing for his disposition. Even Cargo had noticed his dark moods and had warned him that the stress would kill him.

He grunted at the thought of the small man with ebony eyes, his clean, tattered clothes hanging on his wiry frame, giving advice as coolly and professionally as a doctor. Trevan didn't know where the old man lived, only that he could count on him when needed.

Trevan's coffee cup fell from the dashboard to spill

on his lap. He swore, then distractedly wiped with a tissue at the warm liquid soaking into his jeans as he kept his eyes on the black vehicle ahead.

'Damn it, I won't be of much help to her if I get myself killed in a wreck.' His anger evaporated immediately as he caught sight of another vehicle pulling into the far lane of the street. Trevan allowed his car to slow.

'Well, I guess we have a visitor,' he said quietly.

A silver BMW turned abruptly at the corner causing the car behind it to jerk to a stop to avoid a collision. Trevan studied the vehicle, trying to peer into the interior, but the shifting reflections of the buildings off the tinted windows were all he could see.

The car might have nothing to do with the woman he was following, but then again, it might have everything to do with the murders. Gut reaction warned him that it was time for the madman to begin the hunt for a new victim. He would track her, study her, then move in for the kill.

Jocelyn Kendrick's face had been seen on local and national news as she talked with the county coroner. Her image was on the front page of several major newspapers as she stood over Carrie Carter's body. The media had continually flashed her face in front of the killer, tightening the cross hairs of his desire, until she had become the focus of a man with a murderous vision. The killer would not be able to resist the irony of taking the woman who so much resembled the past to replace the one he could never have.

The car turned at the street ahead and Trevan let out a shaky deep breath. He had got little sleep in the past several days, unable to face the shadowy dreams that relentlessly pursued him when he closed his eyes. He wiped at the sweat on his brow and continued to follow the woman. Even in the daylight the images haunted him, forcing him to focus harder on his pursuit. The killing had to stop, he thought.

Every time another body was found, the faceless mask of the murderer would hover in Trevan's dreams to taunt him with his guilt. It had been the driving force to make him adapt to the gadgets and inventions of this time. He did not know why he had been brought forward. But he did know one thing, he had to stop the madman before Jocelyn Kendrick became another victim.

Trevan pulled his truck beside the curb in front of the park behind the woman's house and turned the ignition off to wait. Patience had never been one of his virtues and fortunately he wasn't forced to test it as he caught sight of the ever punctual Cargo.

The thin man walked through the trees to the truck. After he opened the door and slid in, he warmly acknowledged the sack Trevan handed him.

'Thank you, friend. The chill still clings at night,' he said softly.

'I know,' Trevan responded then turned his gaze to the windshield. 'Having you keep an eye on things means a lot to me, Cargo. There is no one I would trust with this but you.'

Cargo stopped opening his dinner and met Trevan's gaze, 'Such elaborate praise for such a simple deed.'

Trevan took a deep breath to calm the threatening

wave of emotions. 'A simple task that could mean life or death for this woman.'

'Yes,' answered Cargo as he pulled a sandwich out and began to unwrap it. 'This one is different, isn't she?'

Trevan frowned, not really caring for the direction this conversation was taking. 'I don't have any idea what you're talking about.'

'Maybe not, but you seem to have a great deal of concern for this woman,' the thin man said quietly. His soft voice filled Trevan's thoughts with too many images of other pretty girls.

'Murder tends to do that, Cargo.'

'Ah, I see I've hit a nerve,' he replied, merely raising an eyebrow at Trevan's word.

Trevan ran his hand through his hair as he shook his head. He realized his words had been harsher than he intended. Cargo had been with him on this hunt almost from the beginning and had helped him too many times in a world he didn't always understand. 'Please accept my apologies, friend. This whole spit of trouble is starting to get to me.'

'The madman you seek,' Cargo asked, his voice dropping, 'or the woman you watch?'

Trevan met his gaze then grinned at the man's uncanny knack for knowing what was on his mind. 'Are you sure you're not one of those psychoanalyzers or whatever they are called?'

Cargo smiled faintly as if in embarrassment, 'I believe some would refer to them as "shrinks", but no, I am not.'

'Too bad,' he said, then turned his gaze to the park to scan it once again. 'Maybe you could figure out why I feel like I know this woman.'

'Does she remind you of someone from your past?'

'A lady I once courted,' he hesitated, realizing his archaic language could reveal too much of his past, as it had with the man beside him. It had not taken long for the observant man to start asking him questions, then later confront him with the statement that he knew Trevan was not from this time. 'I mean dated.'

'What is there about this woman, Jocelyn Kendrick, that reminds you of the woman from your past?'

Trevan took a deep breath as he thought about it; as he had been doing for several hours now. 'She looks incredibly like Justine, not to mention even the similarities of their names, but it's more than that.' He hesitated as he recalled the Kendrick woman's gestures and certain facial expressions. 'The way this woman acts sometimes reminds me of Justine. Things like the way this woman tilts her head when she smiles, or how independent she seems.'

'Perhaps Miss Kendrick is a reincarnation of your Justine,' Cargo offered before he bit into his sandwich.

Trevan frowned unable to keep the skepticism from his face. 'Reincarnation? You mean when Justine died, her soul moved on to this woman?'

With a hint of humor, Cargo nodded. 'One might call it a sort of spiritual recycling of souls.'

'I'll be damned,' he said, giving the idea a serious thought. Then he laughed. 'I don't think so. Justine wasn't nearly as bossy as this woman. I've seen her arguing with that policeman she works with. I guarantee you Justine would never have done that.'

Cargo shrugged, 'It was only a thought.'

Trevan chuckled, then turned his gaze to the park once again. A flash of silver, then a movement of black, pushed all thoughts of Cargo's theory from his mind. He leaned forward to peer through the windshield. The shrubbery behind the trees remained still as he continued to search for who or what had moved in the concealing shadows of the foliage. The inky silhouette of a man shifted, then slowly worked his way from the surrounding darkness into the back yard of the woman's house. A wrist watch flashed briefly in the moonlight as the man moved through the thick shrubs.

Trevan's instincts vibrated with foreboding. He knew without a doubt that the man Jocelyn Kendrick, the police, and the FBI had been searching for was in her very own back yard, threatening the peace of this sleepy, suburban neighborhood.

'Well, I think our "psycho" has just made an appearance,' he said quietly as he opened the truck door. 'The keys are in the ignition, Cargo, if you need them. I'm going to check this out.'

The older man nodded, 'Do you want me to call the police if you don't return within a reasonable amount of time?'

Trevan shook his head, 'Don't worry about me, friend. Neither one of us can afford to talk to the police about this. If I'm not back in twenty minutes, take the truck and head on back to the house. I'll meet you there tomorrow.'

Cargo frowned, 'I don't think this is wise.'

Trevan grinned, 'The way I see it, I wouldn't have been brought here just to die in someone's back yard.'

'No one knows his final destiny,' Cargo reminded him, then slid toward the wheel as Trevan got out of the truck. 'Just remember there are no rules when playing with a madman.'

'Don't worry, Cargo, if I don't like the rules, I'll just change them.' He nodded to his partner then nudged the door shut with a soft click. He took a moment to study the area. Cautiously he made his way to the place where he'd last seen the shadow, his boots silent on the black pavement of the sidewalk. He turned sideways and slipped his large form through the bushes, wincing slightly as the leaves rustled with his progress. Fortunately, the wind picked up at that moment and masked the noise.

Approximately sixty feet ahead of him, the lean frame of the intruder hovered outside the darkness of the kitchen window. His hand ran along the edges as if testing for cracks or openings to nudge the wooden frame up.

Trevan glanced around him. Where, he thought, were the barking dogs keeping the neighbors awake when he needed one. Silently he cursed the fact that he would have to sneak up on the man to subdue him. Trevan didn't want to raise a ruckus so close to the woman's house. Or the woman herself.

He pulled his gun from the shoulder holster under his jean jacket and started to advance on the intruder. Without warning the man spun toward him, his face concealed in the shifting shadows of the trees beside the house.

'Ah, Elliot. I had hoped you were dead,' the low voice whispered with disappointment.

Trevan knew the killer could see his face clearly in the moonlight even as he recognized the man's chuckle from the depths of his own nightmares.

'Fortunately, we've never "officially" met before. We really didn't talk much last time, did we?' The man's silky words caused the heat of Trevan's fury to burn through him in frustration as the moonlight glinted off the gun in the killer's hand. 'But I know you from your sister's description.' He paused a moment as if to let the mocking words bite into him. 'Allysa had your fire, you know,' the figure offered softly. 'That *was* a long time ago, wasn't it?'

'You sick . . .' Trevan began, his words ending in a growl from deep within him. He felt the pain of his sister's loss, dull and deep, start to throb.

'Even in death she tried to tell you.' The man's words were taunting, laced with malice.

Sweat broke in cold beads on Trevan's forehead as flashes, brief and unrevealing, sliced through him. An image of Allysa as a smiling girl with flowing, blonde hair, so unlike his own, pierced his thoughts. Then it changed. A porcelain mask lay within inches of her outstretched fingers. Her face pale, her eyes unseeing. A sense of grievous loss tore through him as fresh as the day he had discovered her battered body.

Trevan glared at the man, his fury igniting every cell in his being. He gritted his teeth as he raised his gun and

55

leveled it on the dark, shadowed features of Allysa's killer. 'You're going to hell if I have to take you there myself.'

'I don't think so, Elliot.'

A burst of flame caused Trevan to dive to the side. He recognized the low whistle of the silencer as he tumbled into the garbage cans. He rolled over the tops and fell into a heap on them as they rattled around him. He struggled with the trash strewn over him, unable to work his left arm fast enough to remove a lid lying across his face.

His adversary chuckled, 'You can't stop me, Elliot. Or my next act with this woman Jocelyn as my leading lady.'

Trevan cringed. He knew the repeated use of his name only served as a scornful reminder that although the menacing shadow knew his identity, he had no idea who the killer was. But worst of all he had made the connection with Jocelyn Kendrick and the past.

He groaned as he heard the man's steps pad softly in a quick jog across the yard, then the soft rustle of bushes as he left. The Porcelain Mask Murderer was gone.

Pain sliced through his arm as he shifted to grip the injured limb. He struggled to sit up. He started to throw the lid off when it was lifted from him and thrown across the yard.

'Don't move or I will shoot.'

He closed his eyes and let his head fall back into the pillow of a trash sack. Standing before him was Jocelyn Kendrick with a snub-nosed, thirty-eight pointed unwaveringly at his face. Things just couldn't get worse, he thought.

Jocelyn gasped as she threw the lid off the man. He met her gaze with a mixture of anger and frustration. The intimidating look was the same one that she had encountered at the crime scene and then again in the grainy images of Carrie Carter's photographs.

The man laid his head back and closed his eyes and for a brief moment Jocelyn thought he might be dead. He was very pale – she shook her head to stop her concern, reminding herself that she had barely caught the other man's threatening words before he ran from the yard. This man lying in her trash had stopped the other one from doing something in her back yard. But what?

She decided it was time to wake up Sleeping Beauty. She nudged his leg with her foot. 'Get up slowly and don't even think about trying anything with me. Put your hand on your head and turn to the wall.'

His eyes opened and Jocelyn felt the strong, mesmerizing pull of his gaze. He was handsome; his features finely chiseled in the dark tan of his face. He obviously hadn't shaved and short stubble framed his face and strengthened his features, giving him a wonderfully all too masculine image. He was a large man, and from what she could see of his partially exposed stomach, had a hard body.

And right now he stank like week-old chicken.

Stranger Number Two groaned and shifted awkwardly in an effort to stand. He glared at her as he turned and slowly placed his hands on the wall.

'Strong, silent type, huh,' she said with confident authority, even though her heart raced with suspicion. Strangely, even though she could not say why, she did not fear for her life. Danger clung to this man, but not from murder. She would have to think on that. Later. Right now she had to find out why he was in her back yard and what it had to do with the other guy who ran away.

Jocelyn wrinkled her nose and was forced to pick off several pieces of garbage from his shoulders and his back before she could begin her search. She kept the gun level on his back with one hand as she skimmed lightly on the outside of his legs with the other.

All too quickly she became aware of his muscular legs encased in his jeans. And yes, she had to admit, the firm ridges of his buttocks were quite nice. She hesitated, her hand hovering by his groin. Nope, she decided, the police could just check that area all by themselves. She then continued up his ribs to his wide shoulders, down his arm, then stopped.

She withdrew her hand and rubbed the sticky substance between her fingers. 'It's blood. What did you do, shoot yourself?'

The low growl coming from his throat instantly had her training her gun on him with both hands. He turned his head slightly, eyed the gun, and took a deep breath as he met her gaze. 'I didn't shoot myself and I don't have a gun on me, as you well know. My gun is lying somewhere in this trash. Now would you please allow me to lower my arm? He shot me, but it's only a scratch.'

With two stiff legged steps, Jocelyn backed away,

giving him room to turn. Seeing his face and his expression, she sensed no danger or fear for herself from him, only a strong curiosity. 'If you're not a klutz, then who shot you?'

The determined expression of a hunter that had earlier burned his image into her memory, returned to his face. He studied her with a grim look as if hesitating, then shrugged. 'I believe you would refer to him as a burglar. Maybe a rapist, I really didn't have time to ask.'

'What?' Why would anyone want to rob her, or worse? Numbing disbelief had her lowering the gun. This guy had to have escaped from the state hospital. The terror-induced thought had her raising her gun on him again. Then something important occurred to her. 'I didn't hear a gun shot.'

'He used a silencer. It looked homemade,' he answered matter-of-factly.

A burglar with a silencer? Yeah, right. Before she could ask the questions filling her mind the bushes rustled noisily, causing them both to turn swiftly in the direction that it came from in the side yard. Jocelyn had her gun ready and noted, with some confusion, how the man had shielded her as he stepped between her and the most recent arrival to their little late night gathering.

The mumbled curses had her lowering her gun and stepping past his tall frame. Instinctively, and by his actions now, she knew he was not something to be feared. If he was going to hurt her, he wouldn't have tried to protect her.

59

Jocelyn worriedly shook her head as she caught a glimpse of large pink curlers encased in a green scarf wobble through the thick bushes. Pushing limbs out of her way, she reached in to gently take her elderly neighbor by the arm to help her out of the thorny tangle of the shrubs. 'Mrs Phillips, what are you doing out here?'

Jocelyn groaned with disbelief as she extracted the large, double-barrel shotgun from the old woman's frail arm. This whole situation was getting crazier by the minute. 'You shouldn't carry this thing around. You could shoot yourself.'

Mrs Phillips straightened to her tiny height of five feet. 'I can handle my gun better than you, little girl. Besides, someone over here shot a hole in my window. Damn ingrates blew a hole two inches wide right in the middle of Mr Phillips's head.'

Jocelyn caught the stranger's look of concern and cleared her throat to catch his attention. 'She's talking about a painting of her late husband.'

The explanation caused his lips to lift in a small smile of amusement. He directed his attention to the petite woman. 'Mrs Phillips, please forgive the intrusion. I will gladly pay for any damage.'

The wrinkles around the woman's eyes almost enfolded them as she squinted at her slim neighbor, then to the tall stranger with what, Jocelyn could only guess, was a look of appreciation. 'Were you trying to shoot this young man? Did he try to take advantage of you? Jocelyn, dear, you don't shoot them to back them off. You have to be coy, my dear, wrap them around your pinky, so to speak.'

60

Jocelyn shook her head in amusement; the elderly woman seemed to think of nothing but sex. Or more accurately, Jocelyn's lack of same. 'Yes, ma'am. I mean, no, ma'am. This man chased off an intruder who apparently also took a shot at him. Or so he claims.' The last part was mumbled so her neighbor could not hear, but did cause a glare from the tall man.

Mrs Phillips frowned, 'Then why are you pointing a gun at him?' Jocelyn was able to keep herself from rolling her eyes as the old woman looked at her with pity. 'Sweetheart, I think we need to talk. You are never going to find a man if you keep threatening them. First, it was that one boy you gave a black eye to, then that man you kicked right in the privates.'

She paused as if considering the action, then shrugged. 'Of course, that one probably deserved it. If someone had asked me to put on leather thigh-high boots and tie him up, I would have – '

'Mrs Phillips, I don't think this is relevant,' Jocelyn interrupted quickly. She shook her head at the elder woman's naive persistence. 'Someone tried to break into my house tonight and I need to call the police.'

Mrs Phillips shook her finger at Jocelyn, the movement causing her curlers to shake. 'That's right young lady, you should. But it still doesn't excuse the fact that you were pointing your gun at the man who just saved your life.'

'I don't know if he did or not,' Jocelyn's brows widened with surprise at the woman's strong words. 'For all we know he's involved in all this.'

Mrs Phillips's gaze swung to the stranger and it made

Jocelyn feel better that he stepped back slightly. 'Young man, were you involved in all this? Did you intend to harm this dear girl?'

He shook his head. The man's lips twitched nervously as if he couldn't decide whether to laugh or take her seriously. He finally held his hand up in an old fashioned gesture as if he were going to swear to his innocence. 'No, ma'am, I give you my word. It was never my intention to cause her harm.'

Her brow rose, then she leaned toward him. 'Are you married?'

'Mrs Phillips, I think it's time for you to go home. Here, let me walk with you,' Jocelyn said quickly, taking her neighbor by the arm and guiding her toward her house.

She had to continually reassure and cajole Mrs Phillips back to her house, and was more than a little surprised when the uninvited handsome man accompanied them, his gaze constantly scanning the area as if he were guarding them. He even kissed the elderly lady's hand with old fashioned flare before he closed the door after her and waited to hear the locks turn before he would leave the porch.

With the door shut firmly behind her busybody neighbor, Jocelyn took a deep breath in relief. Now she could deal with this man and not feel as if she were twenty some years old with an elderly aunt who was terrified she would never marry.

Returning to her home, she kept the man's tall frame at her side so she could keep an eye on him. She also left the safety on her gun switched off. She didn't know what he was doing here, but she would soon enough. The only thing she did know, and it was not confirmed by anything he had said, was he was not here to hurt her. It was obvious that he had followed her and had been here to protect her. But from what and, more importantly, from whom?

She moved to the back of her house and surveyed the damage. The scattered garbage could wait until tomorrow she thought, then gasped as she noted the white lines of pain etched on his face. Just a scratch, he had said. Only a scratch that hurt like hell. 'You need to go to the hospital. After rolling around in my trash there is no telling what sort of germs you've infected yourself with.'

His stubborn expression only confirmed what she already felt; he would not go. A bullet wound would have to be reported to the police and it was obvious, for whatever reason she couldn't fathom, and she just hoped it was a good one, he couldn't afford that.

She shook her head and raised her eyes to the sky and knew she shouldn't let him in her house or anywhere near her. After all, she had caught the man in her back yard and he had been shot, but first impressions were important to her. If she forced him to go to the hospital or called the police, she would never get the answers to the questions plaguing her. She studied him out of the corner of her eye; he reminded her of Tom Selleck in *An Innocent Man*. And who could turn away Tom Selleck – especially when he'd been shot?

She sighed and resigned herself to the fact that she was breaking all of her own rules. 'Come on in and I'll see what I can do about that so-called scratch, but,' she held his gaze long and hard, letting him know she meant business, 'I expect answers or I'll call the cops myself. And if you make one wrong move, I'll finish what the other guy started, is that understood?'

A brief look of grim humor passed across his face before he nodded.

'Oh, Lord,' she muttered. 'What am I getting myself into?'

Yesterday her horoscope had said that a storm was brewing on her personal horizon and she felt like it was going to hit any minute. And she didn't have a raincoat.

The dark figure ran silently around the corner of a garage and pressed himself against the wall. The man's breath came in ragged gulps. Confronting Elliot in the woman's yard had been an unexpected interruption, he thought as he forced himself to breathe deeply to slow down his heart rate. He chuckled and shook his head. It had been a long time since he felt this much energy from facing the thrill of escape.

'No doubt I have Elliot to thank for that,' he murmured in a low voice, scanning the area around him. So far he had not met with any noisy dogs and neither had he heard sirens. Turning, he cautiously looked around the corner to make sure he had not been followed. It occurred to him that perhaps Elliot had approached the woman and together they had realized it would be unwise to contact the police.

His lips twisted upward in an evil smile at the thought. Quietly, he pushed away from the garage wall and calmly began to walk down the drive to his car parked on the street as if he were going for a midnight stroll.

Removing his black gloves he chuckled softly to himself. Destiny had brought him this woman. Did Elliot actually think he could keep him from reaching her?

Did he think he could keep her safe? At the thought, the killer lifted his head and laughed. The dark sound echoed in the stillness of the night.

CHAPTER 4

Jocelyn's mysterious stranger came out of the bathroom after washing up and, with some bickering, allowed her to cleanse the wound. The man was fortunate, since it was only a shallow gash, she thought, then stole a glance at his profile and thought, from the looks of him, he had probably done worse saddling a horse. His worn jeans, the pointy tips of his boots, and the day's growth of beard all suited him. She shrugged at her thoughts. So maybe he could be a real cowboy. If so, then why was he chasing someone from her back yard and getting himself shot?

Lifting her gaze, she found him studying her. It was then she noticed she had finished swabbing his arm with the antiseptic, her hand still lingering on the muscled ridge of his forearm. Dropping her hand to her hip to take a defiant stance in front of him, she met his look head on. Might as well get this show on the road.

'So let me guess. You were leading your boy scout troop on a nighttime expedition to earn their badges in nocturnal foraging, or whatever, when you realized you were lost and decided the evening just couldn't go to waste without at least attempting a good deed, at which time you allegedly confronted some guy in my back yard.' She took a breath, then hesitated. 'Please correct me if I'm wrong.'

'Allegedly confronted?' The rugged stranger's brow furrowed with his glare as he returned her angry look with one of his own. He stood and his bare chest with its inviting mat of hair and the strong column of his neck were suddenly too close to her inspection. She was forced to back away from him to regain her equilibrium and her breath.

'Has anyone ever told you that for a woman you have a sarcastic manner?' His voice was low with anger. Even with its fire, it sent a seductive heat through her.

'Yes, as a matter of fact.' Her temper flared and she decided to let fire fight fire as she lifted her chin to glare at him. 'Especially when I've been awakened at two in the morning by an intruder running from my back yard and I find someone else sprawled in my trash.'

She took a deep breath to calm her anger, then faced him again. 'Despite the fact that it appears you were trying to help me tonight.' His brows rose at her statement as if he were going to argue the point. She went on, not giving him the chance to speak. 'Yes, appears is what I said. You can't blame me for being leery of you and what you're telling me. First, I see you studying the body of a dead girl as if you're looking for something. Then I find you sprawled in the trash of my back yard and some guy is running into the bushes. I have to be crazy for even doing this.'

She looked away to collect her thoughts. Her mind was searching for answers. One of which was that the dead girl, this man, and the one she caught a glimpse of running from her yard were all connected. The thought scared her and she rubbed her hands shakily on her hips, hoping that he could not see the fear building within her.

His hand touched her arm, warming her skin. She looked at his hand on her, then slowly met his gaze as he spoke gently to her. His eyes were soft with understanding and a hint of concern. 'No crazier than I am for being here.'

Jocelyn quickly grabbed a roll of bandaging and determinedly began to wrap it around his arm. She didn't know which unnerved her more, the sensations this man could provoke within her or the questions that hung unanswered between them. 'Now you can tell me what's going on. Starting with your name.'

'All right.' The man winced as she rolled the coarse material in another tight layer. 'All right. What are you trying to do, apply a tourniquet? It's only a flesh wound.'

Jocelyn applied the tape to keep the gauze in place and then moved to lean against the counter, letting him know he had her full attention.

'My name is Trevan Elliot. I won't insult your intelligence by saying I just happened to be strolling by. I have been watching your house.'

'Watching my house?' She snapped, pushing away from the counter. Lack of sleep and her tattered nerves had worn away the last of her patience. 'Watching my house. Well, that part at least is obvious. What I want to know is why? And who was the guy that ran?'

She moved to the coffee pot and started the normal routine of making a fresh pot. 'Caffeine. A good sharp jolt ought to clear things up while you tell me the whole story.'

He studied her for a long moment. Jocelyn found herself straining to hear what he was going to say even as something within her instinctively knew she didn't want to.

'I knew that the man you saw running would come here.'

Jocelyn shook her head, his words were just not making sense to her, 'How would you know he was coming here? Who is he? What does he want?'

'I believe the answer lies in our common interest,' he said quietly as his gaze held her.

Her heart began to pound as she realized what he was getting at. 'The Porcelain Mask Murders,' she said. It was a statement not a question, but her voice still faltered with disbelief.

'Yes,' he answered, then picked last week's newspaper off her counter where she had been saving it for the Carter girl's article. The picture was the one of her standing over the body with Bill Wilson as they discussed the unusual condition of the body for forensic evidence. Trevan dropped the paper with a loud smack in front of her on the counter so she could see it. 'And now he is after you.'

His soft words were like ice water on her already muddled head Jocelyn slammed the coffee can down, brown grains spilling across the smooth counter. She put her hands up and backed away from the man.

'I knew I should've called the cops,' she bit out angrily as she edged toward the end of the counter where her gun rested. Her eyes brimmed with tears, damn her for her own stupidity. How could he know such a thing, maybe he was working with the guy who got away? Unless he was completely insane. Or he was here to . . . she left the thought unfinished. She turned away from him to grab at the weapon. His hand grasped her wrist and she felt herself being hauled against the hard length of his bare chest. The thin fabric of her robe did nothing to hide his muscular body from her sensitive flesh. Her eyes, wide with fright and anger, met his as she stared at him.

'Miss Kendrick, I assure you, you do not need the gun.' His features were calm, if not understanding, and his voice was firm and authoritative. His hands were seductively warm against the tender flesh of her wrists as he held her. She could do little more than stare at the man.

'Jocelyn.'

'What?' His brows knit together as he tilted his head.

She withdrew herself from his grip, knowing that he let her. 'My name is Jocelyn, as opposed to Ms Kendrick.'

She stepped away from him, finding it difficult to think, let alone breathe, when she was near him. Not to mention the bombshell he had just dropped. She rubbed her fingers for a moment on her forehead trying to put her frantic thoughts into some kind of order. The understanding in his eyes and quiet of his words had calmed her, allowing her to think. She was still a long way from feeling comfortable about his statement. 'Now I want to start this over. Why were you in the woods where Carrie Carter's body was found?'

Trevan crossed his arms across his chest and met her gaze. 'To study the area and the body for clues.'

'Okay, I can believe that, but you're not a cop, or a fed.' Again, it was a statement not a question.

'Neither are you,' he returned in the same tone of voice.

Jocelyn frowned, suddenly wary. She crossed her arms, as he had, her guarded expression confronting his. 'How do you know that?'

'A police officer would have had me thrown in jail tonight.' A humorless, small smile quirked the ends of his lips. 'Or shot me.'

She turned back to the coffee and resumed her task. 'Just remember, it's never too late. Besides someone had already done that, hadn't he? So did you find any?'

He hesitated then shrugged, 'I'm sorry, did I find any what?'

'Clues,' she repeated, speaking slowly. 'Did you find any clues at the site of Carrie Carter's murder?'

'No.'

The answer was simple and completely inadequate. Jocelyn drew an exasperated breath. 'I just bet you're fun at parties. Now let's try this again, did you know Carrie Carter?'

'No, I did not.'

'Explain these then,' she demanded angrily as she retrieved a manila envelope from the end of the counter.

She pulled the extra set of pictures she had borrowed from the department out of the thick envelope and dropped them on the kitchen table. The stark images of the photographs fanned across the table like a deck of cards. Jocelyn pulled the picture she had studied intently so many times, and tapped her finger against the matte finish, 'If I'm not mistaken, that is you.'

'Yes, it is.'

She groaned and stalked to where he stood, 'Look, talking to you is like pulling teeth, Mr Urban Cowboy, and this whole evening has really put me on edge, so give me a break. Okay?' Her chest was heaving with anger, she suddenly realized. She hadn't been this angry, this agitated in a long time. She swiped a lock of hair from her forehead and took a deep, calming breath. Keeping her voice cool and reserved, she continued, 'Would you please explain why you are in these pictures?'

Trevan moved to her and raised his hand to smooth away the errant lock from her brow. 'The man I'm trying to find, the one you saw running from your yard, seems to be attracted to theatrical events such as the Renaissance Fair.'

'Okay, I can accept that,' she conceded. Her heart pounded with what felt like a primal anticipation. Of what she did not know. Right now she didn't want to know.

Licking her lips she held the front of her robe in a tight grip. Sometimes the best defense was a good offense, or something like that. She didn't know, but it sounded good anyway.

'As I gather the story so far, you say you followed this man to the fair. You did not know Carrie Carter, yet I witnessed you at the crime scene where, you say, you were looking for clues but did not find any. Now I've caught you lurking in my back yard along with some other guy, who you say you knew would come.'

The whole story sounded ridiculous, like something from a soap opera. His face was expressionless as he studied her. Yet, there was something about him . . . she took a deep breath and raised her chin. 'Are you the murderer?'

His face hardened in anger as he gritted his teeth, the muscles in his jaw beginning to work. Jocelyn moved away, not in fear, but to get the hell out of his way.

'You are insane,' he answered, not quite shouting, but delivering the phrase with loud authority. He stalked past her to stand with his back to her. Running his hands through his hair, he turned around to glare at her. 'The thought is completely ludicrous.'

'Don't get your undies in a bunch. I was only asking. If I really thought you were the murderer, you sure as hell wouldn't be in my house right now,' she retorted as she balled her hands on her hips. 'So how did you know this guy was going to come, who is he, and how do you know he's after me?'

The silence stretched between them, growing uncomfortable with each second that he glared at her. Jocelyn's patience had been pushed past what she considered a very reasonable point. She had been more than accommodating to this man. Hell, she had even bandaged his wound and right now she felt like inflicting a few new ones herself.

'Mr Elliot, this silent response thing may have

worked in the past, but not now. Not here. I have been reasonable, more than reasonable as far as your little story is concerned.'

She only had time to gasp as he moved swiftly to her to grab her by the forearms and haul her against his chest again. His face was only inches from hers. His anger even more evident now that she could see the glitter of the golden brown of his eyes. 'I have told you the truth. If you do not start showing some respect, I have half a mind to turn you over my knee.'

Jocelyn's jaw dropped as she gasped at his audacity. Apparently Mr Urban Cowboy had an attitude. 'Over my dead body,' she muttered.

'Which is exactly what I'm trying to keep from happening,' he answered fiercely. 'The Porcelain Mask Murderer, not "some" guy, came here tonight to learn what he could about you. Possibly even break into your house to go through your things.'

He hesitated and she felt her eyes widen in disbelief. Already her imagination was working ahead of his words and she was afraid she wasn't going to like what he was about to say.

'He and the other guy, as you put it, are one and the same. The man who killed Carrie Carter is now after you. And just like the others, he'll find out about your interests, your likes, your dislikes, and what your passions are. As to how I knew he was after you, that is hardly a moot point since he's made an appearance already. But think about it, how many times have you seen your picture in the paper and on the TV since the last girl's death?'

Jocelyn's gaze shifted away from him and she stared unseeing at the picture in the newspaper. It would be impossible to believe his harsh words, if she hadn't caught a glimpse of the figure leaving the yard. His words began to echo in her brain, his threat now making sense. *You can't stop me, Elliot. Or my next act with this woman Jocelyn as my leading lady.*

A small groan worked from deep within Trevan causing shivers to move through her. His musky scent enveloped her senses, clouding them from everything but his presence. His mouth lowered to take hers, her cry of protest lost in his kiss. She splayed her hands on his chest to push him away, but his tongue stroked the ridge of her lip, igniting a luxurious warmth deep within her. Her fingers curled into the soft mat of his chest hair as she pressed herself against the hard plane of his body. His skin was like satin over steel; her hands slid involuntarily up his torso to the ridge of his collar bones.

His lips left hers and she opened her eyes to find his face still so close. 'Who are you?' she asked huskily.

His lips turned to a lopsided grin and she knew what he was going to say. She found her anger had evaporated somewhere within the heat of his kiss and she returned his smile.

'I don't mean your name. Where are you from?' Self-consciously, she eased herself from the intimate contact. 'You're not from here at any rate.'

'No,' Trevan answered, holding her gaze with a softened look of his own. He took her hand and pressed his lips to the skin of her knuckles, the gesture so old-fashioned and romantic, it had her heart pounding a little harder. 'No, I'm not.'

'If what you say is true, and I'm not saying it isn't,' she said quickly, as his eyes started to harden, 'or is . . . why are you hunting him?'

His hold on her hand changed like the dulling layers of the calluses on his rough hands; his touch became distant, even though his fingers hadn't moved. 'He killed my sister.'

Jocelyn studied Trevan's face as he slept on her recliner. It had surprised her that he didn't seem to know how it worked. But after she had shown him how to lean it back and lift the foot rest, he had fallen asleep. What was it about men and recliners that caused them to fall asleep instantly? She shook her head, it must be that broken chromosome.

He was handsome, she had to admit. She let her gaze move over his face, drawn by the vulnerability of his features softened in sleep.

He had said the Porcelain Mask Murderer killed his sister. Jocelyn didn't have any brothers or sisters, but she imagined something like that would have to be hard. Sipping at her coffee, the pain of a memory sliced through her. Katrina, her best friend all through school, had also been murdered.

Yes, she could understand Trevan's need to find his sister's killer.

Taking a deep breath, Jocelyn went to the kitchen to dump the remainder of her coffee in the sink; her stomach couldn't handle anything more right now. Mr Trevan

Elliot had fallen asleep in her chair last night shortly after dropping his little bombshell. He had also stirred up many hard memories . . . and a lot more.

Jocelyn stood before the kitchen sink to stare out the window as she remembered the feel of his lips on her. The shiver of anticipation moved through her once again as her body began to react. She sighed as she watched the first rays of the morning touch the dew on the grass. It would be nice to cuddle up to a man like him for the warmth of his comfort, the heat of his . . .

'My, you have an active imagination,' she said softly to herself.

'Not really. Not this early in the morning anyway.'

Trevan's sleepy voice startled her and she spun towards him. His hair was rumpled, his beard dark against his face, and he was stretching his arms as he yawned. Jocelyn felt the forgotten tightening of yearning as he gingerly worked his injured arm.

She shook herself from her wayward thoughts; it would be prudent to remember what this man represented; the hunter of a madman.

'Some night watchman you are,' she teased, more to ease herself than to humor him. She moved to get him a fresh cup of coffee. 'Asleep on the job.'

'He wouldn't come back. It's not his style.' Trevan answered. He accepted the coffee with a polite thank you.

This tiny tear in reality almost struck Jocelyn as comical. Here they were talking about a serial killer over a cup of coffee as if they were discussing the morning's paper.

'You seem to know a lot about him,' she said, watching his eyes for his reaction.

She saw a brief glimpse of anger before a mask fell over his emotions.

'I've been following him a long time. Unfortunately, during that time I've also learned a little about his habits.'

Trevan sat at the breakfast bar and studied her for a moment. 'Let me ask you a question. How do you know I'm not the killer?'

The corner of her lip twisted up in a sardonic smile, 'One: you stopped an intruder from breaking into my house. Two: if you were guilty as he was, you would have run like he did.' She paused, 'But you didn't. Three: when Mrs Phillips came crashing through the bushes, you stepped in front of me. I presume that was to protect me?'

She could see by the surprise in his eyes that so far she had been correct in her assumptions. 'Four: if you were going to kill me, you've had plenty of opportunity to do it since then, but you remained here to keep watch. Well, sort of. And finally, I don't know anyone who sleeps in a recliner for the fun of it.'

His eyes watched her with a slight twinkle and a dimple formed on his cheek as he smiled, 'I don't know. I thought it was rather comfortable.'

'That's obvious,' Jocelyn said as she moved to join him at the breakfast bar. She realized the move was a mistake as a vibration of awareness began to course through her when his knee accidentally touched hers. She found herself unable to look at him because of his bare chest. The effect had dimmed little since she had first seen it last night.

'Would you put some clothes on,' she ordered.

She rose quickly and made sure she didn't touch him as she slipped past him; she knew that it would not be wise to make physical contact. She retrieved his shirt from the back of the recliner and headed back to the kitchen.

'I do have clothes on,' he answered, his tone filled with humor.

'You are not fully clothed, Mr Elliot,' she pointed out as she dropped his shirt on his shoulder.

'Trevan.'

She looked at him, her eyebrow rose in question. 'What?'

'As opposed to Mr Elliot,' he smiled.

'Okay, Trevan, put your shirt on.' Jocelyn frowned at his good mood. It made him seem almost . . . likable. 'If Mrs Phillips sees you sitting at my table like that; she'll think we ought to get married before the baby comes.'

'I see some things don't change,' he chuckled.

She returned his look pointedly, 'What does that mean?'

'Nothing. Only an observation.' He took a sip of his coffee and set the cup on the table. He studied her for a moment and Jocelyn found herself growing uneasy at the unreadable look in his eyes.

'Why did you want to become a cop?'

The question came as a surprise. Jocelyn had thought about it many times, but there seemed to be only one reason. She was practical, and pretty much a realist. She knew the drive, the need to be a homicide detective stemmed from the pent up frustration she had never been able to expel, simply because she had never learned who had killed her best friend.

She had waved goodbye to her friend as the girl backed out of her driveway; three days later, Kat's parents had given her the bitter news of her beloved friend's death. Kat had died only a month before her eighteenth birthday, something they had both planned and plotted for. Instead, the deputies had found her decapitated body at the bottom of an old abandoned well.

No one had ever really asked her why she wanted to become a cop before. Jocelyn took a deep breath and picked a cloth napkin from the table to twist it through her fingers. 'A friend of mine was murdered. They never found who did it.'

She looked up and found understanding in his eyes. Yes, he would know exactly how she felt; he had been there himself. Trevan still searched for his sister's killer.

For the first time Jocelyn felt herself become more at ease about discussing her long-held grief. Before, it had always been people nodding and saying they understood, while she knew they truly could not. Trevan had dealt with the same brutal realities she had.

'Katrina's parents had a closed coffin funeral,' Jocelyn shrugged as she remembered vividly walking past the sealed rose coffin. 'I had such a hard time accepting that she was gone. The last time I had seen her, she was smiling and waving to me.'

She hesitated, then cleared her throat of the thickening of her emotions. 'I wanted to know how they knew it was really her in there. I guess I was working through all the stages of grief, or so I have been told by those who mean well, but I never seemed to move past the anger.'

Trevan's hand moved to cover hers, giving her a sense of warmth and comfort. 'I don't know if you ever get past the anger. Especially if it was something so senseless as murder.'

Jocelyn nodded, 'I guess that's what bothered me most. Kat's killer was never found and there didn't seem to be any clear motive as to why he did that to her.'

She looked to him and felt the tears brimming. 'I never had a face, an identity, to focus on . . . to hate with all the hurt of my anger and loss.'

'Is that why you decided to work with the homicide department?' Trevan asked, his voice low. 'So you could find your friend's killer?'

She shrugged. 'Maybe at first.'

With her free hand, she rubbed a finger across her forehead where the throbbing was beginning. She didn't want to let go of his hand and his comfort. The pulsing ache was the same as the day she had persuaded one of the detectives to let her see the file on her friend.

'I talked John into letting me look at the reports. At first they hadn't bothered me because they were so distant and the detail impersonal. But then I noticed the white border of the black and white photographs underneath and my heart began to pound. I knew what was next. Slowly I turned the paper over and it was the picture of how they had found her. It had been brutal.'

Jocelyn continued to look at Trevan, unable to tear her gaze away. It was as if his complete understanding gave her a sense of healing.

She closed her eyes as the image began to swim before her. She realized the shallow gasps she was hearing were those of her own attempts to breathe. She felt Trevan's strong arms embrace her and pull her onto his lap as he held her against him tightly. The security of his touch helped her confront the image flashing through her mind.

'Kat . . . her body lay on its side with her hands tied in front. At first I thought that her head was lying at an unnatural angle, maybe her neck broken when he threw her down the abandoned well. Then . . . then I noticed the jagged edges . . .'

Jocelyn felt the hot tears burn down her cheeks and turned her face into his chest. Her voice sounded muffled against his shirt. 'I had to run to the bathroom because I became violently sick. After I soaked my face and regained control, I headed back to put away the file. You can't believe how much I dreaded seeing that image again. I went back and found the file had already been put away. John never mentioned the incident again, but I know he was the one who put it away for me.'

'I think I like John,' Trevan said huskily. His breath was warm against the top of her head.

Taking a deep breath, Jocelyn inhaled his masculine scent. His arms were around her and his chin on her head; it would be too easy to turn to him and look into his eyes. She knew he would see her need and, perhaps, she would see it reflected in his eyes. No, she thought as she mentally shook herself. What she was feeling was the need to be comforted. And this is not how she wanted it to be. She would want him to want her because he felt something for her. Not just pity. Or a sense of protectiveness.

She withdrew herself from his arms and moved off his lap, feeling awkward. 'Saving damsels in distress and wiping away their tears must be old hat to you,' she joked nervously. 'I need to get ready for work.'

She started putting things away just to keep from having to look at him. 'There's a bathroom in the spare bedroom if you need it. I . . . uh . . . will be down in a while.'

With that she turned and quickly headed up the stairs. Only when she had closed the bathroom door behind her did she finally stop. She leaned against the door and shook her head. 'You know, Kendrick, sometimes you can be a jerk.'

After her shower, she took her time getting ready. Finally she convinced herself that she was being juvenile, that they were both adults and Trevan would understand that what had happened had not been an excuse to cuddle, but had been a natural show of comfort. She hoped so anyway.

Jocelyn worked up her courage and headed downstairs. She didn't know why she felt so awkward, except perhaps that sitting on a man's lap as she cried seemed like an intimate thing. Not exactly something someone should do with a complete stranger, especially one she had just pulled out of the trash. Literally.

Trevan wasn't in the front room and she glanced into the spare bedroom and found it hadn't even been touched. Jocelyn frowned as she stepped into the kitchen and immediately spied the note on the table. She noticed his handwriting was rough and spiky, similar to that of the killer, except Trevan's strokes were open and full.

Opening the note she found it simply said for her to watch herself and that he would be in touch soon. Jocelyn released the deep breath she had been holding, feeling a sense of relief. And regret.

'Boy, Kendrick, you really do know how to scare them off,' she muttered, then gathered her things to head out the door.

Setting herself behind the wheel of her Jeep, Jocelyn drew her brows together and worked to make sense of the events of the last evening. The fleeing image of the intruder had forced a part of her to believe the handsome stranger's words of warning. Yet, the realist within her had not been able to accept the idea of a killer seeking to make her his next victim.

The words flashed in her mind like a bold headline. *Jocelyn Kendrick; another life taken by the Porcelain Mask Murderer.*

She shuddered, trying to push the grizzly thoughts from her mind as she backed from the driveway. Lifting her chin, she checked traffic in the rear view mirror and put the car in gear. Some of what Trevan said seemed logical; part of her felt the truth and sincerity of his words. But there was one thing that neither the murderer, nor the man determined to protect her, had counted on.

Jocelyn Kendrick did not intend to become anyone's victim.

CHAPTER 5

Michelle Slavinsky, Becky Sowers, Halicia Carmichael, Cindy Blake, Lucinda Travers, and Carrie Carter. Jocelyn shook her head in frustration; the women had nothing in common. Location, employment, personality, physical characteristics; their only connection to each other was that they all had been killed by the Porcelain Mask Murderer.

One item was conspicuous by its absence; none of the victims had a brother, or any immediate family, by the name of Trevan Elliot. For the first time, Jocelyn experienced the conflicting pull of logic against something more primitive, less explicable; intuition. Logic dictated that she should turn the handsome stranger in. He was obviously involved deeply in the case. Knew too much to merely be an observer on the sideline. Intuition, if the strong, unwavering feeling deep within her gut could be called such, continued to softly murmur to her. True when she looked into his eyes, she saw the hard edge of a hunter, but she also saw so much more. Reflected in the depths of his eyes were compassion, understanding, and warmth. Could a cold-blooded killer be capable of such emotions? More importantly, she thought, could Trevan Elliot be setting her up to be the next victim of the Porcelain Mask Murderer?

'What are you working on?'

John Cartland's voice startled Jocelyn. She felt her guilt register as the heat of her blush swept across her expression. No sense trying to hide what he has already seen, she thought, as she met his gaze. 'I'm studying the known victims of the Porcelain Mask Murderer.'

John's brow rose in question as he studied her for an intense, silent moment. He turned to the pages to sift through them before turning back to her. 'Any reason? Or did you just feel like it?'

She cleared her throat as she shifted nervously in her chair. She should tell John about the intruder and Trevan Elliot. About Elliot's claim that she was marked to be the next victim of a serial killer. That Trevan's observations about the murderer seeking to know his victims before he approached them had matched parts of the psychological profile she had read over, but the rational part within her stopped her. She had no proof, only a stranger's words, and even that stranger didn't seem to exist. Realizing she was displaying all the reactions of guilt, she forced herself to be still and talk with calm, knowledgeable authority, 'Well uh . . . to develop the background of the serial killer by, uh . . . establishing any physical or personality similarities between the victims.'

'I see,' he answered with a small nod, then glanced to the papers. 'Is that all?'

Jocelyn took a deep breath and tried again to come up with some plausible reason for having investigation files that she really didn't have any business looking at. 'Perhaps to also establish a feel for the enormity of the situation so as to better understand the reaction of the subjects to these heinous crimes.' Her words faltered, finishing more as a question than an answer.

John smiled, then discreetly looked around the department before meeting her gaze, 'Kendrick, you are full of it.'

She ran both hands through her hair, *Where does one start when one wants to make a complete ass out of oneself?*

'What if I told you someone tried to break into my house last night?' At John's tense look she held her hand up. 'He was stopped by another man, and that man says the Porcelain Mask Murderer is after me because I've been on TV so much lately.'

He studied her for a moment. 'Have you run a check on this guy?'

She nodded. 'The preliminary stuff doesn't show anything yet.' She knew that was an understatement considering there seemed to be no record at all of a Trevan Elliot's existence. She had to wait, however, until the full report came back before she made her decision about him.

'What does your gut say?' he asked.

She shrugged, it was hard to say one way or another. It didn't seem realistic that a serial killer was after her. Jocelyn glanced to the list of girls killed by a nameless, faceless killer. Had any of these girls thought they would be a victim? Yet, she remembered vividly the quick flash of pain in his eyes before they had hardened and his manner became distant. Hadn't she felt the same fresh anguish even after all the years that had passed since Kat's death?

'I think he believes what he is saying,' she said cautiously.

John gave her a pointed look. 'And you?'

'Part of me trusts him,' she said finally. 'But it does seem pretty hard to believe.'

His gaze flicked to the paper she held and his voice lowered. 'Probably what those girls would have thought too. Look, I'm not saying trust this guy, but we can't take what he says lightly either considering what we're dealing with. I want to talk to him. I can't do it today, but bring him in tomorrow and we'll find out what he has to do with all this.'

Jocelyn shook her head. 'I don't know, John. He hasn't broken any laws and his only goal seems to be stopping the "PM" murderer before he kills again.'

'Tomorrow,' he repeated, then again scanned the room as he talked. 'Until then keep your butt out of trouble or I'll kick it for you.'

'Right, John. I mean, yes, sir.' She smiled nervously until he winked at her. The muscles in her back and neck relaxed in response to his rough kindness as he walked away. 'And thanks,' she said to his retreating form, receiving only a wave of his hand in acknowledgment as he weaved through the desks.

Jocelyn gathered the copies she had made of the reports and put them in her briefcase. She had put the originals back as soon as she had finished at the copier because it had made her feel a little less guilty. Nervously biting her lip, she reminded herself that she now had John's help, well, sort of, in an unofficial you're-on-your-own way.

She admitted without reservations that she had been checking out Trevan Elliot's little story. He may be who he says he is, or thinks he is, she pointed out mentally, but his sister had not been murdered by this serial killer.

Making her way to the elevator, she nodded goodbye to a huddle of detectives. John was one of the group and gave her a look that she interpreted as a warning to be cautious. Thankfully the elevator arrived, allowing her to duck his gaze and finally sigh in relief.

'You are going to have to learn to ignore your conscience.' Her words bounced with a tinny ring off the walls of the elevator.

The foyer of the county building was filled with people of contrasting personalities. The old man, his clothes clean but obviously worn, sat quietly in the corner. Lawyers and media types swarmed around the center. Not that one was any better than the other, she thought, especially lawyers; she had never really personally cared for them. They were like most medicine; it stinks, doesn't taste good, and no one wants to take it, but sometimes it's what is required to fix a problem. Both cost a lot, too.

Jocelyn had to work her way through the crowd of reporters. The story of the serial killer had them working in a frenzy to get the hottest news. One reporter bumped into her as he scribbled notes on his pad and mumbled an apology. The crowd was getting thick and Jocelyn heard nothing but talk of the latest murder. Last night's conversation with the man calling himself Trevan Elliot filtered through her thoughts and suddenly she wanted desperately to get out of the building. To get away from the talk of murder.

She hit the door at a trot, thankful to have escaped the media circling like vultures over a news story and to be out in the warmth of the sun. The talk of future bodies had caused her insides to turn cold, but the welcoming heat of the afternoon soon dissipated the feeling.

A smile formed on her face until she spotted the broad-shouldered figure of Trevan Elliot appear suddenly at the edge of the activity. He was an immobile force in a tide of emotion, necessity and disregard. Her stomach tightened with the familiar pang of desire before fear and anger quickly replaced it. Fear of what this man represented and anger because she didn't want to believe that a murderer was after her.

People moved, sometimes with a few angry words, as she walked straight through the crowd to him. Determination and anger heated her expression. 'I would ask you why you are here . . .'

'But you already know why,' he interrupted quietly, his gaze holding hers.

'You lied to me.' She bit out the words.

He shifted his stance, forcing her to turn and walk with him as he moved to the edge of the parking lot. 'Everything I've told you is the truth.'

'I checked, Trevan, or whatever your name is. You

had to know I would,' Jocelyn said. 'You told me that "he" killed your sister.'

'He did,' Trevan answered matter-of-factly.

She laughed with annoyed disbelief and shook her head. 'I've found nothing to support your claim.'

With a hooded gaze, Trevan studied her for several moments. He watched her intently as he spoke, 'Will you come with me, if I can prove what I say is true?'

'Now? No, I will not go with you,' she answered. She held her hands up as if to ward off anything he might try to say to persuade her. 'I didn't get much sleep last night, thanks to you, and I've got a lot to do. But I do need to talk to you, later. This evening, maybe?'

A twinkle of amusement and challenge worked its way into his hard expression, 'Are you afraid of me, Jocelyn?'

'No,' she said a little too quickly. Trevan raised an eyebrow and Jocelyn felt the pull of honesty. 'Okay, yes.' *Her damn conscience must be the size of a mountain.*

Trevan looked away in an attempt to hide his smile, but not before she caught the faint twitching of his lips. When he met her gaze once again, a sense of seriousness had dulled his humor and a sliver of caution reflected in his eyes. 'Come with me, Jocelyn, and I'll tell you everything.' He hesitated a moment as if to let her adjust to the idea, 'Everything. Then if you still don't believe me, I will not approach you.'

Her breath quickened as did her heartbeat. His invitation took on many facets as she studied it in her mind. If he proved his statement to be true, it would pull her deeper into the dark derangement of a killer. She would also be in danger of the captivating gaze of the handsome stranger standing before her. The first part was what she was studying for; to try to understand the thoughts or reasoning of a murderer so she could make sure justice was done. As for the second part, Jocelyn had never wanted nor believed a man could affect her with his mere presence in this way.

She did not know which scared her more.

'But you say "he" is after me.'

Trevan hesitated, then he lifted his finger to slowly stroke the curve of her cheek. 'I said I would not approach you. I did not say I would leave you.'

Closing her eyes, she took a deep breath then shook her head. She knew if she said no, he would honor her decision. Trevan reminded her of a time when a person's word was the only thing he needed; a time when lawyers or legal documents were not a necessity to require a man to honor his commitment.

An image of him holding her as she cried over her friend flashed briefly in her mind. She had seen the understanding in his eyes and knew within her that he had experienced the same loss. Perhaps, she should give him the benefit of the doubt.

Groaning softly, she opened her eyes to meet his gaze. 'I don't know why I am doing this, but, okay, let's go see your proof.'

Trevan gently took her elbow and motioned with his other hand toward the parking lot.

Jocelyn stopped, waiting for him to turn back to her. 'This "proof" better be good because even the FBI doesn't seem to know anything about you and as far as the government is concerned . . . you do not even exist. I am warning you, if you try to pull any stunts will turn you in myself.'

Trevan's expression was a mixture of admiration, caution, and disbelief.

She smiled sweetly as she moved past him. 'I checked.'

Out of the corner of her eye, she saw him shake his head. She suspected his words were not meant for her to hear, but she did.

'Somehow that does not surprise me.'

They had been on the road for a while. Jocelyn wasn't really sure how long since her watch seemed to have died. But the landscape on each side of the road had gone from neighborhoods with postage stamp yards to the green stubble carpets of winter wheat fields as they continued driving. Now they were kicking up great pillars of dust on a dirt road in the middle of what, as far as she could tell, was near to nowhere.

She turned to study Trevan as he drove the truck. He seemed perfectly at ease with himself and this whole situation. Still, he hadn't mentioned anything about having to drive quite so far. 'We aren't going out of state are we?'

'No.' He glanced at her, then shook his head with apparent amusement. 'Don't worry, we are almost there.'

'Look, I don't mind telling you I'm starting to get a little nervous,' she said, her irritation building as he only returned her comment with a smile. 'I tend to do

94

that when someone takes me on deserted dirt roads.'

His face suddenly became serious and, if she wasn't mistaken, a little offended. 'I gave you my word I would not harm you.'

Turning to watch the panorama of fall beauty through the side window, she shook her head in disbelief at his naivete. 'I'll bet that's what Jack The Ripper used to say.'

'Who?' he asked.

Facing him, Jocelyn found his brows furrowed in a frown. He honestly didn't seem to know. 'Never mind.'

Silence returned between them as they bumped down the old road. She took the opportunity to study Trevan who seemed lost in his thoughts. His profile was about as good as the rest of him, she thought. His hair was full and dark against the tanned lines of his face. His eyes, now watching the road so intently, made her remember how deeply he could probe into her thoughts. Her heart quickened slightly while her gaze moved over the sensuous curve of his full lips and she remembered all too vividly how they had felt against the hunger of her own. She watched, mesmerized, as they curved . . .

Into a smile.

She focused her attention quickly and intently back on the road ahead when he chuckled, then crossed her arms prudishly over her breasts. She cleared her throat, realizing he had caught her red handed. Well, staring would be more accurate but that didn't mean he had to be so amused by it.

'I think I should let you know that I have a green belt in Karate and I could shove your nose right into your brain and kill you before you ever knew what happened.'

Trevan laughed, 'That's great, but who's going to protect me?'

Growling, then giving him a look of pure fury, Jocelyn felt her fingers curl with the urge to smack him. His grin was devastating, but she would not let it affect her anger. 'You are a despicable jackass.'

He chuckled again, good-naturedly. 'Does your father know you talk like that?'

She scowled as she again faced the windshield. 'Probably not, he's dead. He died in a plane crash with my mom several years ago.'

Trevan was silent for a moment. His hand moved slightly on the steering wheel as if he was about to reach out to her, then he firmed his grip. 'I apologize for my lack of consideration.'

Jocelyn shrugged her shoulders, 'You didn't know. Besides he would kill me if he were here now, for doing something like this.'

Trevan nodded with approval 'I would have to agree with him.'

She looked at him in humoured disbelief. 'Look who's talking. You are the one driving after all.'

'Thank goodness.'

What audacity, she thought. 'What the hell does that mean?'

He studied her for a moment, then watched the road as if it were going to suddenly leap up at him. 'Remember, I've been following you. I've seen you drive.'

Jocelyn sputtered, her anger choking her words. She

started to lean towards him when he pointed to direct her attention. Or most likely distract her, she thought:

'Here we are.'

She followed his indication and noted the small, tree lined cemetery on the side of the road. In Kansas, it was not uncommon at all to find an ancient, isolated burial ground. Probably an old family plot, she shrugged. But what did it have to do with his proof?

'It's a graveyard.' She stated in confusion, then remembered Trevan's sister. After all, he was supposed to be showing her proof of his sister's death. 'I'm sorry, I spoke before I thought. Sometimes it's an annoying habit.'

Trevan parked the truck and disregarded her statement. He started out of the vehicle with a brusque order to follow.

The cemetery was small. Smaller than a standard city lot. Jocelyn was impressed by the neat appearance of the grounds, for such an isolated place. The rough prairie grass was clipped and the old, wind-worn headstones had been cleaned and straightened. Tall oaks, their thick branches sturdy from age, rustled soothingly in the soft wind. Even the harsh sun was gentled as it filtered through the shifting leaves.

Her gaze noted unusual formations in the surrounding fields and, with delight, she could spot the rough planked remainders of what must have once been the houses of an old town.

'This is such a beautiful place,' she murmured more to herself than to Trevan as she followed his broad back.

Old graveyards had always fascinated Jocelyn. She

loved to read the headstones with their names and dates. Unlike the brief information of today's markers, these gave insight to the person. She stopped to gaze at a tall stone with an engraving that resembled a medal: *Capt John Billings, Union Army, Infantry 117, died bravely for his country.*

She was in awe of the history lying before her. At one time this area must have been a bustling town and the captain had lived here with his friends and family. It was all so fascinating. Where had they gone? What had caused the town to die, leaving the gravestones as the only testimony to its existence and time its only witness as the seasons weathered it away?

'Fascinating,' she murmured, as she reverently touched the hand-chiseled face on one of the tall markers, then realized Trevan had stopped to wait for her. She stood and made her way to him. 'Sorry.'

He said nothing, but his rigid stance and the grim tightening of his face warned her to prepare herself for what was to come. The way he held himself and the somber sadness in his eyes revealed more than he probably cared to admit, she thought. She saw then that he stood beside a grave. His gaze was hard as he held hers, then shifted to the stone at the head of the plot.

The marker was beautifully carved with the simple elegance of wildflowers as a border for the inscription. At the base, the curled leaves of black-eyed susans edged the stone as the fall color of mums began to bloom in their wake. A hearty climbing rose had pillared itself on the rough edges to wind up the surface, a few late blooms still clinging to the yellowing vine.

A whirl of wind lifted Jocelyn's hair. She swept it from her eyes with her fingers and watched as several red, withering petals fell softly to the ground in front of the stone. The dark spots fell to pool at the foot of the marker, the blood red color evoking the stark image of Carrie Carter's lifeless expression.

A chill moved through her as she read the words aloud, 'Allysa Elliot, beloved sister and friend, born 6 January, 1854, died 23 May, 1878. By day or night, in weal or woe, that heart, no longer free, must bear the love it cannot show, and silent ache for thee.

'Lord Byron,' Jocelyn acknowledged. Her brows furrowed in doubt as she read the words again to herself. 'Wait a minute, these dates are wrong, Trevan. This is completely irresponsible. You should have had them fix this.'

She looked to his face and found him watching her closely, almost hesitantly. Dread icily filled her like a cold dark wave and her heart began to beat faster. The silence stretched between them, only emphasizing the implication of his somber expression.

'They are not wrong, Jocelyn.'

CHAPTER 6

'I don't think I know what you mean, Trevan,' Jocelyn said. She laughed, then frowned. Unconsciously she stepped away from him. Maybe she didn't want to know. 'What do you mean the dates aren't wrong?'

'I'm saying my sister died on 23 May 1878,' he answered flatly as he watched her intently. She returned his level look as fear mingled in her racing thoughts with shock and denial. She saw hesitation in his eyes and need. The need for her to believe him.

Jocelyn blinked, then blinked again. It was starting to sink in what he was saying to her. She laughed again. But it was impossible. 'This is a really bad joke, right? Are you trying to tell me that you are one hell of a younger brother? By over a hundred years?'

'No,' he shook his head and took a deep breath. He looked as if he was already regretting this whole idea. 'I was older than Allysa by eight years.'

At the mention of the girl's name, something familiar rang within Jocelyn. She looked to the tombstone. 'Allysa Elliot. Isn't she the Allysa of the legend of the Elliot Theater? I remember hearing about that

100

and Thearosa's castle when I was growing up.'

He nodded, a small smile lifting the corners of his lips. 'She was very involved in the community arts. Apparently the town renamed the theater after her murder.'

'Apparently?' she frowned. 'If she's your younger sister, weren't you there?'

'No,' he said.

'Trevan, these monosyllabic answers are completely inadequate,' she said, her voice rising in anger, maybe even from fear of what he was saying. 'How come you were not there?'

He shook his head as he nervously ran his hand through his hair. 'I was not there, because, somehow, I was here.'

'That's it,' Jocelyn fumed as she spun away from him to stalk through the cemetery. How could she even possibly be considering what he was saying was the truth. What he was saying was just not possible. The man was crazy, there was no other explanation. None. 'I don't know why the hell I even thought I might believe you.'

Trevan called her name and when she ignored him and kept walking, he moved behind her to grab her arm and turn her around to face him. 'Jocelyn, I don't know how to explain this to you because I don't know what really happened myself, or even how it happened.'

'Is this all the "proof" you have?' she asked, waving her hand towards the grave. He remained silent for a moment and she could see the sincerity in his eyes as he held her gaze.

'No, I do have other proof,' he answered solemnly, 'but not with me.'

'How come that doesn't surprise me? Look, Trevan, this has gone too far. I thought I could trust you,' Jocelyn snapped at him. The very thought of what he was implying was not possible . . . was not even realistic. 'Even after I discovered you in my back yard and then found out from an FBI check that you didn't exist, I still trusted you.'

Trevan stood in the shadows of a large oak, the sunlight filtered through the leaves to shimmer on his face. He placed his hands in his pockets and studied her. 'Why?'

'What?' she asked. How could she explain her instinct, the inexplicable knowledge within her telling her even now that he was speaking the truth? Or at least thought he was. How could she explain the attraction she felt for him that seemed to override reason and logic. 'I don't . . . don't know.'

'Your instinct, perhaps?'

She sucked in her breath; maybe he did understand. 'Yes. I guess so. But still, this whole idea is ludicrous. I mean, I know they can freeze sperm and embryos, but over a hundred years?' Jocelyn hesitated for a moment at the look of shock on Trevan's face as if she had said *the* four letter word. She wasn't about to get into a freedom of speech debate right now. 'Never mind. Besides it's impossible, they didn't even have the technology.'

'Jocelyn, listen to me,' he tried to interrupt.

She chose to ignore him; there was no telling what

else he was going to try to tell her. '*Star Trek* couldn't even do time-travel, well, except for that one episode with the gate keeper – '

Trevan took her by the upper arms and effectively silenced her tirade of rationalization with a toe-curling, heart-stopping kiss. She stiffened at the searing contact of his lips on hers, then slowly her traitorous body molded against his. But even the incredible effect of his physical proximity could not completely dull the shock of his words. Jocelyn slowly stepped away from him, unable to remove her gaze from the seductive pull of his eyes.

'I can't think when you do that,' she muttered as she ran a shaky hand through her hair, 'and damn it, it still doesn't change the fact that what you're trying to tell me just isn't possible.'

He looked back at the tombstone and his gaze became somber as if the pain of his memories were renewing. 'I have never told this to anyone and I don't expect you to believe me either. I can't explain it to you because I don't even know what really happened, but it did.'

'And I don't want to know either, Trevan,' she said. She recognized his sorrow or sense of mourning, but her own thoughts were muddled with doubt, confusion, and a hint of belief in this man and what he was telling her. They were talking about time-travel here, not whether anything had been achieved by the baseball strike.

His expression silenced her as his eyes darkened with warning. 'You need to know what you are up against.'

'The Porcelain Mask Murderer,' she said softly, as

her muddled thoughts started to crystallize with the icy sensation of shock. Jocelyn glanced back to him with a questioning look.

'Exactly.'

She shook her head in disbelief; too much more and they would be putting the straitjacket on her and not Trevan. 'I don't understand. What does this have to do with him? With me?'

Trevan looked away towards the fields. Jocelyn followed his gaze to the gentle swaying of the thin blades of young wheat and took comfort in the familiar sight. He faced her again and his nostrils flared as he took a slow breath.

'He was brought through time with me.'

> 'By another possest, may she live ever blest!
> Her name still my heart must revere:
> With a sigh I resign what I once thought was
> And forgive her deceit with a Tear.'

The man's voice offered life to Lord Byron's work from so long ago. He moved around the empty stage of the deserted theater. He lifted his upturned hand to emphasize the eloquence of the poem. His form flickered in the dancing shadows of the candles placed with care around the stage. He had never really become accustomed to the harsh brilliance of modern lights. The dark, with its hidden crevices of fear, suited him.

Allysa had been deceitful. He had felt himself warming to the beautiful girl's charming smile and endearing eyes, then she scorned him by telling him that she had only thought of him as a friend. A fellow enthusiast of the theater. That she had already picked someone else for the lead of the new play, even though *his* name had already been announced.

He felt the muscles of his face tightening with anger as he recalled her stunned expression when he'd suggested they could be more than friends. He thought if he could seduce Allysa he could change her mind.

'I'm sorry, I really am.' She had smiled so sweetly as she moved to hold his hands in her own. 'But I just do not share those same feelings for you.'

He had felt all the humiliation and the frustrations of being a bastard well up within him.

I just do not share those same feelings for you. The words had echoed in his mind till they throbbed in him with bitter hate.

His hand had struck her hard, a blemish of red already present when Allysa's head had whipped back from the blow. He watched in shock as she hit the sharp corner of the bricks of the mantel with a sickening thud. Her hand had clutched the porcelain mask he had given her as she tried to stop her fall. Allysa had staggered forward as the blood caressed her face, her eyes never leaving his. Then with slow grace, she had crumpled to the floor and the mask had dropped from her hand and broken. He had watched her gaze when it turned to focus on the split porcelain and the light had dimmed from her eyes.

Allysa had deceived him as had all the others since. As was the Kendrick woman doing now.

'Mr Elliot, I'm afraid, has become quite troublesome,'

he spoke softly as he rubbed the cleft of his chin. He too, had been at the county building this afternoon, in time to see Trevan Elliot speak to the woman. His woman.

He had watched as they had left together. No doubt Elliot would try to persuade the lady to allow him to protect her. Perhaps, he would even tell her the truth in his effort to do so. Perhaps.

He chuckled at the thought. Miss Jocelyn Kendrick was a student of the mind; practical, logical, and reasonable. Would she believe his whimsical story of a murderer being whisked through time with his very own avenger on his heels?

'I think not,' he laughed.

The man turned and caught his reflection in the smoked amber of the mirror covering the wall of the fireplace to the side of the stage. He studied the full length of his appearance, pleased with what he saw. He stepped closer to the image and objectively noticed the hardening of his eyes.

'Still, whether the woman believes him or not, Elliot has forced me to change my plans,' he said slowly as a revision began to form in his mind. He absently stroked the silky petals of a Yellow Jasmine bloom; a beautiful, deadly flower.

'Miss Kendrick, student of the mind, wishes to catch a murderer,' he chuckled. 'Catch a murderer she will.'

Trevan glanced over to Jocelyn as they headed back to town. She had taken everything he had said up till now pretty well. What more could he expect from her? A hint of belief maybe?

He shook his head at the thought, she was a woman of the times; a time with inventions and customs more shocking than he could have ever imagined. If he'd told the same story to a woman from his time, she would have accused him of hitting the moonshine a little too much. When he had come through, he had awakened to find himself soaking wet in the middle of a field. A kindly ranch woman had found him and taken him to her house to recuperate. Jocelyn's voice broke into his thoughts.

'Just for argument's sake, how did you come through – ' Jocelyn swallowed at the thought, 'assuming you're right when you profess to believe you came through time, I mean?'

'A tornado,' he looked toward her and recognized her anger at his short answer. 'I had trailed my sister's killer till I found him and we fought as a storm that had been brewing came upon us in full force.'

He shrugged as he recalled the brief and fleeting images of what happened next. 'I remember the wind whipping me into the center of the tornado and the roar of the storm was deafening, then all of a sudden there was silence. The fear and the anger I had felt was gone. I don't know that I even knew who or what I was as I floated through what I can only describe as curtains of color.'

Jocelyn's eyes were wide with interest when he looked back to her. He had been half afraid that he would see only her bitter disbelief. 'Then what?'

'Then I sort of "woke" up to realize I was sitting in the middle of a field during a storm. The woman who found me, Widow Barker, assumed I had some kind of amnesia from an accident so she didn't question it when I didn't recognize things.'

'Is she the one who taught you how to drive?' Jocelyn asked.

Trevan laughed 'I guess you could say that. We worked out a pretty good deal, I provided muscle and willing labor in exchange for room and board. So Widow Barker taught me how to drive a combine. After that, a car seemed like a pretty simple piece of machinery. Mrs Barker always said I had a natural aptitude for machinery.'

The old woman had needed a strong hand to help her and Trevan had needed a patient teacher. He had remained at the ranch even after he had located his farmstead not too far from the widow's place.

'Do you still work for her?' Jocelyn asked as she watched him intently.

'No.'

He heard her low groan of anger at his short answer. 'No, I eventually started remembering things from before and realized I wasn't too far away from where my ranch used to be. One day I drove out to where the house was . . .'

His voice trailed off as he recalled the image of the overgrown yard of his home with only the birds and the wind for company. 'It was then I realized how truly alone I was. I also remembered the cemetery not being too far from my property and I didn't figure they had moved it since . . . well, since I had last known it. So, I started walking to where I remembered it being located.'

With some relief and dread, he had found the cemetery was still across the section from his ranch house. Trevan's boots had crunched on the frozen ground of winter as he made his way to the small graveyard. There he had found his sister and Duncan, his brother.

Trevan dragged himself from his thoughts as he came to a stop at the sign, then turned to face Jocelyn. 'Duncan, my younger brother, had lived to be an old man and had built the family ranch into a nationally recognized corporation. It made me feel proud that he achieved so much.'

Jocelyn's voice was low, perhaps in deference to his pain. 'The Elliot Foundation?'

Trevan nodded, 'It made me start thinking about this cave that we all used to go hide in when my dad was drunk. We used to call it the family cave. That was the next place I went in search of.'

Curiosity had caused him to search out the family cave in a deep ravine on the property. Stepping inside, he had felt the silky webs of the past brush away. In a chamber deep within the dark confines of the cave, he found several large trunks full of gold bullion. Even as the wood and leather of the containers clung in rotted shreds, the shine of the gold was as brilliant as the day it had been brought to the cave. And a letter from Duncan, its parchment brittle and brown with age, had brought back memories as painful as an open wound.

'It was there I found a letter from my brother, Duncan, saying that Allysa's spirit had come to him to tell him how to help me and so he left several trunks of gold.' Trevan said solemnly as he remembered returning to the cemetery to mourn the family and the life he had lost.

'Gold.' Jocelyn gasped in surprise. 'As in gold coins?'

Trevan shook his head feeling humored by her look of astonishment, 'Gold bullion.' He watched her out of the corner of his eye as she stared out the window for a moment, then shook herself from her thoughts.

'Was it hard adjusting?' she asked. He wondered if she realized she was beginning to sound as if she had tentatively accepted the idea or at least was adjusting to the concept.

He shrugged, 'As far as working the cattle, most things were done differently, but it was toward the same goal. I guess I felt a sort of familiarity with the work and it helped me realize that the world as I had known it, had changed; some for the good, some for the bad. Then Widow Barker said something about the magazine article she was reading about a serial killer who murdered young women and left a mask beside each of his victims. That was the first day I realized that "he" had followed me through. That was when "adjusting" was no longer a priority and learning was. I don't know why I knew it was him, nothing seemed familiar. But somehow deep inside me, I knew it was him.'

At Mrs Barker's words, an image of Allysa had filled his mind, and he had asked to see the article with its grainy photo of a victim covered with a blanket. Only a woman's hand could be seen from within the dark folds, holding a porcelain mask. Trevan's heart had begun to pound heavily and he then knew why he had been brought forward to this time so different from his own: to hunt a killer.

Again, Jocelyn's soft voice broke into his thoughts. She leaned forward, excitement showing on her expression. 'So you know what he looks like.'

He shook his head and self-reproach and anger filled him as it did whenever a new victim was found. His voice wavered with his emotions. 'I had my hands wrapped around his throat. I was ready, more than ready to kill him, but my grip slipped away because of the rain and hail. I had been so intent on killing him that I never removed the handkerchief that he had tied around his head to cover his face. The only thing I did see was his eyes.'

Trevan knew that to his dying day, he would never be able to dispel the fury and the revulsion that had thundered through him as he stared into the murderous gleam of a madman's eyes.

'You said you have never told anyone about this. Then why are you telling me?' she asked, her voice quiet.

'I don't know,' he answered. He took a deep breath and mulled the question over in his mind. He had never felt the need to tell anyone about his presence here, never wanted to take the risk. Yet, he had never met anyone like Jocelyn Kendrick. Trevan met her gaze. 'I was too late to save the other girls. I just don't want to see it happen again.'

Jocelyn laid her hand on his arm. 'Trevan, the only

one responsible for those girls' deaths is the man who killed them. What makes you think you could have saved them? Or your sister?'

'I was her brother. I should have been there when she needed me,' he said, feeling the emotion welling up inside him.

'Even if you had stayed with her, would she have appreciated you hanging around her like a bodyguard?' she asked.

He chuckled softly at the thought. 'No, I guess not.'

Trevan flicked his gaze to her, then smiled to himself. 'You know you're starting to sound as if you just might believe me.'

'Don't get too cocky, Elliot,' she quipped. Rubbing her hands over her face, she groaned, then turned to look out the window. 'I don't know what to believe. In fact, I don't even want to think about it right now. Last night was a nightmare and tonight hasn't gone any better.'

Her words hit him; the impact harder because of the nonchalant way she expressed them. It was then he realized how badly he wanted her to believe him. Needed for her to accept what he was saying as the truth. To accept him.

He shook himself from the dismal trail his thoughts had taken and glanced over at Jocelyn as she quietly studied him, with sympathy and what looked like understanding. He only hoped she would understand. Could only hope she would come to believe what he was telling her. The monster called the Porcelain Mask Murderer was now focusing his murderous vision on her. He silently vowed to himself that he would do whatever it took to protect her.

But would that be enough?

Jocelyn tried to shake herself from her thoughts and the tension Trevan's words had caused. She had read the sincerity, the truth, of his words in his expression, his hands, and his eyes as he recalled his memories of what had been the past. Literally the past from the 1800s, she thought, then suppressed a shudder. She needed time to think about what he had told her and maybe research what she could before she could fully understand, let alone accept the implications of his story.

She scowled as the truck pulled onto her street. She was glad to be home and returning to some sense of normalcy. Pressing her fingers to her throbbing temples, she noticed a man sitting on her front step.

She leaned forward in the seat and studied the man. He appeared to be old and a vagrant, but different from any she had ever seen. He was clean. She sucked in her breath in a mixture of fear and anger as she recognized him. He had been at the county building when she left today. He was following her.

Trevan gave her only a curious glance but said nothing as they pulled into the driveway. As soon as the truck stopped, Jocelyn hopped from the cab.

'Who are you?' she started angrily as she moved towards the man, 'Why are you following me?'

The man stood with eloquent grace and smiled politely at her, but spoke to Trevan as if she wasn't there. 'She is observant, isn't she? That's good.'

'That she is,' Trevan answered, as he grasped the small man's hand to give it a firm shake. 'Come inside and we'll talk.'

Shock was the only word that seemed to describe how Jocelyn felt. Trevan stepped to the door and unlocked it as if it was his own home, motioning the stranger inside. She felt her anger flare hot and white within her as she snapped in irritation. 'Don't mind me, Elliot, after all, I only live here.' He barely acknowledged her retort as he smiled. Apparently his shield of arrogance was back in place, 'Well, are you coming in or not?'

Muttering a few distinct and rather crude epithets, she pushed past him to make her way to the kitchen. Damn the insufferable man, she fumed silently as she got a beer from the refrigerator. Chauvinistic, pig-headed, knuckle-dragging . . .

'Thanks, Jocelyn,' Trevan said good-naturedly as he took the beer from her to pass it to the man, 'and I'll have one while you're at it, if you don't mind.'

. . . Neanderthal, she finished between gritted teeth. 'No, I don't mind at all.'

Returning to the kitchen, she pulled two more beers from the refrigerator. Both men stood automatically when she entered the room and she handed Trevan his drink.

'Thank you,' he said quietly, as the tips of his fingers moved over hers to take the bottle.

She ignored the heat of his touch and the exciting tingles it had invited as she moved to sit in her rocker.

'Jocelyn Kendrick,' Trevan started, then motioned to the man, 'this is Cargo.'

She nodded as he stood to bow silently, 'I guess I don't need to ask if that's your first or last name.'

His ebony eyes twinkled with humor. 'Both.'

Trevan sat beside the man on the couch. 'Cargo and I became friends about two years ago and he has been extremely helpful to me. Tell me, friend, what have you learned?'

The man took an awkward sip of his beer, then began, 'The Carter girl died, I'm afraid, by the same poison as did the others, gelsemicine and other related alkaloids. I believe it is an ingredient derived from *Gelsemium sempervirens*, more commonly known as Yellow Jasmine. Symptoms include weakness, headache, giddiness, paralysis of the tongue, anxiety, low body temperature, tetanic convulsions. In death the victim's face – '

'Becomes mask-like,' Jocelyn finished, 'You're talking about what was in the police file and the coroner's investigation. This sort of information is confidential, how did you find out?'

'I hear things. Most people do not notice individuals like myself,' Cargo's gaze met hers, 'You, however, are different.'

She frowned as she mulled his comment over. Trevan's voice broke into her thoughts, 'Is there anything unusual about this plant, besides the obvious? Is it a common variety or easily accessible?'

Cargo raised his eyebrow, '*Gelsemium sempervirens* is apparently indigenous to all continents but North America and Antarctica. However, I could be mistaken. At one time even the sparrow was not indigenous to North America.'

'How would someone get hold of something like this Yellow Jasmine?' Trevan asked.

The small man shrugged a thin shoulder, 'I'm afraid I don't know that.'

Trevan acknowledged his words with a distracted nod of the head. 'So now we need to track down this plant. Maybe, if we're lucky, it will be rare item around here.'

'I don't think that will be the case,' Cargo said, taking a deep breath and releasing it. 'In fact, I believe it will be just the opposite. I wonder though, whether we could learn if the ingredient is used for any medicinal purposes.'

'Do you mean as an ingredient in a prescription?' Trevan asked. The man nodded and he mulled it over for a moment. 'Cargo, that makes sense. In fact, it makes perfect sense.'

Trevan turned to Jocelyn, 'Is there anyone you can contact that might be able to tell us something, anything about this plant?'

She pursed her lips as she thought for a moment. Thomas worked in the coroner's office and he worked with poisons regularly. 'I think I might know someone. He may not know about the plant itself, but he could definitely give us the name of someone who could. Like a botanist maybe.'

Cargo set his beer down on the table. 'Good, I'm glad the information could be of help. Thank you, Miss Kendrick, for the drink.'

'Thank you, Mr, I mean, Cargo,' she said. The man's genuine concern for her and his willingness to help touched her. Jocelyn regretted her words earlier and noticing the man's clothes, worn, but clean, she wanted to return the favor. 'Uh, Trevan was just getting ready to fix us some sandwiches. Would you like to join us?'

He studied her for a moment, his eyes showing his hesitation. He nodded, 'It would be a pleasure.'

'The pleasure is ours, sir,' she said. Trevan smiled, then rose and started toward the kitchen. He gave Cargo a friendly pat on the shoulder as he passed by him. Jocelyn watched, surprised, as he walked out of the room. When she had said he would make lunch, she had done it more to pay him back for making himself so at home before. Trevan, however, didn't seem to be bothered at all by her volunteering him to domestic duty. Her brow rose at the thought, maybe he wasn't so bad after all.

The doorbell rang and she excused herself to Cargo to go answer it. A tall, awkwardly thin, young messenger stood outside with a brightly wrapped package.

Jocelyn frowned. It was several months to her birthday, what could this be? She thanked the man and brought the package inside. She shook it lightly and heard the contents mysteriously rattle inside. With a puzzled look to Cargo she carried the package to the coffee table and set it down. She started to open it when she caught sight of Trevan entering the room to her right.

At the question in his eyes, she shrugged nervously. 'I guess someone got his dates mixed up.'

She pulled the wrapping paper apart and tore the tape easily from the seam of the box. Jocelyn had to remove several filmy pieces of tissue paper before she uncovered the surprise.

Lifting the last piece of tissue paper, she gasped in revulsion and terror. 'I tried hard not to believe you. I didn't want to believe you,' she whispered, feeling an icy wave of dread wash over her.

Trevan moved beside her, the warmth of his body the only sense of solid security as her world started to spin around her. 'What's wrong, Jocelyn? What is it?'

In the box was a large porcelain mask. The garish expression broken in a zigzag cut from the upper corner of the face, down to the other cheek.

The image stuck in her mind even as the black sand of unconsciousness filled her vision.

CHAPTER 7

Jocelyn had felt herself falling into the buffering safety of unconsciousness. Now a man's insistent voice was threatening to bring her back. Back to where her day had started. At first there was only a small tear in reality, but then it had widened until it became a black hole, sucking away the normalcy of her life.

'Jocelyn.' She recognized Trevan's voice and shook her head. Although the deep sound caused warm tremors to course through her, she did not want to respond to it. To him. 'Jocelyn.'

'What?' she asked crankily as she opened her eyes. She winced as a jolt of pain stabbed through her head. Moving her hand, she tenderly felt a bump with her fingertips.

'Sorry about that,' Trevan soothed, his face so close to her own. 'I wasn't quite fast enough to catch you.'

'Oh, really.' She glared at him, then remembered why she had fainted: The mask; the calling card of a killer. 'I didn't damage it, did I?'

Jocelyn groaned as she sat up, thankful to be off Trevan's lap. Unfortunately his arm remained around her as he sat beside her. He seemed worried that she might have a relapse.

'No, you didn't,' he said. His voice wavered for a moment, causing her to glance at him. She was a little surprised to find his face pale, his eyes filled with concern.

She turned to study the remains of the broken mask and shook her head, a sharp pain reprimanding her for the sudden movement. The mask was much like the others, except, perhaps, more elaborate. The face was topped with a green silky cap and long green plumes embraced the cheek to swirl over the top. A braid of gold framed the face.

Jocelyn hesitated to touch the two pieces. She didn't want to destroy any evidence on the mask left by the killer. She knew within her that he had sent it to her, but why? Surely he would have figured out that she would have it examined for evidence. Gently she held the pieces by the fabric edges and lifted them to turn them over.

Trevan reached beside her to pull something from the box. She almost dropped the mask as she turned to find him holding a piece of paper. 'Trevan, you shouldn't touch anything. He might have left his fingerprints on the paper.'

Trevan's gaze moved from the paper to hers and she didn't like what she saw within their depths. 'He left more than that.'

Jocelyn swallowed nervously as she moved to look over his shoulder at the note. They didn't need any more fingerprints than necessary. She glanced once again to Trevan, noting his eyes had hardened, than focused on the familiar spiky scrawl of the Porcelain Mask Murderer.

Soon, Jocelyn, sweet student of the mind.
We will both have our wishes . . . Soon.

The words innocently shrouded a message; a dark message of sinister intent. Jocelyn felt a cold shiver of fear wash over her. How could she protect herself from a man determined to kill her? A maniacal man who had eluded the authorities quite well so far?

Trevan moved closer to her. Placing the paper back in the box, he put his arms around her and enveloped her within the security of his warmth. For a brief moment, Jocelyn allowed herself to close her eyes and lean against the comfort of his solid chest. For a moment, she allowed herself to believe that he could save her.

With a deep breath, she resolutely stepped away from him and found herself being watched closely by both men. She knew they must believe she was going to become upset, but again, she was determined to prove them wrong. Jocelyn gave Cargo a brief attempt at a smile and returned her attention to the mask in her hands.

'Well, I think we need to get busy,' she said as she again turned the pieces of the mask over to inspect the back. A brief flicker of hope flashed through her as she noticed a stain. On closer inspection, she realized it was a smudge. And it contained the faint ridges of a partial fingerprint.

She felt her confidence return and even the slightest flutter of power. Turning to hold Trevan's gaze, she let him see her determination. 'I think the Porcelain Mask Murderer may have just made his first mistake.'

Trevan's eyes remained on hers for a moment before he looked to the stain she indicated. He glanced back to her. 'How will this help?'

She smiled as she gently replaced the pieces of the mask in the box. 'I think I know someone who can check this out for me. Unofficially of course.' She picked up the package and turned to face him, feeling more in control now. 'We might be able to get a partial fingerprint and maybe, just maybe, an identification of the stain.'

Cargo moved beside her with a knowing smile on his face. 'Perhaps an identification could help you locate the source, am I correct?'

She nodded. 'Fortunately, it doesn't look like paint. That would be too hard to identify or even trace, but it looks like putty of some kind and it's flesh colored. It might be make-up.'

Trevan frowned. 'Call me cynical, but isn't make-up just about as common as paint?'

Jocelyn shrugged, 'Depends on what kind of make-up it is. I did research during my graduate work on face make-up for burn victims.' Trevan's brow arched and she knew he might not be familiar with the implications of her statement. 'There is a firm, perhaps even a couple, that makes face putty to help burn victims cover severe facial scars. And it is specifically made to match each person's unique pigment. The putty on the mask looks similar to this form of make-up.'

Trevan held her gaze, 'Just who is this person who can 'unofficially' look into this for you?'

Jocelyn hesitated a moment, then grinned. 'He works for the coroner's office and I owe him five bucks. I think I can talk him into helping us out. Besides, if he wants his money, he'll have to do it. He can check the composition of the smudge and maybe pull a print for me, and another man I know down at the station can check the prints against records.'

Trevan watched her for a moment, 'You know there will be no record of him.'

'That we know of,' she finished. She hadn't completely made up her mind about what he told her, but she had to check all possibilities. 'Besides, it wouldn't hurt to check them against the AFIS.'

He raised his brows, 'Excuse me, or should I say, excuse you?'

She gave him a dirty look. 'AFIS. Otherwise known as the Automated Fingerprint Identification System. We don't know that he hasn't ever been arrested.'

'Okay,' Trevan shook his head. He showed reluctance in the shrug of his shoulders, but she could see the trust in his eyes. 'You're the boss, so lead the way.'

Thomas Cohen shook his head. 'I don't know, Jocelyn. This could get me, and you, for that matter, into a lot of hot water.'

Jocelyn leaned toward him, placing her hands on the cool shiny surface of the coroner's examination table. 'I'm not asking you to reveal confidential information, Thomas, because I'm the one bringing it in. This package was sent to me and all I want you to do is run a test on the smudge on the back of one of the pieces so I will know if it is over the counter make-up or a specific blend and, if you're not too busy, lift a print.'

Thomas gave her a hard look. 'Why?'

She took a deep breath realizing she hadn't taken the time to think about that. Trevan's voice surprised her as he moved from the shadows he had been standing in.

'Miss Kendrick is assisting me on a case.'

Cohen tilted his head and gave him an exasperated look. 'And you are?'

'A private investigator,' Trevan answered without blinking or hesitating. 'We're working on a possible child pornography ring and we could really use your help. It is imperative we learn the identity of the substance as soon as possible. A young child's life could be at stake.'

Jocelyn had to stop her mouth from falling open and gaping in astonishment at Trevan's improvising. Instead she quickly cleared her throat and turned to look at Thomas as if she knew exactly what Trevan was saying. 'That's right. Just think of that poor mother's relief and gratitude if we can get her little girl back.'

Thomas did not even attempt to look as though he believed their story. He glanced at Jocelyn, then again shook his head. 'Okay, give me a little time and I'll call you with the results as soon as I can.' He grabbed a pad and a pen from his pocket. 'Give me a number where I can reach you.'

Jocelyn smiled sweetly and tried to hide the look of triumph from her expression. 'Thanks, Thomas, someone should write a song about you. I might even be forced to do it myself. Oh, by the way, would you know anything about an alkaloid called gelsemicine?'

'Just make sure the song's a once in a lifetime performance,' Cohen said, giving her a pointed look. He then frowned as he thought for a moment. 'Gelsemicine. No, I can't say I'm familiar with that particular toxin, though I've heard the name. Talk to Pemberton in your department. He knows a botanist that could probably help. I assume this has something to do with a plant called Yellow Jasmine?'

Jocelyn licked her lips nervously, then smiled at him. 'Yes, it does. But it has nothing to do with the Porcelain Mask Murders.'

'Uh huh,' Thomas said, studying her, then Trevan. 'Yeah, well, just remember you owe me ten dollars.'

'Ten dollars. The bet was only for five, that is blackmail,' she sputtered. She started to wave her finger in his face when Trevan grabbed her hand.

Thomas grinned, 'You know, you're right. Make it fifteen.'

Jocelyn started to protest when she felt Trevan's hand on her arm pulling her from the room.

'We are grateful, sir,' Trevan added, then hurried her quickly to the elevator.

'Where did you come up with something like that?' Jocelyn whispered as they hurried down the hall.

'*Magnum, P I*, he answered, then apparently caught her look of doubt. 'It happens to be one of my favorite shows. I catch the reruns.'

'You continually surprise me,' Jocelyn said as they stopped at the elevator.

When Trevan pushed the button and looked impatiently at the lighted numbers she couldn't help quietly laughing. 'What are you afraid of? You sure are in a hurry to get out of here.'

'I can think of a couple of reasons. One: I don't exactly like the idea of being in a morgue,' he answered. 'Two: if you had kept up your "sweet little old me" routine, he just might have changed his mind.'

The doors opened and they stepped in. As the panels slid to close them in the isolated quietness of the elevator, Jocelyn felt a smile touching her lips. 'Why, Mr Elliot, I just might think you were getting a little jealous.'

He glanced to her, then back to the doors. 'There was no reason to be jealous, as far as I was concerned.'

Jocelyn stepped in front of him. She moved her body close to his, but without touching him. Boldly she let her gaze travel up his chest to meet his eyes. 'No reason, Trevan?'

The feeling of being back in control apparently also made her daring. She suddenly wanted to know if she could shake the unshakable force of Trevan Elliot. Slowly she leaned toward him, her gaze on his mouth as she gently touched hers against the warmth of his lips. Closing her eyes, she sighed in appreciation as his opened to her invitation. Suddenly his arms were around her, pulling her firmly against him. She responded by moving her hands over his chest to circle his neck.

Trevan deepened his kiss, tilting her head as his hand slowly stroked her back. A part of her heard the door ding open, then her equilibrium returned in full force as a loud round of applause and whistles broke out in the lobby of the building. Jocelyn started to pull abruptly away but he tightened his hold on her.

He forced her to meet his eyes and a slow smile lit his face. 'No reason at all, Miss Kendrick.'

Jocelyn scowled at his audacity. It burned her that her battle of wills had turned into a full scale attack by a handsome stranger who had worked his way effectively and completely into her life.

As they left the elevator, she ignored the chuckles and knowing smiles of the crowd around them. Trevan, however, nodded and even returned a few winks as they made their way to the door.

Just like a man to gloat, she thought, wishing she could kick him, or something else she evilly imagined, to wipe that smile off his face.

Jocelyn groaned when she saw Gary Pemberton walking toward them with a knowing grin on his face. He chuckled, obviously enjoying her discomfort. 'As usual, Kendrick, you definitely know how to make an entrance.'

Jocelyn introduced the homicide detective to Trevan. 'We were just visiting Thomas.'

Gary laughed, 'I don't know many people who go to a morgue to visit. Especially considering it's Thomas.'

'He said you might be able to help us,' she went on, wondering just how much she should tell him. 'We were curious about an unusual kind of plant and Thomas said you would know of someone who could help us with that.'

He studied her intently for a moment, then lowered his voice. She could tell he knew why she was asking. 'Jocelyn, I don't think I have to tell you that you could be getting yourself into big trouble.'

'I appreciate your concern, but I can't expect you to comprehend why I have to do this,' she said, lifting her chin with determination. 'If you don't want to help me, I would understand.'

'Just remember, this could be the end of your career, before it's even started.' His gaze moved from her to Trevan for a moment, then back to her, as if he was wondering whether he had anything to do with her taking this risk. What Gary didn't know was how desperate the risk really was. 'There's a graduate student at the local university who has helped me with things like this.' He pulled his pad from his pocket and wrote down a name. 'His name is Harvey Miller. He helped me with research on another case. He would be your best bet to get the information you need.'

Jocelyn took the note and gave Gary a quick kiss on the cheek. 'Thanks, this really means a lot to me.'

'If that's all I had to do to get you to kiss me, I would have done it a lot sooner,' he chuckled.

'I wouldn't bet on it, Pemberton,' Jocelyn smiled. She waved to him as they headed to the door.

'What would it take to get you to kiss me?' he asked, his voice low and his breath warm on her ear as he pushed the door open for her.

Jocelyn felt an unexpected tightening of her stomach with desire as his body rubbed against hers. She could all too easily recall how his lips had felt against hers.

How it had felt to run her hands across his chest. She shook the heated images away and forced herself to remember that she could not let this man who was affecting her so completely distract her. She still had to work through what he had told her about where he came from. Quickly she pushed those thoughts from her mind, it was too much to consider. Yet, she couldn't believe how easily her heart was willing to accept the impossibility of what he was saying.

Silently she groaned. When had her life become so complicated, she thought, then immediately knew the answer. When Trevan Elliot had turned up.

'I don't think that would be wise, do you?' She said, then met his gaze. 'Besides, if what you say is true, a man your age shouldn't overdo it.' Before he could reply, she turned and headed for the parking lot.

Glancing at her watch, Jocelyn realized it was getting close to nine. She thought she might as well fix a late dinner for her unique assortment of guests. Cargo had returned shortly after they pulled into the driveway and they had been discussing areas of potential investigation. She excused herself and went to the kitchen to begin fixing sandwiches.

Trevan remained in the front room quietly talking to Cargo. If he was from the past, as he believed, it would probably seem quite natural for him to sit on his butt while she did all the cooking, she thought to herself. With a start, she realized the implication of her thoughts. She reminded herself that, after all, she was cooking for guests. Not divvying up the domestic chores. Trevan was only searching for his sister's killer, not building a relationship with her . . .

She decided to leave that thought unfinished, at least for tonight. Too much had happened today and she needed time to think. About the murder. About the handsome stranger. And her heart.

'Kendrick, you are such a push over,' she murmured as she opened the refrigerator to inspect the contents. The cordless phone rang and she closed the door and answered it.

The low voice of a man greeted her. His words were softly spoken, but not whispered. Jocelyn couldn't quite understand what he was saying but the impression was that of an obscene phone call. Anger flared, hot and indignant, within her, as she started to lower the phone from her ear to slam it back on the base. As if sensing her irritation, the caller's voice became louder.

'I would advise you not to disregard me.'

'What? Who are you?' she whispered hoarsely, fear slamming her heart. Malice had threaded its way into the man's words and something within her recoiled as an image flashed into her mind. A white mask, its lips curled into an evil grin; its empty black sockets invoking fear into her very soul.

'I realize you are afraid,' the low voice reassured her, 'but your fate and mine are intertwined. It was written in the past, for now . . . for always, Jocelyn. I would never hurt you.'

'Wouldn't hurt me?' She barely choked the words, 'You killed those other women and you expect me to – '

It was Trevan's hand, warmly covering hers on the

130

phone which kept her from dropping it. She could feel his heat, the solid assurance of his body as he stood close behind her. It kept the freezing tingles of terror from enveloping her. His other hand was on her hip, the security of his touch keeping the icy fear at bay.

'Unfortunate, I assure you. You, however, are different. They were substitutes,' he chuckled, 'vehicles really. You were my past; now you are my destiny.'

Silence filled the space between them. Jocelyn was too dumbfounded and shocked to even sputter a reply. Trevan turned the phone slightly so that he too could listen.

'I want you to meet me downtown at the service entrance of the library at eleven. Do you know where that is, Jocelyn?'

Trevan's lips moved quietly, soothingly, against her ear as he covered the mouthpiece with his hand, 'Tell him yes, that you will be there.'

Numbly, she nodded, repeating the words to the faceless voice.

'Good. It's a very public place; you will be surrounded by people,' he offered. Then his voice thinned like the end of a knife blade resting against the tender flesh of her throat. 'If you do not come, there will be a price.'

The phone clicked sinisterly into her ear.

Jocelyn punched the off button, dropping the phone to the kitchen table. Terror, heart wrenching, vivid terror consumed her. She wrapped her arms around herself in an effort to stop the shaking.

Trevan turned her to face him, his hands on her shoulders. She was in a daze as she slowly raised her eyes to his. He nodded in answer to the silent question of her expression. She now truly believed that the man who had killed Carrie Carter was after her.

Cargo spoke quietly. 'I believe the game has begun.'

She turned to him, 'What do you mean?'

The gentle pressure of Trevan's fingers made her look at him. 'He is turning this into a game. You are the stake . . . and winner takes all.'

She felt the blood drain from her face. Trevan's hands gripped her tighter, pulling her slightly towards him as if he was going to take her into his arms. He hesitated then wrapped her tightly within his embrace.

Jocelyn turned her face into the crook of his neck and closed her eyes. His touch, his strength, his comfort felt right. She had never really had the luxury of someone to turn to when she was scared or lonely. Not since her parents had died. Now she experienced the same emotions of shock, fear, and anger as she had then. Except a faceless stranger with a penchant for death, had, this time, caused the feelings to surface. A murderer who even now sought another victim.

And if the killer had his way, she too would soon be dead.

'I can't believe this,' she said, pulling away from Trevan's embrace and starting to pace nervously. 'What am I supposed to do, play along with this weirdo's little game. Me come, you kill.'

She laughed, the sound anything but humorous. 'You know what this is, don't you?' She looked at Trevan, the tears of her fear burning down her cheeks. 'The typical idiot in the basement syndrome.'

'The "B" movie black moment where the woman in her satin nightgown goes down into the dark basement to investigate that suspicious little noise that just happens to sound like an ax grinding on a sharpening wheel.'

Jocelyn knew she was rambling, but she was scared. More scared than she had ever been in her life. 'I've always thought that people like that deserved to die. You know, survival of the fittest.'

'Cargo, would you mind staying with her?' Trevan's low voice broke into her frantic thoughts.

'Certainly.' The thin man answered.

'I appreciate the thought, but I'm going with you,' she said, meeting Trevan's gaze determinedly. The words had been out of her mouth before she had realized what she was saying. Now said, the idea appealed to her. Never would she admit it to him, but she felt safe with him. Right now she desperately needed that sense of security. The security that only he seemed able to give her.

'No.' He shook his head as he ran his hand through his hair and paced away from her. 'When I said "winner takes all", I meant life and death.' He stopped to stand before her. 'Yours.'

'He's after me, Trevan. Don't you think he expects your chauvinistic attitude? He could be waiting for you to leave.' She had every reason to believe that very idea could or would happen. Chicken or not, she wanted to be with Trevan. 'I'm going.'

Rubbing her arms against the chill of the fall evening, Jocelyn paced in front of the service door. A light drizzle had turned into a regular fall shower as they waited in the sheltered overhang of the library. She glanced at her watch for what seemed like the hundredth time; it was almost midnight. 'I guess punctuality would not be a murderer's strong suit, huh?'

She felt Trevan's gaze on her as she continued her movements, first to keep warm, then to work off her nervous energy. He, on the other hand, had been leaning quietly against the wall as if nothing dire was going to happen.

'He's manipulating us.'

She shook her head; she was the one with a sociology degree, and still she couldn't figure out what was going on. 'I don't understand. When one manipulates another, it's usually to achieve a goal.'

Sirens suddenly pierced the cool silence of the night. Trevan moved beside her as Jocelyn looked around the corner of the building to see where they were headed. Several police cars wailed past them to turn up the next street.

Trevan's hand moved to the small of her back and he started them in the direction the cars had disappeared. His voice was low and filled with dread. 'And I think we are about to find out what he had hoped to achieve.'

Jocelyn couldn't quite catch her breath as they moved quickly down the block towards the Old Town. A growing apprehension tightened around her chest like wet leather drying in the sun. Turning the corner, she caught sight of the tall fence of McAdam's Park, its large gazebo squatting in the middle of the yellow and red foliage of fall. The glittering lights of the police cars flashed in waves on the walls of adjacent buildings. Despite the weather, huddles of cars and people moved slowly past the spectacle for a view.

She moved closer to Trevan and, as if sensing her uneasiness, he grasped her hand holding it tightly in his. The coldness settling on her came more from the speculation of what might lie ahead than the dampness of the evening. Trevan's warm hands were the only things keeping her teeth from chattering as his heat blended with hers to push her fear away. But it could not completely conquer the feeling of foreboding.

The wind lifted at her hair as they pushed through the hectic activity. Women clutched at their purses, wide-eyed, shifting for a better view. The morbidly curious talked with others about what little was known, making things up to fill the gaps in conversation. Jocelyn was more than surprised to see how many people stood about at such a late hour.

They moved through the crowd, apologizing occasionally as the stirring of the group nudged them into someone else. Jocelyn's gaze narrowed when she caught sight of the hub of the activity over a tall man's shoulder.

On tip-toe, she tried to get a better view until Trevan tugged at her hand and pulled her in front of him. The push of the spectators forced him to press himself intimately against her back. His warmth was welcome, but the distracting effect of his hard body, she did not need.

Turning her attention ahead of her, she was pushed against the familiar barrier of the yellow crime scene tape. She frowned as she saw that the next taped barrier closed off the opening of an alley approximately thirty feet away. A police officer moved from the entrance as the cool drizzle continued. The man's bulky body turned, giving her a view of a dark form lying in the middle of the alley. Lightning illuminated the night sky and Jocelyn's breath choked in her throat as a woman's unfocused gaze briefly appeared.

The flash of a police camera intermittently lit the face of the corpse. Despite the moisture of the fall storm, the dead woman's eyes remained dry, her stare glaring in accusation at Jocelyn.

She could sense the activity around her, but was unable to move her gaze from that of the murdered woman. Murdered because of me, she thought. Her knees jerked with weakness. A fluttering sensation of nausea moved through her and she felt a comforting pressure as Trevan's hands moved around her waist.

The flash of the camera lit the wall under the balcony of the old building the body was lying near. She forced herself to look away from the corpse and shift her attention unsteadily to the overhang of the structure protecting the surface of the wall from the rain. An officer raised his flashlight to study a message.

The letters were awkwardly scrawled on the beige brick, the sticky moisture satin against the gritty texture of the wall. Like the title of a Stephen King movie, the ends of each letter dripped down. Jocelyn's sickened stomach clenched when she realized why.

She scanned the cryptic message; the meaning hitting her physically as she leaned against Trevan's hard chest. The message meant specifically for her.

There is always a price.

The image of the words remained focused in her mind; the nightmarish scene before her swirling into a twister of terror threatening to consume her. Trevan turned her in his arms and held her tightly as he too studied the words of foreboding. She felt the fear move through him as he began to realize how insane this killer was.

And how determined he was to get Jocelyn.

CHAPTER 8

Jocelyn squeezed her eyes shut; when she opened them, the nightmare was still around her. A woman, a stranger, lay dead in an alley beside a park, because of her.

She felt the burn of the tears welling in her eyes as she met Trevan's gaze. 'I don't understand. He wanted me. Why did he kill her?'

'I don't know,' he voice low and soothing as he put his arm around her. He looked toward the alley, his mouth thinning into a grim line of distaste. 'We need to get closer. Can you get us in there?'

She nodded, swallowing the emotions welling up in her throat. 'I'm not a police officer, but I'll see what I can do.'

Jocelyn ducked under the tape and stepped to the nearest officer. Fortunately it was Rose Edwards, one of the few other females in the homicide department. Rose contemplated her request for a moment, then gave her a brusque nod and a sharp order to keep out of the way.

She motioned for Trevan to join her, then waited as he quickly moved beside her with his hands in the pockets of his denim jacket. She kept her voice low, so that only he could hear. 'Just make sure you do not touch anything and we can look things over. But I'm the only one who can get close to the body.'

She could tell by the hardening of his dark eyes that the idea didn't appeal to him. She had to give him credit though, since he did not say anything, only nodded, then began to study the scene.

Jocelyn put her hand on his sleeve and directed his attention to a man examining the body. 'That's Bill Wilson, the coroner. I'm going to talk to him and see if he can tell me anything.'

Trevan pulled at her hand, stopping her. His eyes searched her own for a brief moment. 'Are you sure you want to do this?'

'That woman is dead because of me, Trevan, and I'm going to do whatever it takes to make damn sure he pays.' There was no mistaking whom she meant.

Jocelyn turned and moved to stand beside Bill.

'Jocelyn, glad to see you looking better.' He smiled, then knelt beside the corpse.

'Thanks, Bill. Looks like strangulation,' she said as she studied the purplish bruises left by the killer's hands on the victim's neck. She noted the coroner's dinner suit and tie. 'Interrupted your dinner?'

'Hell yes, and I don't know why. Tom over there says he's busted her for prostitution on several occasions. She probably got in a fight with her pimp.'

'Did he mention her name?' Jocelyn frowned. Even if the woman was a hooker, she didn't deserve to die in an alley because of the whims of a madman.

139

Bill flipped a paper back on his clipboard. 'Ruby Snow. I doubt that's her real name, but you never know.'

She nodded, then turned to kneel beside the body. The woman's eyes had already begun to flatten from loss of fluid but her skin still felt warm. Ruby's legs and arms were turning blue. Jocelyn tilted her head, as she pressed her finger at the purplish color on the woman's lower back which was partially exposed. The area whitened then quickly resumed the dark color once she removed the pressure of her fingertip.

'She's been dead longer than an hour, hasn't she?' Jocelyn said.

Bill nodded as he looked over his glasses. 'You are quite right.'

'I don't understand,' she murmured. The accusing stare of the woman was caused by rigor mortis, she now realized. It usually began in the face, starting with the small muscles of the eyelids and the lower jaw.

'I would say almost three hours. I think rigor mortis started in so quickly because it looks like she put up quite a fight,' he said, as he pointed out the scuffs of her heels on the bricks and her broken fingernails.

'The more strenuous the activity before death, the faster it sets in,' Jocelyn finished. The bastard had killed her before he even made the call. Why?

She thanked Bill quietly. Standing, she turned to get a closer look at the message. *There is always a price.* It was blood all right, but not Ruby Snow's. She had been strangled and there were no puncture wounds or loss of blood from her body.

'Chicken blood.'

'What?' She turned and then nodded when she realized it was John Cartland. 'How do you know it's chicken blood?'

'The carcass is lying in the garbage over there,' he answered, then studied her for a long moment. 'Any connection to what you're working on?'

'He called me tonight.' She didn't know why the maniac had killed the woman, but she knew without a doubt it was the work of the Porcelain Mask Murderer.

'What?' he fumed. Several officers on the scene turned their heads in his direction. John glared at them till they resumed their business, then lowered his voice to a conspiratorial whisper. 'I assume you're talking about the killer.'

She took a deep breath and nodded, knowing his rage was more directed at the fact she hadn't notified him of the call. 'Before you get all bent out of shape, at least let me explain. We both know how overworked the department is. If I had called and said, "John, I was fixing dinner when the Porcelain Mask Murderer telephoned. And guess what, he wants me to meet him at the library!" You and I both know that there are not enough personnel to go chasing after loony stories like that.'

'Damn it.' He crossed his arms and lowered his head as if in thought. 'You work with me. That doesn't make it a loony story. How's this going to look if someone finds out you knew about it beforehand?'

'You know I'm right, John, and I don't actually work with you, do I? I'm only a student and a sociology major, at that. Hell, my emphasis is in deviant behavior and the Porcelain Mask Murderer just happened to call me! Boy, what a coincidence, officer.' She could tell by the softening of his expression that he also knew she was right.

'There still would not have been enough people to check the call out,' she said earnestly. 'Besides, he didn't mention anything about this. I didn't know what to expect after I received the call, but I did not expect him to kill someone. Damn it, part of me kept wanting to believe it was a prank call.'

'So what did he say?' John asked, his eyes scanning the crowd around them.

She paused, running the conversation through her head. 'He said he knew I was afraid, but "your fate and mine are intertwined". Something about "it was written in the past, for now, for always. I would never hurt you". I didn't believe him and he assured me that the others were substitutes. Vehicles. Then he told me to meet him at the library . . .' Jocelyn's smile meant anything but pleasure at the remembrance of the killer's words. 'He said it was a public place and I would be surrounded by people.'

'Was that all?' he asked.

Jocelyn's gaze flicked to the scrawl of the message on the wall, 'No, he also told me if I didn't come, "there would be a price".'

She turned to find John studying the message. He shook his head, his face showing his confusion and frustration. 'This guy is up to something,' he murmured.

'That's what Trevan said. The main thing is, John, I don't have any proof of this guy calling. If you check the phone records I'll bet the call was made from a phone booth around here. And this,' she waved to the body with her hand, 'doesn't make sense. It's not his usual "ritual". All the others he seemed to savor. This one was done for plain malice.'

John crossed his arms over his chest as an intense moment of silence grew between them. 'Or as a distraction.' He met her gaze. 'Or to set someone up.'

Her eyes widened as she took in his words. 'Do you think he is trying to set me up?' she asked, her lips curving into a frown.

He shrugged, 'Hell, I don't know. You're the one with the shrink degree.'

Jocelyn turned and found the dead woman's eyes staring at her. 'As I said before, he did this one for a reason. I talked to Bill Wilson about the time of her death. He said she had been dead for almost three hours, that means he killed her before he even called me.'

John placed his hands on his hips. 'Damn it. This guy is nuts.'

He shook his head, then stopped. Jocelyn followed his gaze to where Trevan stood. John looked back at her.

'Is that the guy you were telling me about this morning?' he asked.

She nodded. John turned to study Trevan for a moment, then he blew his breath out. 'What did you learn about him?'

Jocelyn chewed her lip for a moment, then cleared her throat. There were some things she could tell him. 'The reports showed nothing on him . . .' And some things she could not. At least that much of her statement was true. Trevan didn't exist as far as the reports were concerned.

'And after tonight. After this,' she waved her hand to the body, 'I believe him.'

'Okay,' he said quietly, then rubbed his forehead, 'but I still want to see him . . . tomorrow.'

'Thanks, John.' She attempted a smile. He must think her mad, but he was at least giving her the benefit of the doubt.

She gave him a solemn wave and went to find Trevan. He wasn't in the taped off area where he had been a moment earlier. She moved behind the tape and glanced around, searching the crowd with her eyes. He was nowhere to be found.

He smiled to himself as he suppressed a chuckle. He had enjoyed the glint of fear that he'd witnessed in the woman Jocelyn's eyes almost as much as he had enjoyed watching the life ebb from the street walker.

It had been so pitifully easy and quite necessary to fulfil the role he had chosen. The role of a madman. Of course the media already believed he was. The thought caused him to laugh softly. A woman turned to give him a disapproving look till her eyes met his gaze. He studied her as if she were a specimen, a bug stuck with a needle through its middle on a foam board. He smiled as unease slid into her expression and she moved away from him into the thickness of the crowd. How easily people were manipulated.

The hooker had been a little harder to work, a slight challenge he had relished. Living and working off the street had caused her to be cautious and tough. Yet flashing a wad of money and giving her an approving smile had won her over as effectively as if he had held a gun to her temple.

He had pulled her into the alley and begun breaking down her defenses as he touched and stroked her. He had held her face in his hands as he moved his tongue over the ridge of her lip, lightly teasing. He had let his lips skim over her cheek to her neck where he nuzzled her throat till she had tipped her head back with a soft moan. Even as he softly nipped on her neck, he had slid his hands to her throat and held her for a moment. Pulling back, he tightened his grip and smiled as her neck stiffened in surprise. Her hands had grabbed at his wrists. Her nails tearing into the soft skin of the back of his hands till she drew blood. The drops had slid across the back of his hands in a warm caress as her eyes widened in terror and pain.

Several moments had passed till her hands loosened from his wrists, then fell beside her. Her body had become limp and heavy, forcing him to lay her on the ground. Then he had worked to finish the staging of this act with the proper tools. As he worked, he had heard a garbage bag shift, then fall over. Turning, he'd scanned the dark recesses of the alley seeing nothing till a ragged cat had bolted from a box to run swiftly past him.

'Puss in boots,' a voice slurred behind him.

He smiled to himself as he remembered his discomfort at seeing an old man covered with filth slowly sitting, cardboard pieces falling from him as he sat up.

For a moment he had forgotten the dead prostitute as he'd turned his attention to the vagrant. 'Puss in boots. Puss in boots,' he'd said, rubbing his toothless gums together. 'No food here.'

He'd moved toward the man till he stood in front of him. The homeless man had continued muttering and talking incoherently to himself. Eventually the grimy man's gaze had wandered till it met his briefly.

Blood still fresh on his hands, the killer had been ready to take care of the vagrant till he noticed the old man's eyes. They were milky white and unblinking. If the man wasn't blind, he was very close to it.

He had briefly considered killing the man to put him out of his misery, then quite as easily had dismissed the idea. It didn't play in his thoughts. It would unbalance what he had so carefully staged. No, he smiled as he warmed to the new change he was already calculating in his thoughts, better yet to leave a witness. He had knelt in front of the man and stared till the vagrant had met his gaze. He had leaned closer till the man's eyes showed a brief moment of comprehension, fear, then it was gone.

He chuckled as he watched the woman Jocelyn talk quietly with one of the younger detectives from homicide. Together they approached the old man still sitting in his pile of rags with a steaming cup of coffee in his hands. He watched as she knelt in front of the homeless man with a look of gentle concern on her face. Let her talk to him. Life had already dealt the pitiful man a more wretched blow than he could ever have forced on him. She would learn nothing from his nursery rhymes or his milky eyes.

As he watched them, the old man's eyes briefly seemed to meet his causing him to smile. The woman turned as if to follow the vagrant's gaze and she scanned the crowd.

He turned to move through the onlookers. No, Jocelyn Kendrick, student of the mind, would learn nothing from this lost soul. The thought amused him. A blind man who could only respond to the shadowy specters of his own broken thoughts. He chuckled quietly as he slipped into the crowd and disappeared.

'How come I get the feeling you're about to work yourself into a very tight situation?'

Jocelyn turned, finding Gary Pemberton standing behind her. He was tall and handsome with wide shoulders. With the police lights flashing behind him he looked more like a movie version of a cop than the real thing. Now he was studying her intently.

'You're not my conscience, Pemberton,' she said, taking a deep breath. Again she scanned the crowd behind the tape and still she could find no sign of Trevan.

'I didn't say I was,' he answered, moving to stand beside her. His gaze moved over the body to the forensic technicians moving methodically around it. 'But I get the feeling you're connected with this.'

Jocelyn scanned the body lying on the damp floor of the alley. It was only misting now, but the flashing lights took on a mystic look. She didn't answer him because she was unsure how to. Her heart had withdrawn from the pain, fear, and guilt of what was going on around her. Now she felt tired. Weary of the dark reality threatening to envelop her.

Gary looked at her for a moment, then exhaled slowly. 'I guess this hasn't been easy on any of us.'

'Yeah,' she answered simply, wrapping her arms around herself.

Purposely changing the subject, he nodded toward a group of cops standing on the other side of the alley. 'If you don't mind, there's a guy I want you to come talk to.'

Jocelyn frowned as she followed his gaze. For the first time she noticed an old man sitting with rags and cardboard piled around him. His expression was that of a child as he talked to himself. 'Who is he?'

Pemberton shrugged. 'We haven't been able to get that out of him. He just keeps talking to himself about cats and dogs, stuff like that. But I have a feeling he witnessed the whole thing.'

Gary put his hand on her elbow and led her to the old man. Jocelyn knelt beside the frail vagrant and tried to ignore the stench enveloping him. The man continued talking hoarsely to himself in a whispering voice, the words occasionally slurring one into another. He had mud smudged on the prominent bones of his cheeks and his eyes were sunken, giving him a skeletal look.

She shook her head, turning to meet Gary's gaze. 'He

may have witnessed the prostitute's murder, but he didn't see anything.'

Pemberton frowned, 'What do you mean?'

'He's blind.'

He shook his head with frustration and wiped his hand across his face. Jocelyn could tell he had been hoping the man could help them in some way. 'Do you think he's with it enough to maybe have heard something?'

Jocelyn returned her attention to the small man and spoke softly to him several times. The man's eyes skittered from one point to the next as his wrinkled lips formed words against his toothless gums. Gently she took his hand in hers, surprised that his fingers were so warm.

Maybe it was the contact of her skin against his that caused him to grasp a small hold on reality, but the wild look of the man's face dimmed a bit and he turned to focus unseeing at her. His movements ceased as if he were waiting for her to speak.

In a soft voice she introduced herself and held his hand a little tighter. 'How are you?'

He cocked his head as if processing her words, then answered her in a hoarse sing-song voice, 'I am fine. Fine as wine.'

Jocelyn felt Gary put his hand on her shoulder as he knelt beside her. 'I knew you could get him to talk to you.'

She didn't respond to Gary, afraid it would break the precarious link she had with the man. 'What is your name?'

'Hayden,' the unkempt man said without hesitation. 'Mama calls me Hayden.'

'Hayden, do you know what happened tonight?'

'Puss in boots,' he muttered, starting to rock from side to side. 'Puss in boots. No food here.'

Jocelyn covered the hand she held with the other, enveloping his within her own. 'Hayden, I need to talk to you.'

He turned back to her and his movements quieted. She leaned toward him, unconsciously hoping that her closer proximity would register her presence deeper into his thoughts. 'Hayden, I need to know what happened. Did you know the woman?'

'Snow White,' he said, his voice threaded lightly with pain. 'Snow White took a bite of the apple with blood on her hands.'

Jocelyn felt the excitement building within her. Maybe, just maybe, she was getting through to him. 'Who was with Snow White, Hayden? Was there someone with Snow White?'

'Polyphemus.' The man's eyes widened and his fingers tightened around her hand, 'Polyphemus looked upon her with his sinister eye.'

Polyphemus. The name rang a bell, but she couldn't place it. 'How did he look at her, Hayden?'

'Blue as the sky,' said the old man. His fingers loosened, then no longer gripped at hers. Jocelyn found herself merely holding his hand as the frail vagrant started rocking himself again.

She called his name, but he didn't acknowledge her voice. She exhaled slowly, then patted his hand before she let it go. She rose with Gary and met his gaze. 'He's told us as much as he could.'

'What did it all mean?' Pemberton asked.

'I don't know,' Jocelyn shrugged. Her gaze returned to the old man sitting in a dingy pile of rags that served as his bed and home. Unconsciously she rubbed her hands together, the grime of the vagrant's living conditions gritty against her palm. 'Is there any way you can find out who he is, maybe if he has any family?'

Gary took her elbow and started to lead her away. 'Yeah, I'll look into it.'

Jocelyn nodded, then thanked him as he handed her an antiseptic towelette. She moved away from him and mulled the old man's words over and over in her head. Lost in her thoughts, she almost walked past Trevan without noticing him.

He placed his hand on her arm and remained silent till she looked up to meet his gaze. 'Are you all right?' he asked, his voice low with concern.

'Yes,' she said, not allowing herself to look back at the alley. The image of a dead prostitute and a homeless blind man would stay with her for a long time. She didn't think she would ever forget, but could only hope to begin to understand.

'Was the man any help?' Trevan asked as they started toward the yellow crime scene tape roping back the onlookers.

'He kept rambling about cats, Snow White, and someone or something called Polyphemus.' She frowned as the words ran through her mind, disjointed and incoherent. 'I don't know why, but somehow I feel that what he said should make sense. I just can't figure it out.'

Trevan pulled the tape up for them to cross under it. His hand touched her lightly on the shoulder. 'Don't worry. I know you will figure it out. Maybe tomorrow it will come to you.'

Jocelyn gave in to the urge to look back toward the man. 'Yeah, but will he have a tomorrow? And if he does, will it be any better than today?'

Trevan pulled her into his arms. His chin rested lightly on her head as he spoke to her. 'If any good can come out of this, maybe it will be that at least he is going to get the help he's been needing. If he has a family looking for him, maybe they will finally find him and take him home.'

'Maybe,' she acknowledged, stepping back to give him a small smile to show she was okay. He took her hand and together they moved through the crowd and headed toward her Jeep.

Trevan had a point, she thought, stepping on to the sidewalk as she drew her jacket tighter around her. At least, for a moment, it had given her something to think about other than the senseless murder of a stranger. The rain picked up again and they ended up doing a slow jog the last two blocks to where she had parked the Jeep.

Jocelyn opened her door and unlocked Trevan's. She rubbed her hands together as she waited for them to warm up. It was late and she wanted nothing more than to go home. She would drink a glass of wine and then try to sleep if she could. Somehow she didn't think it would be easy. She knew that as soon as she closed her eyes, the garish image of Ruby Snow's face would again stare at her in accusation.

The streets were slick and Jocelyn had to use all of her concentration to drive. Some dips in the streets had filled, moving like swift little rivers, forcing her to creep slowly through them so the car wouldn't stall. She turned on Maple and accelerated, knowing it was one of the better streets to travel during heavy rain like this, because the sewer drainage was more modern than Old Town's.

Jocelyn started to push the brake to slow for a light. Her foot pushed the pedal too easily to the floor with no effect. 'Oh, no!'

'What?' Trevan asked.

She pumped, trying to breathe life into the brakes. She flicked a brief look of bewilderment to him. 'The brakes are out.'

Fortunately the streets were empty since it was so late at night. Quickly she laid on the horn to warn any cars that might be coming that she couldn't see, before she blazed through.

'Is there any other way to stop it?'

Jocelyn pulled on the emergency brake and it offered no resistance to her effort. She felt the blood drain from her face as she met Trevan's worried expression and his look needed no words.

She turned her attention to the road as her thoughts raced frantically for something, anything, to stop the vehicle. It wasn't exactly as though they taught us how to handle this sort of thing in Driver's Ed, she thought. Or at least she didn't remember them doing it.

They were close to the next intersection as she removed her foot from the gas. Even as she wished fervently for the light to remain green, it yellowed, then flashed red.

'Damn,' she muttered, instinctively checking the cross street. A car picked up speed to move through the intersection as her car hurled towards it. Glancing to the speedometer, she groaned. They had only slowed to 35 mph. She leaned on the horn and slammed her foot on the gas.

They sped through the red light and the other car screeched, then swerved, barely missing the bumper of the Jeep. Her stomach clenched unmercifully and she had to work for every breath as she removed her foot from the gas pedal. The smooth whir of the tires on pavement ended abruptly, replaced with the crunch of gravel pinging the underbelly of the Jeep. The road was scarred with ruts from the onslaught of the rain and her Jeep began to bog down in the mud.

The road turned slightly and Jocelyn glanced to the speedometer to find they were down to 40 mph, but still too fast for a muddy road. She had hoped to stop in a farmer's field, away from traffic.

The vehicle swerved and lurched as she instinctively worked the brakes and swore vehemently at their ineffectiveness. The railings of an old bridge appeared in the beams of her headlights and her chest tightened with terror. The Jeep rattled over the edge of the road before the bridge and hitched with a spray into the swollen creek.

Jocelyn's body jerked forward, then was stopped

abruptly by the pull of the seat belt. Her breath came in deep gulps as she stared in horror out the windshield. The Jeep's headlights illuminated a murky orb in front of the submerged hood.

The rush of the water drowned out the sounds of the night as she turned to make sure Trevan was all right.

'That was pretty good driving,' he yelled over the noise.

'It can't be too good,' she said as she undid her seat belt, 'We're in the middle of a creek.'

As if to emphasize her point, the bulk of the vehicle shifted slightly under the pressure of the driving water.

'Let's get the hell out of here,' he yelled and moved into the back.

Jocelyn didn't need any prodding. She practically crawled on top of him to join him in the back seat. She knew, and apparently so did Trevan, that it would be impossible to open the doors against the current. He moved over the back seat to the rear window. Mud kicked up from the tires during their wild ride had blacked the back half of the windows. Her heart pounded with fear as the darkened interior reminded her of the confining wall of a coffin.

'Stay behind me and cover your face,' Trevan yelled as he fumbled with the latch to the seat where the tool compartment was located.

Jocelyn pressed her cheek to his back and pulled her jacket over her head. The hot breath of fear feathered on her face. Trevan's body moved with the force of his swing. She flinched when she heard metal chinking against the glass causing it to splinter. The surface spidered with a tinkling sound. She jolted as he struck again and again. She felt the pelting of glass chips rain down on her as the window finally smashed from his effort.

Trevan moved through the open wound of the back glass and plunged into the rushing water. Shaking shards of glass from her hair, Jocelyn crawled after him.

The silver gray of the moon lit the dark snaking of the current as it roared past them. Trevan's silhouette stood framed by the window. He grasped her, then pulled her into the water beside him.

As they turned to move towards the bank, the momentum of the water pushed at her and if it wasn't for Trevan's strong hands, it would have swept her away helpless.

Together they fought through the current to the edge of the embankment. Jocelyn's muscles were weak, child-like, as she tried to stagger up the slick incline to the sand. Trevan guided her and she blindly stepped from the wet froth, her breath coming in ragged gasps.

They fell beside each other on the soft sand. Jocelyn lay on her back too tired to sit. Turning her head slightly, she studied Trevan.

'Are you okay?' she asked.

He nodded, working to catch his breath. He leaned forward to rest his forearms on his knees as he looked toward the Jeep.

She followed his gaze through the mist to where the moon eerily illuminated the dark hulk of the Jeep. The metal of the frame groaned, then turned slowly as the pressure of the rushing water conquered its victim.

Awkwardly, the vehicle rolled onto its side, the black swirl of the water instantly filling up the interior.

Jocelyn sucked in her breath. Images flashed through her thoughts. The echoing voice of the man who called her, the dead woman's eyes staring at her accusingly, the words written on the wall with their bloody tendrils dripping down the rough texture. All of them swarmed round her, stinging her with a desire for vengeance.

Icy sweat beaded on her forehead and the back of her neck and she felt her eyes widen with fear as she turned to Trevan. 'The Porcelain Mask Murderer; he did this. He wanted to kill us.'

It was a statement of fact. A fact she knew, the proof coming from within her. Looking into Trevan's eyes, she knew he believed it also. Chills shuddered through her like the dark curls of autumn's leaves skittering across the pavement.

He nodded, his gaze never leaving hers. 'Remember the message? He wanted to collect his price.'

CHAPTER 9

The night had been long and hard. They had been lucky enough to wave down a man with a mobile phone to call the police and a tow truck. Trevan looked the Jeep over and both he and the tow truck driver agreed that the brake lines had been cut enough to start a leak, allowing them to travel the distance they had before the brakes had gone out.

The police, on the other hand, had not been quite so easily convinced. Jocelyn got the distinct impression that the young officers felt she was trying either to get attention, or to concoct some sort of elaborate insurance scam. She had to admit that hypothesis sounded more reasonable than the truth.

It had been after four in the morning when they were finally driven home by the wrecker service. After a brief shower to lose a few layers of mud, Jocelyn had fallen into bed, exhausted, without even attempting to dry her hair. The evening had taken its toll, yet allowed her to slip into a deep slumber. A brief reprieve from murderers and masks and the accusing stare of a dead woman.

A noise made Jocelyn flinch. Even in the dim awareness between sleep and consciousness, she recognized her name.

'Jocelyn.'

She groaned and rolled her face into the pillow. She only wished the offending person would leave her alone.

'Wake up, sleepy head.'

'Go away,' she muttered crankily. She had never been a morning person. In fact, she was downright rude when her sleep was disturbed and there hadn't been much of that last night.

Strong hands rolled her to her back and she groggily opened her eyes to scowl. 'Trevan, leave me alone.'

'Sorry, but we have work to do,' he said with sickening enthusiasm as he sat beside her on the bed. 'It's time to wake up.'

She closed her eyes. She truly hated people who could get up in the morning without feeling like they were dragging themselves out of bed. She hated people who could function, let alone think before the sun was fully up. She hated people who were so happy in the morning.

'What time do you usually get up?' she asked, opening only one sleepy eye.

'Dawn.' He smiled.

'Figures,' she groaned and tried to roll back over.

Trevan stopped her with his hands, then leaned over her as Jocelyn cringed in horror. Oh no, he's going to kiss me, she thought, and I have morning breath.

Instead his lips lightly touched her nose and then he playfully smacked her on the thigh. 'Get up or I'll get you ready myself,' he warned with a lecherous wiggle of his eyebrows.

'Jerk,' she muttered as she scooted out of bed. The threat was more disturbing, or perhaps more accurately, more enticing than she cared to admit.

'Careful.' He paused at the bedroom door. 'Breakfast is almost ready and I won't give you any if you're not nice.'

'It is my kitchen, you know,' she snapped as she headed to the shower. She could hear his chuckle as he went downstairs. So what if he had saved both their lives last night; he didn't have to be so damn cheerful about it.

The shower did not do much to improve her mood; if anything, it only mellowed her grumpiness. She mulled over the events of the night before and no matter how many ways she thought about it, her logical side would not allow her to accept the blame of Ruby Snow's death. There was only one person responsible for that and she was determined to make sure he paid for it.

Jocelyn went down the stairs, slowing when she heard Trevan humming to himself in the kitchen. She stopped at the bottom, her hand on the post, listening to the unfamiliar melody. She wondered if it was a song from his time. Shaking her head, she smiled. Okay, she thought, maybe he could possibly be from the past.

He had already proven himself to be different from any man she had ever met. *Intense*. She had never met anyone with such force. It had struck her when they were at the Carter scene and the crowd had moved out of his way when he left. His animal grace was enough for anyone to recognize that he would be a formidable foe.

Loyal. It was a quality hard to find in a time when a person was a friend only as long as it suited or offered some sort of benefit. Trevan had continued to pursue his sister's killer even after being thrown through time.

Passionate. Jocelyn smiled at the thought. Trevan probably would not like being called passionate, but his eyes told a lot more of him then he knew. She had watched in wonder as his eyes darkened with anger. The way the gold flecks in his eyes brightened when he smiled. And she had not missed the burning of his gaze as it moved over her with a heat that had matched her own.

Shaking her head, she chuckled. Okay, she thought, maybe he is from the past. It could be possible, she reminded herself. After all, there had been a time when man had believed they could not fly or go to the moon.

Still, if he were from the past, another man had come through time with him. A man who, as far as the twentieth century was concerned, did not exist either. Yet he hunted the women of this time with cold blooded efficiency.

Jocelyn walked into the kitchen and watched Trevan working on something at the stove. She took a mug from the cabinet and moved to fill it with fresh coffee. She leaned against the counter and was quickly impressed by his cooking expertise.

She studied his face as he worked. He had shaved, apparently with her razor and had escaped with only one nick on his chin. Tiny laugh lines were beginning to form at the corner of his eyes. She recognized the familiar tightening of desire within the pit of her stomach. Trevan was definitely a handsome man.

'So how old are you?' she asked, then took a sip from her coffee.

'I'm one hundred and forty-nine, if you want to be technical,' he answered. He turned to meet her gaze with a smile she was sure could melt the coldest heart. 'Or you can say I'm thirty-two, give or take a century.'

Her mouth fell open and she couldn't say why, but she felt like laughing. 'Yet you look so young.'

One hundred and forty-nine years. So much had changed during that time. She studied him for a moment. For some reason she had always had this idea that people from the 1800s were dirty, pelt-covered, and homely. Yet, the muscled ridges of Trevan's tall frame were anything but homely. Even his eyes were beautiful, although she was sure he would not appreciate hearing that.

'So what was the first thing that impressed you about the twentieth century?'

'Toilet paper,' he responded promptly.

Jocelyn laughed and received a hard look from Trevan. 'I'm sorry, but we've made so many accomplishments like cars, airplanes, and the space shuttle and you were impressed by toilet paper?'

'Believe me, what we had, honey, was not "squeezably soft"', he muttered, turning back to the stove.

Trevan slid an omelet onto a plate. He put a couple of slices of bacon on the side and handed it to her. 'The toast is on the table.'

Her eyes widened at the quantity of food. 'Do you always eat like this?'

He chuckled. 'No, but today I felt like fixing omelets.'

'That's good. You know the fat and cholesterol content in this could kill you.' She took a bite and thought every puffy gram of fat and cholesterol was worth the exquisite torture. 'This is glorious. Truly glorious.'

Trevan raised an eyebrow as he brought his plate to the table. 'Most people just tell me it's good.'

Jocelyn didn't usually eat breakfast, but his omelets were great. After she finished, she leaned back in her chair and realized with a satisfied sigh that she was going to have to skip lunch to make up for the calories.

'Thank you for breakfast. I'll probably still be full at dinner time.' She picked her plate up and took it to the kitchen to rinse. Putting it in the dishwasher, she started cleaning the kitchen.

'You don't have to do that,' Trevan said, carrying his own empty plate to the sink. 'I made the mess and I'll clean it.'

She shook her head. 'Nope. The house rule is: the one who cooks, doesn't have to clean.'

Despite her house rule, he brought her the dishes from the table and began to help her scrape and rinse them. They were working together when the door bell rang.

'I'll get it,' she said, wiping her hands with a towel as she made her way to the door.

She recognized John Cartland's sparse hair line and

Gary Pemberton's taller frame through the small windows in the door. She pulled the door open and invited them in.

John stepped through and his gaze immediately moved to the kitchen where Trevan was putting soap in the dishwasher. When his eyes met hers, she understood the implication of his thoughts. Gary, fortunately, appeared to have no reaction to Trevan's presence.

'I was getting ready to come in,' Jocelyn explained as she waved them to the sofa.

'You might want to hold off on that for a while,' John said with a slight edge of nerves.

She took a seat on the rocker and shook her head, 'What's going on?'

'I have to be blunt with you. Some pretty hard allegations were made against you this morning.'

'Such as?' she asked quietly, trying to contain the anger welling up within her.

'Such as tampering with evidence, leaking information to the press, and possibly even planting evidence.' John held his hand up, when she started to protest. 'Right now your involvement with our department is under investigation by Internal Affairs. Your college advisors will be contacted regarding disciplinary action and it's possible criminal charges may be brought against you.'

Jocelyn repressed the want, the need, to shout and break something. Instead, she took a deep breath, trying to get her thoughts into some kind of order. Slowly, she leaned back in her chair. 'And what do you believe?'

John gave her a half-hearted smile. 'Don't pull that psychoanalysis crap on me. I know it's a load of bull.'

'So do most of the people you've worked with,' Gary added, his eyes full of concern mixed with anger.

Jocelyn felt part of the tension ease from her shoulders, 'I guess that's more than I could possibly expect from anyone.'

'John Cartland, Gary Pemberton, meet Trevan Elliot,' she said as she motioned for Trevan to join them.

The men shook hands and Trevan moved to stand beside Jocelyn's chair. 'Do you know who might have made these allegations against her?'

The older detective shook his head. 'IA is being as anally retentive as they usually are. It doesn't help that Doctor Richard Lindenmeyer is the one investigating the charges. If anyone should be investigated, it should be him. But after what you told me last night,' he looked at Jocelyn, 'I wondered if whatever you're working on wasn't beginning to stir things up. When I heard what happened to your Jeep, I knew something was going on.'

'How did you . . .' she started, then shook her head. 'Never mind, I keep forgetting that cops are even worse gossips than old women.'

'You're my flunky,' he chuckled. 'The uniforms felt obliged to tell me.'

'Thanks, John you have such a way with words.' She rolled her eyes.

John's face became serious. 'This isn't a school project, Jocelyn. I know you will make a good detective some day, but the way it looks right now, you may never get that chance. I don't care what, if any, evidence you have. Tell me what you know.'

She turned to Trevan and studied his expression. She could see the caution in his eyes, but even more prevalent was the concern. She bit her lip and looked at her hands for a moment. Trevan was leaving the decision to her and she knew he would not stop her either way.

Taking a deep breath, she met John's gaze. 'Like I told you the other morning, as far fetched as it seems, I have reason to believe – '

Trevan interrupted. His hard look confused her. 'We . . . have reason to believe that the man who killed Ruby Snow last night is after Jocelyn.'

John mulled the idea over for a moment. 'She mentioned last night that the serial killer called her. Is there any chance the two are not connected.'

Trevan shook his head firmly. 'Ruby's killer and the Porcelain Mask Murderer are one and the same.'

'It doesn't fit. The "mask" murders are premeditated and Ruby Snow had all the appearances of a grudge,' Gary said.

Jocelyn leaned forward in the rocker. 'We don't know why he changed his MO. We do know that all the previous victims were "courted," so to speak, and then poisoned in a ritualistic fashion.' She frowned for a moment. 'I wonder what the connection is between the masks that he leaves and the poison.'

'What kind of poison does he use?' John asked.

'Yellow Jasmine. Remember Carrie Carter? The poison causes a "mask-like" effect. That, coupled with the masks, is like he's giving us a clue.'

John groaned. The grim tightening of his lips showed his distaste. 'I hate it when you bleeding-heart psycho-analyzers try to say these people are sick and need help.'

She interrupted, 'I didn't say he was sick. I think he's being bold. Perhaps doing it for dramatic effect.' She hesitated for a moment as she tried to find words for what her instinct was telling her. 'He's not just sick, John. He is evil. The man could possibly be so self-centered as to believe he is untouchable.'

John nodded, apparently impressed. 'Okay, we have a serial killer with a superiority complex and a fetish for masks. Why do you think he is after you?'

'I know he is after her,' Trevan stated, meeting John's gaze.

'How? What made him focus on her?'

'Think about it. I saw her the night Carrie Carter's body was found. For the next week a picture of her studying the body appeared in every major newspaper nationwide. Television also carried footage of her. The media basically bombarded him with Jocelyn's face. In fear of inflating her ego even more than it already is, she is a beautiful woman.'

Gary snorted, 'You're right about the inflated ego part.'

Trevan's lips curled into a lopsided smile as he continued. 'She is also obviously intelligent and cap-able. All of the other victims had a similar personality trait: determination.'

Jocelyn noticed a slight hesitation in Trevan's answer and studied his expression. He looked toward her and she saw a brief flicker of guilt. She frowned slightly, then it occurred to her that maybe he knew something more. Something he hadn't wanted to share with her.

Suddenly, she felt her eyes widen at what she realized had been Trevan's praise. She had never really thought of herself as all those things and it was extremely flattering to hear him say them. 'Why, Trevan, thank you . . . I think.'

'You're also a pain in the butt, Kendrick. It detracts from everything else,' John retorted, then turned to Trevan. 'What about last night? The message on the wall: There is always a price?'

Trevan shook his head, 'I wish I knew.'

'That's what I don't understand.' Jocelyn said: 'We did as he asked and he still killed her. In fact, he killed her before he even called. Why? I don't know what the message means. It could be related to something he deeply resents or hates.'

'Like beautiful women with brains,' Trevan supplied.

There was a glint of danger in his expression. His dark eyes hardened as he held her gaze. She felt no fear, because what she saw in his eyes was meant for someone else; the man who killed his sister and was now after her.

'Exactly,' she answered, her heart pounding with the intensity of his look.

'Well, that sheds new light on things,' John said. He seemed oblivious to what was going on between Trevan and her. He stared at the ceiling for a moment as he tapped his finger on his chin. Suddenly he stood. 'Somehow this Porcelain Mask nut is trying to discredit you. And somehow he was able to plant these accusations. I'll do some checking and get back to you.'

Jocelyn turned to Gary. 'How is the old man doing?'

He shrugged. 'He's pretty ill and still talking in nursery rhymes, but we were able to find his family.'

So Trevan had been right. Maybe something good had come of what occurred last night. 'Are they from around here?'

Pemberton shook his head. 'No, up north.'

'Did you ask them about the man?' Jocelyn asked. Somehow she sensed the old man had been trying to tell her something in the only way he knew how. 'Could they tell you anything about him?'

He took his notepad from his pocket and flipped through the pages. 'His name was Hayden. Full name is Hayden Webster. His wife and son died of carbon monoxide poisoning in the late sixties. Apparently it hit him pretty hard. According to the family he always felt responsible for their deaths. He was away for the weekend and had planned to check the furnace when he returned. He started drinking heavily. One day he got up and walked out of the house and never came back. The family lost track of him.'

Trevan shook his head, 'I guess we all have to deal with grief in our own way.'

'I guess till it happens to one of us, we can't truly know how we would deal with it,' Jocelyn said quietly, remembering the milky white of the man's eyes filled with pain. Hayden had never had the chance to be happy. She swallowed back the emotion filling her and turned to Gary. 'What did he do for a living?'

'English teacher,' he answered, closing his notepad.

The old man's words came back to her. He had spoke

of Puss in Boots, Snow White and Polyphemus. Polyphemus, she knew she had heard of it before. Hayden Webster had been an English teacher, it must be some literary reference. She knew eventually recognition would cause the name to click into place.

'Well, we have to leave.' John's words broke into her thoughts. He and Gary stood and faced her. 'Don't worry, Jocelyn. We'll get through this.'

Gary nodded, 'The department's best are working on it.' He smiled at her, attempting to make her feel better.

The world she had been content in only a few days ago seemed to be falling down around her because of other people manipulating her life. She didn't feel like it, but she returned his smile. 'I assume that is supposed to be comforting.'

'Of course,' Gary chuckled. Yet Jocelyn didn't miss the worry in his eyes.

She walked them to the door and placed her hand on the older man's arm. 'John, thanks for believing in me. You too, Gary.'

John gave her an affectionate smile. 'I knew you wouldn't do anything as hair-brained as that crap they've brought against you.' He awkwardly patted her hand. 'Besides, I like having a flunky.'

She shoved him playfully out the door and waved as the two men walked to the car. Quietly she shut the door and turned to face Trevan. His expression had softened and his eyes were watching her with a heated intensity. He came to stand in front of her, then silently lifted his hand to run his fingers through her hair, then cupped the back of her head with his palm.

'I know things seem to have gone from bad to worse,' he said softly, his gaze moving over her face, 'but we will get through this. I promise.'

His eyes never left hers as his lips descended to her mouth. He touched the firm curve of his lips to hers, then deepened his kiss. He pulled her against him and she felt the tip of his tongue caress hers. He pressed her hips to his and the hunger of his strong fingers on her ignited the need within her.

Jocelyn moved her hands to his chest, amazed at the warmth beneath her fingers. Tears of frustration and anger burned at her eyes, but it was the feeling of helplessness that hurt her the most. Never had she not been able to look at a situation and figure a way to solve it. Now, a man was manipulating her, her life, so that he could kill her. She knew if she let it get to her she would lose.

She closed her eyes and let herself awaken under Trevan's touch. She wanted to feel alive and the delicious feelings he was igniting within her proved that she was. She was used to taking care of herself, but for once, just once, it would be okay to let herself get lost in the emotion she was feeling for this man who had so quickly and quietly ingrained himself into her thoughts and her life.

Slowly she traced the hard plane of his chest to his neck, then circled her arms around him. She groaned with pleasure as his hands slipped beneath her shirt to cup the ridge of her ribs. His thumbs smoothed hot circles on her skin.

Deepening his kiss, he pulled her tightly against him

and she felt the very real evidence of his desire for her. His mouth left hers and trailed kisses across her cheek, then to her throat.

Jocelyn let her head fall back as he smoothed her collar from her neck so he could reach the base of her throat with his lips. A yearning so deep she could barely breathe swelled within her.

Exquisite. If ever there was a perfect word for what she felt, she knew that was the closest she could come. Sensation after sensation bombarded her and she felt herself falling even farther within his loving touch.

The shrill beep of the phone broke into the delicious waves of desire Trevan had been causing within her. She closed her eyes once again, more than ready to ignore the phone and lose herself in Trevan's love.

Six. Seven. Eight rings blared through her thoughts, finally pulling her and Trevan slightly apart. She gave a bitter laugh of disappointment as she moved out of his arms to answer it.

'My luck has definitely gone sour. Apparently someone is quite determined to talk to me,' she said as she punched the button, then gave a tight greeting.

Thomas Cohen's voice barked at her in answer. 'Where the hell have you been, Jocelyn? I tried to get hold of you last night. I thought this was some sort of priority case.'

She took a deep breath and exhaled as she ran her hand through her hair. 'I'm sorry, Thomas. I was called out on a . . .' she hesitated a moment, giving Trevan a conspiratorial look, 'case last night. In fact, you probably have the woman in residence now.'

'Oh,' he answered, the anger falling away from his voice. 'You must be talking about the prostitute that was strangled last night.'

Jocelyn's brows rose. 'You wouldn't have had an opportunity to look her over yet, by chance?'

'No,' he answered. 'It will probably be later this afternoon. Maybe tomorrow, but that's not what I called you about.'

'You got the results of the analysis on the smudge?' she asked breathlessly. She knew they might have found their first real lead in their hunt for the Porcelain Mask Murderer.

'You were right about it being the specially blended putty,' Thomas offered, then his voice trailed off for a moment.

'Don't keep me in suspense, Thomas. Were you able to figure out the company who made it?' Jocelyn held Trevan's gaze, knowing he could see the excitement in her eyes.

'Yes, I did. And I've even located the buyer of this particular pigment blend.'

Jocelyn could hear Thomas take a deep breath and release it as if reluctant to give her the answer. 'And?'

'And I'm afraid you've hit a dead end,' he answered. 'In the most literal sense of the word.'

CHAPTER 10

'What do you mean I've hit a "dead end"?' Jocelyn asked, her brows dipping into a frown.

Thomas Cohen cleared his throat nervously, 'This putty was bought by an individual named Lucinda Travers.'

'Damn it,' Jocelyn muttered.

'I guess you know who she is,' he said, 'or was.'

'She was one of the "mask" victims.'

'Which brings up my next question,' Thomas started, his voice dropping low so that perhaps no one could hear his conversation with her. There still was no way to mistake his anger. 'You're working on the "mask" murders, aren't you?'

She took a deep breath, 'Look, Thomas, I'm sorry –'

'That doesn't cut it, Jocelyn,' he interrupted. 'I would still have done it if you had told me the truth. I heard what happened and I can understand why you are working on it unofficially, but I would just like to know what I'm getting into before I get into it.'

'Your point is well taken, Thomas,' she said, running her hand through her hair. 'I appreciate your support and thanks for getting that for me.'

'Just be careful,' he replied.

'Oh, and Thomas,' Jocelyn hesitated, feeling humble from so many people giving her help and showing her support. Especially when the evidence was against her. 'Thanks.'

'No problem,' he answered, his voice sounding almost grudging. 'Let me know if there is anything else I can do.'

'I will,' she said, then hung up the phone and turned to Trevan as she stuck her hands in her pockets. 'I guess you got the gist of that conversation.'

'Yes, I think I figured it out,' he said, his voice low. He studied her for a moment, then moved to envelope her in an embrace, his chin resting on the top of her head.

Jocelyn felt stiff for a second, filled with misgivings. Hesitating at becoming dependent on a man who was so quickly becoming a part of her. She took a deep breath and inhaled his scent and moved her cheek more tightly against his shoulder. If only for the moment, she would return his embrace.

'What about the mask?' Trevan asked, his voice soft against her hair.

She frowned, 'The putty belonged to one of the victims.'

He shook his head, 'I meant the mask itself. It didn't look like any of the masks left beside the victims. It looked bigger, more elaborate.'

Jocelyn raised her face to look at him, a smile working on her lips. 'And probably more expensive.' She kissed him fully on the lips. 'Trevan, you are the greatest.'

His eyes widened and he pulled her back to him as his mouth lowered to hers. His lips moved over her, then he deepened the kiss. Jocelyn let herself fall into the sensations that only he could stir within her. Moments passed before he pulled back to look at her.

'I'd like to keep you thinking like that.'

She smiled and let her gaze move over him. 'So far you're doing a pretty good job keeping that thought in my mind.'

Jocelyn moved away from him to gather her purse. She studied the look on his face and felt a sense of womanly control from the passion sweltering just below the surface. Her lips spread wide in a grin. 'Let's go shopping.'

They stopped by the coroner's office to take a snapshot of the mask. Both Jocelyn and Thomas Cohen agreed it would better protect the 'evidence' by leaving it at the morgue. What little evidence it was, she thought.

Trevan and Jocelyn spent the next two hours traveling from store to store, looking for masks similar to the one she had received. Finally, on a whim, she pointed to the mall and asked him to stop there.

'I know it's pretty far fetched, but it can't hurt to try,' she said, as they got out of his truck. 'There's a store here that carries a lot of china, jewelry, and other breakables.'

They made their way into the store and began to browse through the aisles of sculptures and paintings. Jocelyn felt her heart almost burst with joy as she spotted three masks very much like the one she'd received, hanging in a display.

She pointed them out to Trevan and then looked around for a clerk. Trevan was the first to spot one and wave her over. Jocelyn felt a twinge of instant dislike for the woman the moment she noticed her appreciative look for the man beside her.

'Can I help you?' the lady asked, her eyes focused only on Trevan. The woman placed the tip of her tongue against her lip and looked him up and down as if he were a six foot tall sundae.

'We need a little information about those porcelain masks,' Jocelyn interjected, moving a little closer to Trevan. The way the sales clerk was devouring him with her eyes, she just might have to protect him.

'Oh,' the woman said as if she'd suddenly noticed her. Jocelyn smiled at the look on her face.

'Would you happen to be the salesperson in charge of these masks?' Trevan asked.

The woman again turned to him and smiled almost coyly. 'Of course. How can I . . . help you?'

Start by backing off before I refresh your memory on what real pain is, Jocelyn thought, then forced herself to take a deep breath. They probably wouldn't get any information from the older woman that way. She ignored every part of her that wanted to remind the woman that she was at least ten years his senior . . . then she remembered that technically he was old enough to be her great-great-grandfather.

Jocelyn shook her head at the thought, then handed Trevan the picture and excused herself to go 'browse' a few sculptures while he charmed the sales clerk. He would be able to get any information there might be from the woman more easily if he were by himself. Besides, she thought with a small smile to herself, it would serve him right to have to deal with her. Alone. At her departure, the woman become even more fawning and flirtatious. It was almost worth leaving to watch the fear on Trevan's face as he kept looking over to her with what appeared suspiciously like silent pleas for help.

The clerk moved closer to him and fluttered her eyelashes at him as she gave him a suggestive look. 'Oh, please,' Jocelyn muttered as she rolled her eyes, then almost laughed at the bewildered look on Trevan's face.

The clerk took his arm and showed him the display case, then moved to a computer located discreetly behind the jewelry counter. Jocelyn picked up a figurine to take a closer look at the detail as she waited for the little interview to finish. Her thoughts were interrupted by a polite clearing of someone's throat and she turned to see a male clerk, giving her a pointed look. She glanced at the price tag of the small item and very slowly, very carefully, put it back down.

'Sorry,' she offered, giving him a tight smile. She would have been even more sorry had she dropped the item, as she almost had when she'd noticed the price. *$950 for a little crystal figurine of a caterpillar.* It was time to extract Trevan from the lecherous woman's clutches before she broke something.

As she walked toward him, Trevan gave the saleslady a charming smile and waved. He met Jocelyn in the aisle and took her elbow to head her toward the exit. She noticed the smile remained on his face and it was really starting to bug her, but he released a deep breath of air as soon as they stepped outside.

He shook his head. 'I would almost bet that woman is the descendent of Maybella Lovejoy. I didn't think I was going to get out of there alive.'

Jocelyn chuckled as she recognized his dislike of the situation. 'Now you know how a woman feels when she says a man treats her like a piece of meat.'

Trevan rolled his shoulder as if uncomfortable with the thought. 'I think she thought I was a nice juicy T-bone. Extra rare.'

Jocelyn laughed while they quickly made their way across the parking lot, 'Other than that, did you learn anything?'

'No, I didn't,' he answered as they walked beside his truck. He opened the door and waited for her to get in. He crossed in front of the hood and let himself in.

'I get the distinct impression that you wanted to get out of here,' she said.

Trevan faced her once they were enclosed in the truck. 'You have no idea how much.' He shook his head, 'When did women become so pushy?'

The look of shock amused her. 'Oh, and men aren't.'

He gave her a pointed look, but remained silent. Quickly, she turned away to hide her smile, then cleared her throat. 'You poor thing, you had to go through all that for nothing.'

'It wasn't a complete loss. She was able to tell me a few things,' he shrugged. 'They are distinctive pieces, but not really a collector's item. She even checked the records and found the day it was sold.'

'And?' Jocelyn urged, feeling the excitement build within her.

'Bought and paid for with cash,' he answered with his usual matter-of-fact tone.

'Did she have any idea who might have waited on him?'

He nodded, 'She did. Said she remembered him because he was so handsome.'

Jocelyn rolled her eyes. 'Oh, what a surprise.'

'And that he was almost as charming as me,' Trevan finished.

She gave him a dry look. 'Don't let it get to you. Just remember I've seen how charming you can be,' her brow rose, 'when you're covered with a bunch of stinking trash.'

He groaned and put his hand on the wheel. 'I hoped I had changed that particular impression by now.'

'Oh, but remember what they say,' she happily quipped. 'You'll never get a second chance to change a first impression. So did she happen to remember what he looked like? I'm sure every little detail was pressed intimately into her memory.'

Trevan chuckled, pulling his keys from his pocket to start the truck. 'Tall, but not as tall as me. Well built, but not as well built as me. Extremely handsome, but not as handsome as me, and . . .'

'Conceited, but not as conceited as you,' Jocelyn added with a smirk.

He laughed in response, 'Hey, she said it. Not me. But he was blond with deep blue eyes.'

Jocelyn frowned. 'That doesn't sound right does it? Did the murderer have blond hair or blue eyes?'

Trevan's expression became serious. 'No. I don't really remember details, but my impression was that he had dark hair. I don't remember the color of his eyes, just what I saw in them.'

'Damn it,' she muttered, her flippant good mood instantly evaporated. 'We're not having any luck at all.'

Trevan moved his hand to cover hers. 'Jocelyn, I won't let anything happen to you. The bastard will have to get past me before he can get to you.' He stopped for a moment as he held her gaze. 'I won't let that happen, I promise you.'

She leaned to him and kissed him softly. She pulled back only enough to look into his eyes. 'I know, Trevan. I know.'

'Well, do you have any bright ideas where we should go from here?' she asked as she opened the door, balancing a chocolate shake from lunch in her other hand.

'What about the poison?' he offered as he slid behind the wheel.

'Right now it couldn't hurt, could it. Let's go by the college and check with that botanist Gary suggested. He could probably tell us how readily available it is.'

At the state college, they found Harvey Miller, graduate student in botany. When they asked him about Yellow Jasmine, he smiled and held his hand up for them to wait a moment.

Harvey went into the greenhouse and returned with a small plant. He smiled as he set it before them on a desk. '*Gelsemium sempervirens*. It has a toxicity level of five, which means "honey, it is lethal". All of it is poisonous, but gelsemicine as a drug is mainly used in liquid form.'

'For what?' Jocelyn asked, eyeing the deceiving elegance of the plant.

'Trigeminal neuralgia, mainly, but there are other uses,' Harvey offered, then apparently noticed their looks of confusion. 'Trigeminal neuralgia, jaw-nerve pain. Quite chronic, I understand. There are other variations or similar drugs such as carbamazepine and phenytoin, which have very similar reactions. At least when we talk overdose.'

'As a plant, how hard is it to obtain?' Trevan asked as he lightly touched the beautiful but deadly petals of a new bloom.

Harvey frowned for a moment. 'It is not really indigenous to this area, but I know of several students, besides myself, who have a specimen their own personal collections. And, as a matter of fact, it's the state flower of South Carolina and grows very well in the south.'

'So, in other words, you can get as much as you want pretty easily,' she said disappointed.

'Damn,' Trevan muttered as he met Jocelyn's gaze. She knew he had been hoping, just as she had, that they could trace the madman through his source of poison. Still something about what Harvey said struck a chord within her, but she couldn't figure out what. Yet. She was going to have to get a copy of the 'mask' reports again.

They thanked Harvey for his time, then made their way to the sidewalk that led through the middle of campus. Jocelyn turned her face to the warmth of the afternoon sun on what had turned out to be a beautiful afternoon. 'Well, that was extremely helpful.'

'Yes, now we know anyone can get access to it,' he said as he took her hand in his.

She met his gaze and smiled. His callused hand felt good against her own. Her skin tingled from the memory of his fingers touching her this morning.

An image of Ruby Snow's dead face flashed before her and she reminded herself that they had to find something, anything, to stop the man responsible. There was a killer, a madman, to whom logic did not apply, seeking to make her the next victim. Who was he, she wondered? Of course, the only witnesses who knew that were dead. Or lost in their own world, she thought, thinking of the old man in the alley. Somehow she knew that if they figured out the significance of the masks, they would find the killer.

'You know, I've been thinking of something,' she said as she watched the light of the afternoon sun break through the leaves of a large sycamore.

'My body?' Trevan joked, squeezing her hand in his.

She gave him a pointed look. 'You wish. No, what I was thinking about was what I mentioned earlier about the masks.'

He chuckled as he shook his head. 'Sometimes Jocelyn, I feel I need cue cards to follow you.'

'How would you know what those are?'

'I used to watch Johnny Carson before he retired,' he said. 'Now enlighten me about the masks.'

'Well, our guy leaves a porcelain mask beside each of

his victims. If I remember right all the bodies and the masks are positioned in basically the same way.'

Trevan nodded, 'Meaning.'

'It's almost as if he is reconstructing a scene. A sort of ritualistic act, so to speak. Which could explain a few things,' she murmured, her brows drawing together as bits of memories of photographs and autopsy reports meshed in her thoughts.

'Some of the bodies I was not able to get close enough to study. So what do you mean "it" could explain a few things?' he asked, as they stopped at the edge of the parking lot.

'I've seen the reports on all the known "mask" victims, which I believe to be complete because he seems so proud of his work,' she said as she faced him. 'But the first victim, Michelle Slavinsky, had been moved after her murder. So had Halicia Carmichael and Cindy Blake.'

Trevan's expression was unreadable as he listened. 'How do you know that?'

'The fixed lividity was wrong on all three of them.' Jocelyn knew it had to be hard for him to rehash the murders. The nightmare had started with his own sister, over a hundred years ago. Then it had continued in this century as he had helplessly followed tracks of a serial killer.

Trevan's gaze fell to the tips of his boots, then back to her face. She could tell he was uncomfortable with their conversation. He took a deep breath, his voice gruff as he said, 'I know I'm going to regret this, but tell me what "fixed lividity" is.'

She gave him a reassuring smile and squeezed his hand, before she explained. 'Lividity happens after death. The skin becomes a purplish color because the blood sort of deteriorates and settles into the dependent parts of the body.'

She paused as she watched his face visibly pale. He nodded, his expression hardening as if he were angry at his own weakness. 'Fixed lividity means the liver color of the skin can no longer be shifted by moving the body. This usually occurs six to eight hours after death. For example, Michelle Slavinsky, if I remember correctly . . .'

'And I'm sure you do,' he stated, his expression grim.

She ignored him and went on. 'Was found lying on her right side, as all of the victims were, except Ruby Snow. But the 'fixed lividity' on Michelle's body showed she had died on her back. A subtle, but definite difference.'

Trevan rubbed a hand across his face as he closed his eyes. When he opened them, his look was one of disgust and disbelief. 'They teach this sort of thing to women?'

Jocelyn patted him on the shoulder, 'You are truly an antique, Trevan. Some of the leading forensic pathologists in this country are women. So what do you think?'

He placed a hand over his belly. 'I think we can safely skip dinner now.'

'All stomach, aren't you?' she teased, then started toward the truck thankful that he was at least attempting to ward off his dislike with humor. 'But see what I'm getting at? All the victims were "arranged." Their bodies were placed similarly, and so were the masks.

The poison of the flower causes a "mask-like" expression. He sent me an elaborate, but similar mask.' She paused to let him consider the thought. 'There is a recurrent theme: the masks.'

He held her gaze, his expression hard and unreadable. 'I see. So perhaps by learning what the meaning of the mask is, we may discover what he is hoping to achieve.'

'Exactly,' Jocelyn was having a hard time understanding his quiet anger. She did not know why, but he seemed mad. At her. 'Or, more to the point, what he is seeking to recreate.'

Trevan was a man from another time. A time where a man protected his woman and the woman stood behind him, simple as that. She decided now was not the time to discuss the roles of men and women in today's society. But where her thoughts were headed, and what she was about to say would do more than make Trevan angry. What she was about to say would revive memories of a pain that was over a hundred years old. She did not want to cause him that pain, but she had no choice if they were to find any answers.

'I know this may be hard, Trevan, but I think it's connected in some way to your sister.'

His eyes hardened even more, as she had suspected they would, but it did not diminish the compassion she felt for him and all that he had lost. She gripped her fingers together to stop herself from reaching out to him. His expression let her know the gesture would not be appreciated.

Jocelyn lifted her chin and met his cool gaze with one

of her own. He needed that right now. 'Allysa was the first victim.'

The Porcelain Mask Murders had caused women living alone to lock and bolt their doors at night. And after Ruby Snow, even the toughened ladies of the evening had become more cautious about their visitors.

Yet in the warmth of a brilliant fall afternoon, the man responsible for their fear stood on the steps of Devane Hall. Unknowing young college coeds looked him over and smiled hopefully at him as they walked by. With his dark hair slicked back into a small pony tail and his tight jeans, he looked the part of an older, mature student.

In the shadowed doorway of the stately old building, he waited and watched. He had followed the woman and Elliot here for nothing more than simply to see their disappointment. *Perhaps they had high hopes of locating me through the poison.* He chuckled to himself at the thought. *No, they would learn nothing here.*

But Miss Kendrick was a student of the mind. She possibly could figure out the innuendo of his choice of poison.

When Michelle, the sweet girl, had described the unusual features of a man's face after an overdose of gelsemicine in the emergency room, he knew he had found his weapon. Of course Michelle had been flattered by his interest in her work as a nurse and had helped him research the drug, tracing it back to its source.

Yellow Jasmine.

Yes, it was perfect. So utterly perfect. Shakespeare, Byron, not even Poe's twisted mind could have concocted a more perfect poison for him. It was even said that Cleopatra had used prisoners and her own slaves to test the results of death, in her search for the perfect suicidal poison. She had found her early findings too painful, then later had been disappointed when one poison produced convulsions that contorted the facial features hideously in death. Finally she had found the perfect result. The bite of an African snake called an asp, which would cause a quick and tranquil demise.

Even in death effect is everything, he thought.

He caught sight of Elliot and the woman as they walked through the center of the campus park. He drew his brows together in a frown as he noted their joined hands. His stomach tightened, and his vision blurred momentarily as the need for the power moved through him.

Ruby Snow had not been an effort to satisfy his craving, but only a prop to manipulate the Kendrick woman where he wanted her. Isolated from the police. He had been successful in planting an anonymous tip regarding her 'irresponsible' action.

Yet, here she was flaunting her beauty with another man. His jaw clenched and he balled his fists at his side. When would these pitiful creatures learn that he could see through their deception?

He took a deep breath and slowly straightened his fingers. It was getting harder to control the craving, the need to see the life dim from a woman's eyes. Soon, he would be able to satisfy himself. Soon. He would have the Kendrick woman and she would play the lead opposite him as he recreated his greatest act as an artist. Death.

But the stage had to be perfect. Elliot was being a loathsome thorn in his side and was becoming altogether too close to the woman. His woman.

An evil vision of color flashed into his thoughts causing a wicked smile. There was a little problem, however, that he had learned of only that morning.

A problem he planned to eliminate. 'Then everything will be ready for the next act.'

Watching her with Elliot, he nodded to reassure himself. 'Soon, my dear. Very soon.'

CHAPTER 11

Trevan remained silent as he drove the truck through town. It had been hard to listen to Jocelyn talk so easily about death and things like 'fixed lividity'. There also had been no mistaking the gleam of excitement in her eye from her fascination with the topic.

It was not so much the subject of Allysa's death that disturbed him, but Jocelyn's apparent determination to work in such a field. The four years he had been in this century had helped him learn to deal with his anger over his sister's murder, as had searching for the man responsible.

Yet Jocelyn was unlike any woman he had ever met. The first time he had seen her, she was staring dispassionately at a dead girl's body. Later he had felt her gaze on him and her direct expression told him she would ask questions. Even the knowledge that the Porcelain Mask Murderer was tracking her, working her like a deer hunter pursues his prey, did not dissuade her from her own pursuit of the killer.

She was taking the charges against her personally. He had watched, fascinated, as the bitter fury of the accusations moved through her. It was entirely possible that the madman had made his first mistake. Jocelyn Kendrick was mad as hell for being placed in such a disturbing position. Now she was even more determined to make him pay.

His sister had been the same way. A small smile lifted the corners of his lips as warm memories of his sister washed over him. Her tenacious spirit had driven many a beau away and even kept a few more courageous suitors at bay. Trevan knew that her spirit would never rest until hell, in the name of her murderer, paid the price.

And he had failed her.

Their mother had died when Allysa was a baby and their father had turned to the bottle for comfort. From that moment on, Trevan had been both mother and father to his two younger siblings and occasionally their protector when the elder Elliot came home an angry drunk.

At the age of sixteen, Trevan had been forced to face his father man to man. At the sight of his oldest son hell bent on protecting the younger kids, his father had left. Never to return. The Elliot children had grown up together and were known for their devotion to each other. Trevan had provided for them even as he built the ranch into one of the most successful in the midwest. It was with great pride the day he stepped into the cave, that he found his brother Duncan had carried on the family's unwritten law and provided for him.

Now everything and everyone was gone. Trevan was hard-headed enough to realize he could not dwell on the past, but had to go on. He would build a new life in this overwhelming yet exciting time.

But first he had to put the past to rest. For Allysa's sake, and his own, he had to seek justice.

He had to hunt a killer.

Jocelyn's voice broke into his thoughts and he turned to her. She smiled and repeated what she had said.

'I know this is hard, but we need to discuss the possibility.' She licked her lips. 'I really think your sister's death is the key to this.'

'I understand. What did you need to know?' he asked as he came to a stop at a light.

Jocelyn's voice was soft and she laid her hand briefly on his arm. 'You mentioned you were the one to find your sister.'

'Yes, I was,' he answered grimly. The light changed and he moved on.

'Can you tell me what you remember of the scene?' she started, then paused, 'of her?'

Trevan took a deep breath. He had known he would eventually have to resurrect the memories. Since he had awakened in this time, he had tried to never think of that day. It had been only in his nightmares, after a new body was found, that he had been forced to relive Allysa's death.

He began, his tone low and controlled. 'I walked through the door and put my hat on the hook. I called to her and didn't get an answer. I knew she was at the theater because I'd talked to Maybella Lovejoy before I walked in. I checked her office, but she was not in there. Then I went to the green room, but I didn't see her in the room at first so I started to walk away.'

Trevan hesitated. He had thought a person could get used to a loved one's death. Now he realized that even time could not diminish the pain. 'I glimpsed her foot in front of the sofa. I stepped closer and discovered her lying on the floor in front of the table. I remember calling to her again as I ran to kneel beside her, but she didn't answer. That is when I saw . . .'

He stopped to swallow the grief threatening to overwhelm him. Jocelyn's hand rested on his knee and he studied it as he worked for control. This was hard, harder than anything he had faced in this century, but telling her made facing it a little easier. The pain was not quite as vivid. 'That is when I saw the gash on the side of her head, and I knew she was dead.'

Jocelyn squeezed his knee in comfort, then took his hand in hers. She was considerate enough to give him a few moments before she started the questions he knew she had to ask.

'Do you remember which side she was lying on?'

Trevan tried to recall, but the shock had filtered the brutal images from his mind's eye. 'I don't remember . . . I only remember being terrified that she might be dead.'

'It's all right,' she soothed. 'I know this is rough, but can you remember a mask?'

'No . . . no, I don't,' he snapped. Hadn't he heard too many times when he had attended a funeral for a friend, the people telling the bereaved they 'understood' how they felt. Bitterly he recalled how he too had said the words, knowing now how inadequate they were. 'Damn it, I don't remember anything. Sometimes images flash before me, then they're gone before I can recognize what they are. I only remember how it felt to find her like . . . that.'

He turned to Jocelyn as he gritted his teeth in frustration. 'And don't tell me you know how I feel.'

'I won't,' she said simply.

And she hadn't. Trevan realized he was taking his feelings of guilt and anger out on her. He looked down to their joined hands. She hadn't removed hers when he snapped at her. He lifted her hand and kissed her on her fingers.

'I apologize.'

She gave him an affectionate squeeze. 'Don't worry about it. We will beat this. Together.'

Jocelyn hadn't liked asking Trevan questions about his sister's death, especially when the pain was so evident on his face. Still, there was a connection between Allysa's murder then and the killings now. There had to be, she thought. Trevan had not recalled a mask at the scene, but that was not unusual for someone who had experienced such an emotional shock. He wouldn't like it, but she had to look into the girl's death.

But how would she get around him, she wondered. The time-traveling cowboy seemed to think she was his own personal assignment and was not about to let her do anything on her own.

Drawing her brows together, she gave it some thought. Unless he thought she was someplace safe. She cleared her throat and gave him an innocent smile.

Well, as innocent as she could muster. 'Why don't you drop me off at the newspaper office so I can do some research.'

Trevan's glance flicked over her and he frowned, 'Out of the question.'

So much for being coy. 'I don't believe it was a question. I want to look through the archives and I don't need a baby-sitter.'

His eyes never left the road as he turned left on Douglas, which would take them to the newspaper offices. 'I appreciate you trying to spare my feelings, and all that, but I know you're going there to research my sister's murder.'

He turned to her, his expression unreadable. 'I'm going with you.'

She shook her head, 'I don't think that is a good idea, Trevan.'

'I didn't ask, did I?' he stated, his expression grim, but determined.

They pulled into the lot across the street from the building and parked. Jocelyn stepped from the truck and looked toward the customer service entrance.

'Trevan, isn't that Mr Cargo over there?'

He glanced where she pointed, 'Yes, it is. I wonder what he is doing here.'

'How did he know we were going to be here?' she asked.

'The man has the most uncanny knack for knowing where to be. I've never had to look for him, he's always found me when I needed him,' Trevan answered. He took her by the elbow as they jaywalked across the street.

Cargo smiled as they approached him. 'Mr Elliot, I'm so glad to see you.'

Trevan grasped the older man's hand and shook it firmly. 'What have you heard, my friend?'

'The word on the street is there is a witness to Ruby Snow's untimely death,' he said, then nodded in response to Jocelyn's questioning look.

'The homeless man in the alley? We already know about him, Cargo.' Jocelyn shook her head, feeling frustrated once again. 'I spoke with the man and, unfortunately, he's blind.'

Cargo studied her for a moment. 'The man I'm referring to has quite adequate vision, Miss Kendrick. He witnessed all the brutality and escaped without being seen.'

She frowned at what he was telling her. 'Wait a minute, the police don't know anything about a witness.'

They had been hitting one dead end after another all day. The helplessness and frustration were beginning to get to her, to make her want to kick something. But, if what Cargo was saying was true, they finally had a reliable witness. A witness who knew what the Porcelain Mask Murderer looked like and could identify him when he was apprehended.

Cargo's eyebrow rose as if he could read her thoughts. 'Correct, Miss Kendrick. The police are unaware of his experience.'

A witness, she thought, hope building within her. Obviously the Porcelain Mask Murderer did not know either. Or did he? If he did, the witness could, or more

196

accurately, would be in extreme danger. She turned to Trevan and she could see in his expression that he must be thinking the same thing.

They needed to get to the man before someone more deadly did.

'Do you know who it is?' he asked.

The thin man shrugged, 'I have a suspicion. However, this individual does tend to over indulge, so I believe now would be the most opportune time to approach him before he has found enough change on the street to buy his comfort.'

Trevan nodded and gripped Cargo's shoulder. 'Thanks, I really appreciate your help.'

'I could do no less, especially when Miss Kendrick's safety is concerned. However,' he hesitated, his expression showing a bit of alarm, 'I'm afraid our witness may need your help more.'

The three of them quickly crossed the street and made their way down a series of alleys in the warehouse district in the Old Town. As they passed loading docks and delivery trucks, Jocelyn realized they were not far from where Ruby Snow had been killed. In fact, the alley where she had died very much resembled the darkened areas they were now walking by.

She flicked a cautious glance at Cargo and Trevan. Neither of them seemed bothered that they were walking in a somewhat unsavory part of town. Nervously peering into the shadows of the alleys as they continued searching, she would occasionally meet the hardened gaze of a vagrant. The uncaring glaze of their expression struck a sympathetic chord within her, just as her gut instinct warned her that some of these individuals would not hesitate to turn on her, if the opportunity should arise when she was alone. Moving closer to Trevan, she decided she was going to make sure that didn't happen.

She cleared her throat as she kept her eyes on the area around her and directed her question to Cargo, 'Uh . . . what is this person's name?'

'His name is John Drummand. He may appear quite, how do you say it . . .' He held his hand up in question.

Jocelyn's eyebrow rose, 'Disoriented?'

'Crazy.' Trevan supplied, matter-of-factly.

She turned to study his hard expression and could all too easily imagine him in the old west. High noon, bank robbers, and all that stuff.

Cargo's voice broke into her thoughts. 'Nevertheless, he is quite competent, but he has found it to be less stressful to pretend otherwise. He lives under the loading dock in this alley.'

He raised a bony finger to point to the alley ahead of them. They turned the corner and approached the loading dock closest to the entrance where they now stood.

An eerie sliver of nervous tension moved over Jocelyn as they walked toward the clutter of boxes and rags arranged beneath the cement structure of the dock. She swallowed as she tried to force it back, though still her heart began to race.

The worn boots of a vagrant poked out from the interior of a large refrigerator box. She drew her brows together as a pungent smell reached her nostrils. Trevan stepped forward to look inside the box. He swore vehemently, then straightened to face her. By his hard gaze she knew the Porcelain Mask Murderer had also learned the news of a witness to Ruby Snow's death.

And eliminated it at the source.

The blood began to pound in her ears as she moved past Trevan to kneel beside the corpse. A fly settled on the pale wrinkled skin of the man's cheek. His eyes were open as was his mouth. She touched her fingers to the vagrant's neck, noting the skin was still warm. The smell was overpowering and she covered her nose and mouth with her hand with little effect. Tears burned at her eyes and her stomach churned as her gaze moved over his lifeless form.

'He's dead,' she said, emotion welling within her. She turned to meet Trevan's gaze. '*He* got to him before we could help him.'

'Damn it,' Trevan swore bitterly. 'How did he find out?'

Cargo shook his head. The question was not one that could be answered easily. With more reluctance than she had ever felt, Jocelyn turned back to the body to look for evidence that would help them stop the killer permanently.

She frowned with concentration as she noted Drummand's right hand rested on his chest. Cautiously she leaned over his body to examine the left hand. Turning the hand, palm up, her stomach lurched as she focused on the deep cuts in his wrist. She moved to the man's jacket and lifted the cloth edge from his stomach area. Her fingertips encountered the warm, sticky pool of his blood from a deep gash on the upper right side.

She stood quickly and walked a couple of feet away. The air seemed to whoosh out of her as she bent over and placed her hands on her knees. She took several deep breaths of fresh air and tried to clear her mind of the brutal image. Gratefully she accepted a white handkerchief from Cargo with a silent nod, then wiped the sweat from her face.

Cargo spoke softly. The quiet sound of his voice only slightly veiled the emotion simmering beneath. 'John was a quiet man. Out here no one asks what happened to cause you to live on the street, or perhaps more accurately, make you want to live here. We simply accept. Miss Snow did what she had to do, just as John did.'

Jocelyn turned her face to look up at the man. His clothes were worn, but clean, yet the quiet dignity of his ebony features suited him. She could see the mourning in his eyes for two people whose deaths might not ever warrant a notice in the paper. 'You knew them, didn't you.'

He met her gaze and silently nodded. For a moment he simply looked in her eyes as if trying to probe her thoughts. 'They may have only been street people, but they were people nonetheless. Equal in God's eyes just as you and I.'

He took a deep breath and looked away for a moment as he regained control over his emotions. When he looked back his eyes no longer held the pain of mourning, but the joy of remembering. 'Ruby had a beautiful laugh and a giving soul. Perhaps her means of living were not widely accepted, but her heart was never cold.

200

She made sure that several of the more helpless people always had food.'

'Like Hayden Webster,' she said, beginning to understand the dynamics of the small community living in the shadows of the back streets. She wondered if the cops who had arrested Ruby on several occasions knew that about her. She looked back to John's body. Would the police want to find justice for Ruby and Drummand as much as they did the other victims?

Ruby Snow was dead and now John Drummand would not have to worry about his next meal or finding adequate shelter through another harsh winter, that much was certain. All because he had been in the wrong place and witnessed a murder.

She felt Trevan's hand on her shoulder. 'You okay?'

Jocelyn nodded. She closed her eyes and tried to will her stomach to calm its boiling within her. She opened her eyes, then straightened. Surprised at how calm her voice sounded even to her. 'He hasn't been dead long at all, fifteen to twenty minutes at the most. By the wounds on his hands, I'd say he tried to defend himself from his killer. He died from the stab wound to his upper chest, at least as far as I could tell.'

'Damn it,' Trevan muttered as he scanned the end of the alley leading away from him.

Suddenly he stopped and his body stiffened as he focused on something. She turned to follow his gaze and spotted the tall figure running away from them.

'Stay here with Cargo,' Trevan shouted his order as he bolted off after the man.

'Who the hell does he think he is?' she asked angrily,

her muscles tense with the urge to follow him.

'The closest I could say would be John Wayne,' Cargo offered, then at her pointed look, cleared his throat. 'Perhaps not.'

'I'm sorry, Cargo, but you see what that monster can do.' She pointed to the body of John Drummand. 'Trevan may need me. He needs me.'

'I understand.' His ebony eyes expressed a mixture of concern and regret, but there wasn't much she could do about that at the moment, she thought, as she started racing after Trevan and the shadowy figure.

Jocelyn ran in the direction Trevan had taken. She had seen him turn the corner at the red building and she slid around it, gripping the rail of a stairway to keep from falling over it.

She had never been much of a jogger and already she was huffing, her heart pounding hard against the wall of her chest. She heard a noise not too far ahead, telling her she was not far behind Trevan and the man they pursued, and she was grateful.

'Where are Cagney and Lacey when you need them?' she muttered as she hauled herself on top of a wooden crate to crawl over a fence. She gripped the top ridge of the fence and pulled herself over the top, ignoring the painful protest from her muscles. Landing with a groan, she winced at the sharp splinters of pain shooting up her legs, then sprinted down the narrow lane after them. She was forced to stop at the opening of the alley, at first unable to determine which way they were going. She looked frantically in both directions and saw nothing. Suddenly a cat howled in fright and sprang from her right. Jocelyn ran to the place where the alarmed animal had jumped and quickly scanned the area.

Peering into yet another alley, she spotted the two figures running. All she could see of either man were their backs as they raced away from her. How she desperately wished the fleeing man would turn so she could catch a glance of his profile. Hope leaped within her as she watched them head in the direction of a group of trash cans blocking their path. Both were forced to hurdle several garbage cans as they continued their chase. She ran as fast as she could and although she was not gaining ground, she felt a small moment of relief when she realized she wasn't falling behind either. At least she was keeping them in her sight.

Their suspect, for lack of a better word, slid easily over the hood of a car parked on the side of a one way street. The owner honked and yelled a few obscenities at the fleeing man, then continued to talk on a cellular phone.

Trevan was close behind and also skimmed the hood in one slick move as he pursued the man relentlessly. The driver held the phone away from his head as he stared in disbelief.

Jocelyn was not about to emulate their attempt at stunt doubling and sprinted in front of the car, turning to move through the space between the two parked cars. 'Sorry,' she offered the man as his mouth remained open and the phone fell from his grasp.

They darted into a narrow lane and she heard a roar of anger and then an ominous splintering groan. Her heart beat wildly as pure fear for Trevan speared through her, immediately re-energizing her. She came to the entrance and heard herself gasping in fear as she found him lying on his side in the middle of a pile of small wooden crates, most of which were now broken and lying in slivers around him.

The dark figure had escaped.

'Trevan,' she shrieked, running to kneel beside him. 'Oh, my God Trevan. Are you all right?' she asked breathlessly, tears once again threatening. There were so many things running through her head. Things she wanted to say to him. Do with him. Jocelyn could not stand the thought of losing him now. No, not now, she thought. 'Trevan, please. Please talk to me. I'm going to get that guy and remove his testicles . . . talk to me, please. Are you all right? Trevan.'

His eyes fluttered and he groaned. Slowly he rolled to his back and clutched his left arm.

'Are you hurt, Trevan?' She gently lifted his head onto her lap and stroked his thick hair as a sob racked her throat.

'You really should watch your language,' he hoarsely chided. 'Where I come from, ladies don't talk like that.'

Concern diminished quickly. She felt foolish until anger had her glowing red hot. Exasperated she dropped her load with a plop on the ground.

'Ouch, what are you trying to do, kill me?' he asked as he ruefully rubbed his head. He looked as if he couldn't decide which had hurt worse, landing in a pile of crates or her dropping his head on the ground.

'I don't know why I even worried.' She held her hands up in exaggerated astonishment. The fear of his having been injured, or worse, filled her with irritation again. She paced away from him and started to count to ten. She got to three before she decided to hell with it and whirled towards him to point her finger at him. It annoyed her even more as she realized she was still shaking with fear. 'Damn it, Trevan, he got away. Did you at least get a good look at him?'

'No,' he admitted, then shifted to rub his arm with a small grunt of pain. 'Just the two by four he hit me with. I thought I told you to stay with Cargo?'

She narrowed her eyes and gave him an irritated look. 'That only works on dogs.'

'Insufferable, damn . . .' He hesitated, then his face became hard and his eyes gleamed with anger. 'Sneaky, low down, cocky, son-of-a . . .'

Jocelyn gasped, shocked by the string of oaths that erupted from his mouth. How dare he! 'Trevan, that is completely uncalled for.'

She recognized the look on his face. Following his gaze, she spotted his assailant, the man who might be Drummand's murderer, moving stealthily along the other side of the road.

'Get up damn it. He's going to get away,' she said sharply, her eyes never leaving the man's back as if that alone would keep them from losing him again.

Jocelyn helped haul Trevan to his feet and together they sprinted to the street. The Porcelain Mask Murderer had forced them to participate in his sadistic game of life and death. It was a game she was determined to make him lose.

CHAPTER 12

Trevan and Jocelyn crossed the street almost casually, trying to catch up with their prey. The man they had been chasing, and who was now walking almost a block ahead, was tall with raven black, shiny hair. He wore black jeans with a bright blue shirt open over a turtleneck the same color as his jeans. Occasionally he would look to his left or right and Jocelyn would see part of a profile, but the image was obscured by dark sunglasses.

It was an uneasy feeling to realize that she was being maneuvered by the man. Jocelyn frowned at the thought, but there was no other explanation. The killer's movements were too casual, too visible, as if he were trying to stay within their sight. He wanted them to follow him. Silently she wondered what kind of situation he was manipulating them into.

He stopped at a silver BMW and went to the driver's side to get in. Jocelyn yanked at Trevan's jacket without thinking about it. She glanced at him distractedly when he gasped, then realized she had grabbed his sore arm.

'Sorry, but he's getting into a car,' she explained, her gaze trained on the man. 'He's going to get away. We've got to stop him.'

'You really are observant,' Trevan muttered as he glanced around them. He walked to a car and tried the passenger door. Finding it unlocked, he opened it and slid in over to the driver's side.

Jocelyn sucked her breath in shock and guiltily looked around quickly to see if a cop or even a concerned citizen might try to stop them. She leaned in the door and whispered loudly, 'This isn't your car.'

He gave her a frustrated look at this observation, 'Just get in.'

'I can't do this,' she said as quietly as she could, considering she was obviously hallucinating. Trevan could not be hot wiring the car as she watched fascinated by his swift and experienced movements. The car turned over and roared to life and she knew it wasn't a dream. He was going to steal a car.

She shook her head in disbelief. 'I can't believe this. I'm studying to be a cop. I can't go and steal a ca – '

She was interrupted when he grabbed her by the hand and hauled her head first into the car. She landed uncomfortably with her face in his lap. The car surged forward with a screech of the wheels and the door slammed shut behind her with the momentum.

'You aren't stealing it, I am,' Trevan explained. She could feel his arms move above her as he steered the wheel. 'And you're not going to have a career remember? He set you up. If we don't stop him, it will be a miracle if we don't both end up in jail.'

Considering the position of her head, Jocelyn quickly tried to sit up. Instead she found herself tangled with Trevan's arm.

'Move it, will ya?' he ordered, trying to peer around her head.

She didn't apologize but ducked and pulled herself from his lap. She gave him a glare; he didn't deserve an apology. If anything he deserved a swift kick. She turned to study the street and could not see the car anywhere.

'You didn't lose him did you?' She asked.

He gave her a dry look, but didn't say anything.

She had always been good at highway bingo, she thought, scanning the cars around them. She caught sight of the shiny, silver car with tinted windows. She bit her lip in frustration, she wished they would outlaw those windows. You couldn't see anything through them. Every time a cop walked up to one of those windows, they had no idea what might be behind them.

'There it is, the silver beemer.' She squinted, trying to make out the tag. 'How convenient, the jerk has a temporary tag and no way to trace it.'

Their car jerked sideways as Trevan swerved around a truck to pass. He gassed the accelerator, speeding them forward then wheeled back in front of the pick-up. Jocelyn glanced back in time to see the driver telling them they were number one with his middle finger extended before she was slammed against the passenger door again by Trevan's wild driving.

'Watch it, will you?' She yelled and leaned forward to scan the road ahead of them. She slapped the dashboard and pointed as he cut yet another driver off. 'The car, Trevan . . . watch out for the car.'

'I see it, damn it,' he snapped, his eyes never left the street. 'Quit being a back seat driver.'

'I'm in the front seat in case you haven't noticed. And where did you learn to hot wire a car?' she asked.

He jerked the wheel in his hand and they passed two more cars. 'It's a long story and I'm sort of . . .' He almost side-swiped a station wagon, then accelerated to get ahead of it. 'Busy right now.'

The silver BMW was suddenly in front of them. Try as she might, Jocelyn simply could not see anything through the darkened rear window. Her head jerked back when Trevan gunned the car and they bumped the beemer forward.

'Any closer, Elliot, and we'll be in his back seat,' she snapped, grabbing for a secure hold on the door and the dash.

He started cussing and she knew his attention was centered on the man and the car ahead of them. Out of the corner of her eye, she caught the movement of something sliding in the back seat of the vehicle.

She turned and focused on the object, feeling the smile spread on her face. 'There's a cellular phone in the back.'

'Hallelujah. Call in a pizza,' Trevan retorted, his expression intense and his gaze focused.

'You know, you really can be a jerk,' she said angrily. 'We can use it to call the police for help.'

'Then what are you waiting for?' he asked.

Jocelyn leaned over the seat to retrieve the phone, but they swerved violently and she fell half way into the back seat with her legs flailing in the front. Her face smashed into the upholstery, she tried to get leverage with her feet so she could remove herself from the uncomfortable, not to mention suffocating, position.

'Jocelyn, move your leg.'

'If you had been watching your driving, I wouldn't be hanging – ' She was not able to stop the scream as another lurch shoved her face deeper into the seat. 'Here like a . . .' The vehicle hurtled forward with a symphony of screeching tires, honking and beeping. 'I think I'm going to be sick.'

Trevan swore again and she realized the thing she kept hitting with her knee must be the side of his head. He pushed at her with his hands and she found herself straddling his neck in a most unbecoming fashion. Finally he grabbed her legs and roughly shoved the rest of her into the back seat. She landed on top of herself in an extremely embarrassing, acrobatic position.

She struggled in the small area and sat up to glance around them. They had somehow ended up on Kellogg and the silver car was nowhere to be seen.

'I thought cowboys were supposed to be the good guys?' she snapped grumpily, wishing for a few Rolaids.

'They are,' he said, then slammed his hand against the wheel in frustration. 'Damn it, we lost him . . .' Through the rearview mirror she saw his eyes dart to the back window. 'But it looks like we found someone else.'

She turned to follow his gaze, then groaned. 'Oh no, it's the cops.'

'Like I said, Jocelyn, you are observant.'

Jocelyn didn't appreciate the compliment.

The police had arrested them, as well they should, considering the circumstances. At the station, Jocelyn recognized one of the officers and asked him to get John Cartland for her.

Half an hour later she sat in an interrogation room with her wrist handcuffed to a steel loop mounted on the wall next to the table while she prepared herself to face John's anger when he showed up. That is, if he even decided to come.

The door opened and John stopped to glower at her for a few intense moments. She knew he would be angry, but she had definitely underestimated him. He was furious.

He shut the door and moved quietly to the table. Resting his hands on the surface he leaned towards her so she could get the full effect of his ire.

His words were low and soft, all the more intimidating to Jocelyn. 'You steal a car, then rack up who knows how many violations, then ask to speak to me? Your butt was in enough trouble as it was. What were you doing, Kendrick?'

She lifted her chin to face him and meet his gaze. 'Research, John.'

He shoved himself from the table as he snarled with frustration. 'Don't fool with me or I'll arrest you myself. I know you've been checking around. Now spill it. What are you up to?'

His manner left no room for argument. He was not asking, but demanding she tell him. She chewed her lower lip for a moment; he had helped her before and was helping her now. She had to give him the truth.

'The killer sent me a mask and I had the coroner's office check out a smudge on it.' At his impatient look

211

she continued. 'It was a special kind of face putty and it belonged to one of the mask victims.'

'Dead end,' John stated.

'Exactly,' Jocelyn took a deep breath, wishing he would make it easier for her. 'We then checked out the mask itself because it is somewhat unusual. The clerk at the store remembered the man who purchased it, but that didn't help. He didn't match the description we had, so we believe he's altering his appearance.'

'We don't have a description of the killer,' John snapped, giving her a pointed look.

'Trevan's seen him before. Three times,' she swallowed. 'But it was more impressions of the man that he remembered, since he's never actually seen his face.'

'Go on,' John said between clenched teeth.

'And we checked out the flower that I believe he uses for his poison.'

'You and that Elliot character. And?'

She shrugged, 'And nothing. In Kansas it's hard to get, but not impossible. In fact, it's an ingredient in a prescription used to treat jaw nerve pain.'

Jocelyn started to put her hands on the table, when the handcuff clinked against the loop, restricting the movement. She hated this feeling. The Porcelain Mask Murderer had effectively and masterfully maneuvered her and Trevan into this position. Why?

Instead she placed her left hand on the table and met John's hard gaze. She knew he wouldn't like the audacity of the questions she was going to ask, but she had been forced into this position by a madman. She had no choice.

'Were any of the mask victims a doctor, nurse, or

anything in the medical profession? Or maybe even a botanist?'

His brow rose and he took a deep breath as his face grew red. He looked as if he was about to explode. She winced in preparation for the bellow, instead she was shocked by the quiet shriek of his voice. 'Who's asking the questions here?'

'John, please. This could be important.'

'I knew you were a pain in the butt. You're too smart for your own good,' he muttered as rose then stormed out of the room.

Jocelyn blinked, trying to decide if he was finished with her or not. A few minutes later, the door swung open with John carrying a load of files.

'You know I'm breaking big time rules here,' he said with a critical eye. Then he turned to leaf through the files.

'I know, John.' She said it quietly. She had to clear her name, if not for herself, then so she could repay this man for his faith in her even when the evidence was overwhelming.

He frowned and his voice lost the edge of anger. 'Carrie Carter, coed; Lucinda Travers, marketing assistant; and Cindy Blake, florist; Halicia Carmichael, pharmacist; Becky Sowers, paralegal; and Michelle Slavinsky, nurse.'

'Nurse, huh. Interesting,' she murmured, leaning toward him to try to see the file he held. 'That list started from the most recent back to the first victim right?'

'Exactly, but you seem to be missing the point.' John slapped the file closed on the table. He rubbed his hand roughly on his forehead and paced the length of the small room. 'You are not in a position to examine anything. Nothing. You are the one in trouble here.'

Jocelyn stood and her hand jerked against the handcuff. A desperate urge to break into tears swelled within her. She swallowed the frustration and the anger.

'Don't you think I realize that? He set me up with those trumped up charges and you know that, John.' She hesitated for a moment, how could she make him understand this whole crazy situation? The cold, hard truth would have made an excellent episode for the *X-Files*.

'Don't you see, it's like you said. He's manipulating us,' she said slowly. 'Manipulating me. That's not all . . . he's killed again.'

John's eyes widened. 'When?'

Jocelyn shook her head, trying to force away the image of the old man's brutal death that was still fresh in her memory. She cleared her throat. 'This afternoon. The victim was a vagrant who had witnessed the murder of Ruby Snow.'

John took a deep breath and exhaled slowly. 'You don't know the two are even connected.'

'I do know, John,' she said bitterly, then frustration filled her as she fought back a sob. 'That's the problem, I do know. A man came to us, someone Trevan and I know, and he told us about this man and what he had seen. As soon as we learned about this we went to the vagrant, but he was dead.'

Jocelyn pressed the palm of her hand against her forehead as she schooled her breath. 'Last night I looked down at the body of Ruby Snow, then today

214

I find John Drummand stabbed in an alley. Their eyes . . . their eyes stared at me.'

The accusation she had met in their unseeing eyes had haunted her. How could anyone understand unless it was directed at them? 'It was as if they wanted to know why I had let this happen to them.'

'You can not accept blame for this, Jocelyn. Ruby Snow was a prostitute. Prostitutes get killed by their pimps and sometimes even the johns they pick up. This old man could've been rolled by another vagrant looking for pocket change to get more booze.'

'But he wasn't, John.' Jocelyn ran her hand through her hair. She needed for him to understand. 'Ruby Snow was a prostitute, that much is known. But did you, or any of the cops who ever arrested her, know that she took care of a lot of people on the street who could barely take care of themselves? She bought food for them and clothes just so they could survive. The man I found today, John Drummand, was a quiet and gentle man. Now both of them are dead because of some sick man's little scheme to manipulate me where he wants me.'

'Jocelyn, you didn't kill them, he did.' John waited till she met his gaze. 'All of us have had to face this at one time or another. Whether it was losing a partner or an innocent bystander who was caught in the cross fire. You don't have to accept it necessarily, but you just have to learn to deal with it.'

'I don't plan on accepting this,' she said quietly.

'Let me talk to a few people,' he said, his eyes asking her to agree. 'We'll get you out of here and take you somewhere safe till we can get this guy.'

215

She shook her head as she laughed, the sound weary to her own ears. 'You know I can't do that. He's after me. I didn't want to believe it, but now I've been forced to accept that he is. I don't want any more people to be used as props for this man, John.'

Jocelyn's eyes brimmed with tears. 'Ruby Snow and John Drummand may not have been the cream of society, but they didn't deserve to die. I have to see this through. The Porcelain Mask Murderer is after me and he won't stop till he gets me.'

John gripped the back of a chair with both of his hands and hung his head for a moment as if waging an internal war. 'Don't you see, Kendrick, that you're getting in way over your head? This can kill your career, not to mention you.'

'I don't have a chance at a career, John. He's made sure of that.' Jocelyn hesitated knowing that what she was about to ask could have repercussions for both of them. 'The only chance in hell I have of getting out of this is if I can prove that he set me up and stop him from killing anyone else. I know the evidence is stacked against me, but I need help. I have no right to ask, but will you help me?'

When he raised his eyes to hers, his expression had lost most of its anger and was now resigned as he blew out his breath. His eyes were filled with concern. 'I realize he killed the prostitute to set you up on those asinine charges, Jocelyn, but did you ever think of why he did it? I'll tell you why. It's because he's isolating you so he can get to you, don't you see that? This maniac's not going to stop till he's proven his point.'

She held his gaze as a wave of apprehension moved through her, matching that which was reflected in John's eyes. 'I know, but I don't think it will be long before he tries to make his "statement" again.'

Images of the three bodies the madman had left behind since coming to this part of the country, flashed through her mind. 'And when he does . . . he'll punctuate it with deadly emphasis.'

Trevan leaned against a wall and wished for a cigarette. He had quit smoking as soon as he began learning how dangerous they were. He had always thought the things to be unhealthy. Even so when his back was up against a wall, one would sure hit the spot.

He studied the people in the cell with him. He hadn't been booked, charged, or anything since he was brought in. One of the arresting officers had been about to sit down and talk to him, when a load of gang members were brought in. Most of them had been covered with blood and all of them were cussing and showing complete disrespect for the law.

Trevan shook his head at the thought. Stealing a car had been considered low priority compared to a gang war where several members of both sides were clinging to life and one was already dead. Apparently, because he had shown them respect, the officers treated him well and promised to get to him as soon as they could.

Now he watched a vagrant sleeping on the floor in the corner and marveled again at how far civilization had come. And how far it had regressed.

Trevan's thoughts drifted to Jocelyn and he wondered where they had taken her and how she was doing. Pride washed over him as he recalled her courage when the police brought them in wearing handcuffs. She had kept her head high and calmly asked to see John Cartland. He had to admit to himself, she was one hell of a lady.

The smile slowly fell from his lips. The Porcelain Mask Murderer had killed again. Trevan had almost had him when the man had unexpectedly swung at him with a board. His fists balled with futile anger. This had been the third time he had confronted the madman, and the third time the murderer had escaped. And he still did not know what the man looked like, this time because of the black sunglasses.

A guard came to the door, 'Come on, Elliot. They want to talk to you.'

Trevan pushed from the wall and nodded to the officer as he stepped through the open door. He noted that the short man did not cuff him as they climbed a set of stairs. They came to a door and the man opened it and waved him through.

'Thanks,' he offered, then lifted his gaze to find Jocelyn sitting at a table with John Cartland. A smile of relief spread across his face to see her uncuffed and in the law's favor instead of in its scrutiny.

'Trevan,' she said, her face brightening. He hoped it was because of him.

John stood to shake his hand then moved to shut the door and motioned him to a chair. 'Jocelyn has told me a pretty amazing story.'

Trevan turned to her and held her gaze, he wondered

how much she had told him. She shook her head slightly and he knew then that she hadn't told him everything.

'I was telling John about the man under the dock and he sent a car out to confirm what I had said.' She nodded to John.

'I've pulled in a lot of favors to get them to hold off on charging you two with grand theft auto,' John's look was straightforward as was his manner. Trevan admired the man for it. 'I have to tell you, however, that because Jocelyn is not an officer and neither are you, your involvement in this "mask" case could get both of you in a lot of trouble.'

He raised his hand to quiet Jocelyn's protest, 'But I think you've told me more than enough to convince me now that this serial killer is really after you.'

He turned to Trevan and studied him for a moment, 'I know people, Elliot. And I know you won't back down from this even if I tell you it isn't your job. I'm giving you both a chance to clear yourself on these charges and everything else.'

Trevan's expression hardened and he prepared himself for the conditions he knew must be made.

'That is off the record.' John rapped the table top with his knuckles. 'Now, we know the murderer has contacted Jocelyn by phone and we have checked the phone company records, and, of course, it was a pay phone as you had expected.'

'Figures,' she muttered.

'They found the body,' said Gary, catching the last of their conversation as he pushed open the door. He dropped several Polaroids on the table in front of John. 'The blues found a vagrant in his late fifties under the loading dock just like she said. Forensics is going over everything there now.'

'Did they have any preliminaries?' John asked, spreading the pictures out.

'He was attacked with a six to eight inch bladed knife and two of the wounds appear to have been fatal.' Gary rubbed his hand across his forehead in a familiar gesture of worry. 'He hasn't been dead that long according to what the coroner estimated. It's just like she said.'

For a moment the room remained quiet as everyone looked to the photos of the dead man spread on the table. The old man's blood showed vividly in the washed out pictures. A reminder of what they were up against.

'He left her a message at Ruby Snow's murder scene,' John turned to Jocelyn and his voice lowered slightly, a thread of caution woven through it. 'I have a feeling he's going to contact you again.'

An icy wave of dread washed over Trevan and he leaned forward in his chair to put his arms on the table. He stared at the photos as an image flashed through his mind of Allysa with bright streaks of blood covering the one side of her face. Jocelyn's face superimposed itself over his sister's face causing him to shudder.

His eyes moved to his fingers laced together and he studied them as he forced the horrific images from his mind, then his gaze moved to Jocelyn. 'And when he does, I don't think we're going to like what he has to say.'

CHAPTER 13

The murderer Jocelyn and Trevan hunted was standing in a mall, outside a book store, watching a young woman with long blonde hair stock the shelves with the latest best sellers. He smiled to himself as he thought of the events of the day before.

He had learned while discreetly talking with the unfortunate people of the street, that there had been a witness to his little act of manipulation.

The old street man had licked his lips as he stared fixedly at the amber liquid in the bottle, 'Yeah. Yeah, I know him. Name's Drummer. No. Drummand. Something like that anyway, lives under the loading dock behind Fiesta Merchants. He says he saw the whole damn thing, but kept hid because he was afraid the guy would kill him.'

'Did he say what the killer looked like?' the man had asked with an encouraging smile, moving the bottle a fraction closer to the old man's shaking grasp.

'No, not really,' the little man offered, nervously watching him as if he would run away with the liquor. 'But, uh, he said the guy was dressed all neat

221

and everything. Real uptown. Wasn't one of us, that's for sure.'

'Thank you, my friend. You have been extremely helpful.' And with that he had tossed the bottle to the beggar, then watched with a feeling of distaste as the little scavenger of a man panted and worked to get the container open. He knew the man had been too busy eyeing the liquor in his hand to even notice his disguise.

He'd turned away from the pitiful show then, and begun to seek the vagrant called Drummand. He was not ready for anyone to ruin what might be his best achievement ever.

He had found the contemptible specimen of a man exactly where the drunkard had said he would be. He had leaned over the sleeping form and raised his knife. Unexpectedly, the large fellow opened his eyes and immediately sought to defend himself against the attack, something which the killer had not expected. He had been forced to strike at the dirty loafer, the long blade of the knife hitting him in the arm.

The murderer had struggled with his victim, then felt a euphoric rush as his knife sank thickly into the miserable vagrant's chest. He had watched the shock register in his eyes as he realized he was dying. The man's smile had slowly spread across his face as he regarded the expiring wretch and his struggling attempts to breathe. The old fellow took one last rattling breath, then stopped. He gazed down on the unseeing stare of the vagrant as a drop of blood slid slowly from the dead man's open mouth.

It had almost made up for the fallacy of his thinking

that he had been so careful when he killed the whore in the alley.

He had not, however, expected the Kendrick woman and Elliot to be so close behind. He chuckled as he recalled their chase through the alleys. It had been fortunate that he had taken the precaution of wearing a disguise. Even if Elliot had seen him without the sunglasses, he would never have recognized him.

That was his job as an actor; to be recognized as the persona of the role. Not as himself.

He had wanted them to find the vagrant, had wanted them to follow him. To realize they would never stop him. Still, Elliot had come quite close, but fortunately he had been able to steal away. Only to be pursued once again in his car. At one time he had liked the prestige of having a nemesis from his own time, but now Elliot was becoming too troublesome. A problem that needed to be eliminated just as the old man had been.

He narrowed his eyes as he observed the store manager, an average looking man with a thick middle, give the woman permission to go to lunch. She gathered her purse and began to make her way to the food court.

The Porcelain Mask Murderer shook his head as he thought of how he had strived to achieve the perfection of Allysa's demise. Yet he had never been able to quite recapture the intoxicating feel of the mastery of her death. This time, however, would be perfection. Instead of seeking the Kendrick woman out, he would merely lead her to him.

A corner of his mouth lifted in a lop-sided smile,

calculated to be disarming as he approached the woman from the bookstore. He needed something to woo the Kendrick woman. As he had anticipated, the mouse of a maiden turned to him and smiled awkwardly.

More importantly, he needed someone.

'Excuse me, madam. I couldn't help but notice that you would be dining alone. I wondered if you might be interested in joining me,' he asked, his voice dropping seductively low.

The woman looked at him with a cautious glint of fear in her eyes. He smiled to put her at ease and offered her his hand. She licked her lips timidly as her gaze moved to his hand, then flicked back to his eyes. He watched as the fear in her eyes was replaced with hope. And hunger.

When she took his outstretched hand into her own and he felt the slick sheen of her nervousness on her palms, he knew he had found who he needed.

Jocelyn studied the black and white pictures taken at the Porcelain Mask Murders. They had not left the police station till a little after seven the night before. John had gone over their stories of finding Drummand and their 'alleged' pursuit of the serial killer. Finally, satisfied they were telling him about all the events that had transpired, John had granted her request for copies of the files of the Mask murders. She hoped studying them would help her better understand the clue of the mask. The answer was in there somewhere.

She had to find it. It could be the only thing to save her from a killer.

Jocelyn pulled a black and white photograph of

Lucinda Travers's body from her file and began to study it. This time she looked at it from a psychological point of view, instead of a forensic one. Out of the corner of her eye, she noted Trevan's expression harden at the picture in her hand, then focus back on the report he was reading.

Laying the photograph down, she leaned back in her chair to study him. He'd been quiet ever since they'd left the police station. His attitude had become distant and impersonal whenever he talked to her. 'Is there something bothering you?'

'No,' he said without shifting his attention from the page in his hand.

She leaned forward and clasped her hands together in front of her. 'Does it have anything to do with being thrown in jail yesterday?'

'No. I've been in jail before.'

She raised her brow at his statement. It had never occurred to her that at one time he could have been on the wrong side of the law. Of course, they were talking over a hundred years. He could have reformed since then. Maybe. 'For what?'

'Rustlin',' he said his gaze meeting hers briefly.

She felt her eyes widen, 'You were a cattle rustler?'

'No, I was a rancher,' he explained, putting down the report. 'But rustlin' was a problem. I was on my way home from the stockyards where I had purchased some livestock when a group of local ranchers looking for a rustler came across a couple of strangers.'

Jocelyn listened, trying to absorb the fact that he had really been there to experience the 'old west'.

225

'Those strangers were me and my men. My foreman had lost the stockyard receipt and they threw us all in jail and confiscated my cattle.'

Amazing, she thought. Even with all the hardships, it must have been an exciting time to live in. She shook her head, 'How did they know those weren't your cattle? I mean, I've always thought all cows looked alike.'

He chuckled, 'There is such a thing as a brand. And I felt damn lucky they only put me in jail. Rustlin' was a serious crime then and a rancher dealt with it seriously. When a rustler was caught red-handed, there usually wasn't a judge or a jury to plead his case to. They simply threw a rope over a branch and the case was decided. Guilty.'

Had she imagined the 1800s to be exciting? It sounded more barbaric than anything. She swallowed, the feeling of being so naive forming into a hard ball in her throat. 'That seems so harsh.'

'It was a harsh time,' he answered matter-of-factly. He picked up a pencil and tapped it rhythmically on the table.

Jocelyn's parents had died together in a plane crash several years ago. She had aunts, uncles, and cousins, but in one hard instant she had lost her family. Trevan must have felt the same feeling of grief when he . . . traveled through time to the 1990s.

'Do you miss it?' she asked quietly.

'I miss my family and I guess I miss the simplicity,' he said slowly as if measuring his words. The pencil stopped tapping. 'And I miss the decency.'

She had to agree with that, and she had almost felt sympathetic until his gaze had flicked to the pictures and his expression had darkened once again. 'And you miss women "knowing" their place?'

'Wait a minute now,' he said quickly, dropping the pencil to hold his hands up as if to ward off her anger. 'I've been here long enough to know those are fighting words. And I did not say anything to that effect.'

'You didn't have to.' Jocelyn pushed back her chair and stood. Right now she felt like pushing his knuckle dragging chauvinistic attitude just a little. 'I've seen it in your eyes, Trevan. Especially when I'm studying a corpse or looking at pictures like these,' she said, sliding one of the photos toward him.

He studied it quietly, dispassionately. When his eyes met hers, he had sealed off his emotions. 'I do not understand how you can look at such things.'

'You don't have to understand you only need to know why. I have to do this, Trevan. We have to.' she amended quietly. Jocelyn looked to her hands for a moment, not knowing what to say to him. It bothered her slightly that she cared so much what he thought of her. Of how much she cared for him.

'It's what I've been trained to do,' she went on to explain, her voice stronger now. Somehow she couldn't help feeling there was more at stake here than his chauvinism. A part of her was becoming wildly attracted to this man, but she couldn't turn her back on her sense of self and her duty. She stepped closer, her voice husky and warm. 'Would you prefer a soft, demure lady with her hair up in a bun?'

His gaze never left hers and he made no move to answer her. After a moment his silence angered her. A small part of her wanted to be that kind of lady, if only it would make her more attractive to him. She balled her fists on her hips, 'Well, I'm not that kind of woman. The only ones I know of like that are about eighty-six years old and soak their teeth at night.'

Trevan slid his chair back and stood slowly, his gaze never leaving hers. The golden brown of his eyes darkened and his lips curled in an unfriendly smile. Jocelyn refused to back down to his intimidation as he walked slowly to her, stopping inches from her body.

She could feel the heat from him and memories, all too vivid, reminded her of the enticing appeal of his chest. Her heart drummed within her and suddenly it took most of her concentration to breathe evenly. She stiffened even as she tilted her chin defiantly up at him to squarely meet his gaze.

His voice was low and coaxing like a gentle touch of a fingertip. 'And what do you prefer, Jocelyn? A man in a three-piece suit who coordinates his socks with his ties? A man who kisses his wife and ruffles his kid's hair in the morning when he says goodbye? A man who, when he comes home late at night, like every other night, crawls into bed, gives his wife a tired peck on the cheek, and then rolls over?'

She blinked. How had he gotten so close to her? The smell of his aftershave, mixed with his own scent, was an intoxicating combination. He was standing next to her now, so close his body almost touched hers, the heat radiating from him, searing her skin.

'Or would you prefer a man who respects and cherishes a woman? And when he makes love to her in their bed, or on the kitchen table . . .' he paused, his voice low and seductive, causing her gaze to move instinctively to the wooden surface beside them. The image, all too enticing, caused her to swallow in alarm.

'. . . she would feel his love as he touched her with his fingers.' Lightly he skimmed his fingertips across the ridge of her jaw till he reached her mouth. Then he feathered his thumb across the soft curves of her lower lip.

'She would feel the unspoken words of his love as he touched his lips to hers . . .' He said the words as he slowly lowered his mouth to take hers.

Jocelyn had no idea what to do. She could barely form a coherent thought, much less decide whether this was a good idea or not. His hands slid from her neck to skim her arm, then down to her hips and he pulled her against him.

The heat moving through her was liquid and molten. Her hands rested on his chest, then moved of their own will to encircle his neck. She ran her fingers through his hair, the silky texture caressing her hand.

Trevan's lips were firm and coaxing as he ran the tip of his tongue across her lower lip. He groaned and pulled her closer as if he wanted to pull her within him.

Jocelyn was not innocent, but she had thought herself experienced till Trevan's hand lightly skimmed her breast and the tightening deep within her flamed her need for him.

She felt his breath against her cheek; her lips regretted his departure but only for a small moment. His mouth caressed, tasted the length of her neck before placing a tender kiss in the hollow of her throat.

'Is this what you prefer?' Trevan's voice was husky, thick with desire.

His words pushed through the misty shroud of her sensations. The gist of their earlier conversation returned. 'Yes . . . no. I don't know.'

She withdrew herself from his embrace and moved to sit heavily in her chair. Shakily she ran her hands through her hair, she could still feel the warmth of his lips on her own. Now her trembling equilibrium had returned as had her sense of reason. She would not let this time-traveling cowboy seduce her so easily. A part of her knew without a doubt that giving herself to him could entail yielding a lot more than she could give.

Her sense of self.

Trevan had begun working his way into her heart, until the icy threat of a murderer had cooled the growing heat between them. She took a shaky breath and raised her chin, meeting his dark eyes with her own. 'We weren't discussing what I prefer, Trevan. I can't change who I am. I have to look at these, especially now.'

She pulled a photo in front of her and glanced at the brutal image captured within the frame. 'He's after me, remember. The answer's here.' She tapped her finger against the matte finish.

She knew they would have nothing between them till the madman's threat had been removed. Before it was too late. The thought caused her throat to tighten with emotion. 'We only have to find it.'

His gaze held hers as he studied her for a moment. She could see the tightening of his jaw and she wondered what his decision would be.

'What are we looking for?'

She sighed a silent whisper of relief and swallowed the threatening tears. Maybe there was hope for him yet. Hope for them both. 'I'm not an expert, so this is only an educated guess. But remember how I told you about the fixed lividity on a couple of the victims?'

Trevan nodded. A good sign considering it had been a hesitant one.

'Okay. Here is Michelle Slavinsky, the first victim . . .' His brow rose and she could tell he was thinking of another time and another place.

Another body. That of his own sister.

'In this century,' she amended. 'I know with the picture being black and white it's hard to tell, but here are the marks of the fixed lividity. She died on her stomach.'

She pulled two more pictures from the files and placed them beside the first. 'It's the same with Halicia Carmichael and Cindy Blake. They were moved and I have to wonder why?'

Carefully she lined all the photos of the victims in a row beside each other. The images were all very similar. Only the participants were different.

'I'm sure the experts have already come to the same conclusion as I have. He positions all the bodies the same. Their hands, their faces, and the masks are all the same. He's recreating a scene.'

She paused a moment. 'But here is where I'm one

step ahead of the experts. I think I know why he's doing it.'

Trevan's gaze met hers and his jaw tightened. 'Why?'

'Remember I said I thought it was connected somehow to your sister?' She took a deep breath, her eyes never leaving his. 'I believe he's trying to recreate her murder.'

CHAPTER 14

Trevan hadn't appeared shocked or even upset at her words. He merely continued to study her with an unreadable expression. 'You think he's recreating Allysa's murder, yet you said yourself there was no connection between any of the victims in this time.'

'Logic does not apply in his case, I'm afraid.' Jocelyn crossed her arms and moved past him so she had room to pace. To think. 'But Allysa was his "first". He may have felt, I don't know, a sense of power from her death. I've read studies to the effect. And, like an addict, he will continually seek that high again.'

She turned to face him. 'To figure out if I'm right, though, we need to search the newspaper archives.'

'Why?' he asked, leaning against the table.

'I would think the murder of a young woman would make the news, even in the 1800s. And maybe they have a picture of the murder scene.' She snapped her fingers with excitement. Jocelyn really had the feeling they were getting close to learning the identity of the Porcelain Mask Murderer. And then, hopefully, they would be able to stop him before he claimed another innocent person. Or found her.

Trevan's voice broke into her thoughts, 'I've explained to you what I saw that day when I found her.'

Jocelyn nodded in agreement, then stepped closer to him. She lowered her voice in concern for the pain Allysa's death still caused him. As they dug deeper into her murder, the wound of his grief would only become more painful.

'You also said you were quite upset and couldn't remember a mask. I believe if we find a picture, we'll find a mask. And I think we will indeed find one.'

She moved to stand in front of him. Placing her hand on his arm, she met his gaze. She was confident that they would find one, but sensitive enough to know it would be hard for him to face. 'He's arrogant, Trevan. He's practically waving the answer in our face. He positions the bodies like Allysa's and he leaves a mask. Even the poison he uses gives the victims a mask-like expression.'

He took a deep breath, his emotions sealed within him. 'The common theme.'

'Exactly,' she said softly. 'We figure the mask out and we will know who he is.'

Trevan took her hand in his. 'Then let's get going. I've been waiting a long time to make him pay.'

Jocelyn began to feel apprehensive as soon as she saw the smoke rising from the general direction of the newspaper headquarters. When they were only blocks away, her hopes sank. She knew what would await them.

Two large fire trucks were blocking the four lanes of the street. The men in their heavy, protective gear moved efficiently around the area. Police were keeping the gathering crowd at a safe distance as she and Trevan worked their way to the front to get a better look.

Several windows were broken, the glass shattered on the sidewalk below. The frames were charred and the bricks above the openings were blackened from the lick of the flames that had been extinguished. Several firemen steadied a light spray of water into the affected area to cool any lingering embers.

Steam still escaped from the windows, but now it had lightened to a gray column. Jocelyn searched the people within the off limits area and was relieved to see that most of the employees with soot blackened faces appeared to be all right.

She glanced to Trevan and recognized the look of anger. His lips were pressed into a grim line as he shook his head.

'Damn it. The manipulative bastard beat us again.' He stopped to take a deep breath as if trying to control his anger. 'And I bet the files we wanted to look at will be gone.'

She nodded and raised a brow. 'I think you're right.'

He turned to her with a skeptical look. 'I guess that should brighten my day.'

'I choose to ignore that,' she sniffed and slid her gaze to the building. 'But still you are right. He is manipulating us. And he always seems to be one step ahead.'

The crowd shifted and she felt someone step close to her. It was Gary. 'How come wherever you are there seems to be trouble? You know what they say about where there's smoke . . .'

'There's fire. I know, Pemberton,' she finished, then waved to the building. 'But I didn't have anything to do with this.'

'Yeah, but I bet you have an idea who did.'

She gave him a pointed look. 'Do you know where the fire was started?'

'The fire fighters haven't had much time to check, but several people reported seeing smoke and flames coming from the library resource room,' Gary answered softly. His gaze moved to the crowd of people who had escaped and she saw his concern. 'Fortunately, we were able to get everyone out safely.'

'You were here?' she asked. Her gaze moved over him. For the first time she noticed he was covered with soot. 'Are you okay?'

Jocelyn took Gary's hands and turned them over to look at his palms. 'Gary, you've been burned. What are you doing here? You should be at the hospital.'

'It looks worse than it is. Believe me,' he shrugged. He held her gaze for a moment and she didn't like what she saw in his eyes.

'What is it?' she asked.

'I was here because someone called in a tip,' Gary hesitated for a moment. 'The man mentioned your name and said we would find you here.'

'Damn it.' Jocelyn felt Trevan's grip tighten on her shoulder and she knew his thoughts were following hers. They were on the trail of a madman. A trail he was effectively erasing with no regard to the cost. And implicating her.

She released his hands and ran her fingers shakily

through her hair. 'I didn't have anything to do with this, Gary.'

'I know and John knows that, but it's IA that's going to get a hold of this.' Pemberton bit the words out, his heated resentment clear.

Jocelyn frowned. 'What is it? What's going on?'

'Damn this to hell.' He took a deep breath and shook his head. 'But you're going to hear about this sooner or later.'

'What?' she asked. Her throat tightened with apprehension. She shivered with dread and welcomed the reassuring heat of Trevan's hand on her elbow.

'IA's down here. John's with the guy now.' He rubbed the back of his hand across his forehead in a sign of frustration. 'It's none other than Doctor Dick.'

Trevan shifted closer to her. 'I hope you're referring to his name.'

'It's his name all right,' Jocelyn answered, muttering a few low oaths. The feeling of being pulled deeper into a dark whirlpool without any chance of escape was threatening her reasoning. At the moment, part of her wanted to run. To run and hide from the dark shadow of the murderer who was playing her like a pawn in a deadly game. 'Doctor Richard Lindenmeyer. I've never had the pleasure of meeting him, but I've heard a lot about him.'

'Even though he's a cop he hates cops if you know what I mean,' Gary supplied, noticing Trevan's look. 'And he especially loves busting female cops.'

'Hell of a guy,' Trevan quipped. 'What do you think he's going to do?'

Gary shrugged, he turned to look toward the building. 'I don't know, but my guess is, at the very least, he will make sure she never has a career in law enforcement. But he's looking for blood on this one, exposure and all that. I think he's going to press for criminal charges.'

Jocelyn resisted the urge to throw her hands over her face and cry hot tears of despair. 'You said John's with him. What's he doing here?'

'A friend of mine at IA knew about you and me. After he got the call he phoned me to let me know what was going on.' He studied her for a moment, then chuckled. 'John likes you and has been calling in a lot of favors to help you, Jocelyn.'

Tears welled in her eyes and her voice was thick as she looked at Trevan, then turned back to Gary. 'I know, but he also enjoys having a flunky.'

Trevan rubbed her shoulder. 'John's a good man.'

Gary nodded, 'He's one of the most respected men in the department. He's with Lindenmeyer right now trying to get him to back off a little.'

Her brows drew together at what he said. 'Does John know him?'

'I've heard they go way back together,' he answered. 'but John won't talk about it. In fact, he said he would personally handle Lindenmeyer. I have a feeling there is a strong dislike between the two men. What I don't know is why. John's usually very vocal about what he thinks, but with Lindenmeyer he's completely different. Very tight lipped.'

'You were here when the fire started then?' Trevan asked, returning to the original subject.

Gary nodded, turning his hands to look at them. 'The fire alarms didn't go off like they were supposed to and several people were trapped.'

The dull throbbings of a major headache were beginning to work their torture on Jocelyn. Distractedly, she rubbed at her temple for a moment. 'I wonder how he figured out we were coming here?'

'He'd have figured the next logical step for us was to come here to look at the archives,' Trevan answered. 'Or it may have been a coincidence.'

'He's right,' Gary added. 'The caller never said you would be here, just that you might be involved or would know something about this.'

'Damn, I hate this.' Jocelyn's lips tightened with anger. 'He's backing us into a corner and we can't even fight back because he keeps killing our leads.'

She flinched at her choice of words, but was thankful the two men did not say anything.

'So you were coming down here to go through the resource library?' Pemberton asked.

Trevan nodded. 'Now everything is gone.'

'I don't know what you're looking for but the state college has an extensive library,' Gary said, then looked to Jocelyn. 'What are you looking for?'

She shook her head and chuckled at the thought. 'It really doesn't have much to do with these cases. We thought it might be helpful to do some background research, that's all.'

'Uh, huh,' he gave her a pointed look. 'If you don't want to tell me, that's okay. It's your ass that's in the fire, not mine.'

'It's not that,' Jocelyn said quickly, reaching up to his face to pull him down for a quick kiss. 'You wouldn't believe me if I told you anyway. When, and if, we get things figured out, I'll spill my guts to you.'

'That's an enticing thought,' he said, his eyes widening as he casually put his arm around her. 'Maybe while you're at it you could take care of my wounds. I was injured in the line of duty.'

Jocelyn playfully nudged him in the ribs with her elbow. 'You have my sympathy. Now go take care of your hands. Maybe you'll luck out and the nurse will be good looking.'

He made a face at her. 'Just keep yourself out of trouble.'

Jocelyn waved to him as they moved through the crowd and made their way to the truck. Trevan remained silent till they reached the parking lot.

'What did he mean the guy at Internal Affairs knew about you and Gary?'

She smothered a chuckle. Clearing her throat, she shook her head and shrugged. 'Nothing really. We went out to dinner once. As you can tell by the looks of him, Gary is quite popular with the ladies. People at work were betting on how long it would take for me to succumb.'

She glanced to Trevan and noted his scowl. She smiled at the green-eyed monster beginning to emerge from within him, 'Why, Trevan. I would almost think you were jealous.'

'Jealous?' He gave her a frustrated look of disgust. 'Of him? No, I'm not. I like Gary. He's a hard working, respectable man.'

240

'And he is awfully good looking isn't he?' Jocelyn asked.

Trevan looked flustered for a moment. 'I wouldn't know.'

Jocelyn chuckled, but his expression darkened as he frowned at her. 'Oh, don't feel awkward, Trevan. I'm sure, compared to his good looks and smooth charm, it would be normal for your masculinity to feel just a little threatened.'

Her retort was meant to be humorous, but the look in Trevan's eyes was anything but. They were beside his truck now and he began to advance slowly toward her, forcing her to back away till she bumped into the door.

His voice was confident, seductive. 'There is no doubt about my masculinity, Miss Kendrick.' He allowed his gaze to move in a slow caress down her body, then back to her face. His smile was arrogant and bold. 'A point I would be more than happy to prove.'

Jocelyn moved her hand across the smooth surface of the truck door till she found the handle and quickly opened it, forcing Trevan to step back. 'We need to go to the college.'

She didn't know which was more infuriating, Trevan's chuckle as he moved around the front end to get in, or the realization that for a small moment she had hoped he would prove his point.

'Are you sure?' Jocelyn asked.

The blonde bimbo behind the counter in the history department appeared flustered by her question. The girl gave her a confused smile. 'Uh . . . positive, well, sort of. Mr Stephens won't be back till sometime in the next couple of days.'

Jocelyn had little patience for perky little cheer-leaders with a bra size bigger than their IQ. She tilted her head and raised her eyebrow. 'Sometime in the next couple of days? Doesn't he have classes to teach?'

The girl smiled quickly. Finally they'd asked something she knew. 'Yes, ma'am.' The excited look faded. 'But I don't know when he'll be back because I'm not the regular clerk.' She looked to Trevan and finished her explanation. 'I'm covering for the lady who works here. She's at the doctor's right now.'

Trevan gave the girl an encouraging smile dripping with charm. 'Would she be able to let us into the archives?'

Jocelyn felt like giving him a swift kick; instead she decided to ignore the nausea caused by his sweetness. The girl's eyes widened and she smiled shyly at him, even though Jocelyn would bet a fifty there wasn't a shy bone in her curvaceous body.

'Well, I don't know about that,' she giggled. 'Mr Stephens is very picky about that sort of thing. I really think you'll have to wait for him to come back from Hawaii.'

Trevan nodded to the girl and thanked her, while Jocelyn glared at him and wished for a chunk of cement to throw at a window. Or maybe at him.

'Nice girl,' he said casually, but there was no mistaking the thread of humor woven through his comment.

'Yeah, if you like 'em built like a brick, sh . . .' she caught herself.

She noticed him studying her with an odd look and didn't miss the effort it took for him to hide his smile. But she had to give him credit; he didn't say anything. And she did not intend to offer to prove her femininity.

They walked to the parking lot and Jocelyn waited for him to unlock the door. She climbed into the truck and crossed her arms over her breasts. Trevan slid behind the wheel, his gaze flicked to her arms and he cleared his throat looking out the windshield in front of him.

She realized the way she was holding her body only proved how mad she was. He might even think she had been intimidated by Betty Boob. She uncrossed her arms and ignored his chuckle as she shifted several times to position herself in a calmer, more confident fashion.

Trevan laughed giving her a side-long look. 'Don't worry, Jocelyn. Remember experience is better than youth.'

Her mouth fell open as she slowly turned to him and gave him the full benefit of her glare. 'Coming from a man who is older than dirt, that really means a lot.'

'If her youth didn't intimidate you, it must have been her b-'

'Trevan, I was not intimidated by her anything,' she interrupted.

'Brains,' he finished with a laugh.

Right now, the urge to wrap her fingers around his throat did seem very appealing. Instead she turned away and counted to ten.

'As if you noticed that she even had one,' she said, trying to sound nonchalant.

243

'Who could miss them,' he offered and then broke into a laugh when her mouth flew open again.

Jocelyn refused to be pushed by him. She sat stoically as he finally quieted to an occasional chuckle, then he leaned towards her and said quietly, 'Now whose sexuality is insecure?'

She popped her fist into his arm, not as hard as she would have liked, but enough to get the point across.

Trevan had finally stopped chuckling but still continued to smile in his infuriating and charming way. Jocelyn ignored him as he started the truck and they left the campus.

'Well, I'm glad you were so amused by our trip to the college, but we still haven't been able to find what we've been looking for. We've hit nothing but dead ends,' she muttered.

Trevan remained silent for a moment and she glanced to him to find his brows furrowed in a thoughtful frown.

'I may have a copy of the article we're looking for,' he said distractedly.

'And you're just now telling me?' she retorted.

He held his hand up to silence her. 'I don't know if I have it, but my brother left me a trunk in the cave I told you about. I opened it when I first found the cave and it had some of our family photographs and letters from friends. At the time it was too painful to go through. I've never opened it after that.'

All her anger slipped away and she watched him for a moment. When she finally spoke, her voice was soft, throaty with concern, 'Do you think you're ready now?'

His gaze met hers. 'Right now, I don't think I really have a choice. Do you?'

Jocelyn did not know what to say. He was right, they really didn't have a choice any more. Yet, she hated to see anyone, even arrogant, intimidating, hard bodied Trevan Elliot, have to face something that would cause him so much pain.

He turned away, his expression unreadable. 'It's a little after noon right now, still early enough so we can stop at your house and pack an overnight bag. Then we'll head out to Widow Barker's place and borrow a couple of horses.'

'Where is this cave, anyway?' she asked, after his comment about the horses. It had been years since she had ridden a horse; she wasn't sure if she still knew how to ride, but she wasn't about to admit that little item to John Wayne beside her.

'Basically out in the middle of nowhere,' he smiled, his attention on the road.

'How come no one has ever found it?' She had always loved to explore caves, and it would have been even more fun to find one full of gold.

'The land remained in the family for a long time. I learned that eventually my family quit working the land and ranching and leased it out, but the section where the cave is located is unfit for raising anything.' He paused for a moment, then shrugged. 'I don't believe Duncan passed our secret on. When I found out that the town was gone, but our house and the land was still intact, I bought the place from my own great, great nephew.'

Jocelyn listened, her eyes widening in disbelief, 'I bet that was weird.'

Trevan chuckled as if the thought also struck him as funny, 'In a way it was, but he looked a lot like Duncan.'

'That must have been comforting,' Jocelyn murmured. Didn't most people wonder about immortality and the generations that would come from their own selves?

'Yes,' he agreed. 'My brother's descendent, who was older than I am, said it had to be fate that a man named Trevan Elliot came to purchase the land. Then he went on to tell me about my own life and how I disappeared in a tornado seeking my sister's murderer. Never to be seen again.'

A chill rippled up her neck. 'So you're a legend.'

'Not much of one by my standards,' he remarked. 'But Widow Cook is the head of the Historical Society. She could tell you all about it.'

Jocelyn looked at him. 'Is there anyone around there that isn't a widow?'

'Obviously you've never been to western Kansas. It's almost a ghost town,' he said with a hint of regret.

Images of a cave, a dead girl, and a murderer from the past, swirled in Jocelyn's mind. What once was Trevan's home town may be gone, the memories of what it used to be the only thing left of its heritage, but its ghost held the key to the identity of a madman.

A cold-blooded, methodical individual who had killed before, and no doubt would kill again.

The Porcelain Mask Murderer.

CHAPTER 15

They made a stop at Jocelyn's house to pack overnight bags and after loading their bags into Trevan's truck, they headed out of town.

Jocelyn leaned her head back against the seat to rest her thoughts. Her mind, however, refused to rest. They were headed to a ghost town to search out a cave where Trevan might or might not have a picture of his dead sister's murder scene.

She shook her head and remembered it had not been that long ago that she would have scoffed at such a ludicrous idea. Time-travel, faceless murderers, and a deadly poison. It might make great fiction, but it was causing too many sleepless nights as she tried to sort out the mess she had stumbled into.

Finally she turned to the window and studied the passing scenery. The houses began to be farther and farther apart and life seemed to lose a few of its complications. What would it have been like to live in a time when walking to the neighbor's house was a three hour ordeal? Right now it sounded like a little slice of heaven.

Jocelyn had drifted off to sleep and was awakened with a jolt as they bounced on the rain washed dirt roads she recognized from her last visit here. Well, they looked like the last roads she had been on, but after a while she wasn't so sure. It wasn't until she saw the small, tree-lined cemetery that she knew they were the correct roads.

They bumped past the little graveyard and Jocelyn could barely make out the headstone of Allysa Elliot's grave. She shuddered at the thought of Trevan's sister lying so cold in the ground. She had died at the hands of the Porcelain Mask Murderer and knew his identity. Jocelyn turned her head to keep it in her sights as long as she could.

If only she could help them, she wished silently.

Facing the road again, she scanned the area around them as they continued to go deeper into the red-earth country of southwestern Kansas. They turned onto a small road, the longest drive-way she had ever seen.

'I bet she gets all the exercise she needs just going for the mail,' she commented as they pulled in front of the newly painted farmhouse.

Trevan chuckled and slid from behind the wheel. 'Wait till you meet Widow Barker.'

Widow Barker was a sixty-year old feminine version of John Wayne. Jocelyn caught her giggle as it occurred to her that the notion would make Mrs Barker a Jane Wayne. Boy, she really needed sleep, she thought.

Widow Barker had emerged from the barn and then gave a big whoop when she caught sight of Trevan. She trotted over on her stout legs and embraced him in a mammoth hug. She slapped him on the back a couple of times, then held him away from her to study his face.

'Trevan Elliot, it's been too long,' she smiled, then hauled off and hit him on the shoulder. She dropped her hands to her hips and gave him a pouting glare. 'Where the hell have you been?'

Jocelyn chuckled as she realized it was his left arm which was still healing from a flesh wound and being hit with a two-by-four. Now a one hundred and seventy pound granny was releasing her fury on it.

'Damn it, Millie. That's my sore arm,' Trevan grumbled, rubbing at his arm, then cautiously moved to hug her again.

'Well, it's going to be a lot worse now isn't it?' she laughed, then caught sight of Jocelyn. Her eyes lit up and she grinned, giving him a knowing wink. 'Well, what do we have here. Who's your friend, Trevan?'

'Millie Barker, meet Jocelyn Kendrick.' He held his hand out for her to come meet the amicable woman.

Jocelyn nodded and extended her hand to the lady for a introductory handshake, only to become the recipient of one of Widow Barker's bear hugs. She thought she was going to be squeezed to death until the woman pounded her sharply on the back, then held her out for inspection.

'She's a bit skinny, but I like the fire in her eyes,' Millie announced.

'Thank you, ma'am.' Jocelyn offered mildly, stopping herself from rubbing at the bruise that surely would be left from the robust woman's grip on her arms.

'Call me Millie. Now Trevan, tell me what you're doing out here, because I know it wasn't to introduce me to your woman,' she said taking him by the arm.

'I need to borrow a couple of horses,' he answered, matter-of-factly.

'Going out to the cave again, huh? Well, you go on out and pick out a couple of horses and Jocelyn can come help me fix you a saddle bag to take along with you.'

Jocelyn's gaze swung to Trevan at Mrs Barker's mention of the cave. She had thought it was sort of a secret, but apparently it wasn't. She wondered who else might know about the cave? As soon as she could, she was going to get him to answer a couple of questions.

Millie took her into the house and marched her into the kitchen. She was ordered to retrieve the saddle bag from a peg on the back porch.

Returning to the kitchen, she didn't see the widow right away, until she caught sight of the woman's rump sticking out from the refrigerator. Finally she emerged, loaded with food, and they began to make a meal which Jocelyn thought was large enough to feed at least four people. Maybe more.

She shook her head and started to protest, 'Millie, you really shouldn't go to so much trouble. Trevan said it wouldn't take long to get to the cave.'

'That's because he's a man.' Millie finished packing the saddle bag and offered her a wide grin. 'He's used to riding all day, then falling onto a roll and sleeping till dawn. But I don't think you've done that in a while, so he needs to take it a little easier. Besides, a person should always be prepared. You never know what might come up.'

Jocelyn shrugged. The woman made sense, and she couldn't argue with that. 'I guess you're right.'

'I'm old,' Millie announced, 'So I know I'm right. It's already afternoon and he would really be pushing it to get out there and back before night fall.'

Jocelyn felt her eyes widen, 'You mean he's planning on us spending the night out there?'

Millie nodded, hoisting the saddle bag from the table, 'That's the way Trevan is. I can tell he's in a hurry to get to that cave for whatever reason, and if he waits till morning to go, he's wasted this afternoon and the evening. He hates waste.'

She moved around the table to stand in front of Jocelyn, giving her a bawdy wink, 'And, in case you haven't noticed, he is quite a stud. If I were about thirty years younger I wouldn't mind spending a night with him in a cave myself, if you know what I mean.'

Jocelyn knew exactly what the woman meant and the thought caused her mouth to dry. She realized he must have been thinking the same thing.

'I would rather kiss a snake,' she muttered finally.

The widow laughed and put her hand on Jocelyn's shoulder as they started to walk outside. 'There are few of those out there too, if you want. Personally, I'd prefer Trevan.'

Outside they found the human snake in question finishing up with the two horses. Trevan flirted and charmed old Millie, then gave her a hug before he helped Jocelyn climb unsteadily onto her horse. He stepped easily into his saddle and they were off.

It hadn't taken long for Jocelyn to get the hang of horseback riding again, and the ride became quite enjoyable. She looked out over the sloping hills of the land and only occasionally would see a house; she could almost imagine what it had been like in Trevan's time. She could pretend there were no cars and airplanes, only a horse as a mode of transportation.

'It must have been peaceful to live out here,' Jocelyn said with a dreamy smile on her face.

'Sometimes,' he answered with his usual matter-of-factness.

She shifted in the saddle. 'Come on, Trevan. I couldn't even imagine it. No telephones, no television, no hassles.'

He turned to give her a pointed look. 'I admit there probably weren't as many hassles, maybe just a different kind.'

She shrugged, the good mood she was in had her feeling at ease with him. An inquisitiveness she did not know she possessed grew within her as she tried to comprehend the changes he had been forced to make. 'What was it like out here?'

He remained quiet for a while as if thinking about her question. 'It could get lonely sometimes out here, but most of the time I enjoyed it.' He turned back to give her a small smile. 'Sometimes I come out here just to be alone and gather my thoughts.'

'Getting yourself centered,' she said. She noticed his frown and went on to explain. 'I guess you would call it getting in touch with yourself. Maybe achieving balance in your life.'

'Well, I wouldn't know about that,' he said with a soft chuckle. 'I know I need the time to help me deal with everything.'

'Re-energize yourself,' she said quietly. Her gaze moved over the warm orange of the tall prairie grass covering the land with an occasional clump of yuccas to break up the scenery. It was beautiful land that could be hard, even deadly, to those who didn't know enough to treat it with the respect that was demanded.

Her eyes moved back to Trevan and she realized how this land was truly suited to him. Somewhere in the time since she had met Trevan Elliot, she didn't know when or even how, but she had come to accept that he was from the past.

He was from a different time and a different place. He had acclimatized very well to this time and showed no discomfort with the changes modern technology had made. But that didn't mean his own personal beliefs had changed or would.

Jocelyn's good mood dampened a little as she re-membered the hardening of his eyes and his distant attitude when she worked with the files of the murders. He had relented because he was forced to as they worked against a serial killer, but how would he feel down the road when, and if, this was over? Could this man from the past accept what she chose for her future?

She took a slow steady breath at the thought. Part of her hoped that he would at least learn to accept and deal with it, but part of her feared the other possibility more. What if he didn't?

They rode at an easy pace for almost an hour without stopping and the pleasure she had first enjoyed wore off; her bottom hurt, her back was tired, and worst of all, she needed to use the bathroom.

'Trevan, how much farther to your cave?'

'Just a ways,' he said, flicking her only a brief glance over his shoulder.

She rolled her eyes. The man could be excruciatingly irritating when he wanted to be. 'Just a ways? Could you translate that from "cowboyeze" to English? Is that a mile or so, or what?' she asked grumpily.

'As in over the second hill,' he answered, waving towards the area they were headed.

She studied the direction he'd indicated. The hill didn't seem that far away, maybe a couple of miles. She could make it if she set her mind to it. 'Okay, that is great.' She smiled, suddenly feeling slightly better. 'In fact, that is excellent.'

Trevan stopped his horse and turned to her. 'In case you were wondering, there is no plumbing there. We can stop here if you need to.'

What had she been thinking? Of course a cave wouldn't have indoor plumbing. Regardless, she lifted her chin and gave him a frosty glare. 'I knew that and, yes, I would like to stop for a minute.'

She slid from the horse and was forced to hold to the saddle for a moment so her shaky legs could get used to standing once again. They were in a rocky terrain with ravines cutting deeply into the ground in jagged slashes. She would definitely need her balance.

She nodded to him and moved towards a large boulder. 'I'll just find a favorite bush or rock.'

She could see Trevan out of the corner of her eye as he slid his Stetson back and glanced up to check the position of the sun. 'I'd be careful if I were you. It's starting to cool off a little and those rattlers like to catch those last few rays on a sunny rock to keep them warm.'

She stopped and turned towards him. She balled her hands on her hips defiantly as she gave him a hard glare. 'Don't give me that load of bull, Elliot.'

His face remained serious, although she couldn't tell whether his eyes were holding a hint of humor or not. His lip twitched a little as he spoke. 'If you see one just throw a rock on its head.' He paused a moment as if in thought, then nodded wisely. 'That should kill it.'

'Jerk,' she muttered over her shoulder as she walked away from him.

She moved around the large boulder and caught sight of the spindly spray of a bush. Stepping behind it, she saw that she was safely hidden from the sight of any curious cowboys by a high ledge of rock to one side of her and a fringe of rugged, wind worn cedars on the other.

Having taken care of a very pressing matter, she felt immensely better as she emerged from the skimpy bush. Out the corner of her eye, she caught sight of a brown coil curled on a flat surface of a rock. Jocelyn froze as she recognized it as a snake, what particular species she didn't know. Probably didn't want to know, but did not want to take the chance of being wrong. With a slow tilt of her head, she tried to look around her for Trevan, but was too afraid to move. A part of her mind tried to remember what she knew about snakes, like weren't they supposed to hibernate or something during the winter? Obviously, she reminded herself, it's not winter yet. In fact, they had been having an unusually warm fall. She also recalled something about poisonous snakes having vertical slits for pupils. Without moving, there was no way to see what kind of eyes it had, and she wasn't about to press the issue.

Slowly she slid her foot backwards, then moved the other. Rotating the two, she was able to put several feet of ground between her and the unidentified snake. The little visitor, she would assume he was little since he was coiled, was not rattling or showing any signs of anger, yet. But it was alive. She knew that because she could see its little forked tongue flicking at her occasionally.

The back of her heel bumped against something, causing Jocelyn to startle. She glanced cautiously behind her and realized that it was a rock. A rather large, flat rock. She flicked her gaze back to the little critter on the ledge. Hadn't Trevan said 'throw a rock on it'? Slowly she bent at the knees to pick up the stone. It weighed about ten pounds and had a nice smooth surface to it. She hoped the other side was just as smooth. She didn't want any hidden crevices helping the reptile to survive.

Biting her lower lip with caution, she raised the rock to her side. Pulling her arm and the rock back, she swung it forward and plopped it on the outstretched head of the slithering little fiend. The body of the snake rolled out of its coil and even rattled its tail a time or two before it wormed to a stop.

'It was a rattler,' she said hoarsely. Her stomach soured as she swallowed at the bile burning in her throat and her knees began to shake unsteadily. She put her hands on her knees to keep her from falling the rest of the way to the ground.

She released the breath she had been holding and suddenly realized her heart had been beating like a wild drum. Her head hurt and she pressed her fingers against her temples.

She didn't want to pretend she was in the wild west any more.

Jocelyn rose slowly, then staggered with short, jerky movements back to her horse and quietly climbed into the saddle unassisted. Trevan's worried gaze studied her for a moment as she gave him a tired look.

'What happened?'

'I did what you said to,' she answered, frowning as a wave of nausea rolled over her. Again. 'I threw a rock on it.'

His eyes widened in disbelief, 'You killed a snake?'

She nodded slowly. Her tongue felt thick and pasty, slurring her words. 'A rattlesnake, I believe. At least it rattled anyway. If you want to skin it or eat it, or whatever you guys do with snakes, it's under a big rock behind that boulder.'

'We usually avoid them when possible,' he said, wiping a hand across his face.

She gave him a withering glare, 'Thanks a lot,

Trevan. Do you think you can keep your sage advice to yourself from now on?'

Trevan ignored her comment and dismounted from his horse. He walked behind the boulder and his gaze immediately found the snake in question under the rock she threw on it. He swallowed, feeling guilty for having teased her.

He picked up a stout stick and poked at it to make sure it was dead. Stretching the reptile out, he figured the cold-blooded creature had to be a little over five feet. Taking a closer look at the tail, since the head wouldn't do him any good, he cursed himself six ways to Sunday. He had teased her about throwing a rock on a rattler, and that was exactly what she had killed. A rattlesnake.

The table was beautifully set. The linen tablecloth had been pressed and the napkins were folded neatly, then placed in their decorative holders. He had prepared a simple, yet elegant, meal; filet mignon wrapped in bacon, baked potato, and a green salad with fresh chunks of blue cheese sprinkled on top. White Zinfandel chilled in a bucket of ice beside the table, and an elegant arrangement of white roses sat to the side of the table. After all, he did not want his view to be obstructed.

The man studied himself in the mirror as he knotted the black bow tie to his tuxedo. His hair was not in its usual slicked back style, but fell in loose waves around the collar of his shirt. Stepping back he moved his gaze down his image and back to his face.

Yes, it was perfect.

The key to his success had been the ability to adapt himself to the role of the perfect man for each of his victims. For Michelle Slavinsky, it had been a sensitive and caring individual with a fondness for reading the classics. Becky Sowers had required a leather jacket and a chin of rough stubble. Each of the ladies had developed a fantasy, and he had adapted himself to fill the requirement.

Ellianna Vernon had required a dashing adventurer. A modern version of a white knight.

It had been easy to soften her to him, as he had planned, and without any difficulty she had agreed to meet him for an informal lunch at the park. She had awkwardly tucked her skirt beneath her and laughed with him over their wine and cheese basket. He had taken her hand and held it till she shyly raised her gaze to his, then he had asked her to come to dinner.

He chuckled as he recalled her reaction. At first it had been shock, quickly passing to exhilaration, then calculation, as the little wheels of her mind spun in an effort to juggle the lies, excuses, and promises it would take for her to step out on her family.

He struck a match and made a slow circle around the room as he lit the slender, white tapers of the candles. The small flames danced in the darkness of the room, shifting and spinning to create a seductive glow around him. He assessed the room with a critical eye, then smiled slowly. Yes, it was perfect, he thought to himself. Ellianna Vernon would experience the fantasy which had so warmly brightened her dismal little life.

Although she wasn't what he would consider beautiful, she did have a certain delicateness about her.

His gaze hardened and he watched the flame of the match burn almost to his fingertips. Gently he blew out the yellow glow. Beauty is only temporary, he thought. Then she becomes useless. *Unwanted*.

Dead.

The door bell rang and he smiled. Ellianna Vernon was right on cue.

And the curtain rose . . .

CHAPTER 16

Jocelyn remained quiet the rest of the ride. Bashing a rattlesnake had really taken a toll on her energy. The horses ambled into a wide, shallow valley – well, as much of a valley as southwestern Kansas could muster. They traveled past several cedar-filled ravines carved deep into the sides then descended into a particularly deep cleft.

Tall cedars, fat with green boughs, filled the large chasm. They jockeyed their horses into single file and slowly made their way to the middle. Jocelyn frowned as she twisted in the saddle, scanning for the cave. She was beginning to eye Trevan with a wary suspicion. Maybe that tornado had done more to him than shove him through time, she thought. As far as she could tell, there was not a cave to be found anywhere.

Trevan stopped his horse in front of a darkened overhang. Dismounting, he moved to the ledge, then hunkered over and disappeared into the black shadow.

Jocelyn blinked, then drew her brows together. 'Trevan?' she called, uncertainty filling her voice.

He emerged with his hat off and nodded to the cave. 'It's unoccupied.'

'Well, that's comforting,' she said, sliding from the saddle. She stroked the silky nose of the horse as she studied the almost invisible entrance to Trevan's family lair.

'I didn't know we had caves in Kansas,' she said.

'Actually, there are quite a few here in the Gyp Hills,' he answered.

'How did you find it?' It wasn't as if a person searched one of these out, or looked in the phone book.

'When I was young, we used to have a small house not too far from here. My brother, sister, and I were playing one day when we stumbled onto it. Or more accurately, into it,' he answered. He stopped removing the gear from the horse to point above the wall of the cave. 'There's a hole up there, a secret entrance, I guess you could call it.'

'Your parents let you roam like that?' she murmured, thinking of how her friends kept very close eyes on their own kids.

'I didn't have parents.' He glanced to her briefly then returned to his horse. 'As I told you, mother died after Allysa was born and my father was a drunk. He was never home much. If he was home, we usually tried to avoid him. It was safer that way.'

Jocelyn tried to imagine Trevan as a lonely little boy who lost not only his mother, but his father too. A child forced to mature and bear the responsibility of raising his younger brother and sister. She glanced at her hands and bit her lip. Words seemed so inadequate.

'It must have been rough,' she finally offered, knowing it could never be a consolation for the harsh reality of his childhood.

'It was life,' he said. He slid his hat back and glanced to the ridge of the valley where Jocelyn could see the pink rays of the sun as it lowered itself into evening. She understood now a small part of Trevan Elliot. No matter what life handed him, he would deal with it and go on.

'It's going to get dark pretty soon. I'll finish untying the rolls and you can help me take them inside. We're going to have to spend the night here.'

Jocelyn's sympathy for him quickly faded. She gave him a dry look as she remembered Millie's statement. 'Oh, what a surprise.'

He stopped to look at her. 'What does that mean?'

She put her hands on her hips. 'Millie said you knew there wouldn't be enough time for us to get back tonight.'

'Are you afraid I brought you out here so you couldn't run away if I tried to seduce you?' His expression was of cool amusement and his lips curved into a smile filled with charm. 'I wouldn't be totally honest if I said that I did not want to accommodate your distrust.'

Jocelyn was beginning to realize Trevan Elliot's talent at turning things against her. To make her feel uncomfortable and awkward in his presence. 'I did not say that I wanted you to accommodate anything like that for me. I'm not a bubble-headed cheerleader who melts whenever you smile.'

'No, you are not.' He walked to her till he stood in front of her. The smell of leather and the outdoors were intoxicating to her senses as his gaze heated with his desire. He touched her cheek softly as his finger caressed her skin. 'You are much more than that, Jocelyn.'

His gaze lowered to her mouth and she knew she should not let him kiss her, but she didn't stop him. She realized she wanted him to kiss her. Wanted to be with him away from the city and its endless interruptions. Wanted to be with him here where he belonged.

His lips moved over hers and she moaned a soft sigh of pleasure as she returned his kiss. Trevan's arm circled her waist and pulled her to him. Her breasts pressed against the muscled ridge of his chest and her hands tightened on his shoulders in response.

Jocelyn slid her hands around his neck and wove her fingers through the dark silk of his hair. Everything faded from her as Trevan filled her senses. She reveled in the feel of him and the taste of him. His hands, his exquisite hands, moved over her till he cupped her breast and rubbed his thumb over the hardening peak of her nipple.

His lips moved softly down her throat and she whispered his name. She wanted to give in to the passion building within her. Give herself to him. Trevan was pushing her collar open as his mouth moved over her collar bone when suddenly Jocelyn was shoved roughly against him. He swore bitterly as he moved her away from the horse.

Reality crashed back to her senses and her eyes flew open. 'What was that?'

She turned and realized they had been leaning heavily against the horse while Trevan had been kissing her senseless. She began to wonder just what kind of luck she had when even in the middle of nowhere, they still were being interrupted.

She turned back to him and opened her mouth to suggest that they find a more secluded spot, when he handed her one of the rolls.

'We better get things taken care of before it gets dark,' he said, moving past her to lean over and slip into the cave.

Her mouth still open she simply stood there for a moment in shock, her hormones raging. Finally she closed her mouth and silently cursed her luck, Trevan Elliot, and the damn horse, as she stalked toward the cave.

Ellianna Vernon accepted the glass of white wine from the handsome man. She shook her head every time she thought of this virile man asking her to dinner. She would be thirty-five next month and had been married for sixteen years to Carl, who was an assistant manager at a small grocery store. They had two kids, a mortgage, and last week the car's engine had begun to make a threatening, very expensive-sounding noise.

She had never had the opportunity to go to college; a steamy night in the back seat of Carl's car had robbed her of that. She had accepted her lot in life though and tried to cope with each day as it came. But she couldn't help feeling there was something more.

A nameless, faceless, something that would make her life perfect. She still hadn't figured that one out, however. Instead she absorbed herself in her romance books of true happiness with fulfilling love where in the end everyone found their reason in life. Her fixation with the romance books had helped her land a job in the bookstore. She had felt lucky to get it, considering she had not worked one day outside the home since her marriage.

But still she couldn't help wondering if there was more.

Where was the heart-pounding, mind-numbing, soul-wrenching pleasure she had read about? She snickered into her third glass of wine; it sure wasn't Carl and his accordion-like body.

Hungrily her gaze moved up Brent Masters' athletic form and she felt an unfamiliar burn of desire. Never had such a good looking man given her a second glance, let alone invited her to a private affair. She had noticed him watching her at the mall and then he had caught her completely off guard by introducing himself and asking her to lunch. Even now, as she sipped wine with Brent, she still couldn't believe it.

A part of her knew she would never have the guts to leave her safe little family and the security of her home, but for one night, one blessedly sinful night, she wanted to live as she had never done before. Without worrying about the consequences.

She wanted to live dangerously.

Brent turned the music on, the melody softly filling the room. He removed his jacket and draped it casually across the back of a chair. He advanced slowly, almost casually toward her, his eyes bold and demanding. Ellianna shuddered with excitement unable to stop herself from imagining that she was his sultry captive and he was determined to make her his. That he would use his seductive force to bend her will till she mindlessly did as he wished.

He held his hand to her. 'Dance with me.'

She set her glass on the table and rose, suddenly feeling woozy from the combination of the wine, and her fantasy turning to reality as he led her to the middle of the room.

He pulled her against him and Elli placed her hands awkwardly on his wide shoulders. She could feel the hard muscles of his body move beneath her fingers and wondered what it would be like to touch him without his shirt on. To touch the inviting mat of hair on his chest. She wanted to run her hands down the rippled hardness of his torso to the button of his slacks.

Timidly she stared at the buttoned front of his shirt and damned her nervous habit of sweaty palms. Flicking her glance briefly to his face, she realized he didn't seem to notice or care that her hands were sopping his white shirt.

His finger gently cupped her chin and tilted her gaze to meet his. She stared, mesmerized, fascinated as he returned her look and swayed his hips in a seductive brush against hers.

Her heart fluttered and her breath came in shallow little gasps. She realized this was what they wrote about in her books. The thought of the joyous rapture Brent would give her, that Carl had never been able to fulfil, had her heart beating loudly in her ears with excitement.

'Ellianna,' he murmured, placing his cheek against

hers. She could feel the erotic touch of his breath against her ear. His lips feathered lightly against her skin, causing delicious waves of pleasure to wash over her. 'That is a pretty name.'

'It's . . . uh . . . the name of an Egyptian slave,' she started nervously. She tried to will her body to relax as his arms embraced her waist, his hands firmly holding her hips. 'My mo . . . mother heard it in the movie about the ten commandments and, well, named me after the g . . . girl.'

He pulled back to gaze into her face, his expression knowing. 'And do you feel like the Egyptian girl?'

She blinked as she frowned at his question. 'I don't understand, what do you mean?'

'Trapped by the bondage of your life,' he said, his eyes a warm offering of much more. His fingers smoothed small circles against her hips in a slow invitation.

'Yes . . . Yes, I do,' she whispered hesitantly.

He leaned to her, his lips skimming the heat of her cheeks. 'Then let me take you away.'

His words came to her like the pillowy softness of a dream. Elli let her head fall back and her eyes closed as his lips masterfully claimed hers. Never, never had it been like this.

Brent Masters released her slowly, then led her to the table and pulled the chair back for her to sit down. He leaned forward and plucked a white rose from the vase. He smoothed the silky petals gently down her cheek, then handed it to her.

'Please allow me to serve you,' he offered huskily and moved to the kitchen.

She felt her eyes widen and took a deep breath. How had she become so lucky? He served her with sophisticated expertise. At least she thought so, the fanciest she and Carl ever got was their anniversary dinner at the cafeteria, where she got to walk along a buffet and pick out what she wanted.

He placed before her a little steak with bacon wrapped around it and a baked potato with a salad. It smelled good and she smiled as he filled her wine glass once again.

Brent took his chair and started cutting into his steak. He glanced at her and paused. His smile was slow and enticing. 'My dear, tonight you will need your energy.'

Elli looked down at her steak and nodded. Her mouth dried at the image of this man's naked body rising above her. She shivered voluptuously as she thought of him taking her. Touching and bewitching her body till she stood at the edge of oblivion. His masterful fingers forcing her over the edge into the heated shower of fulfilment.

The image began to wave in her mind's eye and she frowned in confusion. She shook her head; she tried to remember the dream. To clutch it desperately and force it back into focus. She struggled for a moment; how many glasses of wine had she had? Three? Four?

She cut into the tender meat and reveled in the rich flavor. Brent watched her, then raised his glass of wine. 'To us, my sweet . . . to you.'

Elli looked away shyly and took a deep breath. If only for once, she wanted this night more than anything. Even if there was hell to pay. She raised her full glass of wine and clinked it against his. 'To you, Brent, for making my dreams come true.'

He sipped at his wine, his eyes never leaving hers as she did the same. She started to put the glass down when he stopped her.

'No, Ellianna. It's customary to finish the glass,' he said softly, his eyes holding hers. When he spoke again his voice was a whisper laced with promise. 'It's like a wish. What is your wish, Ellianna?'

She tipped the glass back and drained the contents. The liquid left a bitter taste in her mouth and it caused her to smack her lips. She returned her blurry gaze to Brent and smiled timidly.

'What is your wish, Ellianna? Only ask, so that I may give it to you.'

'My wish.' She tingled from the wine; heady, brazen, seductive. Licking her lips, her thoughts flashed in a whirl of heated emotion. A wish? There were so many things she had dreamed of. Wanted. Needed.

Desired.

She leaned forward and her hand fell to her lap. Elli frowned, looking at it in confusion. Her head started to hurt desperately and she wanted to push the pain away with her hand, but it refused to cooperate.

She glanced at Brent to find him smiling at her as if she were the most beautiful woman in the world and she wanted to smile too, but couldn't seem to get her body to cooperate. It occurred to her that she should feel fear, but reason did not seem to want to recognize its duty. Finally she was able to raise her hand and distantly, from somewhere within herself, she noticed the tremor of her fingers. When had that happened, she wondered?

Elli heard a woman giggle and she tried to turn to see

who it was, but it was as if she was a participant in a dream. Unable to move, only to watch the drunken movements of the woman sitting in her place. She tried to stand and in response her leg would only kick awkwardly out in front of her. She watched fascinated, then realized it was her leg and not that of a wooden dummy. Why couldn't she feel it? What was happening to her perfect dream? To her?

Her mouth was so dry. She couldn't even feel the burn of her own tears on her face. Brent was there talking to her soothingly, giving her more wine. She tried to shake her head to tell him no, but her muscles would not move. They would only jerk and shake, making her feel like gelatin as the cool liquid spilled over her cheeks. Her voice sounded like a dim gurgle, incoherent and slurred. Finally fear worked into her consciousness and connected with her thoughts. The dream was fading, leaving terror in its wake. It grew and festered within her as she tried again to move.

She could hear a slow swoosh, swoosh, a slowing rhythmic beating. Her head rolled and she watched the room move before her like a horrible slow motion movie of a woman dying.

Intense horror stiffened her very soul as she realized it was not a movie, only her very own participation. A sob tore through her as she realized how truly helpless she was.

She struggled loudly for a breath, could hear the ragged wheezing, but strangely she did not feel anything. There was no pain and even the terror was slowly beginning to fade. Suddenly her vision seemed to jump from one point in the room to another. Lights, there were so many of them. Flickering licks of yellow tapered from the white candles. Sensations of color caused her body to jerk and bolt. The legs of the chair bucked beneath her frantic movements and she hit the table causing some of the dishes to spill to the floor.

She was the next to fall, her hand and her arm landing in front of her face. Her breath came slowly. Ever so slowly. She could hear the rhythmic sound slowing within her, around her, through her.

She heard the muffled beat of her own heart. Images flowed through her mind of her family from the past and now. Images of her parents long dead . . . and her children so young.

Another beat. Her husband Carl. She could not deny he was a good man. He had taken care of her and the children. Perhaps she should have told him she loved him more often.

A beat. Dreams, so many dreams. Most never fulfilled and never would be. Yet there was a sense of calm about her. She knew God would take care of her.

A beat. Brent's face swam before her and she could hear a slow intake of breath rattling through her lungs. He kissed her cheek and told her she was beautiful. The dream, the lovely dream of fulfilment, fluttered before her.

Now she would always be beautiful, Brent was telling her. His voice was deep, the enticing richness of his words swirled around her in a warm caress.

A beat. The air slid slowly from her lungs and her eyes saw no more.

CHAPTER 17

'It's like a little maze in here,' Jocelyn said. Her voice bounced off the cave walls with a tinny sound, eerie and hollow.

Trevan walked ahead of her holding a kerosene lantern out in front of him. The warm light moved over the uneven surface of the walls causing the shadows to dance and jolt around them. The passageway was so narrow at some points, they had to turn sideways to squeeze through.

Jocelyn felt the cold surface scrape against her front and back giving her a brief moment of fear. The confined feeling forced unfamiliar bolts of alarm to thunder through her. She had never liked restricted areas and some parts of the cave were about as restricted as it came.

'It basically consists of the large cavern back there where we just passed and the three smaller chambers ahead of us.' He stepped over a small rock, then turned sharply to the left and appeared to walk right into a wall of stone. He stopped at the opening of the chamber and waited for her to move beside him. 'This was Allysa's.

She used to play dolls in here and pretend she was a famous actress.'

Jocelyn tried to look at his face to see what emotion registered in his eyes, but the kerosene lamp only shone around them and she was unable to make out his expression through the shadows that covered his face.

'I'm sure she was happy,' she said softly.

'She was.' His voice was low, but she could hear the cautious amusement in his tone. 'Here it was safe to be happy.'

Jocelyn turned to study the chamber. The beam from the lamp illuminated the room filled with cobwebs. Shrouded beneath the dusty silk were small figures; their dull, glass eyes staring back at them. A delicate tea set sat on the rough surface of an old crate, the webs providing a ruffle around the make-shift table.

Sweep away the shrouds of time and imagine the rough walls of the cave as a room; it would have surely appeared to be the remnants of a little girl's sweet imagination. Jocelyn recognized it for what it was, a child's haven from the brutal reality of a dead mother, a drunken father, and a family that never was.

She moved past him to pick up a doll. She blew away the years of dust and marveled at the fragile porcelain of the head. Jocelyn traced her finger over the contours of the doll's face where time had darkened her features and exposed small blemishes to the ravages of the cave. Jocelyn fingered a delicate curl and admired the beauty of its little dress, still amazingly intact.

She turned to Trevan and noted his softened smile. 'They're beautiful.'

He shifted and the light of the lamp moved over his face. He said quietly, his voice filled with the emotions of his past, his eyes reflecting so many memories. 'She had to leave them here. Otherwise, when my father occasionally showed up, he would take them and . . . burn them.' His gaze moved from the doll to hold hers. 'After he left, I guess she decided they would always be safe here.'

His expression became unreadable and Jocelyn delicately set the doll back at her party. She did not try to give him words of comfort, but remained silent. Some things were better left alone.

She moved beside him and they continued through the small passageway. She could barely make out a wide opening ahead of them.

'This next chamber was Duncan's,' he nodded to the dark hole with his head. 'I need to warn you about – '

The beam from the lamp washed across the bleached face of a skull, its black sockets wide with surprise and its skeletal teeth bared in the wide grin of death. Jocelyn screamed.

'. . . Charlie,' Trevan finished with a note of humor, then chuckled.

She backed away from him and the ghoulish smirk of the skeleton till her back bumped roughly against the wall of the cave. Her heart thumped wildly and still she covered her mouth shakily with her hand, muffling her voice. 'Trevan, did you kill . . . I mean, did you do this?'

He slid her a sideways look of mild irritation. 'No, he was here when we found the cave. If you look closely you'll see he is wearing the remnants of a Confederate uniform.'

She glanced uneasily at 'Charlie' and, yes indeed, he was wearing a tattered and faded gray uniform; complete with pants and bony feet. 'I thought you said the cave was unoccupied. I would definitely call that occupied,' she snapped, waving a hand toward the skeleton.

'He is dead, Jocelyn. I don't think that his remains would count in a census.'

She felt her eyes widen with disbelief and horror, part of it transforming to her words. 'You didn't play with it, did you?'

He gave her a pointed look, then joked. 'Again, no. Charlie sort of became our confidant. We always knew he would listen.'

Jocelyn shook her head as she tried to suppress a shudder, 'And you thought I was morbid.'

She stepped a little closer and frowned as she looked at him with timid curiosity. 'Why didn't you bury him or something?'

His look of revulsion matched that of her own. 'We were just children, Jocelyn. Would you want to move him?'

'No, I wouldn't,' she answered truthfully. She swallowed and her lips curled in a grimace at the thought of handling the stained bones of the Confederate soldier. 'But still, you're a grown man now. Surely, you've developed your courage since then.'

He looked at her, his expression a mixture of leeriness and distaste. 'Sure, and you're going to be right there beside me to give me a hand, aren't you?'

'I think there are laws against moving remains and improper burials.' She straightened and rubbed her hand uneasily against her jeans. 'Maybe it would be a good idea just to leave him there.'

'That's what I thought,' he answered, his voice smug.

Trevan turned, removing the security of the halo of light. She hurriedly caught up with him and stuck close to his side in the dismal passageway. She didn't want to be caught off guard again, in case there were any more occupants of the cave.

'The trunk is in the next chamber,' he said.

His chamber, she thought to herself. The first two had given a small hint at the personality of the individual. Allysa's had shown a frightened little girl seeking her comfort in the dirt floors of a cave where she had the security to play out her childhood dreams. Duncan's had, well, she didn't know exactly what his had shown. She had never really gotten past 'Charlie' to see what else was in the chamber. But what would Trevan's area hold, she wondered? He had been the eldest and forced to grow years in a matter of months.

The entrance of the chamber was a narrow opening, but wide enough so that she wouldn't have to squeeze through it. She frowned as the light moved across a large boulder to the right side of the entrance. It looked remarkably like a gigantic dog. Part of it was the natural formation of the rock, and only time could explain the basic shape. But she could make out the faint chip marks as if a small, but very determined, little boy had scraped at the surface to make his own statue.

She glanced at Trevan, but was unable to read anything in his expression.

He slowly walked through the entrance and the orb of light illuminated the chamber. Unlike the other two rooms that were filled with cobwebs accumulated over more than a hundred years, Trevan's room was clean. For a cave, anyway.

Jocelyn had to admit to herself that this room did reveal a lot about Trevan. Probably more than he cared to admit. The chamber was arranged like a one room home. A haven for a man ripped from the past.

An old barn ladder leaned against the far wall with quilts folded over the rungs, probably in an effort to deter 'critters,' though she did not know how effective that would be. Chiseled into the cave wall not too far away was a sort of built in fireplace with a natural chimney. She walked over and leaned into it. Looking up into the opening, she could see the pink and orange of the fading evening sky.

'This is great, Trevan,' she said, 'but wouldn't people see the smoke?'

'They probably would, if they were in the area,' he answered matter-of-factly. 'But, I only use oak. It's a hard wood, burns hot, and causes less smoke. An old friend of mine taught me that.'

'Are we talking just old, or really old?' she asked hesitantly.

He gave her a lopsided smile. 'A really old friend.'

She stepped back and continued her inspection of the room. Her gaze moved to a large, flat rock that was about the height of a bed. She assumed that was what he used it for though there were no pillows or mattress.

Without warning, a heated image of Trevan's hard body intertwined with hers on their bed rolls worked its way into her thoughts, the warm caress of the fireplace licking at their skin like a fervent kiss.

She shook herself and was thankful for the shadows caused by the kerosene lamp hiding the blush she felt warming her face. Purposely she moved away from the bed and walked toward Trevan as he stepped to the back of the chamber.

Outside she had been more than ready to join him, but fortunately she had been saved from herself by the horse. They were here to try to find answers to the identity of the killer who worked in the shadows to get to them. To her. Neither she, nor Trevan, could afford to be distracted by the pleasures they most surely could give each other. Jocelyn made a silent resolve to herself to keep that thought foremost in her mind and not allow herself to succumb again to his touch.

Jocelyn moved to stand beside him. She blinked and drew a deep breath. Awestruck, she absorbed the sight before her. Two large crates, their tops opened to expose the glint of smooth gold bricks. From the size of the crates, she couldn't even begin to comprehend how much the gold must be worth.

'Are you sure you weren't a bank robber?' she asked in awe.

Trevan chuckled, 'No. I used to keep my money here because of my father. He would drink it away if he found it and I needed it to feed and clothe us. As my ranch grew, it seemed only natural to continue keeping my money here. I guess Duncan felt the same way. He didn't keep all the family fortune here, of course. He reinvested most of it and made a pretty good business for himself with cattle, then the railroad.'

'Elliot Enterprises,' Jocelyn said in wonder. 'Your brother was the founder of one of the largest corporations in America.'

Trevan smiled proudly, 'I thought this would help you believe me.'

'Too bad you don't have any access to the family fortune,' she said as she moved to timidly touch the shiny bars of gold.

'It's where it belongs, with Duncan's descendants. Besides,' he said with a hint of humor, 'I don't think my coming forward with the story of me being his long lost brother would hold much water, do you?'

'No, probably not. That would sound a little fishy, wouldn't it?' she admitted.

Trevan stepped to a large, humpbacked trunk beside the crates. He quickly removed an ancient hasp from the ring. 'The lock rusted a long time ago.'

He slid the trunk forward a little, then opened the lid. Jocelyn moved beside him smiling to herself. She was finally going to find out about his childhood and his family.

The chamber itself was not the room of a child as had been Duncan's and Allysa's. This room spoke of a mature Trevan Elliot, a man who had been torn from his family and his life. A man who perhaps considered himself a ghost in a time when he realistically should be dead.

Trevan set the lamp beside them on a crate. The light exposed the neatly packed contents of the trunk. Albums of tin-types and yellowed letters were stacked in one corner. Tiny infant clothes with beautifully embroidered borders were pressed between thick sheets of paper that smelled strongly of camphor. The most notable item in the trunk, however, was a lop-eared dog with button eyes and a quilted body resting lovingly in the middle of small, quilted baby blanket.

Jocelyn smiled and lifted the little dog, 'Who is this?'

He quickly, but gently removed the toy from her hands to replace it in the trunk. He seemed determined to avoid her gaze. 'It's Sir Puppy.'

Her eyes widened in disbelief and she laughed. Trevan Elliot had a stuffed toy named Sir Puppy! 'Such an original name. I bet you had dreams of being a knight in shining armor, didn't you?'

He slid her a dry sideways glance and disregarded her question. Carefully he began to remove, shift, and thumb through the contents of the trunk in an obvious attempt to ignore her.

'It looks like this is a lost cause,' he muttered as he picked through several papers.

'I don't know, I think it's been rather enlightening, Sir Elliot,' she said with a teasing tone. At his look she suppressed her laughter. 'Hand me the albums and you can keep looking through the trunk.'

Jocelyn turned through pages showing pictures of solemn and sometimes severe looking men and women. Even the children never seemed to smile. Except for Allysa. She had turned the page to find a photo of two boys and a girl. The eldest was Trevan, there was no mistaking his direct gaze. Duncan was a shorter, lighter version of his older brother. But Allysa smiled at the camera, her expression one of delighted surprise.

Jocelyn smiled to herself and quietly glanced at Trevan as he continued to move through the trunk. For an unguarded moment he had allowed his emotions to show on his face. Going through the old items, his expression moved from tenderness to pain, all with a thread of mourning woven through it as he held an age worn photograph in his hand. He stroked his thumb slowly over the surface, then placed the item in the pocket of his shirt.

Jocelyn returned her gaze to the book, feeling as if she had intruded on a very personal moment for Trevan. She sighed and turned the page. Her eyes widened as she glanced over an old article. She delicately removed the yellowed document from the page to turn to him.

'Did you find something?' he asked as he shifted to look over her shoulder.

'It's a cutout of the article about your sister's murder, but the picture has been removed,' she said quietly, hoping to tread lightly over the sensitive subject.

'That was the kind of man Duncan was. He always wanted to protect us.' Trevan's breath brushed against her ear and Jocelyn felt a chill of awareness prick through her.

He was entirely too close. She could feel the heat of him caressing her back and the desire to lean into the seductive warmth was overwhelming. She reminded herself of her resolve as she cleared her throat and shifted away from him to read the article.

'The community was shocked by the murder of one of Niola's leading citizens . . .' Jocelyn paused, furrowing her brows. The name sounded familiar. 'Isn't that near Pratt?'

'Yes,' he answered, 'but this was the original Niola.'

'*Patron of the Arts, Allysa Elliot,*' she read, '*was found by her elder brother Trevan, brutally murdered in the theater early yesterday afternoon. There was no known motive and the victim apparently expired from a harsh blow to the head. Sheriff Jarboe, as of yet, has not been able to determine any suspects. On the same note, it has been discovered that the before mentioned brother, Mr Elliot, disappeared only hours after the murder. Apparently he set out to trail the killer, who some speculate . . .*'

Jocelyn paused, leafing through the book, 'Where's the rest?'

'Damn it,' Trevan muttered, taking the page from her to glance at the other side. 'It looks like the part sticking from the book was accidentally ripped away when it was packed.'

He stepped back to the trunk and shifted through the contents. 'It must have turned to dust a long time ago.'

Jocelyn frowned in thought, 'What about the historical society you mentioned? Maybe they have the sheriff's records or know who might have them.'

'It's worth a try, but we'll have to wait till morning. It's really too late to head back.' He gave a frustrated shrug. 'I'll go get the saddle bags.'

'You're not leaving me in here by myself,' she said. 'I'll go with you.'

'Jocelyn, there is nothing to be scared of.' Trevan's frustration had now turned to amusement at her unease. 'I'll be right back, I promise.'

'I'm not scared, I just want some fresh air, that's all.' She noticed he tried to conceal his smile. 'That is all.'

'Whatever you say.'

Trevan grabbed the lantern and they headed back through the passageway to the front of the cave. Nearing the entrance, noises from outside caused a note of alarm to shoot through Jocelyn. They could hear the frightened sounds of the horses and the snarling growls of what sounded to Jocelyn like vicious dogs. He ordered her to stay inside as he pulled a shotgun from his pack lying beside the entrance and moved outside.

He ran to where the horses were hobbled. Jocelyn ventured cautiously outside the cave, unable to think of him facing the dogs alone. She shifted, trying to see in the darkening shadows of the trees. She saw a horse rear on its back legs in wild fright, then the snap of the tree limb as it broke its bond.

She jumped as the gun fired. The brief illumination lighting a horrific scene. Coyotes were frightening the horses. Trevan's mount bolted into a desperate run. He fired again and she heard the shrill yelp of the coyote as it fell. The rest of the pack scattered, blending back into the darkness surrounding them.

She ran to him where he stood looking at the dead animal. She looked from it to him then out into the night where she could still hear the riderless horse running away.

'Now what do we do?' she asked, her breath coming in short gasps.

'Nothing,' he said, turning without a glance in her direction. He went to soothe the remaining horse.

The man was positively maddening, she thought. 'What do you mean, nothing? The coyotes frightened off your horse. Aren't you even worried about him?'

Trevan moved her mount closer to the entrance of the cave. 'He will head back to Millie's place. It's not the first time out here that a horse has been scared off by a coyote.'

'Well, it's the first time it's happened to me,' she snapped. 'What about the historical society? Does this mean we're going to have to ride together?'

He slid her a frustrated sideways glance, 'Unless you plan on walking all the way, that is exactly what we're going to have do. Maybe we'll get lucky and my horse will come back here later tonight.'

She glared at him as she moved past him to the cave muttering a few low oaths. At least with two horses, there had always been the option that they could leave if they had to. Now they were forced to stay the night, alone with each other.

She did not look forward to spending the night in a cave with Trevan Elliot. Unless one of them slept on the floor, or with Charlie, they would have to share the ledge. Neither choice was attractive to her.

Grabbing the lantern, she stalked carefully back to his cavern, deliberately not glancing in on the bony resident in Duncan's chamber as she moved past it. She moved into the third room and promptly sat on the ledge with a determined look of possession. She opened the saddle bag she had brought with her and pulled a sandwich out.

He could sleep with Charlie, she thought as she took a bite.

Several moments later, Trevan entered carrying a load of wood for the fireplace. He headed to the pit and began arranging the bundle. Soon he had a small flame of yellow licking at the twigs he used for starter.

Trevan stood, then moved to the bed rolls. He picked one up and tossed it to her, then retrieved his own. 'I see you figured out where the bed was.'

'Yes,' she said, prudishly clearing her throat. 'Where . . . where were you planning to sleep?'

'Right where you're sitting,' he smiled easily.

He began to move towards her and she jumped from the ledge. 'You can't, I mean, then where am I going to sleep?'

Trevan shrugged as he untied his roll and began to smooth it out, 'That is entirely up to you.'

Jocelyn started to glance around her at the dirt floor and couldn't really convince herself to sleep so close to whatever might scamper across it, or more frightening, scamper across her at night. She noticed him watching her with a faint twist of his lips.

'I guess your choices are Charlie or me,' he said with quiet patience. 'I have to warn you though, that he snores. Loudly.'

She didn't smile at his comment and she felt her eyes

widen with uncertainty. How strong would her resolve be with temptation lying only a touch away? She shifted nervously as she quickly tried to think of another option.

His gaze softened. 'I give you my word, Jocelyn, I will not try anything.' His promise relaxed her only a little.

'Unless you want me to.'

That statement did not. Her hands dropped stiffly to her sides and she gave him a pointed glare. 'Keep to your side of the roll, Trevan, or you will be sleeping with Charlie.'

'Probably would be better company,' he muttered as he turned away from her.

Jocelyn made a face at his back, then picked her roll up to arrange it beside his. She opened out the length of the bedding, purposely avoiding his gaze while she did it.

The task done, she straightened and stepped to the lantern. 'I need to borrow this.'

'Don't go too far,' he responded distractedly.

He didn't need to worry about that; first sight of a coyote and bodily functions or not, she would simply have to wait till morning.

It didn't take her long to take care of her necessities and she quickly ducked back into the cave. Entering Trevan's cavern, she fumed at the sight of him stretched out on the front edge of the makeshift bed. It was not that she was picky, but she didn't relish the idea of crawling over him.

Jocelyn nudged him none too gently with her finger. 'Move over.'

He opened one eye. 'Does that mean you want to get up in the middle of the night to put more wood on the fire when it starts to die down?'

Okay, she thought, let him be a hero.

There was no way for her to get into the makeshift bed from the end, she noted with disappointment. Jocelyn determinedly lifted her chin, then started to crawl over him, trying not to touch him any more than necessary. She had barely put her knee over, warily straddling him as a cat would a puddle of water, when he opened his eyes to grin at her. His gaze moved down her suspended body, then back to the heat of her burning cheeks.

'Good night, sweetheart,' he drawled with a knowing quirk of his lips.

Jocelyn growled as she dove over him, then quickly folded herself in her roll. Damn insufferable, egotistical male, she thought angrily. She settled with her back to him and worked hard to ignore the seductive heat of his body so close to hers.

Self-consciously she shifted farther away from him, but she did not want to get too close to the wall. Trevan was right about one thing, she thought, Charlie probably would be safer company than the enticing man beside her. His teasing, suggestive glances, and his touch, were already working their spell on her resistance. She then realized resistance was all she had left, Trevan Elliot had already stolen her heart long ago.

She groaned quietly at the long hours ahead that she would be lying beside him forcing herself not to think of how his every movement was an enticement to her eyes.

A seductive lure to her senses. Who was she trying to fool? she thought to herself. If sleep came to her tonight, he would be in her dreams touching her, tasting her as she longed for him to do. She shifted again as her thoughts continued to torture her.

It was going to be a long night.

He sat at the table and absently traced the tip of his finger down the stem of his wine glass. The remains of their dinner were still on the table and he reached over and plucked a slice of bread from the basket. Silently he pulled a section of the crust from the bread and ate it.

The bread was good and he enjoyed the subtle bite of garlic as he tilted his head to study the form lying before him on the floor. The woman was not like the others. She had not been chosen for the same purpose as the others. His gaze moved over the woman's body as a painter would study his canvas. Ellianna would need color, he thought to himself. She would not have been so drab, so unnoticeable if she had only learned to effectively use color to enhance herself.

He flicked the slice of garlic bread onto the dead woman's plate and wiped his hands together briskly to brush away the crumbs.

It was time.

CHAPTER 18

Jocelyn woke with a start. The unfamiliar surroundings confused her for a moment till she remembered they were in Trevan's cave. She glanced beside her, unconsciously whispering his name as she discovered with a twinge of fear that he was not next to her.

Raising her head, she looked toward the fire to see him down on one knee staring into the flames. He had removed his shirt; the light of the fire reflecting the gold highlights of the dark hair of his chest, the warm glow illuminating the defined ridges. She watched in fascination as he moved his arm to poke at the fire with a thick stick. His body was muscular, but not brawny. Every ridge, every definition of muscle was a seductive lure to her eyes.

It had been a long time since she had been interested in a man. It had been even longer since she had felt attracted to one. Trevan Elliot was as irritating as they came, but something within her heart was determined to give him a chance. She couldn't identify what it was, but it had been the reason she had allowed him in her home the night she found him sprawled in her trash. It had been the reason she had accompanied him to his sister's grave, when every shred of evidence had been against the story he had told her. It was the reason she now watched his softened expression as he looked into the flames and hoped she could understand the loneliness and sadness she saw reflected in his eyes.

Jocelyn lifted herself to her elbow, the movement causing Trevan to glance toward her. His gaze held hers as the fire haloed the outline of his body against the flames. She read the longing in his eyes, the uncertainty. The need.

Trevan was from a time when a man and a woman were married for life; till death did them part. He had talked of respecting and cherishing a woman. The unspoken love contained within a touch. His touch.

There would be no backing out with Trevan. No speedy quick fixes or a divorce. The responsibility overwhelmed Jocelyn, causing a moment of fear to well up within her. She knew without a doubt in her heart, if they took the next step, there would be no going back. Yet, even as the commitment caused her to hesitate, there was a sense of security in the idea. He would put up with her grouchiness and waspish temper he had already been witness to on several occasions . . .

'You are thinking too much,' he said, causing her to stop the mental tirade of excuses and attempts to convince herself.

She swallowed nervously as she met his gaze. 'Actually, I don't know what to think any more, Trevan. This is all so different for me.'

'I see.' He turned back to the fire, a small smile lifting the ends of his lips. 'You're scared of me.'

'Well, I wouldn't say scared . . . exactly, maybe leery, hesitant, confused.' She laughed softly as she shook her head. The sound caused him to turn back to her. 'Okay, maybe I am scared of you.'

'Why?'

She glanced at her fingers. How does a person explain being scared of forever? Or the more realistic possibility of being scared of the pain of a failed relationship?

He stood to face her, his jaw strong with a hint of a cleft on his chin. His shoulders were wide with the dark mat of his hair continuing to dip enticingly into the waist of his jeans. His stance was proud, as he was, she thought to herself, her gaze moving up his body to meet his eyes.

He studied her for a moment as if he could read her thoughts, then took a slow deep breath. His voice was low when he spoke to her. 'Neither one of us can see the future, Jocelyn. Perhaps that is for the best.'

She let her gaze move over his face, noting the honesty. Taking comfort in the strength. 'I thought you could.'

Trevan's eyebrows furrowed into a deep frown and he shook his head. 'I never said I could see the future, Jocelyn.'

'Didn't you?' she said softly as she shifted to sit up. She wrapped her arms around her legs and leaned her chin on her knees as she returned his gaze thoughtfully. 'Didn't you foresee the future when you predicted that the murderer would come after me?' She hesitated a moment, feeling an ounce of uncertainty. 'And now he is.'

'I never predicted that he would come, Jocelyn.' He returned her gaze for a moment, conflicting emotions warring in his eyes. 'I said I knew he would come.'

'That's what I don't understand. How?' she asked, raising her head. 'I know you've been keeping something from me.'

Trevan turned away from her, his gaze once again looking into the yellow depths of the fire. 'It's hard to explain. It all happened a very long time ago.'

'Then try, Trevan,' she said softly. 'I know that there had to be a logical reason why you knew he would come after me. I've heard it in your words. I've seen it in your eyes.'

His forearm rested against the wall above the fire, his face hidden in the shadows as he stared into the fire. For a long time he didn't speak, when he did his voice was low, almost a whisper. 'It wasn't too long after I . . . I came here that I knew my sister's killer had also been brought forward. As I pursued him, I learned to deal with the loss of everything I had ever had. There were so few reminders left to even provoke any of the painful memories for me. But that changed when I saw you. When I saw you standing there I knew he would not be able to resist taking you from me.'

'Me?' Jocelyn asked. She frowned as she tried to understand what he meant. Then she remembered the first time she had seen him. There had been the shocked look of surprise, then his lips had moved. Even though she had not been able to completely understand his words, at the time she thought he had said her name. 'What do you mean?'

'Your face. Your hair,' he answered, holding her gaze. 'Even your name.'

'What? Did I remind you of your favorite mule or something?' she joked nervously. She could read in his eyes that he was very serious. A sliver of fear worked its way into her thoughts and she began to wonder if she really wanted to know what he was about to tell her.

He shook his head, a hint of a smile lifting his lips. 'Even your sense of humor.' He shifted to pull an old photo from his shirt pocket. He moved to quietly hand it to her.

She took the tin-type in her hands. Her brows lifted in shocked surprise as she stared at the image of a woman. Her pose was similar to those she had found in the album from his trunk earlier, but it was the woman's face that caused her heart to beat faster. The face was the ghostly image of herself. 'Trevan, she looks just like me.'

He nodded slowly. His gaze never moved from hers as if he were trying to judge her reaction. 'Her name is . . . was Justine. We were very close at one time. I guess people these days would call it being "involved" with each other.'

'So that's why it looked like you said my name the first time I saw you.' Jocelyn felt a stab of jealousy as she studied the woman's features so like her own. For him she felt a moment of pain at the love he had lost. For herself, she wondered if the attraction between them was real. Or the illusion he wanted to recreate because she reminded him so much of the girl dead for so long.

'Were you engaged to be married?' she asked quietly.

He shrugged. 'We were never officially engaged, but, yes, I guess we were. Most everyone in the town expected us to, others couldn't wait to cause trouble between us. Just before I found Allysa's body, Maybella had caught me on the front porch and couldn't wait to tell me about Justine's other man. I never did learn if that was true or not.'

She bit her lip in a moment of indecision, then asked the question that burned within her. It may be a sadistic move, but she had to know. 'Did you love her?'

'I had strong feelings for her,' Trevan answered softly as he moved into the firelight. The soft glow illuminated his features and she could see the warmth in his eyes. 'Now I realize they were nothing compared to what I feel for you.'

Jocelyn's gaze flicked to meet his. Her heart beat faster at the depth of his words. For several moments they remained that way. Looking at each other. Within each other.

She slowly licked her lips as his eyes held hers. The nerves within her gradually melted. Out of the corner of her eye the image of the other woman caught her attention and she tore her gaze from him to look at the picture she held in her hand.

'Do you think I'm her . . . Justine's spirit reincarnated?'

Trevan moved to stand beside the ledge of their makeshift bed. He reached to her to smooth his thumb across her cheek as he smiled. She tilted her chin to look up at him. 'No. Justine was never as mouthy or opinionated as you are. You are beautiful and intelligent. The only woman I'm attracted to. The only kind I want to be attracted to.'

Jocelyn's lips opened in mixed protest to his contradictary words. The objection died on a slow breath as she noted the look of controlled passion in his eyes. She saw what he intended for her in his look. His desire. Her heart beat a wild tattoo as she held his gaze. Tonight she would make love to Trevan. She would give him anything and everything. Including her heart.

Trevan put his knee on the ledge and leaned over her to put a hand on each side of her. Slowly he lowered his mouth to hers and Jocelyn felt the heat of his desire burn from his kiss to ignite her own. He raised his lips from her and his eyes searched hers.

'I never knew how truly alone I was till I met you, Jocelyn Kendrick. Or how much I could need someone.' He stroked his hand over her hair. His voice was husky with emotion, his gaze showing the barest hint of fear. 'Now I know that all through time it could only be you for me.'

Jocelyn stroked her thumb across the day's growth of beard on his chin. 'Now you know why I'm so scared of you.'

His eyes wrinkled with humor, his low chuckle causing delicious vibrations to course through her. 'And here I thought it had something to do with the difference in our ages.'

'I don't know, for an old man . . . you seem to do all right.' She smiled as he softly muzzled her cheek.

He moved to gently nibble on her neck, 'I'll show you what an old man can do.'

She arched her throat against his lips, running her hands from his chest to encircle his neck. The light feathering of his lips on her skin caused her to groan softly. 'Then shut up and give me a demonstration.'

He drew back to meet her gaze, his face appearing serious except for the amused twinkle in his eyes. His words sounded almost sincere as he drawled, 'Yes ma'am. I do aim to please.'

Jocelyn started to laugh when his mouth covered hers in a hungry kiss, smothering her humor. He held his hand beneath her as he lowered her to their makeshift bed. Trevan laid himself beside her and tightened his embrace. Leaning on one arm, his hand moved from her hip to gently brush against her breast. With deft fingers, he started to unbutton her blouse, his lips following the creamy flesh of her skin in a hot trail.

Jocelyn forgot about the cave and searching for the answer that could stop a murderer. Her heart and her body pushed away thoughts of reason as they slowly began to help each other with their clothes.

Trevan brushed aside her collar so his lips could move to the swell of her breast. Jocelyn murmured in pleasure as his thumb moved lightly, delicately over her nipple till it hardened under his touch.

'I've wanted to make love to you for so long,' he said huskily against her skin.

Jocelyn ran her hands over his wide shoulders, then to the smooth silk of his hair. She framed his face with her hands and brought him up to her, then pressed her lips against his. Her need was endless as she deepened their kiss. Her silent resolve forgotten the moment he had touched her.

She shifted under him as he removed her shirt. Expertly he unsnapped her bra and for a very brief moment she wondered how he could have learned that skill, till his hands seduced her thoughts elsewhere.

Sensation after sensation washed over her as his hand moved lightly over her rib cage to the snap of her jeans. Trevan unbuttoned them, then slowly opened the zipper. She started to shift to help him remove them when his hand moved to her thigh by her knee and stilled her.

His fingers spread over her leg and he held her for a moment as he nibbled at the soft skin of her throat. Slowly his hand began a heated journey to her hip. He brushed his hand over her stomach, then dipped it into the opening of her jeans. His fingers cupped her warmth and moved in torturous circles over her. Her fingers dug into his shoulders as the pleasure speared through her at his touch and she turned her face into his neck.

Jocelyn's breath came in shaky gasps as Trevan finally moved to slip her jeans and underclothes from her. She reached for him and helped remove the last barrier of cloth between them, that of his own jeans.

He rejoined her and she felt the seductive touch of his warm flesh along the length of her. He moved his muscular thigh between hers as he leaned over her to kiss her with a longing born of pleasure. He cupped her breast in his callused hand, then moved to take the peak in his mouth.

Jocelyn arched against him as he lightly nipped at her, then ran the tip of his tongue over the crown. A soft throaty moan escaped from her as he took the other nipple delicately between his teeth, then suckled her with torturing leisure.

'Trevan, please.' Her words were a soft plea against the top of his hair as she moved under him.

She moved her hips against his leg in an enticing invitation. His face raised till he met her gaze and his hand moved over her stomach to silence her movements with his touch. He lowered his mouth to hers and kissed her softly, gently. His lips left hers to move over her cheek.

'Jocelyn, you are so beautiful,' he murmured, his voice thick with arousal.

She rubbed her thumbs over the smooth ridge of his collar bone, then reveled in the strength of his shoulders. She ran her palms over his back down to the narrowing of his waist, then to flat muscles of his lower stomach. Boldly she took him in her hands and stroked the silky flesh till Trevan groaned against her throat. In one quick move he was on top of her. His gaze held her mesmerized as he joined with her the heat of him causing Jocelyn to arch against him as he began to move with her. Her breasts brushed against the soft hairs of his chest and hardened.

Lover met lover as they moved slowly against each other, with each other, in a sensual rhythm. Slowly the tightening began deep within Jocelyn. Growing warmer, hotter, till it flared into a climactic haze. Her body tightened, then loosened again and again around the hot length of him.

She held him tightly as her lips tasted his skin. She lightly traced her tongue over his shoulder till he groaned. His arms braced on each side of her, his movements quickened, then subsided only for a moment as he shuddered within her, a slow moan escaping his lips.

Several moments passed and they remained joined. Trevan kissed her lovingly, then began to move his lips slowly and lazily over her face. He stroked, then held the tips of her hair in his hands as he nipped tiredly at her throat.

Slowly their breathing returned to normal as Trevan nuzzled her cheek with his lips. He moved beside her and pulled her back against him. The warmth of their bodies enveloped her and she closed her eyes, the tired smile still on her face as she started to drift off to sleep.

In that last moment before she slipped into her dreams, she thought she heard him softly whisper against her hair, 'I love you.'

Trevan woke her early the next morning. So early she watched the last of the sunrise from horseback while she rested her cheek tiredly against his shoulder. The only redeeming aspect of watching it was enjoying the feel of his body within her arms. She rode behind him in the saddle, shifting for a comfortable position on the horse's wide rump. After a while she became used to the lopsided gait of the back end.

When Trevan had first nuzzled her with his lips and the bristle of his beard, she had turned to him hoping for another 'demonstration'. He was all business today, however, as he had slapped her on the bottom and told her to get up. She had groaned irritably in frustration, then had rose to get dressed. It wasn't until later, when she was staring at the sunrise, that the foggy sound of his words came back to her from last night.

She drew her brows together in a frown, but for the life of her she couldn't remember if they had been real or the filmy edge of one of her dreams. Jocelyn rubbed her cheek against the warmth of his back and closed her eyes. She was rewarded with a tender squeeze of his hand on her arm and she smiled.

And she prayed the words had been real.

Millie was leaning against the fence as they ambled into the widow's yard. Her eyes moved over Jocelyn, then widened with a knowing grin. She took the saddle bag Trevan handed her and chuckled. 'Glad to see you both back, I got kind of worried when Roan came home by himself last night.' Millie turned to Jocelyn with a bawdy wink. 'Hope Charlie didn't scare you too bad.'

Jocelyn slid from the horse and arched her back to stretch the kinks from riding. 'No, but he does snore too much.'

The older woman laughed as she took the saddle bag into the house. Jocelyn chewed her lip, then turned to Trevan with narrowed eyes wanting an answer to yet another unanswered question. 'I thought you said no one knew about the cave?'

He removed the saddle from the horse, stopping to smile at her. 'Well, no one does know, except Millie, and now you.'

His way of reasoning could drive a person mad, she

thought. She put her hands on her hips as she followed him to the tack room. 'Remind me to explain to you what "no one" actually means. I believe some people would call it the fine art of communication.'

Putting the saddle away, he turned to her and kissed her lightly on the nose. 'No one that I do not trust knows. Is that better?'

'Slightly,' she conceded. She put her hands on his shoulders to stop him from moving past her. Boldly she covered his mouth with hers. Trevan did not hesitate, but moved his arms around her to hold her in a warm embrace. Jocelyn circled her arms around his neck and wove her hand through his hair. His hands moved to pull her hips against him and she moaned softly in pleasure to feel him harden against her.

'Why don't the two of you come on in here for some lunch,' Widow Barker called loudly as she strolled towards them.

Trevan chuckled, then brushed his lips lightly over Jocelyn's before he turned to Millie. 'I'm afraid we'll have to pass. We need to go see Mrs Cook as soon as we can.'

She frowned slightly. Jocelyn noticed that the response had thrown Millie off guard for a moment. 'Rachael? She's probably at the museum. You know how she is about that stuff, Trevan, always hovering over it like an old mother hen.'

Jocelyn tilted her head as she studied his reaction to what Millie said. If she didn't know better, she would swear he was nervous. She tried to imagine what would cause a grown man to be so uptight about seeing the old widow who ran the historical society.

His gaze flicked to Jocelyn before he turned back to Millie. 'Yes, I remember. I appreciate you letting me use the horses. Jocelyn and I will come back to visit as soon as we can.'

The old woman's eyes widened in disbelief, then her smile spread into an almost motherly joy. She grabbed Trevan in a tight hug, then held him before her. 'You do that.'

Before Jocelyn could prepare herself, Millie grabbed her in an enthusiastic embrace. When she pulled away, she gave her a suggestive wink. 'Told you he was stud, didn't I?'

Jocelyn met Trevan's embarrassed gaze and laughed. 'Well, I don't know about that, Millie. I thought that rattlesnake had his fine points too.'

It didn't take them very long to drive to the museum where Widow Cook worked. The town itself, as Trevan remembered it, no longer existed, but there was a small populated stretch along the highway that could almost pass for a community. It had a gas station with a combination convenience store and restaurant, a hardware/department store, and the Niola County Historical Museum.

Everything paradise needed, Jocelyn thought. Except a pizza joint.

The house was set a way from the road in scenic backdrop of trees complete with a barn full of ducks and chickens pecking around a small pond. Jocelyn spotted a woman's figure standing in the front yard and a sudden suspicion started working its way through her thoughts. She frowned as she leaned forward in the seat to note that the figure was that of a shapely young woman with beautiful waist length hair. The lady's hair swirled around her as she turned to see Trevan stepping from the truck.

Standing on the other side of his pick-up, the long haired nymph had not yet caught sight of Jocelyn. Her eyes, it seemed, were only for Trevan as she ran excitedly up to him and jumped into his arms with a delighted squeal, giving him an enthusiastic kiss on the lips.

Jocelyn felt her fingers curl into fists, then forced herself to calm the murderous urge that surged through her to take a large pair of scissors to the woman's hair or anything else for that matter. She didn't want to be accused of being jealous. Instead she moved behind Trevan to line herself up in the squeaking female's vision and loudly cleared her throat.

Trevan had the good sense to detach himself from the widow before he turned sheepishly to face Jocelyn.

Jocelyn smiled, hoping her urge to bare her teeth didn't show through. Not too much, anyway. 'Widow Cook, I presume?'

He nervously coughed into his hand, then moved beside Jocelyn to pat her arm. 'Rachael, I would like to introduce you to Jocelyn Kendrick.'

The merry widow eyed Jocelyn with a narrowed gaze, then lifted her chin as if coming to a silent conclusion. With more graciousness than Jocelyn felt, Rachael 'the widow' Cook extended her hand. 'I see. It is nice to meet you, Jocelyn. Trevan and I are . . . old acquaintances.'

Trevan removed his hat and ran a quick hand through his hair. He apparently wanted to change the subject as quickly as possible. It amused Jocelyn greatly and relieved a considerable amount of her nervousness to see him so edgy. 'Rachael, we came to see you about an old newspaper article. Would you have any copies of the old *Niola Journal* from, say 1878?'

She nodded, then gestured with her hand towards the house. 'At least I'm pretty sure we do, but we'll just go on into the house and take a quick look.'

Trevan started to put his hand on Jocelyn's elbow to escort her and gave her a nervous smile. She returned it with a saccharine twist of her lips then swept past him as regally as she could. She couldn't wait to have a little talk with him about the subtle art of communication. Or his exceptional lack thereof.

At a quizzical look from Rachael, Trevan held back. She studied him for a moment, then smiled at him. 'You're in love,' she said simply.

He chuckled as he shook his head and looked away from her for a moment. 'I don't think that's any of your business, Rachael.'

'You're right, it's not,' she said good-naturedly. 'But I'm still happy for you.'

'Thank you,' Trevan answered, feeling a little nervous to be discussing his new love with a former lover.

She laughed at his unease, then lowered her voice. 'You don't need to feel so nervous, Trevan. What we had was nice, maybe even special, but we were never really meant to be more than just friends. That's okay isn't it? To be just friends?'

She leaned forward a little to look into his eyes. Trevan laughed softly, realizing she was right. 'You are a good friend and thank you for making me realize it.'

'No problem,' she said with a smile. 'You better get in there before she comes back out here and gets mad at us.'

He started toward the house, then stopped to look back at her. 'How did you know?'

She shrugged easily as if the answer was very simple. 'You were never that nervous around me.' Her smile widened into a grin as she started to walk past him. 'Of course, there is that hickey on your neck.'

Trevan frowned as his hand automatically went to his neck. Rachael laughed at his gesture, then headed to the house. He rubbed his throat thoughtfully and wondered if she was joking with him.

The museum was a beautifully restored farm house with smooth oak flooring. The rooms were decorated as they would have been in the late 1800s, complete with mannequins in costumes. Jocelyn was impressed by the size of the civil war sword collections displayed under glass in the hallway and the length to which the museum had gone to display photographs of the everyday life of the people. Several signs acknowledged the generosity of the local families for donating the items displayed.

As they moved through the first level to climb the stairs, a picture caught Jocelyn's attention. She stopped and sucked in her breath as she studied the grainy image. It was the hard, direct gaze of the man's eyes that gave him away, she thought.

She read the caption under the picture in a quiet

whisper. 'The Elliot family at the grand opening of a doctor's office they furnished. They have not only used the influence of the Elliot name, but the family money as well to bring needed services to the community.'

Her gaze returned to the handsome man with an incredible curling mustache in the photograph. Quietly she turned to Trevan and found him watching her, his expression unreadable. His hair was shorter, the mustache not as elaborate, but there was no denying the same look in the eyes. The eyes of a hunter.

'The family resemblance is incredible, isn't it?' Rachael's voice stirred her from her thoughts.

'Yes.' Jocelyn blinked, then faced her, 'Yes, it is.'

The woman frowned for a moment as she studied her, then motioned them to follow her. 'I've always thought it was a great thing for a family to pass their heritage on, especially if they name their children after a relative who did so much for the community such as the Elliot family. I can honestly say the Elliots were a moving force in helping people keep their ranches out here. Without their help, a lot of families over the years would have been forced to sell and move away.'

'As you see, I'm named for my great grandfather,' Trevan supplied, his hand on Jocelyn's hip as they climbed the stairs.

Rachael flicked a brief glance over her shoulder. 'He was your great, great grandfather,' she corrected.

Jocelyn turned to give him a wry look. 'Isn't that just double great.'

He blew his breath out and muttered something she couldn't hear as they went up the narrow stairway.

They followed the widow as she moved around the staircase banister. They made their way down the hallway to a door at the end. Rachael removed a key from her pocket and inserted it into the hole under the glass door knob.

'This is where I keep the smaller stuff like old editions of the paper,' she said, holding the door open for them.

Jocelyn had thought the other stairway was narrow; this one could make a person feel positively claustrophobic as their tread echoed around them on the way to the top.

They emerged into the attic and she was surprised at how neatly organized it was. There was no denying that Rachael Cook was efficient and dedicated to the running of the museum. She led them to a dark corner and switched on a light. She asked Trevan for a helping hand and together they pulled a large flat drawer from a tall cabinet.

They moved the steel file to the surface of a table in the middle of the room. Rachael lifted the cover to expose neatly sealed pages of the old editions of the Niola paper.

'We have almost a complete set of the papers, thanks to old lady packrats, and efficient wives around here who lined their trunks with these,' Rachael said.

Jocelyn murmured her thanks and began to carefully turn through the brittle pages. 'We're looking for May of 1878.'

'Okay,' Rachael answered, moving next to her to help go through the pages. 'The paper, as you can tell, was put out weekly. Unless something really notable happened.'

Jocelyn was glad Rachael had decided to help look through the pages. The yellowed sheets of pages were sealed to protect them, but the delicate paper looked brittle. Breakable.

Jocelyn scanned for dates as the woman turned through the journals. They were nearing the end of April and she flipped the next page. The same headline she had read only the night before appeared before her, except now accompanying it was the grainy and badly reproduced picture of Allysa's dead body.

She leaned closer to study the old newspaper photo. Her heart began to thud heavily in her breast as her eyes moved over the picture. She felt Trevan lightly touch her elbow as he leaned beside her to look.

Details were lost in the fuzz of the printing process, but what she had hoped to find appeared in a distorted mass of white. There was no mistaking the broken features with gaping black sockets and a sardonic grin.

It was a porcelain mask.

He pulled the car to a stop in the darkened shadows of the street. Switching off the engine, he simply sat and studied the area around him. He was parked to the back of an apartment complex that was beginning to slide quietly into deterioration. He leaned slightly forward and scanned the parking lot. It was perfect, he thought, without a soul in sight.

Earlier that morning, it hadn't been like that.

Carefully he had wrapped Ellianna in an old blanket,

then placed her in a cardboard TV box. It had been awkward moving the heavy box down his back steps, then out to his driveway. It had been after two in the morning and the street was heavy with the silence of the night. He had approached his car with his load and contemplated how he was going to get the back passenger door open without having to lower the box. The unexpected sound of a voice behind him had shot fear through him, icy and hot. For the first time in a very long time, he had felt the sweat bead on his forehead.

'Let me help you with that, neighbor.'

He lowered the large box onto the back seat and slid it in. Slowly he turned and found his next door neighbor standing behind him. His unease diminished as he noted the old man's extreme state of intoxication.

The drunken neighbor had swayed unsteadily, then took another drink of the beer he held in his fingers. Rubbing a fat hand over his stubble of beard, he had given only a blurry glance at the box in the car.

'Good idea to move your stuff at night. That way your old lady can't get to it like mine did,' he had said, then tried to muffle a belch. The old man's flannel robe opened to show the yellow stained T-shirt he wore underneath it. 'When the old lady and I split the sheets, she took everything. The damn judge didn't care one way or another whether I even had a pot to piss in.'

Distractedly, the man had rubbed at his bulbous nose. 'Twenty-five years. Can you believe that? We'd been married twenty-five years and she just up and left one day. Said she needed to grow. Hell, I thought she was grown when I married her.'

The killer's hard stare eased as the man just turned without another word and started to walk away. The old man shuffled toward his yard, then stopped at the front porch and raised his beer in a solemn salute. 'Good luck to ya.'

He chuckled to himself as he wondered what his drunken neighbor would have thought had he known what was in the box. Or more accurately who.

He scanned the area around the apartment complex one last time and when he saw no one, he opened the car door and got out. He moved around the car and opened the passenger door. Sliding the box to the edge of the seat, he gripped the top and quickly tore the side panel away. There would be no need to carry the cumbersome load in the box, now that he was so close to the trees surrounding the golf course.

It took him almost fifteen minutes to carry her across the rolling greens of the golf course, but the task was made significantly easier by the silvery light of the full moon washing over them. He trudged ahead with his load as the sweat rolled freely down the sides of his face.

His eyes focused on the spot that he knew would be perfect for Ellianna. He moved through the slight opening between two bushes to the tiny moonlit clearing of a stand of trees. The brittle, brown fall foliage of the trees provided a fragile carpet under his feet as he stepped to the center of the clearing.

The killer lowered the body to the ground, letting her head rest against his bent knee. He unwrapped the blanket from around her cooling body and studied the woman's face. Smiling softly as his gaze moved over her still features, he thought of the dreams the woman had hoped to fulfil. Really, he had done her a favor, he thought to himself. Ellianna Vernon would never have had the will, the determination, to achieve those dreams. She would have spent the rest of her uneventful little life wishing for what she never would have reached out to obtain. At least this way she would always be remembered.

She would always be beautiful.

Slowly he raised his hand to her face and closed her eyelids. He shifted her body over to the bed of leaves and slid the blanket from under her. He straightened the dead woman's legs, the dry crunching of the leaves the only noise in the quiet of the night. He folded her arms over her breasts, then moved his gaze over her. Smoothing a strand of her blonde hair from her face, he decided he was pleased with the arrangement.

As he knelt beside the body, the killer pulled the white roses from his pocket. He lifted the pale flowers to his nose and inhaled the lingering scent as he looked to the vivid blue of the night sky.

In the dark blanket of the stars, an image of the woman, Jocelyn, appeared silently into his thoughts and he smiled. She was beautiful, as beautiful as Allysa had been, he remembered warmly.

Then like a ruthless intruder, the man Elliot invaded his thoughts and the killer's lips thinned into a grim thin line of distaste and anger. Damn Elliot, he fumed silently, the woman was his. He needed her. He would have her.

The killer forced himself to take a deep breath to calm

312

the fury building within him as he realized his hands were clenched into fists. Slowly he opened his fingers and looked at the crushed pale petals of the roses he held. The velvet texture of the delicate blossoms were now bruised and torn. Again, he blamed Elliot. Carefully he arranged them in the woman's hair, then stood over her.

The Porcelain Mask Murderer looked down at the body of Ellianna Vernon. Her corpse was softly veiled in the moonlight and he wondered how long it would take them to find her.

CHAPTER 19

Trevan's gaze moved from the old reproduction to Jocelyn. His voice was husky with emotion. 'You were right. I can't believe I didn't re – '

Rachael eyed the two of them curiously. 'Did this help with what you were looking for?'

'Yes, it does very much,' Jocelyn answered distractedly. She studied Trevan for a moment, hoping that this was not too painful for him. Slowly she turned back to the newspaper article. 'Listen to this: on the same note, it has been discovered that the before mentioned brother, Mr Elliot . . .' She gave Trevan a meaningful glance, hoping to dispel some of his sorrow with humor. 'That would be your double great grandpa.' She turned back to the paper to finish reading. '. . . has disappeared. He was apparently trailing the murderer, who, some speculate, to be the gentleman who had been courting the young Allysa's attention as of late.'

'The article is written by Lisa Brown.' Rachael pointed to the byline and shook her head. 'According to the diaries of some of the townsfolk, and from what I gather from most of the articles I've read by her, she

314

was a notorious gossip. Lisa Brown would not hesitate to speculate on anything and everything. Even if she didn't know what the hell she was talking about.'

'Especially if she didn't know what the hell she was talking about,' Trevan muttered. He remembered all too well the irritating woman.

Rachael chuckled good-naturedly. 'Isn't that the truth. Lisa Brown gave "yellow journalism" and the gutter press a whole new emphasis.'

Jocelyn wasn't feeling very comfortable with their camaraderie, but she reminded herself that Trevan hadn't been a virgin, before they made love. Neither had she for that matter. She could not have realistically expected him to have never had a relationship with another woman. Hell, he was almost a hundred and fifty years old; he could take care of himself. She just wished the widow had been ugly, or at least suffering from an acute lack of muscle tone in the area of her bottom.

Jocelyn took a deep breath as she wondered where the green-eyed monster had come from; it had never bothered her before. But she had never felt so . . . in love with a man before either. The thought scared her, even as the memories of their lovemaking last night brushed over her. The images caused her stomach to tighten with desire as deliciously as if Trevan had touched her himself. She shook her head and quickly pulled herself back into the conversation. 'So we don't know who the boyfriend would have been? Could he have been mentioned in other articles or in letters?'

'No, old Lisa was meticulous about only treading slightly into the gray area of libel and not into the

315

black,' Rachael shrugged as she crossed her arms. 'As to letters or articles, many of the townsfolk would gossip, but few were willing to talk badly about the Elliots. They were self-made and always worked hard to help the community. Not to mention that Allysa Elliot was a young and beautiful woman. She was seen with a lot of men, but none she was serious about or so it seemed. From what I've found, she was just a nice girl enjoying life. I have found nothing in my research of personal correspondence that has helped me find the name of the man. There is nothing in any of the community records I have seen to even give me a clue.'

'Such as the man's occupation or lifestyle?' Jocelyn questioned, frowning when the woman shook her head. She put her hands on her hips as she studied the reproduction in the journal and was frustrated by the lack of detail. She turned back to their host. 'Obviously we know they took a picture. Where would the original be?'

Out of the corner of her eye she noticed Trevan's expression became distant as he looked at the publication photo. 'Sheriff Jarboe's son, Jacob, worked occasionally as the newspaper's photographer. It would have either stayed with him or the sheriff.' He glanced up as if he suddenly realized what he had said. 'Or so I have heard from Millie.'

Jocelyn tried to swallow her smile. 'Probably the sheriff. It would have been evidence, after all, of the original condition of the crime scene.'

She looked at Rachael, glad to see the woman's expression had not altered at Trevan's slip. The young widow only continued to look at the yellowed newspaper and nodded at his statement. 'Trevan's right. If anyone would know, Millie would. She's helped me a lot with the maintenance of this place and her grandmama used to work at the mortuary.'

Jocelyn frowned at her statement and Trevan explained. 'The funeral home was the Jarboe family's main occupation.'

'Sheriff, newspaper photographer, and mortician, what a resourceful kind of guy,' she said, chuckling softly.

'He was probably considered the town's most eligible bachelor,' Rachael laughed. 'But, if you think about it, the positions are all sort of inter-related.'

'Do you have the sheriff's records?' Trevan turned to ask her.

'I think I do,' she said, walking to the other side of the attic. She motioned with her hand for Trevan to follow her. 'Help me move these boxes over here and we'll take a look.'

Jocelyn couldn't help scrutinizing the widow's rear again as the woman bent over to read the labels on the boxes. She only wished she looked half as good, she thought to herself, rubbing her hands down her thighs nervously. Of course the widow probably walked to work every day; or, like Jocelyn's grandpa always used to say, six miles in the driving wind, uphill both ways.

'Fowler, James, and here we have Jarboe.' Rachael handed boxes to Trevan for him to set aside till she got to the sheriff's box. Lifting it, she moved back to the table. When she removed the lid, her eyebrows rose at the small number of documents in the box. 'As you can tell, murder wasn't exactly a nightly occurrence back then. Or I should clarify that and say a lot of times if a couple of cowpokes got in a gunfight and one was killed, it wasn't considered too notable. However, Allysa Elliot's murder was. As you can tell by the legend of the Niola Theater.'

She lifted the folder from the box and opened it on the table for them to look at. 'Especially considering the murderer was never found and her brother disappeared.' Rachael pointed to Trevan for him to take the other end of the flat file so they could replace it. 'Some people even speculated, quietly of course, that your great-great-grandpa might have done it.'

Trevan closed the flat drawer with a slam. 'That is ridiculous.'

'I agree,' Rachael said as she wiped her hands on her jeans. 'They said the girl may have done something to embarrass the family in some way. The way I see it, from everything I've researched, the Elliots were too devoted to each other. If anything, the other Trevan would have stood by his sister no matter what the scandal might be.'

Jocelyn met his gaze, wishing she could smooth away the anger and sadness in his eyes. 'Rachael's right,' she said quietly, letting him know with her expression that she believed in him. In fact, there had never been a doubt, as far as she was concerned, that he was not involved.

A phone rang loudly from somewhere downstairs and Rachael moved quickly to the stairway. 'If you'll excuse me, I'm expecting an important delivery and they always seem to mess up the directions.'

When Rachael left, Jocelyn moved to Trevan and did what she had been wanting to do. She smoothed her thumb across his cheek to the lines at the corner of his eyes. 'I know it's hard to hear, but it was only speculation. Allysa was very lucky to have a brother like you.'

Gently she cupped his face with both hands and pulled him to her kiss. She slowly stroked her tongue across the firm ridge of his lips, then sighed when he opened himself to her. His hands pulled her against him and she felt him take his comfort as he tightened his arms around her. Her palms moved up his chest to encircle his neck, her hands finding the short silk of his hair.

Trevan's lips were exquisitely gentle. He held her tightly, his touch more in want of solace than the hungry need of passion. He pulled back from her, then buried his face in her hair as he took a slow steadying breath.

'You make a man feel good, Jocelyn.' His voice was muffled. 'Thank you.'

Jocelyn turned to him to claim another quick kiss. 'We'll talk about how you can repay me later. Now let's get back to work.'

She turned back to the file spread before them and began to look through the papers. 'Here's the autopsy report, well, at least as much as they could decipher back then.' She skimmed down the page, 'They came to the conclusion that she died of a severe blow to the head.'

'And here's the picture.' Trevan's voice was husky with a tremor of emotion.

Jocelyn met his gaze and found that the hard, direct look was back. It saddened her, but she knew that was what he would need to go through these items.

Her attention returned to the picture. The original was definitely more detailed, as Jocelyn had hoped it would be.

Trevan dropped the picture to the surface of the table, his words quiet with a tight thread of tension pulled through, them. 'This was taken after I found her, so her . . . body had been moved. But I would say it is similar to the murders committed since then. Those in this time.'

Jocelyn took his hand in hers and gave it a gentle squeeze of reassurance. 'Now we know he is trying to recreate the original scene. But this doesn't look right to me either.'

'How?' he asked quietly as he held her gaze.

She took a deep breath, then turned to study the picture, trying to pinpoint what caused the feeling for her. Her mind began to pick out observations and sensations from the crime scene. The print of the rug was bold in the frame of the picture. The mask broken in two, but the pieces were aligned evenly without touching. The autopsy report had stated Allysa had died from a blow to the head, but where was the blood Trevan had mentioned? Even her hair and her dress were neatly ordered. Everything was too groomed, too clearly organized. Jocelyn couldn't say why, but she felt that the killing had been done accidentally, maybe in heated moment of a passionate argument. But then the murderer had taken the time to tidy things up, suggesting to her that he had done so as part of his remorse. As part of his affection for the dead girl.

'He arranged her too,' Jocelyn murmured. 'Look, Trevan, it's like he's trying to create an effect. Her hair, her dress, the mask. Everything is arranged. I'm not positive about the dress. I mean the only long dress I've ever worn was to my junior and senior proms. At my junior prom, I fell and my dress billowed everywhere but where it should have.'

Trevan frowned and she pointed to the girl's feet in the picture. 'Allysa's dress is neatly tucked around her. Almost modestly.'

'Exactly,' she said.

His gaze moved over the grainy black and white image. 'I didn't move anything except her head, so her dress is pretty much as it was.'

'The answer is in this picture.' He continued, picking up the old photograph. Jocelyn felt a chill move through her at his cold expression. 'I only wish we could see it. Then I would find that animal . . . before he strikes again.'

They heard Rachael come up the stairs. She smiled as her head appeared over the stair railing. 'Sorry about that. You would think as often as I get deliveries here, they would remember the directions to this place. It's not like this town is a sprawling metropolis.'

She joined them at the table and looked at the picture. She noticed their tense silence, and took the picture from Trevan to look at it more closely. Rachael's gaze

321

moved over the image and her mouth turned down in a frown. 'There is no dignity in death.'

'It happened a long time ago,' Trevan said gruffly.

Rachael turned to him, her gaze holding a hint of anger. 'Just because it happened over a hundred years ago, doesn't make it any less significant, Trevan. The girl was murdered, her killer never found, and her brother lost. Allysa Elliot deserves justice just as much as you or I.'

Jocelyn's eyes widened in amazement at Rachael's passionate words. She had sorely misjudged the Widow Cook. To them, Allysa's murder was as recent as Carrie Carter's, and the other victims, but to Rachael Cook the girl's death even a hundred years earlier affected her as strongly as it did them.

Trevan looked at Rachael. His gaze was not angry, but tense. 'I am fully aware of that.'

He turned and went to the staircase. The two women looked at each other as his departure echoed down the steps.

Rachael turned to Jocelyn. 'He's truly involved with this, isn't he?'

Jocelyn looked at the woman for a moment. 'Yes, he is. Learning about his . . . his family's history has been quite eventful for him.'

Rachael pursed her lips. 'I guess it would affect some people more deeply than it would others. Trevan has always been a very sensitive man.' As if realizing suddenly what she had just said, and the intimacy it implied, Rachael sputtered for a moment. 'What I meant was – '

Jocelyn chuckled. It became clear to her that it would be impossible to not like Rachael Cook. Her unease slipped away as she patted the woman's hand reassuringly. 'I know exactly what you mean, and you are right. I feel I need to be honest with you, Rachael. When I first met you and realized that you and Trevan had shared . . . well, had shared a relationship together, I was jealous. I can see now, however, that you are friends and I would like to start over.'

Rachael grinned and extended her hand. 'That makes two of us.'

Jocelyn took her hand and shook it. 'I can't tell you how much I appreciate you letting us look through your archives.'

'That's what they're here for,' she said. The woman studied Jocelyn briefly, then spoke slowly, as if choosing her words carefully. 'I can see why he loves you now. I hope you can help him realize that the past is not nearly as important as the future.'

Jocelyn nodded. If only the woman had an idea of how right her words were. Trevan would have to deal with his past, in his own way. She glanced back to the photo. They would have to resolve the past if there was to be any hope for their future. 'Rachael, would it be possible for me to borrow this photograph for a while?'

Trevan thanked Rachael Cook for her help. They had started to walk out of the house when the picture of Trevan, his brother and sister caught Jocelyn's eye once again.

She didn't know when, but she had grown accustomed to the thought of him being brought forward in time. At first it had seemed ludicrous, like maybe he had been thrown from the old bull one too many times. Yet, it hadn't been too long ago, Trevan's time in fact, that people had never even considered the idea of walking on the moon or a contraption like the space shuttle being able to orbit the outer atmosphere. Even though she had come to accept the notion of time-travel, a small part of her had wanted evidence. Cold, hard, can't deny it, in-your-face evidence.

And there it hung on the wall in front of her.

Trevan Elliot with his impressive handle bar mustache standing in a portrait for a local opening with the woman she now recognized as Justine. The picture had reminded her of the prop photos of the old west where one could pay five dollars and put on a costume. Except the clothes he had been wearing were not a costume.

As they got into the truck, she thought of how everything had changed since his time. Food, clothes, medicine, civil rights, transportation; she couldn't even imagine not having cable TV.

Jocelyn felt the goose bumps rise on her arms as she was overwhelmed with all Trevan had been forced to learn and become accustomed to. She glanced at him out of the corner of her eye and traced the ridge of his handsome face with her gaze.

She respected his accomplishments and his determination. She admired his adaptability and intelligence. She loved his fierce loyalty and pride.

She loved him.

Jocelyn took a deep breath and immediately felt the

tight band of fear as it wrapped around her chest. She concentrated on schooling her breathing to keep herself from hyperventilating as she closed her eyes and rested her head against the back of the truck seat. It had been a lot easier to accept the idea last night with his hands brushing over her, touching her. It had been only them then, the cave a haven from the harsh reality that awaited them.

She had finally done it. Jocelyn Kendrick had admitted she was in love. It had been only to herself, but that had to count for something. Didn't it? She would have to work up to saying the words out loud to him.

She felt Trevan's warm hand on her knee. 'Are you all right?'

She opened her eyes and playfully slapped his hand away. 'I'm fine.'

'You don't look fine,' he said, as his gaze moved worriedly over her, then back to the road ahead. 'Do we need to stop to get you something?'

'No.' She didn't feel fine either, she thought. In fact she felt sick, but wasn't about to explain that to the 'stud' as Widow Barker had referred to him. She studied him for a moment, remembering how nervous he had been with Rachael Cook as he introduced her to Jocelyn.

She swallowed her smile, working to keep her voice even. 'So just how old is your acquaintance with the delightful widow?'

Trevan didn't hesitate. 'I've known Millie ever since I've been here.'

He didn't want to rise to the bait, that was okay, she

thought. She could push it a little closer. 'I meant the merry Widow Cook.'

He took a deep breath, then flicked his glance to his door. Jocelyn wondered if, for a moment, he thought of jumping from the truck while it was moving. 'Rachael and I were close friends for a brief time.'

'Friends, huh?' Jocelyn smiled, then cleared her throat to mask it. 'She seemed quite excited to see you for being "only" a friend.'

'I won't deny we had a relationship, but that was a long time . . .' Trevan looked to her to find her grinning mischievously at his nervous state. He laughed and pointed a warning finger at her. 'You really are a sadist, you know that.'

'Rachael and I had a nice talk, Trevan, and I can understand why she is your friend. Besides she is an attractive woman.' Jocelyn chuckled good-naturedly. The nausea she had been feeling was gone as was the panic that had threatened to overwhelm her. 'Besides it's nice to know that even an old cowboy like you can be flustered now and then.'

Trevan removed his hat to set it on the seat, then ran his hand through his wavy hair. 'No, the definition of flustered is waking to find an Apache brave standing over you.'

She frowned, her history wasn't the best in the world, but she was sure the Indians had already been torn from their lands by the 1870s. 'I am embarrassed to admit it, but I'm not that familiar with Native American History. Weren't the majority of the Indians forced onto reservations?'

He nodded, his lip thinning to a grim line. 'As you said, the majority, but not all of them. I never could condone people, especially the government, stealing land from the rightful owner.'

'So what did the brave do?' she asked.

'Nothing. We watched each other for a while, then I offered him some coffee,' Trevan shrugged, then his expression became distant. 'Now I know how he felt. His way of life was gone and he was simply trying to adjust. To survive.'

Jocelyn said nothing. There were no words she could say to tell him she understood how he felt. The honest truth was she couldn't. Might never be able to. She was living in the time she was born in. She had grown up with her world and was no longer awed by its inventions.

Yet Trevan hadn't been born in this time and he had adapted very well. His survival abilities had given him advantages over the law of this century. In his time, the officers had followed the tracks left by the criminal's horse, the breaking of a twig as the animal moved by, and people had lived by their own gut instinct. Trevan's instinct had helped him to survive in the late 1800s and now in the 1990s.

There was one other with the same skills as Trevan and even now he was hunting another woman. The Porcelain Mask Murderer. And now he was after her.

Trevan trailed a murderer. The murderer hunted women, seeking to obtain the power of the kill. The vicious race had to end sometime. But how, Jocelyn wondered. And who would be the victor?

She pulled the photograph from the dash and began to study it once again. Allysa Elliot was very much like her brother. They both had the same unwavering gaze. Jocelyn studied the dull eyes of the dead girl. The dark photo seemed to emphasize the beseeching look. It was only a feeling, a sensation, that Allysa was trying to tell them the answer. Even in death.

Jocelyn's head began to pound and she pinched the bridge of her nose between her fingers to drive away the pressure. They were close. So very close to finding the answer. She again studied the picture, systematically considering every item.

Trying to decipher the message of the mask.

CHAPTER 20

The shadows from the late afternoon sun were beginning to stretch across the front of Jocelyn's yard as they pulled into the driveway. A radio news bulletin had said the county was under a severe thunderstorm watch, which seemed impossible considering the unseasonable warmth of the fall day. Tornado Alley, as Kansas was sometimes known, usually dealt with the deadly storms in early spring. Yet, everyone knew they could hit at any time of the year, if the conditions were right. This helped start an old saying in Kansas, 'If you don't like the weather, wait five minutes.'

Jocelyn heard the persistent ringing of her phone when she opened the truck door. Running to the porch, she hurriedly unlocked the front door.

Throwing it open, she muttered an oath as she practically tripped over the coffee table to get to the phone. She answered it, working around the shortness of breath from her little sprint.

'Where the hell have you been?' John Cartland yelled into the receiver. She could tell by the tinny sound he was talking on the department's cellular. 'I've been trying to get hold of you for over an hour.'

'Gee, John. Here I thought you missed me,' she said. 'Trevan and I were checking some stuff out. What's going on?'

'Well, you can come do some of your research here then,' he said gruffly. 'He's done another one.'

'Oh, no,' Jocelyn gasped. There was no need to identify who 'he' was or what he had done. She looked up to find Trevan watching her with the hard look of his determination.

'Give me the address, John.' She snatched a notepad from the end table and scribbled the directions down. 'We'll be there in fifteen minutes.'

Jocelyn replaced the receiver and turned to face Trevan.

'Where at?' he asked, his stance tense. Ready to move.

'On the golf course at the campus,' she answered, moving with him to the door.

The drive would normally have taken fifteen minutes, if one drove the speed limit and obeyed all the laws. Trevan made it in ten.

They parked in the university parking lot and jogged across a circular campus drive to the green of the golf course. Their destination was easily marked by the gathering crowd of people and the media across the green of the course. Police officers were holding the crowd back from the scene in the trees.

Jocelyn moved to one of the officers and explained who she was. 'Detective Cartland sent for me.'

'Yes, ma'am. Believe me, we all heard,' the handsome black man said. He leaned closer and lowered his voice. 'He's not exactly quiet.'

She nodded in agreement, giving the man a brief smile. 'Tell me about it.'

'Kendrick, get your butt over here.' John Cartland yelled from the edge of the tiny grove of trees.

Jocelyn and Trevan covered the short distance to John. He was red in the face and she wasn't sure whether it was from exertion or the result of the anger that was evident in his scowl. 'A couple of early bird golfers found her when one of them sliced into these trees. She's on the fifteenth hole, so it took a while for them to stumble across her.'

Following the detective, they stepped over the second barrier in front of the bushes to the location of the body. The corpse of the woman lay nestled in a bed of fall leaves. The vivid autumn colors provided a vibrant border to the drab clothes of her body. Jocelyn frowned as she studied the victim. The dead woman was lying on her back, hands folded across the chest. A definite change in pattern.

John shook his head and muttered a few choice oaths. 'I tell you he's messing with us. If this guy wants to play games, I could dream up a few for him.'

'Like Russian roulette,' Trevan said, grimly.

He stood with his arms crossed across his chest and a very intense, cold look. Jocelyn shivered at the complete lack of warmth in his eyes. Although she personally did not fear him, she knew what would happen to the man responsible for this death if Trevan found him. Turning back to the body, she questioned whether she would stop him. Or help.

John grunted at Trevan's suggestion. 'Yeah, for

starters. Forensics is going over the area while we wait for Bill to show up. We figure she's been dead at least twenty-four hours.'

Jocelyn carefully knelt beside the dead woman and tried not to breathe too deeply. The corpse had begun to smell like a slab of beef left outside for too long. She gingerly touched the victim's exposed arm, shivering at the coldness of the woman's skin, the texture of it dry and pasty. The drab blonde, straight hair of the victim clung to her pale face. The color of the corpse's skin was starting to turn to a greenish red around the cheeks and neck. At the moment, Jocelyn had only a faint idea of what the victim might have looked like, the woman's features had become swollen and distorted in death from exposure. Yet, the face of the corpse still held a ghostly reflection of the mask-like effect of the poison.

Jocelyn's stomach tightened with a sickening lurch causing her to stand abruptly. She avoided Trevan's eyes, not wanting to see his protective expression. It wasn't that she was 'sick,' but sick of seeing innocent women murdered by this sadistic crazy man, only because he was trying to recreate a thrill.

That much she was more than sure of by now. The madman was trying to obtain the delusion of power he had experienced with Allysa and it didn't matter how many women he had to use to achieve it.

Glancing toward the body again, she focused past the physical remains before her. The woman was not positioned as the others and one item was conspicuous by its absence. There was a message here. A message for her and Trevan.

She knew because there was no porcelain mask by the body.

'Do we know her name?' she asked, her voice tight with regret and anger.

John flipped open his pocket notepad and flipped through the pages. 'Ellianna Vernon, age thirty-four, married, with two kids. That's her husband over there,' he said, pointing to a distraught man standing with two officers.

Her gaze flicked over the man. He was balding slightly and dressed conservatively in neutral colors. She shook her head as she compared the similarities of the husband to his dead wife. For him, it would be as if he had lost all sense of his security by losing her.

'Married,' she repeated, watching the man cover his face with a white handkerchief. 'He's never done a married one before.'

John's gaze too was on the husband. 'I know and he's never stuck in one area so long.'

The officer that she had talked with before, jogged over to them. 'Detective Cartland, one of the guys may have found something.'

'Thanks,' he said, then waved to the body with his hand. 'Put your mind to that, Jocelyn. Tell me if all that money you've been spending on psychoanalysis can come up with anything.'

She felt the heat of Trevan behind her as he put his hands on her shoulders, his voice a cold statement against her ear. 'It tells me he won't stop until he's dead.'

Jocelyn rubbed her face with her hands, trying to wipe away her feelings of frustration. 'I'd be more than willing to suggest a few options to help him achieve that.'

She did as John had asked and began to look the corpse over, point by point. She started with the woman's hair and stopped. There seemed to be something in the stringy, mouse-blonde strands. She frowned and knelt beside the body to touch the item.

'Look, Trevan, she has flowers in her hair, petals actually. I didn't notice them before, because it looks like they've shriveled and lost their color.'

He moved beside her, 'He's never done that before.'

'Why start now?' she asked, meeting his gaze.

John's booming voice interrupted her thoughts as he lumbered towards them. 'This maniac is sick. He even left her a love note.'

'Where did your men find it?' Trevan asked.

'In her bag. A dog probably pulled it under a bush on the other side of this tree. Her money, what little there was, was still in her purse.'

He turned the paper so they could read, holding the edge with his rubber-gloved fingertips. Jocelyn read the words aloud:

'Now hate rules a heart which in love's easy chains
Once passion's tumultuous blandishments
Despair now inflames the dark tide of his veins;
He ponders in frenzy on love's last adieu.'

'I've never seen anything like this,' John stated brusquely. 'The guy's crazy and he likes playing mind games, which leaves us completely in the dark trying to figure this one out. Which reminds me, does your psychoanalysis come up with anything on her?' The way he emphasized 'psychoanalysis' told her exactly what his red-necked opinion of it was.

'Nothing screams at me, if that's what you mean,' she replied, giving him a dark look. 'I'll have to go over it again.'

Out of the corner of her eye, the victim's husband caught her attention. He was no longer weeping over the heart wrenching loss of his wife, but had moved on to quiet shock. Or the blurry buffer of denial. He leaned against a patrol car, dry eyed, staring sadly.

Jocelyn pressed her lips together and breathed deeply, then nodded toward the man. 'Have you talked to the husband?'

John was gripping his forehead with his hands as if trying to alleviate a headache. She could sympathize, hers was pounding too. 'We tried to, but he's understandably upset by the whole deal. He kept saying his wife would never do something like this. I don't know what the hell he is talking about and I don't think he does either.'

'Who's the lady with him?' Jocelyn motioned with her chin. The tall woman was pretty, dressed in vibrant colors with her hair fashionably styled. A complete opposite of the conservative couple's drab, unnoticeable attire.

'The victim's friend. We haven't talked to her yet.'

Jocelyn studied the woman, noting the tears welled in her eyes and the worry in her expression. 'Maybe now would be a good time, and I think we need to start with the friend of the victim.'

Trevan muttered under his breath so that only she could hear as they walked to the car. 'When is something like this ever a good time?'

John touched the woman's elbow gently, his words soft and respectful of the grief shared between the pair huddled together. 'Mrs Meade, may we speak to you please?'

'Of course,' she sniffed. She then grasped the thin man's hand and gave it a reassuring squeeze. 'Carl, I'll be back in a few moments.'

He shrugged and blew his nose heartily into the handkerchief. 'Thanks, Mary. I'm okay, really.' He turned to them as if trying to offer an explanation, or maybe ask for advice. 'I don't know how to explain this to the kids. To find out she was murdered and then . . . that she might have been having an affair.'

The brightly dressed woman patted him awkwardly on the arm. 'Now, Carl, we don't know that.'

He met her gaze with a tight lipped frown, 'I heard the officers talking, Mary. They said they thought she may have been seeing this guy.'

John quickly ran his hand through his hair. His expression was consoling, but the anger of his eyes warned Jocelyn that he planned to chew out a few of those tactless officers before all of this was over. 'I assure you, Mr Vernon, that was only one person's speculation. We do not have any evidence to support that theory.'

The man looked hopeful, 'Are you sure? Elli was so responsible. I just can't imagine she would have done something like that.'

John quietly reassured the man as did the victim's friend, leaving the husband in slightly better spirits when they moved away.

Mrs Meade glanced anxiously back at the husband, then turned to them with a reluctant expression. 'There may have been a possibility of her having an affair. I didn't want to say anything in front of Carl. He is already taking this very hard,' she offered quietly.

John nodded. 'I understand, Mrs Meade. I'm sorry I can't promise to keep any of this quiet.'

'I know,' she took a deep breath, then glanced at Jocelyn and Trevan. She studied them for a moment. 'Ellianna was going through a very hard time emotionally,' she said finally.

John removed a pen from his pocket to take notes. 'Marital problems?'

'No, they had a pretty solid relationship,' she answered nervously. Her hands shook and she wrung one then the other as if trying to figure out what to do with her hands. She finally hugged her arms around her. 'I guess that could have been the problem, if you can understand that. Elli had talked of the predictability of their marriage and the routine of their everyday lives. I didn't find that hard to believe. After all, they had been married for over sixteen years.'

Jocelyn watched the woman's face and recognized her reluctance to talk about her friend. Especially now that the friend was dead. 'Was she feeling anxious about anything?'

'Yes, her birthday is next month, and she had been doing a lot of self-assessment lately.' Mrs Meade chewed at her lip for a moment, pain filling her eyes. 'And I don't think she liked what she was coming up with. Which was not much of anything. I didn't know what to say to help her. I remember hating myself for thinking it was true.'

Jocelyn stepped closer to the tall woman, hoping to give her a sense of comfort and closeness. 'So do you think she was feeling that her life lacked . . . something?'

A tear fell silently down Mary Meade's cheek. Her lips quivered and she fought to control the grief threatening to overwhelm her. She ran her two heavily jeweled hands through her hair, then started to dig through her bag as she sniffed noisily.

Trevan handed her his handkerchief and gave her a gentle smile. She returned his look for a few moments, as if she took comfort from the understanding in his eyes. The understanding of one who also had a loved one murdered. She graciously thanked him and held the cloth to her nose.

'This is so hard to say,' Mary started, her voice thick with emotion, 'but Elli was not what you would call . . . spectacular.' She glanced to each of them, then continued, her words running swiftly into each other. 'She could have been, maybe, if she had tried something different with her hair color and the style. But she was basically a timid mouse on the outside with a Loni Anderson inside, wanting like crazy to bust out.' She paused to laugh at the thought, warm humor filling her expression as if recalling a good memory. Her eyes began to sadden and Jocelyn could see the mental images being replaced with others. Images that were hard to face, or acknowledge in a close friend. 'I think . . . I think it was hard for her to balance the conflict between the two and . . .'

The woman's words trailed off. Jocelyn gave her the space she needed to work through her grief. After a moment, she quietly interrupted the woman's thoughts. 'Please forgive me for asking, but do you feel Ellianna may have been . . . looking for something to, perhaps, help balance the two?'

'Yes,' she answered quickly, quietly. Mary Meade stole a glance at Carl Vernon then turned back to them. 'The only reason I think that, is a comment she made not too long ago. Elli had finished reading a particularly good romance novel I had given her. She said she wished a white knight in shining armor would sweep her away. Literally.'

She began to rhythmically twine the handkerchief Trevan had given her between her fingers as she paused. 'At the time I didn't think much about it and teased her. I asked her what about Carl and the kids and she laughed and said she really wasn't worried. She said she doubted there were any white knights any more and why would any of them be interested in her. She said it was just a fantasy she had. That she could never leave her kids or her husband . . .' Mrs Meade's voice broke for a moment. 'She said she loved her family too much to leave them.'

She held Jocelyn's gaze as if trying to make her understand her dead friend. 'She may have uncon-sciously looked for this white knight as a fantasy, but never did she have the guts to approach him even if she did find him. She never had and she never did.'

Jocelyn glanced to Trevan and read in his expression that he come to the same conclusion she had. Ellianna Vernon had been looking for something to balance out the lack of adventure in her life and its confines.

And the Porcelain Mask Murderer had found it for her.

'Damn him to hell,' Trevan muttered, his voice filled with the bitter sound of anger.

'What the hell is she doing here, Detective Cartland?' A voice suddenly barked from behind them.

John grimaced and thanked Mary Meade for speaking to them. The woman flicked a disapproving glance at the approaching man, then moved away.

Jocelyn turned to see a man in a dark suit, advancing on them with angry strides with Gary Pemberton hot on his tail. The thin man's gaze flicked briefly over Trevan before he dismissed him, then leveled on Jocelyn with a glare. 'I thought she was expelled from your department until we had completely investigated her actions.'

John's chest puffed up with anger and he moved in front of the man's face, forcing him to look him in the eye. Gary stopped beside John and placed his hand on the older man's arm. Jocelyn couldn't decide whether it was in reassurance or, more likely, restraint. 'Allegations, remember? Innocent until proven guilty and all that.'

'Of course, detective, but that still does not answer my question.'

The irritating stranger was tall with dark little eyes

and a nose that reminded Jocelyn of Ichabod Crane. In fact, she thought as her gaze moved over him, he looked a lot like the nervous school teacher who had disappeared one dark night.

'What is she doing here?' he asked with a sneer.

Raising a brow, she wished this petty little man would vanish too.

John stepped back and nodded toward the disapproving man. He spoke through clenched teeth. 'Jocelyn, this is Dr Dick Lindenmeyer. He's the guy in Internal Affairs handling your case. I told you about it the other day.'

Her lips twitched with amusement. Doctor Dick, Internal Affairs, how appropriate. Noting his disapproving look she purposely held her hand out to him. 'Dr Lindenmeyer, how unfortunate that we had to meet under such circumstances.'

As she had expected, he frowned, then reluctantly grasped her hand. 'Since the detective seems to choose to ignore my questions, would you like to answer why you are here?'

'I invited her, Lindenmeyer,' John growled before she could speak. 'What are you doing here?'

Lindenmeyer continued to study Jocelyn as if she were an unusual bug specimen. 'I received word that she was here. Unauthorized and ransacking a crime scene.'

'Who called you?' Trevan's voice rang with formidable authority, completely throwing Lindenmeyer off guard.

The doctor opened his mouth a couple of times, then

blinked at Trevan. He pursed his lips, then squared his shoulders. 'I don't recall your name, sir.'

'I never said it.' Trevan's lips curled with his anger.

'Mr Elliot is with the media,' Gary interjected. Jocelyn knew he was backing Lindenmeyer off with the threat of public exposure. Pemberton's expression was as dark as Trevan's and John's.

She glanced toward Trevan and sucked in her breath. She could tell he was mad. Very, very mad. She cleared her throat quietly which seemed to remind Trevan of their original purpose and he eased his rigid stance.

'I believe Mr Elliot has a valid question, Dick,' John said, obviously amused at Lindenmeyer's discomfort. 'Who did call you?'

Lindenmeyer lifted his chin in a nervous gesture as he adjusted the lapels of his suit. 'I don't really know. It was an anonymous call.'

Jocelyn glanced around her at the crowd gathered behind the barricades. There were many people here observing the police. The media were represented heavily by television, radio, and the newspaper. Scanning the curious faces, she could not make out a familiar one. Yet there had to be one person here who was determined to discredit her with the police department. A nameless, faceless individual who was even now luring her into his deadly trap. She knew he was there, somewhere. The icy tingle of fear moved over her as she felt his eyes on her. Watching her.

And waiting to make his move.

Her heart quickened and her breath caught in her chest. The fear tightened around her chest and she swallowed. She tried to logically explain the warning her gut instinct was giving her, but she couldn't.

There was no denying it any more. Jocelyn knew she was next.

The killer watched her as she scanned the crowd. She was afraid. He could see it in her eyes and the rigid way she held herself. In her pale expression he could see that she knew the time was coming. Time to reach the climactic conclusion of their drama. He checked his watch, smiling to himself.

It was time.

Time. How he loved that word, he thought. Time can be your worst enemy, he thought. And hadn't he already proved that he was the master of time?

CHAPTER 21

The idea of a murderer, a madman, working to lure her into his deadly trap had been present in Jocelyn's thoughts for a long time. Now it was more than an idea or a possibility; she knew he had been here watching her. His eyes had moved over her as she knelt by Ellianna Vernon's body. He had once again tried to discredit her in the eyes of the department. Why?

Jocelyn chewed her lip as she thought it over. The only explanation she could come up with was the killer's need to get access to her. With the department against her, she would not be under their protective noses. Her gaze moved to Trevan and she knew that would leave him as the one last obstacle for the murderer to overcome. She had to make sure that grisly prospect never happened.

John's voice rose in irritation and dragged her attention back to the conversation. Doctor Dick of Internal Affairs and the detective were still going at it. Lindenmeyer had made it more than apparent that he had some sort of personal beef against Jocelyn and she had no idea why. John seemed to know, but he was not letting her in on it. The two of them were discussing, very loudly, whether Jocelyn could remain at the scene.

'What evidence do you have against her?' John asked angrily, then rubbed his hands over his hair. The movement roughed it out even more from the side of his head. 'There were dozens of people around the whole time she was at the site. Tell me how she could have removed or planted evidence?'

He stabbed a finger at the tall man from Internal Affairs. 'Hell, you've never even stated what she did or did not remove from where the prostitute was killed.'

Lindenmeyer's chin rose and he arched an eyebrow. 'This is not open for discussion, Cartland.'

'I say it is,' John barked. 'You're doing your best to ruin her career before it's even started and I want to know why. Tell me who made the charges.'

Lindenmeyer leaned forward and his lips curled into an unbecoming snarl. 'As I said, this is not open for discussion. Your questions and concerns can be addressed at the preliminary hearing scheduled for next week.' He sniffed haughtily and readjusted his tie. 'Now, Officer Harris, please escort Ms Kendrick and her friend from the area.'

The nervous young man nodded briefly, then motioned with his hand for them to precede him. Gary and John both stepped forward. John held the man back with a wave of his hand.

'Back off,' John snapped. 'I'm a cop and I'll walk them to their car.' He stepped closer to Lindenmeyer and his voice dropped to a furious whisper that Jocelyn barely caught. 'I guarantee you are going to address a lot of things next week, and I don't mean just this case, Dick. I should've done it a long time ago.'

A flash of fear, then animosity moved through the doctor's gaze. The man's anger contorted his face into an ugly sneer. 'I don't appreciate your petty attempts at a threat, Detective Cartland. I suggest you watch your actions from here on out . . . you can be sure that I will.'

John moved beside Jocelyn and Trevan, then waved them ahead with his hand. Gary remained with the young officer for a moment. She noticed his expression was solemn as he spoke quietly with the man. The nervous cop nodded at what Gary said, then his expression showed his relief. Pemberton clasped the man's shoulder briefly before he turned to catch up with them.

Jocelyn glanced back to Lindenmeyer and noted that the man still watched them. His face showed a mixture of fear, doubt, and hate. John had hinted at knowing something about the good doctor and apparently it was a lot more than just unpaid parking tickets.

'I have to say your defense of my reputation was pretty admirable, John,' she said, quietly. 'Especially since you don't know that the allegations are not the truth.'

John loosened his tie with an angry jerk of his hand. 'I know the whole thing is a pack of lies and it stinks to high heaven of a set up. We just need to figure out who did it and stop him.'

Trevan had remained silent during Lindenmeyer's tirade. Jocelyn knew it was only because he realized she did not need any more trouble than she already had with Internal Affairs. Now he walked with his hands in his jean pockets, his face dark with anger.

'Just how well do you know this Lindenmeyer, John?' Trevan asked. 'I gathered from your conversation that you knew a few things he would rather keep quiet.'

She glanced over at him and smiled to herself. Apparently she was not the only one wondering about John's knowledge of the obnoxious man.

'You're good, Elliot,' John said, then scanned the area around them. 'I knew Dick back when we were in the academy. He had a penchant for young girls and leather. His family kept his little excursions under wraps.'

He took a deep breath and the lines of his face tightened with disgust. 'After one particular episode when the girl had to be hospitalized, his father threatened him. Told him to control his urges or get used to being poor. Of course they paid the girl's hospital bill.'

'Of course,' Jocelyn said, disliking Lindenmeyer even more.

Gary pinched his nose between his fingers as he shook his head. He ran his hand through his hair and looked at John. 'I never have liked the man, but now I see why you've always been so hostile toward him.'

John nodded, then took a slow breath. He raised his hand to his hair as he realized his ends were sticking out like a clown's and smoothed it back. He stopped, then studied the crowd around the crime tape. 'The girl blackmailed him for a while, at least that's what she claimed. Ever since then old Dick has had a real dislike for women. Other than, well, obviously you can figure that one out.'

Jocelyn shook her head. How could they not arrest the man for whatever they could come up with? 'So old

Ichabod is a pervert. Why did the girl tell you she had blackmailed Lindenmeyer?'

He leaned over to pick up a branch twig and began to strip the leaves from the tiny stem. 'She told me that particular bit of information just before she died. She was a prostitute and worked in a bad part of town. Got herself shot one night.'

He threw the stick down to the ground. 'It wasn't like I could tell anyone about him. I had no real evidence; only a dead prostitute's word and her hospital bill. His family is big, prominent, charitable. They could say they were just helping the poor and unfortunate. That was years ago when I was only a snot nosed rookie.'

John paused. She could tell by the unease in his face that he was remembering similar words she had spoken to him not so long ago as they stood over the body of Ruby Snow. 'Anyway, that is why Lindenmeyer will personally do his best to make sure you don't become a cop. You're smart and you're female. He hates that in a person. And I think he's afraid of you, although I don't know why.'

'He acted like Jocelyn knew something,' Gary said, his gaze moved to her. 'Have you met him before or run across his name in any of your research?'

'No, I haven't.' She shrugged. What Gary was saying made sense, but she knew nothing about the man. Her eyes moved to Trevan. 'But he does sound like someone else we know.'

Trevan nodded. 'Yes, he was here tonight and he called Lindenmeyer to tell him you were here. If there was a call at all, for that matter. I wish he had been man enough to tell us who made the allegations.'

348

'Well, we've already established that he's anything but decent,' Gary stated.

The four turned to the man they were discussing to find him still watching them with an intense gaze of dislike.

'And he's going to keep riding this and me until you two are out of here. Go home and get some rest. I'll give you a call if I find out anything.' John muttered.

Jocelyn softly punched him in the arm. 'Thanks, John. You are a real hero.'

He chuckled and shook his head as some of the strain left his face. 'I can't say that I've ever been called that before. Trevan, take her home and order a pizza or something. I'm counting on you to keep her out of trouble for at least a little while.'

Trevan gave a small salute. 'Yes, sir. Although I don't know if that can be accomplished by only one person.'

John waved, then headed back to the scene. Jocelyn smiled when he walked past the irritated Lindenmeyer, ignoring him as if he weren't there. Gary turned back to them.

'I thought I should give you an update on the old man that you talked to that night in the alley,' he said. He put his hands on his hips and studied the grass in front of him before he met her gaze. 'He isn't completely blind.'

'What?' Jocelyn felt a small flaring of hope. If the man wasn't blind it meant he had seen the killer's face. 'Has he been able to tell you anything?'

Gary shook his head. 'No, he's still talking in riddles. I did talk to the doctor, however, and it wasn't as encouraging as I had hoped. He has pretty advanced glaucoma and it affects the peripheral vision, then sort of fills in toward the center. But the doctor said he would not have been able to see anything too clearly, unless the killer had practically stared him in the face.'

Polyphemus. Now Jocelyn recognized the name and suddenly everything made sense. Her eyes grew wide in realization. 'Oh my, God. He did.'

'He did what?' Gary asked. He looked at her, then back to Trevan.

An image filled her mind. The old man waking to noises of two people struggling, then sitting up in the pile of rags where he had been sleeping. The murderer's hands gripped tightly around Ruby Snow's throat till the woman slid bonelessly to the ground. He had turned to study the old man, then noticed the milky eyes skittering wildly around the alley. The murderer walked to the vagrant and squatted in front of the man till his face was even with that of the vagrant. The killer slowly leaned forward till the old man's eyes finally met and held his gaze.

Jocelyn felt an icy shiver move through her. Hayden Webster had been lucky that night. He had stared death in the face. And lived.

She licked her lips, then turned to find both men studying her nervously. 'Gary, remember Hayden talking about Polyphemus?'

He nodded, 'I'm not that good on classic literature, what does it mean?'

'You're better than you think,' she smiled. 'It is from the classics, Greek mythology as a matter of fact. Polyphemus was the Cyclops.'

'Okay, so he had one eye, I still don't get it,' Gary said, looking to Trevan.

350

Trevan shrugged, 'It doesn't make sense.'

'It does if you put everything Hayden said together. He had said that "Polyphemus looked upon her with his sinister eye," or something like that. Then he had said, "Blue as the sky."'

Trevan nodded. 'The killer had blue eyes.'

'Well, now we know he has blue eyes,' Gary hesitated. Jocelyn could tell that he was reluctant to dispel her hope, 'but we can't use the old man as a reliable source. Not to mention, you thought the killer was altering his appearance anyway.'

Jocelyn took a deep breath. 'I know, but at least we know Hayden did see what happened.'

She heard her name being called and turned to see Thomas heading toward them. She swore quietly and grabbed Gary's arm. 'Give me fifteen bucks, Pemberton.'

He eyed curiously. 'For what?'

'Just give it to me,' she said, distractedly. 'Quick before he gets here.'

Gary took his wallet out and opened it. 'I only have ten dollars on me.'

Trevan was looking through his wallet and pulled a bill out. 'Here's another five.'

'Thanks,' she said, taking the money from the two men. 'Thomas, I was hoping I would see you. Have you had a chance to look the victim over?'

'You know I can't tell you anything,' Thomas answered. 'Besides, you owe me.'

She handed him the money and offered him a wide smile. 'There you go.'

He looked at the money for a moment in surprise,

then folded it and put it in his pocket. 'I guess I should take back all the things I said about you, Kendrick.'

'I'll settle for what you can tell me,' Jocelyn offered.

'John told me you'd already seen her,' he said, rubbing his chin. 'I'd say it was the same poison he used on the other victims, but that's where the similarities end.'

Trevan nodded, 'He's good at covering his tracks.'

The excitement of solving one tiny piece of the puzzle that had briefly buoyed her spirits was beginning to fade. Her gaze was drawn back to the small clearing of trees and in her mind's eyes, she could see Ellianna Vernon's body nestled within. She was surprised to realize that the fear had lost its grip on her, then mentally shook herself. She felt as if she were about to accept that the killer was coming for her. No, she thought vehemently. She would not accept it. That was too close to giving in and she was going to fight him. She was not going to be his next victim.

They excused themselves from the two men as Trevan took her arm and they made their way to the truck. They walked together silently, each lost in thought.

Getting in, Jocelyn pulled the door closed, then began to rub her fingers in soothing circles on her temples. Trevan slid behind the wheel and studied her. She glanced at him and gave him an encouraging smile.

'How are you feeling?' he asked quietly.

'Tired,' she shrugged. Taking a deep breath, Jocelyn picked up a pencil from the dash. She held it in front of her and snapped it in two with a satisfying crunch as frustration flared through her. It would definitely have been more fulfilling to smash something, but she had an idea that Trevan might need his windshield.

'I'm tired of being manipulated and toyed with, Trevan, and now he's got us backed against the proverbial wall.' She looked out the window to study the people walking in front of the parking lot. Strangers, each with their own problems and idiosyncrasies. Text book examples, or were they? 'I've spent years in school learning how to deal with guys like this and right now the only thing I can think of is he's coming after me. That I'll be the next one to die.'

'Don't say that.' He gathered her into his arms and almost crushed her with his embrace. He pressed his lips to the top of her head, his words muffled in her hair. 'Don't ever say that, Jocelyn.'

He held her away from him waiting till she met his gaze. 'I know you're scared. I am too, but I'll do whatever it takes to stop this guy.'

'How? We don't know who he is. He could be anyone. He's even changed his ritual of killing.' She shook her head, then ran her hands roughly through her hair. 'Why did he kill this woman?'

Trevan lifted his hand to touch her cheek. 'Then that's what we should be focusing on, the why. Why did he suddenly change his method now?'

She leaned into his touch and nodded. 'You're right.'

He returned her smile, then his gaze dropped to her lips. Her heart quickened as she watched his eyes darken. The flecks of gold within them a warm contrast to the honeyed brown of their depths. Slowly his mouth lowered to hers. She sighed as his firm lips caressed the contours of her mouth and she responded to their gentle invitation. Jocelyn slid her hand into the short satin of his hair and he pulled her closer.

The tip of his tongue stroked her lips and she felt her breath catch in her throat as a quick shiver of pleasure speared through her. He skimmed his hands up her arms and his thumbs lightly brushed the sensitive peaks of her breasts. Jocelyn arched against him, but his fingers had already found their way into her hair as he slanted her head to deepen his kiss.

Trevan's lips left her and he pressed his forehead against her own. She closed her eyes again, wishing the dreamy sensation of his touch could go on. His chuckle washed warmly over her cheek. 'I think we need to hold that thought.'

Jocelyn found herself laughing with him. 'Again, you are right. Head west, young son, and you just might get lucky.'

'Keep talking like that, young lady,' Trevan drawled in a very horrible impression of John Wayne, 'and I might just get a speeding ticket on the way home. Yah ha.'

Jocelyn could no longer contain herself and she doubled over in laughter. After a few moments, she wiped away her tears and found Trevan staring at her with an arched eyebrow as he tried to suppress his smile.

'Am I to assume it was a bad imitation?' he asked.

'Well, Trevan.' She paused to clear her throat in an

attempt to hide her mirth and failed miserably. 'Let's just say, you shouldn't give up your day job yet.'

'Everyone's a critic,' he returned.

His smile dispelled any thoughts she might have had that she had hurt his feelings. She saw the warmth in his eyes and her smile softened.

'Thanks, Trevan. It's really nice having someone know how to make you feel better.'

He stroked his thumb in a slow caress across the ridge of her cheek. 'It's something I plan to keep working on.'

He pulled the truck onto the street, then merged smoothly into the thick traffic exiting from the college. Jocelyn looked out the window and thought of Ellianna Vernon's husband. The smile slid from her lips as she tried to imagine him explaining to his children about their mother's death.

Anger and frustration filled Jocelyn. An image of a closed rose colored coffin flashed through her mind. Kat, her childhood best friend, had died at the hands of a nameless, faceless stranger, just as Ellianna Vernon had.

Jocelyn swallowed her tears and let the anger fill her. It strengthened her resolve. She had been forced to go on without her friend. Never having known the identity of Kat's killer. She refused, however, to let Ellianna's children grow up with the same sense of futility.

The Porcelain Mask Murderer had killed so many, apparently without a thought to the repercussions of his crime. Had he ever considered how many people he affected when he murdered a person? Murder was like throwing a rock into a quiet pool of water; the splash of the stone causing ripples to wave to the edge of the pond. For every person he killed, there were friends and family who felt the ripples of the brutality and were forced to realize that the person they had loved would no longer be a part of their lives.

She again resolved that not only would she not become his next victim, but that she would make him remember the women and the man he had killed in cold blood.

Jocelyn closed her eyes and an image of Ellianna Vernon appeared. She had been poisoned like the others, but positioned differently. And what was the significance of the flowers in her hair?

Opening her eyes, she straightened herself in the seat. They were leaving the outskirts of Old Town and she was relieved to realize it wouldn't be too much longer before they were home.

'Trevan, I keep going over this woman's murder and I can't figure it out,' she said, frowning as she watched the darkening storm shorten what little daylight they had left. 'She was lying on her back with her hands crossed over her chest like she was in a coffin and he didn't leave a mask like he did the other women.'

'Maybe she's an offering,' he added quietly.

'What?' she said. She turned to him and an unwanted thought, perhaps following his, worked its way into her mind.

He kept his gaze on the road, but his voice was tense with concentration. 'It's only an idea, but the flowers in her hair and the position of the body, put together with the note and it's like she's an offering.'

'Oh, God, you're right. It all makes sense now.' Understanding shivered through her and her lips tightened with anger. 'He knew it was my goal to catch murderers and make them face the law. He killed Ellianna Vernon so I could try to catch him.'

'Exactly,' Trevan said, glancing to her. 'We've already established that he studies his victims so that he can accommodate their fantasies.'

'So this murder was supposed to be part of my fantasy,' she stated with grim acceptance. 'We both know what comes next.'

Trevan's knuckles whitened as he gripped the wheel. A low snarl escaped from his lips. 'He'll have to get past me before he touches you.'

She blew out her breath. 'And he will try. He turned the department against me, except for John, and you're the only obstacle left.'

The thought tightened the thick band of fear wrapping around her chest. The murderer would strike soon and they had to figure out a way to stop him. She had to, or the man she had come to love would die. And so would she.

They pulled into her driveway as a man on the radio announced that the area was still under a tornado watch. Jocelyn climbed from the truck and shut the door with a firm shove. They walked to the house and she pulled her keys from her jacket to unlock the door. Lightning flashed in a bright glare reflecting from the window panes and she turned to look back at the sky.

She opened the door and flicked the light switch on. Fatigue weighed heavy on her, but she knew there would be no time for rest, at least for now. 'I'm going to take a shower.'

Jocelyn climbed the stairs, then headed to her room. Turning on her light, she took a deep breath and started undressing. A hot shower was what she needed most right now to ease her nerves and dispel part of the ache from her muscles. She'd forgotten how sore horseback riding could make an unpractised rider.

Undressed, she padded into the bathroom and turned the water on. She adjusted it, then stepped inside. Jocelyn closed the glass door and the relaxing steam drifted around her. Moisture beaded over her body. She turned her back into the shower and let the water wash over her head in a warm caress.

The glass door started to slide open, causing fear to flash briefly through her till she met Trevan's heated gaze. Silently, he stepped into the shower with her and her eyes moved over his naked body. Jocelyn knew she would never tire of looking at him. He was splendid and the mere sight of him caused her heart to race with desire.

His legs were muscular, defined: his wide shoulders tapered to his narrow waist, and the hair covering his chest all combined to seduce her. She put the palms of her hands on him. She could feel his nipples hardening under her touch and she felt a stab of pleasure shoot through her.

Trevan's hands moved to her waist, then pulled her slowly to his kiss. His lips sought her hungrily as his hands cupped her to him. His mouth left hers, then worked slowly, torturously down her neck till he bent and took her nipple into his lips.

Jocelyn moaned softly, running her hands through

his hair. Trevan released her and straightened. He turned her away from him and she could hear him picking up the bar of soap. His arms came around her and she leaned against his chest. He kissed her neck as his hands slowly brought her arms beside her head. She held him behind her as the soap on his hands smoothed over her body like satin. He lathered her stomach, then moved to circle her breasts. He caressed her skin with his touch as he rubbed the soap over her.

Jocelyn bit her lip, her desire growing red hot within her. She turned to him and took the soap into her own hands. She touched him, running the lather over the hard muscles of his stomach. She took pleasure when his muscles tightened in response and she moved lower. Jocelyn stroked him till Trevan moaned and pulled her roughly against him. His mouth found hers, taking her with a sense of urgency. His need was as strong as hers.

'Let's get out of here before we drown,' he said huskily against her cheek.

Quickly they rinsed off, then stepped out of the shower. Trevan took her by the hand before she could grab a towel and led her to the bed. He turned her to him and lowered himself with her to the mattress.

She gasped in pleasure as he entered her. Their need for each other was wild, almost desperate as they moved against each other, with each other. Trevan's hands moved boldly over her body, touching her, skimming her as he moved within her. She couldn't touch him enough, taste him enough, as her fingers moved over the slick sheen of moisture covering him. The need burned within her, consuming her till she arched against him as it seized her. His hands gripped her and he shuddered within her.

For several minutes they lay joined together, enjoying the warmth of each other's bodies. Jocelyn turned her face into his neck and smiled. 'I'll never be able to look at a bar of soap again without becoming highly aroused.'

Trevan lifted his face, then kissed her. He pulled his head back to look her in the face and he grinned. 'Now I know what to get you for Christmas.'

Jocelyn wrapped her arms around him. 'Only if you come with it.'

Trevan shifted beside her, then rolled from the bed. He started pulling his clothes on. He snapped his jeans, then put his hands on his hips. 'Are you just going to lie there?'

Jocelyn raised her arms above her head and gave him a satiated wink as she smiled playfully. 'I might.'

He chuckled as he put his arms through his shirt sleeves. He swatted her on the thigh, then left the room.

'Coward,' she groaned in frustration. She wouldn't have minded spending the rest of the evening in his arms. The image brought a smile to her lips and she sat up. She decided to get dressed and went to the dresser to get clean clothes.

Jocelyn found herself humming as her hands moved down the buttons of her shirt. Her movements froze as her gaze fell on the old photograph of Allysa. She studied the dead girl's face, her unseeing eyes staring at the mask. As if she were looking at the mask.

'Look to the mask,' Jocelyn murmured. She felt the

answer hovering on the filmy edge of her thoughts. 'Damn it, think,' she muttered, but it refused to reveal itself.

Quickly she pulled her jeans on, then snatched her shoes from the foot of the bed. She picked up the picture in the other hand and headed out the door. She went down the stairs two at a time, then hurried to the kitchen. Jocelyn found Trevan in the kitchen pouring himself a glass of milk.

She put the picture on the counter, hopping on one foot, then the other as she put her shoes on.

'You're in a hurry,' he said with a smile. He drank the milk, then set the glass on the counter before moving over to her. It pained Jocelyn to see the relaxed humor slide from his face as his gaze rested on the photo.

'The answer is right here, damn it,' Jocelyn said. Placing her hand gently on his forearm, she studied his expression for a moment. 'I just can't see it.'

'I can't either,' Trevan added, then blew his breath out in angry frustration. He turned abruptly away from the picture and moved to lean against the breakfast bar. 'We've already established he studies his victims so he can create the perfect "fantasy" man for them.'

'So he's a good actor,' Jocelyn murmured. A fragment of the phone conversation she had with the killer the night of Ruby Snow's murder flicked through her mind. A phrase struck a chord within her and she felt her eyes widen. 'Remember the night he called? He said the women he killed were "vehicles".'

She opened the copy of the file John had given her.

She flipped through the pages till she found what she wanted. 'Michelle Slavinsky, nurse. Becky Sowers, paralegal. Halicia Carmichael, pharmacist. Cindy Blake, florist, and so on.' She looked to Trevan and held his gaze. 'He picked these women to be his vehicles. To teach him what he wanted or needed to know.'

Trevan pushed from the bar, his brows drawn in concentration. 'That night I followed him into your back yard, he said something like that then. At the time, I thought he was being sarcastic, but now maybe it makes sense. He said that even my sister tried to tell me.'

Jocelyn took a deep breath. 'Look to the mask.'

She picked the picture up and studied the grainy image of the porcelain mask. Jocelyn chewed her lip as she squinted at the photograph. Look to the mask. Allysa's eyes stared intensely at the eyeless cracked face. A thread of understanding started to weave through her thoughts.

'Look to the mask,' she repeated quietly. Handing the picture to Trevan, she tapped her finger on the broken porcelain. 'Where did she get it?'

He shook his head. 'I don't know really, I assumed it was a gift. The people at the theater were always giving her tokens of their appreciation.'

'Patron of the Arts, Allysa Elliot.' Jocelyn remembered the article of depicting the girl's death. 'To accommodate each victim's fantasy, he would become her perfect man.'

Her eyes met Trevan's. She could see by the tension in his face, he was thinking the same thing she was.

'An actor,' he said. 'The beau in the article was more than

362

likely an actor.' He hesitated, then swore in anger. 'Remember I told you about how Maybella had been so eager to tell me about Justine and how she thought she might be seeing some other man? She also mentioned Allysa's unseemly behavior with a new actor. I've already thought that it may have been the same man after Justine. It wasn't like there were an abundance of strangers in Niola.'

'Would Rachael have any play bills from the old theater?' she asked, hope growing within her. Every cell of her body was tight with anticipation. They were on the verge of discovering the identity of the Porcelain Mask Murderer.

'I'll call and find out.' He picked the phone up and dialed the widow's number. The fact that he knew the number by memory amused Jocelyn. That was not important now, she decided with an arched brow. Even so, after this was over, she was going to make sure he forgot the merry widow's number.

Luck was with them; Rachael was still at the museum. Jocelyn felt her tension building as Trevan quickly asked her to check the theater bill for the week of Allysa's murder. After a few moments, his face lit with a smile and he nodded to her to let her know that the museum did have a copy.

'Do you have a fax modem on your computer?' he asked after a moment.

Jocelyn's felt her brows raise. It should not surprise her that the little museum had a computer with a fax. But it did. 'Of course, I'll go turn it on.'

She wrote the number down and handed it to him, then hurried to turn on her computer. She heard

Trevan hang the phone up and his footsteps as he moved to stand beside her.

'Rachael's going to scan the play bill and fax us a copy,' he said quietly. He held her gaze and took her hand. 'We'll get him, Jocelyn. This will finally be over. For the both of us.'

She smiled and gripped his hand tighter with her own. 'I am more than ready for that.'

The minutes slowly clicked by. Finally the fax began to beep, signaling it was receiving a message. The first sheet slid noisily from the machine revealing the title of the play. The page was dark because of the document's age and slightly distorted from the scanner.

The second sheet started to slide from the machine and Jocelyn felt her breath quicken. The name of the actor starring in the show appeared in the flowery scrawl of the late 1800s. Her eyes widened and she heard Trevan mutter a bitter oath.

The page dropped from the fax and Trevan picked it up. The face of the actor was drawn with the blade of his sword covering part of his face. The artist had captured, only too well, the hard glint of the man's eyes.

The evil gaze was that of the killer. The name of the man was Lucas Vandemeer.

Jocelyn gasped as her hand went to her throat, 'Trevan, he's the man I ran into that night when the Carter girl was found. I've since found out he's a reporter.' Her frightened gaze moved till she met his. 'He's the Porcelain Mask Murderer.'

CHAPTER 22

Trevan looked down at the face of his sister's killer. The malevolent gaze of the man he had held within his grasp before the tornado stared back at him. Trevan's jaw clenched and he felt the same burning rage he had the day he discovered his sister's body.

'Now he'll pay,' Trevan swore.

'We'll have to notify John,' Jocelyn reminded him quietly. 'We can't go and just string him up on the nearest branch.'

She placed her hand on his arm and he studied her worried expression. 'There are procedures we have to follow, Trevan,' she said softly.

He took a deep breath and was forced to recognize the truth of what she said. He had been here long enough to know she was right. He gave her a slight nod and she reached for the phone.

She dialed the number, then waited. He watched as her eyes widened and she moved to tap the phone against the palm of her hand.

'What's wrong?' he asked.

'It's dead.' She looked to him and he felt his fury renew at the fear he saw in her eyes.

'We can't wait here till the phones are working again, Jocelyn.' He slid Allysa's picture in front of her, then opened the file to the black and white photos of the other mask victims. 'He's out there right now and we can't take a chance on him killing another woman.'

His voice dropped to a whisper and he held her gaze. 'Or he could come after you and I can't take that chance.'

Trevan watched her swallow as she looked to the pictures. She lifted her eyes to him, then nodded.

'Let's go stop him,' she said.

He took her hand and they headed to the door. 'We'll go by the newspaper first and see if he's there. If not, they might have an address on him here in town.'

'I just want this to be over,' she said, locking the door behind them.

Walking down the sidewalk to the truck, a rustle of leaves from the side yard caught Trevan's attention. Jocelyn was already climbing into the truck as he stood by the front bumper and listened. He heard the noise again and caught the quick stir of the bushes out of the corner of his eye.

Apprehension speared through him and he held his hand up for Jocelyn to stay in the truck. Quietly he made his way to the gate, his gut tightening in warning when he found it open. Silently he cursed the fact he didn't have his hand gun. It was still being repaired from the last time he had used it. Thank the Lord he still had the rifle.

Noiselessly he moved through the dark opening. Too late he caught a movement and a flash of silver coming at him. It struck the side of his head and he fell with a groan to his knees. He heard the low ominous chuckle of the killer who had haunted his nightmares, then his vision filled with black.

Jocelyn opened her eyes. She could see nothing and she felt a sharp jolt of fear. Quickly attempting to sit up, she hit her head on a hard surface and the surrounding darkness erupted into tiny pin points of color.

'Damn it,' she muttered, letting her head fall back to what felt like a carpeted floor. 'Where the hell am I?'

In answer, her body thumped against the bottom as if she were hitting a rut on a road. She felt her eyes widen and knew then where she was. Or to be more exact, what she was in.

'The stinking jerk put me in the trunk,' she shrieked.

She skimmed her fingers around her to investigate her enclosure. It wasn't a very large compartment, so she had to assume she was in the mysterious silver BMW.

Jocelyn swore vehemently under her breath. She had no idea where Trevan was or how he was doing. Earlier he had disappeared into the back yard. It had really riled her that he had pulled his macho crap again and had expected her to sit in the truck like a whimpering, chicken hearted female. She may have the heart of a chicken, but she wasn't a wimp.

Following the direction he'd taken, she had found him lying unconscious just inside the gate. Then someone had grabbed her and stuck a needle in her arm. She remembered turning as the drug began to hit her system. The smiling face of Lucas Vandemeer had been the last thing she'd seen.

Now she was in his trunk.

Her thoughts turned to Trevan again and she said a silent prayer, hoping he would be all right. Somehow she knew he was. The Porcelain Mask Murderer, or Lucas, had enjoyed taunting him too much to be satisfied with just killing him in her back yard.

No, she figured he had something else in mind. Instinctively she knew he would want to use her to recreate his thrill and jeer at Trevan one last time before he killed the two of them. A shiver of desperation rippled through her. She didn't want to become another victim of a serial killer. To make sure that didn't happen she had to be prepared. But how?

She wondered where they were going. She felt around her, knowing full well that the killer would have removed everything from the trunk. Her fingers found nothing, not even a screw driver to try to pop the lock.

The vehicle began to jostle as from a rough road. He must be taking her into the country he realized. Her thoughts raced as she wondered where he would take her. Then she knew; to ultimately recreate Allysa's murder, he would have to return to the theater. She hoped Trevan would come to the same conclusion.

The car stopped. Her chest tightened in response to the silence of the engine. Her heart was pounding so hard she could barely hear. She strained to listen for any noise that might give her warning.

She heard a door open, then click softly as it closed.

For the first time she caught the deep rumble of the thunder. It shook the ground and the metallic plop of rain began to pelt heavily on the lid of the trunk.

She worked to slow her breathing. The pounding rain masked all other noise. The sensation of being completely vulnerable was unnerving as she waited. Lucas would be coming for her soon and she had to be ready.

Having no weapons, she thought frantically to try to come up with something, anything, to get her out of this. She groaned and ran her hands through her hair in frustration. Nothing.

One small idea began to snake its way into her mind. Surprise. He probably expected her to still be sedated, or at least somewhat subdued. He wouldn't be prepared, for her to jump at him, kick him in the groin, and run like hell.

Seconds ticked by into minutes. Jocelyn began to sweat, the moisture beading in a cold pool on her forehead. *Where was he?* She really didn't care to see him, but she couldn't stay in the trunk.

The trunk lid suddenly raised. Lightning flashed with a loud grumble of thunder in its wake as it silhouetted the tall figure. Lucas Vandemeer grabbed her by the hands and hauled her out of the small compartment. The heavy rain had already saturated the earth, turning it to mud. It caused her to slip in the slime and fall into his arms.

'Be careful, my dear, the storm is going to be a dangerous one,' he said quietly in her ear. His lips were pressed against her hair in order to be heard over the noise of the thunderstorm.

She leaned away from him and tried to pull her hands free. She found his touch repulsive and shuddered in response. His eyes, the color of ice, moved over her. Noting her shiver, his gaze hardened.

Jocelyn drove her knee at him. Vandemeer easily sidestepped her, then swung her around in his grasp. He forced her back against his chest and before she could react, he clicked a pair of handcuffs on her wrists.

'Damn you,' she yelled, struggling against the metal grips.

Chuckling, he spun her to face him. 'I see Mr Elliot has been working on your vocabulary.'

'Bite it, Vandemeer,' she spat at him. Images of Ellianna Vernon and Ruby Snow flashed into her mind. She felt her anger for the needless pain and suffering he had caused for so many families of the girls he had murdered. 'Don't make the mistake of thinking I'll be an easy victim. I've seen the results of your charm.'

'Ms Kendrick,' he leaned forward, then casually caressed her cheek with his fingertip. 'Jocelyn. I had hoped to do this easily, but I can improvise if you force me to.'

He held the cuffs with his hand and she tried to yank away from him. 'What are you going to do, drug me again?' she yelled as she glared at him. The release of her anger cleared her head. Vandemeer had played mind games with them by forcing them to decipher the message of the mask. Maybe she could use his own technique against him. Her gaze hardened and she lifted her chin. 'It wouldn't have the same effect, you know.

The sense of power would only be a dull pulse. Isn't that why you brought me here? To achieve the same feeling that you experienced with Allysa Elliot?'

He studied her for an intense moment. The lightning flashed around them and the rain slicked down his hard face. 'I knew you were perceptive. In fact, I had counted on it. No, I'm not going to drug you.' He swept his hand in front of him with a slight bow. 'But I do think we need to go into the house. The weather out here is quite treacherous.'

Jocelyn looked at him, making no attempt to hide the animosity she felt for him. Lifting her chin, she stepped carefully past him and moved to the theater. Stopping at the door, she refused to meet his gaze as he opened it. He motioned for her to enter.

'I took the liberty of placing a change of clothes in this room for you,' Vandemeer said with a friendly smile.

She studied him, her gaze moving over his face. Part of her might believe he felt guilty, almost awkward, but the dark soulless depths of his eyes reminded her how accomplished an actor he really was.

His nostrils flared, and his voice was low with a thread of menace as he removed the cuffs from her wrists. 'Please do not try to escape through the window. It is old and squeaks. If I hear any noise, I will kill you. Then I'll kill Elliot when he arrives.'

Jocelyn stepped into the room, not so much to do as he asked, but to give herself time to think. And to escape the icy evil of his voice.

The room was small with tall windows. The shifting

shadows of several candles revealed a beautifully ornate stamped tin ceiling. Closing the door behind her, she scanned the room. It held little furniture she thought, then recognized it as a dressing room.

And it had no other doors.

An elegant burgundy dressing sacque was draped across the back of a leather upholstered sofa, along with what looked like the minimum number of required undergarments it would take to achieve the full effect. She fingered the fine lace of the white ruffle knowing that anywhere else she would have admired the delicate beauty. Not now, she thought, then flung it back on top of the dress in frustration.

'Damn it,' she whispered, looking around her. She had thoughts of attempting to escape, despite the killer's warning, except that he had mentioned Trevan coming. The only comfort in that was it meant he was still alive. Chewing her lip, she realized how isolated she really was. She didn't know her way around this area and more than likely would only get herself lost. That would do neither of them any good. She had to stay and give whatever help she could to Trevan.

Lightning illuminated the room and the storm roared its fury. A new sense of fear washed over her as she looked out the window at the sky. She'd lived in Kansas all of her life and knew only too well the feel of tornado weather. The dread she felt, coupled with the apprehension of knowing a murderer was waiting for her to join him, tightened around her.

'Might as well get this over with,' she muttered, pulling her shirt over her head.

She was not familiar with the antiquated attire, but finally struggled her way into the confining undergarments, then battled with the hooks and eyes up the front of the gown. When she had finished putting it on, she refused to check her reflection in the mirror. It would serve Vandemeer right if she looked downright ugly.

Taking a deep breath, Jocelyn opened the door wide and lifted her chin. The flicker of candlelight in the next room signaled her destination. The warm flames in the fireplace backstage beckoned to her, but she forced herself to refuse its siren call.

Vandemeer, leaning against the mantel, stared into the flames. He was dressed in similar attire from the late 1800s. His hat rested on the corner of a high backed chair with his black duster slung over the back. The vest with its satin back was an odd contrast to the rough material of his dark jeans.

Spurs clicked as he slowly turned to her. She swallowed back the bile in her throat when she noted the appreciative gleam in his eyes.

You are beautiful, my dear,' he said, his voice husky. He motioned with his hand for her to join him. 'Please have a seat and I'll fix you a drink.'

'This is Allysa's theater,' she stated. Part of her was torn between the realization that she was seeing part of his history for the first time and the possibility that it might be the last.

'Again, you are very perceptive,' he said as he poured the wine into the glasses. The bottle had already been open when she entered the room. She watched the sparkling bubbles float to the top with a sense of dread. 'Yes, this is the theater their money funded. In fact, Allysa died in this very room. Just off the stage.' He met her gaze. 'Somewhat appropriate, don't you think?'

The old photograph of the dead girl flashed in her thoughts and she glanced to the carpet. Turning back to Vandemeer, she narrowed her gaze. 'You mean when you murdered her.'

'It was an accident.' Picking up his glass of wine, he took a slow sip as he looked into her eyes. For a moment she saw a weary sadness in his expression. 'I loved her, you see. So much so that I even proclaimed my love to her. She held my hands and told me we would never be more than friends

'I really don't remember hitting her.' He stared at the floor in the middle of the room. She could see in his distant expression that he was seeing the room as it was that day so long ago. His brows rose and she watched a shadow of evil move across his face. 'I cannot adequately describe the fascination I felt as I watched the life dim from her eyes, even as I shuddered in revulsion for what I had done. Nothing could have compared to that; the mixture of guilt, horror, grief. The power. It was an overwhelming experience to know that I had wielded the God-like control of life and death.'

'Is that why you killed the others?' she asked quietly. Her heart was pounding with the terror she felt from the insanity she was witnessing. The maniacal thoughts of a madman.

Vandemeer shook his head as if disappointed with her question. 'Sweet student of the mind. It is a physical need the same as breathing or thirst. It builds within me.' He hesitated, then shrugged. 'I simply have to fulfil it.'

Anger speared through her, matching the intensity of the driving rain against the window pane. How dare he reduce someone's life to an insignificant thought? 'What about the other victims? Carrie Carter was so young. She had her whole life ahead of her. Now her mother is left to mourn the death of her child.'

He sipped his wine. 'We are all victims and we will all mourn in our lifetime.'

She jumped from the chair to stand in front of him. 'You took advantage of Ellianna Vernon's dreams, then killed her with them. She had two children who will now grow up without their mother. Do you ever feel remorse for hurting so many innocent people?'

'I do not have to justify myself to you, Ms Kendrick,' he yelled, angrily throwing his glass into the fireplace. 'I grew up a bastard in a time when it was a brutal stigma. My mother fell in love with a man who left the moment he discovered she was pregnant with me. She raised me alone and worked herself into an early grave.'

He stepped toward her, his voice lowering to a whisper of pain. 'She was twenty-six when she died, yet she looked as old and haggard as a grandmother.'

Vandemeer's face contorted with a mixture of pain and hatred. Whirling away from her, he returned to stare into the fireplace. 'Women are insignificant.'

Jocelyn looked at the bottle of wine and noticed a small brown vial beside it. She'd started toward it when he turned away from the fire and caught the look in her eyes. Quickly he snatched the vial from the table. The drumming of her heart pounded in her ears as he poured several drops of the liquid into the remaining glass. He swirled the wine to mix it in, then met her gaze.

Her eyes widened. The tingling cloak of shock enfolding her within its depths. She opened her mouth to protest, only to find no words could escape her lips. Dully she shook her head.

'Drink up, my dear. The alternative is not nearly as appealing,' he said.

Her gaze flicked to his hand. Lightning struck nearby, the white flash illuminating the metal of the small deadly gun in his grasp.

Finally finding her voice, she stumbled over her words. 'Sh . . . shooting me would only ruin the effect, Lucas.'

A glint of malice flickered in his eyes. His face tightened with his shaking anger. 'Enough talk. Drink.' He nudged the gun at her. 'Now.'

'Drop the gun, Vandemeer,' Trevan ordered, stepping into the room with a rifle.

Vandemeer grabbed Jocelyn and hauled her to his chest. His arm was wrapped around her throat as he used her body as a shield. 'I doubt you will shoot me, Elliot.' He skimmed the lip of the gun across her cheek and she strained away from the touch. 'You wouldn't want to mar Ms Kendrick's beautiful skin.'

Trevan's expression was unreadable as his rifle remained raised. The loathing in his eyes was the only thing he allowed to show. Jocelyn could not see Vandemeer's face but felt his grip tighten painfully around her throat.

'Come along, dear.' The killer forced her to back with him to the door. When they reached the darkened entrance he stopped. 'Reminds me of another night long, long ago. Do you remember, Elliot?' he asked, his voice an ugly sneer.

Trevan's gaze moved to hers. Jocelyn felt a sense of comfort in the familiar direct look of intensity, then his eyes flicked back to the killer. 'I won't let you take her, Vandemeer.'

Lucas laughed. The sound rang with an ominous echo in the old theater. 'And how do you propose to stop me?' he asked confidently. 'No, we will walk out of here and you won't make a move or I'll kill her like I did Allysa and all the other women you tried to save.' He hesitated as if enjoying the pain he was inflicting. 'You wouldn't want her death on your conscience too, would you, Elliot?'

Trevan's lips thinned with his rage and his glare reflected his frustration. 'Damn you to hell.'

'I'll see you there,' Vandemeer retorted.

He jerked her towards the door, throwing it open with a bang against the wall. Jocelyn balked when she realized the pounding noise was that of hail. The icy spheres were the size of golf balls and growing. Her gaze frantically searched the sky in fear, knowing too well the thunderstorm could easily produce an even deadlier menace.

He shoved her off the porch, grabbing her wrist in his hand as he pulled her across the yard. Unused to long

377

skirts, she tripped several times. Awkwardly she tried to shield herself from the sharp pain of the hail but not before she felt the scrapes on her cheek.

She fell to her knees and Vandemeer hauled her to her feet with a yank. The hail suddenly stopped and she scanned the area around them. The sky was still dark with a tinge of orange. The wind whipped around her, pulling at the muddy length of her skirt. The roar of the storm drowned out any noise of their progress through the mud.

Jocelyn realized he was taking her out into the open range. Frantically she searched the landscape. The rocky terrain was riddled with cedars and scraggy trees bent from the constant deforming force of the Kansas wind. She glanced back to see the theater about the length of two city blocks away. Trevan, with the rifle still in his hand, moved closely behind with a grim look as he waited for an opportunity.

She quickened her steps to look at Vandemeer's face trying to see if he had noticed Trevan following them. Apprehension coursed through her as she noted his eyes. They were focused ahead with a determined intensity. Following his gaze, she cried out in terror. The sound was lost in the oppressive clamor of the storm.

A wall cloud was boiling ahead of them, its swollen shape swirling in an attempt to form a tornado. Even as she watched, the tip of a deadly finger lowered from the blue-gray of the storm.

'No,' Jocelyn screamed, the echo was ripped away in the wind before it could reach her own ears.

She yanked fiercely at his hand on her wrist. The sudden movement caught him off guard and allowed her to pull free. Stepping forward, she drove her elbow into his stomach with a force born of desperation.

Vandemeer doubled over as she backed away. She felt a sense of satisfaction for inflicting only a small amount of the pain he had forced others to suffer. Wicked streaks of lightning snaked around them as Trevan quickly shoved Lucas into a standing position and hit him with his fist.

Blood slid from the cut to his lip and Vandemeer yelled with fury. The two men faced each other with the same naked hatred in their eyes. Vandemeer lunged forward and grabbed Trevan by the throat. They slipped in the mud and fell to the ground. Trevan's hands grasped the killer's throat and the two men stiffened as they closed their deadly hold on each other. Vandemeer removed his right hand. It shook as he reached to his side.

Jocelyn saw the glint of silver and gasped when she realized it was the smooth edge of a blade. 'Trevan, he has a knife.'

Trevan pushed his heels into the mud till he found a hold, then flipped himself on top of the man. He held him by the throat with one hand pushing the one with the knife away.

Hopping beside the two men, she lifted her skirts and aimed a hard kick at Lucas's forearm. She felt a rush of relief as the lethal blade fell, disappearing in the thick soup of the mud ten feet away.

The men continued to struggle against each other,

their muscles bunching and working with the effort. An ominous, whining roar caused her heart to slam within her. She lifted her gaze and saw the murderous fury of the tornado had won its freedom from the sky.

'My, God,' she whispered, unable to hear the words. 'Trevan, it's a tornado,' she cried. 'Trevan.'

The two men remained in their fight with each other to the death. Both had started to weaken from their struggle. Jocelyn pulled at Trevan, yelling and begging him to come with her to shelter. His gaze remained locked on the evil gleam of Vandemeer's eyes.

Growling in anger, she grabbed Trevan's shoulders and yanked at him fiercely. He turned to her and she pointed to the twister. He rose shakily, then grabbed her hand. With her skirts bunched in her other hand, they ran towards the theater. Trevan glanced back to the danger following swiftly behind them. Tugging at her, he yelled and pointed toward a ravine on their left.

The wind whipped heavily around them with a force strong enough to knock Jocelyn to her knees. Trevan hauled her to her feet and his arm slipped around her waist. Together they fell into the waist deep ditch.

Trevan pulled her beside him and wrapped his arms around her as they huddled against the steep side. Jocelyn found herself looking up into the swirling charcoal depths of the storm as it passed above them. The cloud boiled and heaved as it released its fury on the land.

She thought of Vandemeer and with a stab of guilt realized they had left him out there. She turned to Trevan, her lips moving against his ear as she said

Vandemeer's name. His hands tightened on her waist and she knew his anger was still very raw. Cautiously they sat up to peer over the edge of the ravine.

Jocelyn gasped at the sight before her. Vandemeer was standing where they had left him, facing towards them. His expression was calm, except for the sneer of his smug smile. His dark hair whipped in a frenzy around his head as his body jerked and shifted from the heavy blow of the winds. Even though he was forced to squint because of the blinding dust, Jocelyn could still see that his eyes were bright with his madness. His gaze moved to hers, his eyes widened and she saw the insanity within them. His mouth shaped the words that the storm stole from his lips.

Fate brings us together.
Time can never tear us apart.

Lucas Vandemeer laughed at his victory, then turned to lift his arms to embrace the black murderous tornado bearing down on him. Ice flushed through Jocelyn's veins as she watched his body being sucked quickly into the swirling mass like a rag doll and disappear.

EPILOGUE

As far as the world knew, the Porcelain Mask Murderer's identity would forever remain a mystery. The authorities had a face and a name, but no history. At least not one they would want to believe. And only Jocelyn and Trevan knew the truth.

Fate brings us together.
Time can never tear us apart.

When Lucas Vandemeer had held out his arms to the deadly storm, had he met his death? Or, as his expression had caused Jocelyn to wonder many times since then, had he fooled destiny one last time? She shook her head; they probably would never know.

'Jocelyn Kendrick, the panel has come to its decision.'

She looked up quickly, realizing that she had not heard the somber and grim-faced men that made up the Internal Affairs panel come in. They had been adjourned for over an hour now. She had an hour to sweat about what their decision would be regarding her future.

Dan Gates opened a file and scanned the contents briefly, then looked over his glasses at her. 'Ms Kendrick, this is perhaps one of the most unusual situations we have ever had to deal with.'

Jocelyn looked at her hands for a moment, hoping she could hide the small smile. She cleared her throat, then looked back to Mr Gates. 'I'm very aware of that, sir.'

She found Gates returning her smile. 'Ms Kendrick, tell me, what is it like to be one of the homicide department's most notable detectives when you haven't even graduated the academy yet?'

Jocelyn felt the flush of her embarrassment. 'I uh . . . to be honest, sir, I don't feel that I am one of the most notable. There are plenty of others who deserve that credit.'

'I must remind you that you are still under oath,' Mr Gates said, causing the other panel members to chuckle. 'However, I'll let you off the hook and go on. As you know, very damaging allegations were made against you regarding tampering with evidence and so on. During our investigation we have discovered no foundation for these charges, nor have we found any evidence of inappropriate behavior.'

Gates took off his glasses and held them in his hand. After a brief pause, he looked to her and held her gaze. 'We found that the allegations made against you were not based on any concrete evidence, but on information supplied by an anonymous individual. Dr Lindenmeyer did not follow the correct procedures when he canceled your internship with the homicide department.'

Gates looked to one of his panel members, Addison

Taber. Taber folded his hands over his copy of the file. 'We've had Dr Lindenmeyer under investigation for several months now, Ms Kendrick, and it is with deep regret that these charges were made against you before the conclusion of our inquiry. I realize the discomfort caused by the allegations cannot be removed with only an apology, but the panel would like you to know that all information regarding this proceeding will be completely confidential.'

Jocelyn took a deep breath, then slowly let it out. She knew all too well what 'completely confidential' meant. Some of her thoughts must have shown on her face because Gates spoke up once again.

'I know that is not entirely comforting, Ms Kendrick,' he said, his face serious. 'To perhaps ward off some of the whiplash of this incident, the panel has decided to enclose letters from each of the members describing the circumstances behind this whole situation. Again, we apologize that you were brought in on this.'

Jocelyn looked to each one of the panel members before she spoke. 'I appreciate the board's sincerity regarding the effects this proceeding may have on my possibilities of a law enforcement career.'

She knew there would always be one officer who would question her involvement, question her tactics in an investigation; she was prepared for that. But it was the memory of Trevan's face as he watched her go over the 'mask' case files that caused her to hesitate. Would he be able to accept what she chose to do?

'Ms Kendrick, I can understand your hesitation,

384

however, I would like to let you know the kind of support you have had during this investigation.' Gates flipped through his file. 'Our panel has heard not only from several members of the coroner's office, but from many of the detectives in the homicide department. All have vouched for your character and for your actions during this incident with the investigation of the Porcelain Mask Murders. One of your defenders went so far as to tell us we would be "complete idiots if we believed the crap that was being piled on you." I believe those were his exact words.'

Jocelyn frowned. 'I don't understand.'

Taber chuckled, flipping to a page. 'I'm sure you are acquainted with a Mr John Cartland?'

'Yes, sir, I am,' she answered with a smile.

'He has done everything, including threaten to turn in his badge, if this panel were to find you guilty of the allegations made against you.' Taber folded his hands and smiled as he looked to her. 'Mr Cartland is one of the most respected people in this force, Ms Kendrick, and it was his testimony that helped the panel decide to not only continue the investigation into Dr Linden-meyer's conduct, but to once again look at your case. This time from a different perspective. Dr Linden-meyer apparently thought you had knowledge of his involvement with known prostitutes and sought to cover it up. He used the anonymous tip to substantiate his allegation. However, we felt that when a man of John Cartland's reputation stakes his career on that of a relatively unknown individual, that individual must have some very fine qualities.'

Jocelyn's eyes brimmed with tears and she looked away for a moment. She cleared her throat and faced the panel once again. 'Could you do me a favor and not tell him that you told me about this? He'll never let me live this down.'

The panel laughed at her statement, then they rose and each one of the five men shook her hand and wished her luck in her career. Jocelyn was relieved that the Internal Affairs investigation was over, but part of her regretted walking out the door.

Would Trevan be out there waiting for her? The night they had confronted Lucas Vandemeer, after the police had finally let them go home, they had made love, slowly and desperately. They had caressed each other with an intensity born of fear. The realization that destiny had brought her the only man she could ever love had speared through her that night and she had wanted to hold him, touch him. Never let him go.

And now he was gone.

Jocelyn had remembered all too vividly the terror that had gripped her when she watched Vandemeer's body being whipped into the frenzy of the tornado that night. She'd been frightened that whatever force had brought Trevan to her, would also take him away.

Except this time it had not been a tornado that had taken him.

She had awakened to find Trevan gone with only a note propped against the coffee pot. He said he'd had to go see if Millie and Rachael had weathered the storm safely. It had been hard to deal with the realization that perhaps he had been unable to accept what she planned to do with her life.

Jocelyn pushed the depressing thoughts away and gathered her material to leave. She would walk out the door and face the obstacles ahead of her and hope that Trevan wouldn't be one of them.

Quietly she pushed the door open and started to walk toward the elevator. She felt a hand on her shoulder and she turned.

Trevan stood before her as he gently studied her. She could read the concern mixed with the hunger in his eyes. He lifted his hand to touch her cheek. 'What did they say?'

'They dropped everything,' Jocelyn said softly. Her gaze moved over him reliving every sweet detail that she had already committed to memory.

He frowned, then a moment of fear flashed in his eyes as he noticed her look. 'Jocelyn what's wrong?'

She looked away trying to swallow the emotion welling in her throat. 'I didn't know if you were going to come back,' she said simply.

'Not come back,' he said hoarsely. Trevan pulled her roughly to him. 'I'm so sorry, Jocelyn. I thought you knew I would come back.'

She buried her face in his chest and inhaled the masculine scent of him. 'You hadn't said anything about going back, then I found the note.'

He cupped the back of her head and brought his mouth to hers. He kissed her till she didn't know whether she could stand on her own. He pulled back till his gaze met hers and she could see the desire, the hunger in his eyes. 'You'd had a rough evening and I knew that you would be busy with paperwork for the investigation and taking care of this proceeding, so I let you sleep in. I knew it would be impossible for you to go back with me for a couple of days.' He hugged her to him tightly. 'I didn't realize that you would think that I wasn't coming back.'

Jocelyn didn't want words as she pulled him to her and kissed him with all the fear she had felt. She ran her hands from his shoulders down his chest to his waist. Rubbing her hands around him to his rear where she cupped him. Trevan groaned against her throat. She slapped him on the buttock and pulled back to look at him with mock anger. 'Don't ever do that again, Trevan Elliot.'

He grinned as he pulled her toward the elevator. 'Let's go home and you can punish me all you want.'

Jocelyn laughed at him. 'You won't like my punishment, Elliot. It involves cooking and cleaning.'

The elevator slid open and he pulled her inside. His arms went around her and lips sought hers. Once again, she found herself getting lost in the sensations that only he could evoke within her. She had wrapped her arms around him and was enjoying the feel of her fingers in his hair when the elevator door opened and she heard whistles and loud applause.

Jocelyn chuckled as she dropped her forehead against his chest. 'Please tell me that they aren't here waiting for me.'

'We are, Jocelyn, and as usual we've enjoyed your entrance,' Gary laughed, pulling her from Trevan to hug her, then swing her around. She heard the pop of several champagne bottles. 'We just got the news, congratulations.'

She gave him a smacking kiss on the cheek, then stepped into Thomas's and Bill Wilson's embrace. Straightening his glasses, Bill chuckled as he handed her a paper cup of champagne. 'Best we could do, dear. I want you to know that you had us worried there for a while, young lady,' he said.

'You should've seen John,' Gary said over Jocelyn's shoulder. 'When we got Trevan's call, I thought the man was going to wreck the car at least three times as he sped to get out there.'

John glared at Pemberton. 'The hell I did. I wasn't worried about her scrawny self; I was mad as hell that she'd pulled a stunt like that.'

Jocelyn laughed as she wrapped Cartland in a tight embrace. 'It wasn't like I asked to be kidnapped, you know.' She kissed him on the cheek. 'But I appreciate you caring about me anyway. And thanks for everything, John.'

'I'm just glad you're okay, kid,' he said quietly where no one could hear him. John awkwardly patted her on the shoulder, then cleared his throat. 'I would like to propose a toast. I would like to toast to another case closed and I guess a tiny part of the credit should go to Jocelyn, although we know what a pain she can be.'

Jocelyn laughed with everyone at his statement, then raised her cup. 'Cheers.'

The informal celebration went on around Jocelyn as people congratulated her and briefly discussed the outcome of the case. It would be a while before she could go to sleep at night without reliving the night that the Porcelain Mask Murderer had finally captured her, but she knew that she would. It was hard, but she was learning to deal with the many deaths Lucas Vandemeer had caused, and more painfully those victims he had killed to manipulate her.

Jocelyn looked around her for Trevan and was unable to find him. Then she felt the warmth of his touch on her lower back and the deep stirring of pleasure as his breath touched her ear. 'How about I take you home and give you a demonstration of old fashioned hospitality?' he asked, his voice seductive against her hair.

She chuckled softly as her lips grazed his cheek. 'I don't know if a man your age is up to it.'

They said goodbye to everyone, then together they stepped outside. Jocelyn stood in the sun for a moment and realized how much she enjoyed having Trevan's hand in hers. She smiled as she met his gaze and for a brief moment she remembered Lucas Vandemeer's last words, but now it had lost its veiled threat. Jocelyn held Trevan's gaze and the words took on a whole new meaning.

> *Fate brings us together.*
> *Time can never tear us apart.*

THE EXCITING NEW NAME
IN WOMEN'S FICTION!

PLEASE HELP ME TO HELP YOU!

Dear *Scarlet* Reader,

As Editor of *Scarlet* Books I want to make sure that the books I offer you every month are up to the high standards *Scarlet* readers expect. And to do that I need to know a little more about you and your reading likes and dislikes. So please spare a few minutes to fill in the short questionnaire on the following pages and send it to me. I'll send *you* a surprise gift as a thank you!*

Looking forward to hearing from you,

Sally Cooper

Editor-in-Chief, *Scarlet*

*Offer applies only in the UK, only one offer per household.

QUESTIONNAIRE

Please tick the appropriate boxes to indicate your answers

1 Where did you get this Scarlet title?
Bought in supermarket ☐
Bought at my local bookstore ☐ Bought at chain bookstore ☐
Bought at book exchange or used bookstore ☐
Borrowed from a friend ☐
Other (please indicate) _____

2 Did you enjoy reading it?
A lot ☐   A little ☐   Not at all ☐

3 What did you particularly like about this book?
Believable characters ☐   Easy to read ☐
Good value for money ☐   Enjoyable locations ☐
Interesting story ☐   Modern setting ☐
Other _____

4 What did you particularly dislike about this book?
_____

5 Would you buy another Scarlet book?
Yes ☐   No ☐

6 What other kinds of book do you enjoy reading?
Horror ☐   Puzzle books ☐   Historical fiction ☐
General fiction ☐   Crime/Detective ☐   Cookery ☐
Other (please indicate) _____

7 Which magazines do you enjoy reading?
1. _____
2. _____
3. _____

And now a little about you –
8 How old are you?
Under 25 ☐   25–34 ☐   35–44 ☐
45–54 ☐   55–64 ☐   over 65 ☐

cont.

9 What is your marital status?

Single ☐   Married/living with partner ☐
Widowed ☐   Separated/divorced ☐

10 What is your current occupation?

Employed full-time ☐   Employed part-time ☐
Student ☐   Housewife full-time ☐
Unemployed ☐   Retired ☐

11 Do you have children? If so, how many and how old are they?

_____

_____

12 What is your annual household income?

under $15,000	☐	or	£10,000	☐
$15–25,000	☐	or	£10–20,000	☐
$25–35,000	☐	or	£20–30,000	☐
$35–50,000	☐	or	£30–40,000	☐
over $50,000	☐	or	£40,000	☐

Miss/Mrs/Ms _____

Address _____

_____

_____

Thank you for completing this questionnaire. Now tear it out – put it in an envelope and send it before 31 May, 1997, to:

Sally Cooper, Editor-in-Chief

USA/Can. address
SCARLET c/o London Bridge
85 River Rock Drive
Suite 202
Buffalo
NY 14207
USA

UK address/No stamp required
SCARLET
FREEPOST LON 3335
LONDON W8 4BR
Please use block capitals for address

THTIM/11/96

Scarlet titles coming next month:

WICKED IN SILK Andrea Young

Claudia is promised a large sum of money for her favourite charity if she will act as a kissagram at Guy Hamilton's birthday lunch. What she doesn't know is that his headstrong daughter, Anoushka, has arranged the whole thing. So when Claudia finds herself in Greece with Guy and Anoushka, anything might happen . . . and it does!

COME HOME FOR EVER Jan McDaniel

Matt and Sierra were lovers ten years ago . . . then she betrayed him by marrying another man. Matt hadn't married Sierra because he didn't want to bring a child into the world. What he doesn't know is that the child Sierra brings home for Christmas is *his*!

WOMAN OF DREAMS Angela Drake

Zoe has a secret which she finds difficult to accept . . . and when she falls in love with François, the gift seems to become a curse. To avert disaster, Zoe decides never to see François again . . . but *can* she survive a marriage without love?

NEVER SAY NEVER Tina Leonard

Dustin Reed needs a housekeeper . . . Jill McCall needs a job. What Dustin doesn't need is a single mother with a baby to care for, though that seems to be exactly what Jill is! Oh, of course, she denies the baby is hers . . . telling Dustin that the little girl was left on his doorstep! Whether he believes Jill or not, this is clearly going to be one Christmas Dustin will never forget.